Spore

Spore

Tamara Jones

SAMHAIN
PUBLISHING

Samhain Publishing, Ltd.
11821 Mason Montgomery Road, 4B
Cincinnati, OH 45249
www.samhainpublishing.com

Print ISBN: 978-1-61922-977-8
Digital ISBN: 978-1-61922-691-3

Editing by Don D'Auria
Cover by Scott Carpenter

First Samhain Publishing, Ltd. electronic publication: June 2015
First Samhain Publishing, Ltd. print publication: June 2015

For Laura
Love you, Punkin.

Part One
Seeding

Chapter One

Head pounding from another fitful night of summer storm and nightmare laced insomnia, Sean Casey plucked an email printout from the mirror and skimmed it as he brushed his teeth.

Black Pawn's art director had emailed rough content and graphic specs for Ghoulie's January issue. Murphy's script—saving inner city kids from kidnappers—was early for once, and editorial changes should arrive that afternoon. *Cool.*

His girlfriend's handwritten note said the script was on his drawing table. Also cool. And that it was decent, if cliché in places, with good detail options for the illustrations. Triple cool. Despite having woken from a typical pursuer-munching-on-his-entrails nightmare, Sean had apparently stumbled into a good morning.

"Mare?" he called out as he left the bathroom with the paper. "You still home?"

Of course she's not home on a Sunday morning, he reminded himself. Their wheezy AC had been running non-stop since late May. She always jumped at the chance to work a little Sunday overtime at the nursing home, and maybe get the power bill caught up.

Sean padded to the kitchen and flicked on the radio by the microwave to drown out the neighbor's barking dog. No music, just the end of a soggy farm report, then a quick update on the ongoing flooding of the Des Moines River basin and incredible fishing near Juniper Creek. Mare's note set aside, Sean dry-swallowed a couple of Excedrin as news gave way to *Alice in Chains*. He stood at the sink, humming and filling the pot for morning coffee as he planned his day: prelim sketches by noon, a couple of rounds of layout changes with Murph and editorial, and maybe get started on pencil work for the finals tonight. Be ahead of the game for a change instead of scrambling to make deadline.

Movement outside caught his eye. He looked up and muttered, "What the hell?"

Someone stood at the edge of the Christmas tree farm behind his half-acre lot—a man, partially obscured by branches, his shape a thick, dark slash beside a drenched and drooping fir.

Sean leaned forward, squinting into morning sunlight filtering through bland, efficient rows of conifers. He barely noticed cold water run over his hand. "Is he *naked*?" he whispered.

Yep, the bastard's naked. Sean flinched as branches shifted, leaving little obscuring coverage. Had to be his imagination, a relic from the nightmare—in all the years living in the neighborhood beside Hobson's farm, he'd seen no one but the farm's mowing crew there during the summer. This year had brought more rain than mowing, so much rain that some of the trees had drowned. Sean closed his eyes and counted to ten before opening them again.

Nope. Still there.

We have kids around here, he thought as he flicked off the water and rushed to the laundry room. *Families. What kind of sick freak runs around a Christmas tree farm naked on Sunday morning?*

He found Mare's aluminum softball bat in its corner by the dryer. Hefty assurance in hand, Sean strode to the back door and flung it open. Beads of sweat erupted on his skin; at not quite seven in the morning, it was already sweltering outside and reeking of hot, wet evergreen.

Sean silenced the fear inside his head and stomped across the yard, pausing at the edge of a rippling puddle that had grown to infect every yard on his side of the neighborhood. "What the hell do you think you're doing?" he managed to bark at the man in the tree line. The guy was taller than he looked from the kitchen. As he slowly turned his gaze to Sean, Sean tightened his grip on the bat, steadying its tremble.

Before the man could respond, a plumpish young woman stumbled out a couple of trees away. She, too, wore not a stitch of clothes, and she let out a low, terrified moan as she blinked at Sean. She fought through shin-deep water and rubbed her ears, turning aside and shaking her head as if to cower from a loud noise only she could hear.

Sean's gaze darted to the man. "What the hell have you done to her?" he snapped as he splashed out to the woman.

"Hey, you all right?" he asked, nearly touching her shoulder before pulling his hand away. Vaguely familiar, she was in her mid-twenties and smelled like stale sheets. Her skin looked slick, almost oily, and pinkish slime dripped from her dark, curling hair. When the naked guy stepped out of the trees, Sean raised the bat as a warning and kept himself between the man and the woman. "C'mon," Sean told her, "let's get you to the house—"

The woman's startled lurch splashed water halfway up his thighs. "What's going on?" she asked, looking around, apparently oblivious to her own nudity. "Where am I? Who *are* you?"

"I'm Sean Casey. You're in my backyard, in Pinell," Sean said, turning to keep his attention on the man who strode out of the puddle and toward the garden shed as if he were royalty. "And I have no idea what's going on." He glanced at the woman's face. "Are you hurt? Were you drugged?"

"What?" She shook her head, still wobbly on her feet. "Me? Drugged?" She tilted her head, concerned, then she blinked and her eyes grew wide. "Oh my *God*!" she squeaked, scrambling away from him. "Why am I naked?"

"I have no idea," Sean said, avoiding looking at her. "You just walked into my yard like that."

"I *what*?" she asked, voice rising. "Why would I… He's nak— Holy crap, what's going on? Have I lost my mind?"

Maybe it's me, Sean thought as the woman babbled. *But I haven't had lucid hallucinations for years.* He shook his head, looking between the two naked strangers. Unlike the usual companions in his nightmares, they weren't bleeding, gutted, or being eaten. And it was a sticky morning in broad daylight, not a cold, dank night. Sean clenched his left hand, nails biting into his palm.

Daylight or not, maybe it's just another nightmare.

He opened his fist to see welts, one threatening to bleed. *I'm still here. In my backyard. With two naked strangers. No, three. Did a nudist cult have a party in the tree farm?*

Another drenched nude woman stumbled out of the trees. Skinny and going gray, she gazed mindlessly at the sky and walked through Sean's drowned peonies.

Sean took a breath and asked the first woman, "Do you remember what happened? Was there an accident? You and your friends okay?"

"I don't know who they are," she said, covering herself with her hands. She blushed as far down as Sean dared to look. "Do you have a towel? A blanket? *Something?*"

He didn't want to let crazies into the house, but he couldn't let naked women stand around his flooded backyard, either.

"Um, sure," he said. "There's a quilt over the couch in the living room, straight through, and sheets and towels are in the linen closet, down the hall by the bathroom door. Help yourself."

Sean winced as the other woman tripped and fell against the old brick barbecue before landing on her ass in the puddle. Letting the first woman manage on her own, he rushed to help the second to her feet. "It's okay, ma'am," he said, turning slightly to point to his back door. "Go on in and have that other lady help you get covered up, okay?"

He guessed her to be about forty. She looked up at him, her eyes wide and afraid. "Who are you?" she asked, gripping his arm as if he was the first solid thing she'd seen. She had a faint dirty-sock aroma about her, and her palm felt slimy and cold against his forearm. "Where am I? Why is it so wet and hot?"

Taking a quick glance at the still-silent man staring into the shed as if he'd never seen a lawn tractor before, Sean started to lead her toward the house. "Sean Casey, ma'am. You're in my backyard. At my house, in Pinell. On Hobson Road. It's been raining a lot and it's the middle of July. It's supposed to be hot and wet."

The woman's fingers clenched tighter. "Hobson? *In* Pinell? There ain't no houses on Hobson, other than Hobson Holiday Farm, and the Caseys live in Boone, on Third."

Confused, Sean stopped and stared at the woman. "I grew up in the house on Third. My mother still lives there. Helene? Do you know Helene Casey?"

The woman nodded eagerly. "Of course I do! She and Pat bought that little house just last summer, right after the baby came."

Okaaay, he thought. *She seems to believe it's thirty years ago.* "Ma'am, I think you're confused," he said, coaxing her toward the back door. "Maybe too much sun. You need to go sit—"

A child screamed next door, and Sean turned, wrenching his arm out of the confused woman's grip. "Steffie! You okay?"

Steffie Mathers, six years old and already wearing her swimsuit, stood on her deck screaming bloody murder and pointing at a nude, old man staggering out from between two trees.

Another one? What the hell's happening out there?

Steffie's mother ran onto the deck. She grabbed Steffie and dragged her toward the patio doors. Then she saw Sean.

"Sean! What's happening?" Nicole called out, holding Steffie's face against her belly.

He had been keeping an eye out for Nic and the kids while her husband, Aaron, was on his second tour in the Middle East.

"I have no idea," Sean said, walking to her deck. A middle-aged man staggered out of the trees as the other grasped onto the swing set. Sean shook his head and turned away from the men. "I have three at my place, too."

Nic blinked at him. "Three? I only see one. Please tell me you didn't let any in your house?!"

"Well, I…" he said, voice sounding timid in his own ears. "They seem really confused." He shrugged over at the silent man in his own yard. "The other two are women. I can't—"

Nicole pushed her daughter into the house. "Hell yes, you can. Women will steal you blind just as quickly as a man. And God knows what they've been doing out there," she said, gesturing toward the tidy rows of fir and spruce poking out of the water. She grimaced and shook her head. "Always knew you were crazy, but damn, Sean, can't you—"

Sean looked toward his own yard. A naked child splashed toward the rhubarb marking the property line with his other neighbor.

Crap.

He interrupted Nicole. "Call the sheriff. Find something to cover them up. In or out, I'll try to corral them at my place."

"I'll bring some towels," she sighed.

Sean ran, sprinting across his own yard to the Simmons'. When they weren't turning Earl's consulting job into a vacation, their anti-social mutt, Peaches, had full run of the place, contained only by invisible fencing that kept her inches inside the property line. The Simmons found it funny when she chased off Girl Scouts, old men collecting for the veterans, or Jehovah's Witnesses. A confused grade-schooler wouldn't stand a chance.

"Ho there!" Sean hollered, waving for the little boy to stop.

Her hackles raised, Peaches silently ran back and forth along her demarcation line while the kid splashed toward her as if she were a regular, friendly dog.

Why, oh why, couldn't the Simmons be on vacation again? Sean hustled across the yard. "Stay away from that dog! She bites!"

The kid blinked, stopping not two steps from Peaches, then whined and rubbed his ears as if they suddenly hurt.

Sean tucked the bat under his arm and snatched up the little boy, almost coughing at the low reek of his skin. "You all right?"

Peaches stopped pacing and growled, baring her teeth. The boy nodded, shuddering, while one hand ground at his ear.

In the middle of his own yard, Sean set the boy on his feet and pointed him toward the back door. "Ask one of the women inside to get you covered up. Okay?"

The man at the shed finally spoke. "Where's my motorcycle?"

Sean took a breath and turned, managing to hold his voice to a polite timbre. "Excuse me?"

The man turned and said, "Where the hell's my Kawasaki? And what do you all think you're doing in my yard?"

Sean thought for a moment he recognized the man's face, but then he wasn't sure. He was about Sean's age and build, and had a sprawling, lumpy mole on his right forearm. Nothing remarkable, but somehow the guy's presence was distressing.

"Look, dude," Sean said, shifting the bat to his hand again, "this isn't your house, it's mine. Lived here eight years."

"Eight years my ass. I built that fire pit, laid the patio brick, and expanded the back bedroom. This is my house!"

Sean started to say that the bank surely would disagree, but he clamped his mouth shut as Nicole walked toward them. Grimacing, she escorted the elderly man, who was struggling to hold up the towel sagging around his waist. The middle-aged man wore a snug towel and walked behind them, eyes wide and darting about as if he couldn't believe what he was seeing.

They were just guys. Harmless, naked, confused guys. Arm-mole-guy on the other hand… Just looking at him made Sean feel edgy.

"Sheriff's on the way," Nicole said. Steffie trailed behind the adults, leading her toddler brother and angling her free hand over her eyes to block the view past her feet.

The guy with the mole glared at Sean and Nicole, then stomped into the house and slammed the screen door behind him.

Chapter Two

Twenty minutes later, Sean leaned in the archway between his kitchen and living room, glancing often to the trees. They'd picked up a couple more strangers before a deputy arrived to herd them all inside for interviews.

Sean frowned at his kitchen phone, lying disconnected on the counter. He wanted to call Mare, but anything less than a life-or-death emergency would get her into trouble with her asshat boss. And if he did plug the phone back in and call her, the strangers would be clamoring for their chance to suck up his long distance minutes again. According to their small town phone co-op, almost anywhere worth calling was long distance from Pinell, Iowa, and he'd already had to pry three of them off the phone.

Across the room, Sean's lifelong buddy, Todd Anderson, sat with a pad of paper on the kitchen table and his Boone County Sheriff's hat on his knee as he talked with the wild-haired woman. Sweat dripped down his cheeks; not surprising, since Todd had probably put on fifty pounds since high school and July temperatures in Iowa hovered between scalding and Hades. Todd smiled thankfully at Nicole as she freshened his iced tea, then returned to interviewing the woman.

The rest of the strangers waited in the living room, wrapped in sheets, like a surreal, multi-generational toga party. They watched SpongeBob tittering on the TV because Sean had grown tired of their squabbling and had taken the remote. The guy with the mole stared sullenly ahead, but at least he had stopped arguing about the house.

As Nicole brushed past Sean with the pitcher of tea and a stack of plastic cups, she nodded her head toward the wild-haired woman talking to the deputy. She whispered, "I think I know her."

Sean winced. In all the craziness, he'd forgotten to ask anyone their name. "You do?"

"Yeah. No. I mean, I can't place her face, but I've seen her before. I know I have. Maybe she's an adult student or something?"

"Maybe," he whispered, nodding. Nic worked at the college and students on a psychedelic bender made at least some sense. "I got that familiar feeling too, about her and the guy with the mole. It's like I should know him from somewhere." He met the man's glowering gaze. *Whoever he is, he definitely gives me the creeps.*

Nic looked over her shoulder and forced a smile. "Yeah. Hard to forget a charmer like that."

Sean nodded. "That other lady says she knows my mom."

Nicole mouthed, "Weird," then continued on to the guests.

Sean glanced out at the trees lined up just past his property line—no new arrivals—then smiled at Steffie and her little brother coloring on the laundry room floor. Hot-press illustration panels and markers were scattered around them. Pip, not quite three, had decided he wanted purple fingers. Steffie held up her picture, a house and a pony, and Sean gave her a thumbs up. They were being quiet and good, the illustration board and markers a small price to pay to keep them entertained and safe from the nudists in his living room.

"I wanna know why I get some pizza joint when I call home!" the woman with Todd said, drawing Sean's attention as she burst to her feet. "And don't you tell me I misdialed. I called twice!"

Sean didn't hear Todd's reply, but the woman crossed her arms over her chest. "He's not at the bank, either. I called and it's closed, but today is *supposed* to be the day after Thanksgiving! Instead, it's summertime! What the hell's going on?"

The adults in the living room glanced at each other, mumbling about what day it was. None seemed to agree. The old man covered his eyes and turned away, his hands shaking.

The woman's voice rose with each syllable. "What are you not telling me? Where's Jeff? Why can't I call my husband? He's a very important man and you do not want to piss him off!"

Todd tried to get her to sit again. "Mrs. Howard, please."

In the living room, Nicole clenched the pitcher to her chest and turned to blink at Sean. "No way," she managed. "It *can't* be her. It isn't possible."

Howard? Sean thought, scowling at Todd and the woman. *Jeff Howard? Wasn't he a bank manager in Boone?*

He'd heard of no other Jeff Howard. *But something happened a couple of years ago. A scandal. All over the news. He'd built a house. A new wife and a brand new house, with the insurance—*

Sean backed a step toward the kids, shaking his head. Jeff's first wife—*Cindy? No... Mindy. Wasn't her name Mindy?*—had had a car accident. She'd totaled the car. And she'd died. Mindy Howard had *died.*

But there she stood, wrapped in his sheet, in his kitchen, arguing with Todd Anderson while two kids colored quietly on his laundry room floor.

Sean sat on a lawn chair and watched a helicopter fly over the trees. He had a piss-warm bottle of hard lemonade in his hand and three empties beside the pile of sheets at his feet. It was maybe ten thirty. On a Sunday morning, no less.

They're dead, he thought, taking a sip. *Or they're batshit crazy. And here comes another one.*

The forty-something woman claimed to be Evelyn Fischer. As a teenager, Evelyn had babysat his mother; she'd died thirty years ago, when he was two. The kid almost eaten by Peaches said he was Tobey Dunders, hit by a car about five years ago. And Sean had overheard the deputies mention the skinny teenage girl getting wasted at a barn party in 1974 and suffocating on her own puke.

He didn't know about the rest. Wasn't sure he wanted to. *That's what I get for eavesdropping on the deputies. I find out there are nine... no, ten, dead people in my house who don't even know they died,* he thought. He took another drink and sighed. *Only two bottles left. Gonna have to run out for more.*

Todd had called for additional officers, and Nicole had taken the kids to her sister's. Sean polished off the bottle and tossed it aside. *Probably the best thing for Nic to do. Wouldn't want Steffie and Pip hanging out with dead people.* He sighed and ran a hand through his hair. The whole mess would be easier to accept as a nightmare.

The door opened behind him and someone came out. Sean glanced back to see Todd and two other deputies approaching. He stood, steady, and wondered if it was too hot to get drunk. "So, what's the deal? What's next?"

"They all come from that Christmas tree farm?" the tallest deputy asked. Six foot four if he was an inch, he had the sheared-hair and hard-eyed, ass-kicking look that Todd, even on his best days, could never approach. The shiny nameplate above his badge said Hendrix.

"Yes, sir," Sean said. "Just like that one, there."

Hendrix nodded toward the trees and the other deputy splashed out to intercept the newest arrival, a dazed nude man who might have been thirty, might have been forty, or anywhere between.

"We're taking them all to the hospital," Todd said. "The van's out front. You'll get your house back before you know it."

"Glad I could help," Sean said, nodding a silent greeting to the nude man as he was led past. "But I'd like to know where they're coming from and why they're wandering into my yard."

"We think they—" Todd started, but Hendrix cut him off.

"That is none of your concern, Mr. Casey," Hendrix said, glaring down at Sean.

Sean stretched a little and glared back. At a hair's breadth shy of six feet, he didn't like feeling short. "It's my house, my yard. They're wearing my sheets for chrissake. I think that qualifies as my concern."

"They're wearing paper scrubs now," Hendrix said. "And, speaking of your house, I have some questions." He opened a leather-covered notebook and clicked a pen. "There are some rather disturbing images hanging on your walls, Mr. Casey. Torture. Maiming. Desecration of graves. Would you care to explain them?"

You should see the ones in my portfolio, Sean thought, his smile hardening. "They're art."

"I told you, John, he's a—" Todd started, but a warning glare from Hendrix silenced him.

"Art? Corpses eating naked women?"

"Actually, that's a ghoul. Ghouls eat, corpses don't."

"You getting smart with me, Mr. Casey?"

"Nope. I'm telling you I'm an illustrator. Black Pawn comics and graphic novels, mostly, but every now and then I do a book or album cover. Did a movie poster once." Sean shrugged. "I do horror. It keeps food in the fridge."

Hendrix just stared. "Interesting. Any idea why these…individuals chose to invade your yard, Mr. Casey?"

"I have no idea," Sean said, shrugging again. "Just my lucky spin on the surreal-o-meter, I guess." He clenched his fingernails into his palm again until the pain made him unclench. He said calmly, "I don't know why they came here. This is a *Twilight Zone* episode. Or a nightmare. "

Hendrix showed a ghost of a smile. "Have many nightmares, Mr. Casey?"

Every night, asshole. And today's gonna be great fodder. "You my shrink?"

Hendrix's eyes narrowed, then his radio squawked. He snapped his notebook closed. "We'll talk again, Mr. Casey." Hendrix plucked the radio from his belt and walked away, listening.

"Sorry, man," Todd said, giving Hendrix a furtive glance. "He's usually not this pissy. I heard he's having money problems and was gonna do a favor for cash, but instead he's working OT that'll mostly get taken by taxes."

We all have money trouble, I think. "It's okay. Any idea why they all wandered into my yard?"

Hendrix had taken his radio around the side of the house, but Todd craned his neck, looking about, before he spoke. "Nothing I can say, not really," he whispered, "but don't let Hendrix get to you. It's been a crazy morning. You're not the only one to call about naked people wandering around."

They turned to watch the helicopter bank hard and fly east.

"We're heading out," a deputy called from the door.

Todd waved him off. "One last thing," he said to Sean. "That guy, the one who keeps insisting this is his house…"

"Yeah?"

"He says his name's Paul Casey. Your dad's brother."

"Oh frickin' great. My dad always said his brother was a shit," Sean muttered as worry slammed in his gut. *Thought I recognized him from somewhere. Does this mean the dead really did come back?* Uncle Paul had died in a hit and run accident when Sean was a kid, and he barely remembered the guy. His father and Paul had parted ways long before, but his dad still inherited the house after Paul's death. He had rented out Paul's place then sold it to Sean after college for next to nothing.

"Then it is his house. Or was. There's no way he can take it from me, is there?" He unclenched his fists. *Be just my luck he'd boot us out.* "Mare and I can't afford to lose it right now."

"Sean…" Todd said, shaking his head.

"I know I draw some weird shit, but I never thought dead people could come back and walk around."

"They can't," Todd said. "Dead's dead. These folks are impersonators. It's just a twisted scheme or hoax, or they've been taking some weird new psychotic drug." He took a cleansing breath and resumed his deputy posture. "We're taking all of them to the hospital to be checked out for drugs, and we'll run their prints and background checks, warn the families to watch for scams, that sort of thing. Now that we've gathered them up, everything will be fine."

He paused, then said, "You might want to warn your mom, though, that someone's pretending to be her dead brother-in-law."

Sean nodded, unconvinced. Mindy Howard didn't seem like she wanted to trick anyone. She just seemed scared. And a little kid like Tobey surely wasn't a grifter. "Yeah. Thanks," Sean said, shaking Todd's hand. "I'll tell her. Good to see you. Give Hailey a hug from us."

"I will. Wish I'd bumped into you under saner circumstances." His radio squawked and he released Sean's hand. "Gotta go. It's been too long. We should get together later, maybe grab a beer or something."

Sean nodded and followed Todd into the house. Other than a pile of rumpled sheets, dirty foam plates and plastic cups, and a pair of deputies lingering in the living room, the place looked almost normal. It smelled musty though, like a shower desperate for a cleaning. *From all the sweat?* Sean thought as he thanked the deputies and told them goodbye. *Or something else?*

Sean frowned out the kitchen window and decided the answers waited out there, in the rows of trees. Or the cemetery beyond the far side of the farm.

Dead people walking from a cemetery. Maybe Hendrix was right. Nightmare or not, this IS the kind of thing I illustrate.

He sighed and went to find his shoes.

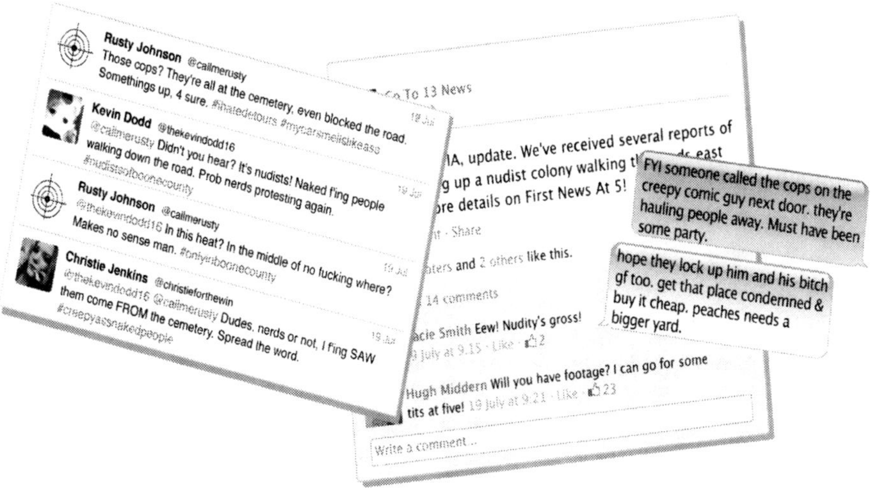

Chapter Three

Mindy Howard clasped her hands between her thighs as the police panel van pulled away from the house. A metal bench ran along both sides of the van, and the Pine People, as the deputies were calling them, sat in two rows facing each other. They wore scrubs, paper shoes, and disoriented, confused expressions. An older woman near the back door sneezed.

Mindy wrinkled her nose at the weird, moldy reek. The house had stunk, too.

The old man to Mindy's left leaned close and whispered, "I ain't never been arrested in my life," while the skinny teenage girl to her right merely wept.

"We're not handcuffed," Mindy whispered back. "So we're surely not—"

"We're in a paddy fucking wagon, you dumb bitch," the guy across from them muttered.

Mindy stared at him, but held her tongue.

"Please don't," the teenage girl said, drawing her knees up to her chest and clenching them to her. "Don't fight."

The old man sat straighter and glared at the grumbly guy. "Mind your tongue around these ladies."

"Any woman that walks around outside naked ain't a lady," he replied, sighing and resting the back of his head against the van wall. He closed his eyes. "We're all headed to processing and a wait in a jail cell as they figure out what to charge us with. Indecent exposure, most likely." He opened one eye and smiled. "I don't know about the rest of you, but I haven't done anything else worth getting arrested for."

"I was just coming home from church. Christmas service," Evelyn, the older lady at the back, said. She blinked and looked at the others, her lower lip quivering. "This makes no sense."

The occupants shifted uneasily, barely meeting one another's gazes. The teenage girl peered over her knees. "I was at a party. Just a party. Now everything looks weird. Skinny TVs and curvy cars and, and…" She lowered her face to her knees again.

The little boy curled against a woman sitting next to him. "I was just riding my bike to the gas station for a pop. Next thing I knew, that guy told me the dog bites and sent me to his house."

"Harvesting beans," the old man beside Mindy said. "And then high summer with that little black girl screaming and pointing at me." He snapped his fingers. "Yeah, just like that."

"Tubing on the Des Moines River, then I'm drinking iced tea in that dude's living room. The season's right, but it's still fucked up," a young guy said, looking at Mindy. "You?"

Mindy blushed. "Coming home from shopping on Black Friday. Suddenly I'm naked in a strange man's backyard."

"What about you?" the old farmer asked the grumbly guy with the mole.

"Just walking my dog, then I'm back home, only it's daytime instead of night."

"It's not your house," Mindy said as the van eased to a stop. "The deputy said that guy Sean—"

The doors opened, and everyone turned to see a crew of medical personnel peer in. "Okay, folks," the man in front said, reaching to help Evelyn out of the van. "Let's get you checked out so we can figure out what's going on."

They'd made her change from scrubs to a hospital gown and Mindy had lost track of how many people had taken her vitals, looked down her throat, or poked and prodded her abdomen. She'd agreed to samples of her hair, fingernails, spit, and sweat. She'd refused a vaginal swab, informing them that last she knew it was still America and no one but her regular doc was looking at her girly bits without a court order. Even now, a nurse repeated her requests for a urine sample. Mindy refused that too, claiming she didn't have to pee.

Mindy offered an apologetic smile but thought, *I peed at Sean's, and that was enough, thank-you-very-much. If I told you what I saw, you'd put me in the psych ward and there's no way you're going to get me to drink anything, either.* The nurse shrugged and scribbled in a chart as the phlebotomist arrived.

Alone again, Mindy sat on the examination table and picked at the cheery Band-Aid taping down the cotton ball at her elbow. Her blood had been dark purple, not bricky red, she was sure of it, even though the phlebotomist had tried not to let her see.

She peeled off the Band-Aid—she'd always been a quick clotter—and, yep, a reddish purple speck. About the color of grape juice.

Mindy flinched. *Purple again?*

Another nurse opened the door and bustled in. "How are we feeling?" she asked, reaching for the blood pressure cuff hanging on the wall beside the exam table.

"Still fine. Still confused," Mindy said, hiding the Band-Aid in her fist while offering her arm for the umpteenth BP check of the day. "Getting tired of sitting here, though. What's going on? Where's Jeff? Have you found him?" *Will he even bother to come?*

"I don't know," the nurse said, pumping up the cuff. "The sheriff is supposed to locate everyone's relatives. I'm not sure who's been found and who hasn't. As for the rest, they're still investigating. I'm sure someone will come to talk to you." She finished checking blood pressure, looked in Mindy's throat, then patted her knee and left.

Time dragged, interrupted by medical personnel wanting to poke, prod, and measure her over and over. No TV, no magazine, nothing but an exam room, a jar of Q-tips, another of tongue depressors, and a rack of ear-exam cones to entertain her.

Somewhere, out past the door, Mindy heard weeping.

She pushed herself off the exam table. *I'm tired of waiting for Jeff to decide to get me. We only live a few blocks away, I'll just walk home.* She found another hospital gown in the cupboard over the sink and pulled it around her, covering her back half. Taking a breath, she opened the door and peered out.

Doctors and a couple of deputies stood together talking softly as nurses and technicians moved from one exam room to the next. One nurse immediately noticed Mindy.

"You need to wait inside," she said, already continuing on.

"Finally have to pee," Mindy replied with an embarrassed smile. "Is there a ladies room…"

The nurse pointed past the doctors and deputies. "Third door on the right. Write your name on one of the cups, please, and after you've given a sample, put it in the cubby behind the little door. Then you come right back, okay?"

Not likely, Mindy thought, but nodded. "Sure."

Mindy scooted toward the doctors and deputies, ready to claim a trip to the ladies room as an excuse for her presence, but none noticed her scurry past. A half-full laundry rack and an empty gurney stood in the hall a couple of doors past the restroom, but no other people. Inside the restroom and the door locked behind her, Mindy took a deep breath and tried to settle her hammering heart. *I'm out. I'm free,* she thought. Then she realized she really did have to pee.

She ignored the cups on the back of the toilet as she sat to relieve her bladder. Afterward, she noticed that her urine was a delicate pale pink.

At least it doesn't stink this time. What's going on? Are all of us like this? she thought as she peeked into the cubby. The two cups inside held raspberry colored fluid. The cubby smelled like mold, not urine.

She flinched. Her urine at Sean's had been a dark berry color and had left the same stink lingering in the air, despite her spraying air-freshener everywhere. She closed the door with a shaking hand and pressed down her panic as she took a single step to the sink and turned on the hot water.

Can't be happening, she thought as she squooged a third splurt of soap onto already sudsy hands. *My blood isn't purple and I don't pee pink. Jeff's just busy at home and everything's fine.*

After rinsing and drying her hands, she flushed the toilet without looking at its contents, and settled herself before opening the restroom door. Two doctors walked past, and she heard the closer one ask, "How can they be alert and functional and in apparent good health? It's in their blood, their urine, the space between their damned cells. This much fungus, they should all be dead."

"I don't know," the other said, "but they need to be quarantined, just in case. CDC's on the way."

Oh shit, oh hell, Mindy thought, easing the door closed again. She pressed her spine against it and took one deep breath after another. *Quarantine? For what? Some stupid fungal infection that turned my blood purple? I can't let them lock me up, but what can I do? I'm in a hospital gown. No money, no ID, no anything. I don't even have shoes!*

She scrunched her eyes closed and allowed herself one moment of trembling panic before she set it aside. *I'm fine. Just fine. Screw these doctors, I have to GO.* She took a breath and opened the door again. Head held high, she strode into the hall as if she belonged there, snatched an armload of scrubs off the laundry cart, and kept walking until she found an unlocked room.

Chapter Four

Hobson's Holiday Tree Farm was crawling with cops: police from nearby towns, deputies from several counties, even a helicopter circling overhead. Despite nearly an hour of creeping around acres of soggy fir, pine, and spruce, Sean had found no way past the cops to see whatever had happened at the cemetery side of the farm.

Can't say I didn't try, but at least it's still early enough for me to get some work done. Sean took another photograph of the copter over the trees, then trudged to his own flooded yard. He paused at the back door and scraped his soggy mud-and-pine-needle-caked tennis shoes across the edge of the top step. Once the worst of the gloppy mess was hanging in thick, black ribbons, he went inside and kicked off one shoe before he tracked mud through the house. *Might as well get started on those sket—*

"Where have you been?" his mother asked, her voice a tight panic as she hurried from the living room, her hands clenched together. "I heard there were a dozen police cars here this morning, then when you didn't answer your phone…"

"Shit," he muttered under his breath. *What's she doing here? And how'd she get in? She never touches anything, not even the front doorknob.*

He took a breath and pasted on a stiff smile as he turned to face her, hoping to disarm her nerves before they led to a full-blown meltdown. "There weren't a dozen. Maybe three. Early this morning. Been an adult a long time now, Ma. I'm managing fine. Really."

"Still, the police… They were here, and they've blocked Juniper Road. I was worried!"

He clenched his teeth and took a steadying breath. *She probably called the hospital, too, to make sure I wasn't in the ER.* "So the sheriff blocking a road east of town makes it okay for you to barge in?" Remaining on the rug by the door, Sean balanced on one foot to peel off his drippy, needle-coated sock before it drove him insane.

As he snatched the sock loose, he glanced at the kitchen phone. Eleven messages. And he'd been gone maybe an hour, tops. *Goddammit.* "You even stuck around though we obviously weren't home. Don't you think that's a bit overboard, Ma? You could have just waited for me to call you back. Stuck a note on the door, something besides freaking out again?"

Helene Casey grimaced at his shoes and socks, his tendency to attract grime a constant affront to her germophobia. "The door was unlocked, Rosemary's car was gone, and you weren't home. I was worried. I am still your mother, after all. Are you going to tell us what happened or not?"

Us? I know you can't stand Mare, but maybe if you were crazy worried… Sean flung the sock into the laundry room and yanked off the other shoe. "Who else is here?" When he saw his mother's frown, he silently cursed and said, "Please tell me you didn't call Mare. You know how her boss is."

"I didn't call Rosemary," Helene said, grimacing. "Why should I? It's not like she listens to anything I say."

Just gotta keep gnawing that bone, don't ya, Ma? Sean wrestled off the other sock and hurled it away. His mother knew Mare hated to be called by her full name. "Don't, Ma. Just don't, okay?" He marched across the kitchen and jerked a glass out of the cupboard. He filled it with water, drank it down, and filled it again. *Damn, it's hot.*

"Don't what? Don't worry about where my only child's been or what he's been doing? Don't wonder why the police were here? Don't be concerned over what he's involved in? Don't ask why he's reeking of booze on a Sunday?" She paused as he finished draining the second glass of water.

"Don't badger me about Mare," he said, slamming the glass on the counter.

"Yes, the… The woman who stole my son." She paused before pointing a shaking finger at the narrow garbage can and its fresh bag, empty save for the morning's plastic cups and a couple of paper towels. "Moldy garbage stinking up the place. There are no grandchildren in my scrapbook…" She tucked her hands behind her crossed arms again. "What good is she?"

"Here we go again," Sean said, stomping past her. Helene imagined filth lurking in every cranny, and Mare had long insisted her fertility issues were no one else's business, especially his mother's.

He reached the archway to the living room and stopped when he saw the man examining the print over the sofa. "And of course you brought Pastor Bailey. Thanks, Ma, for dragging him over to hear all that." Sean nodded hello. "Pastor."

Bailey returned the greeting. "Sean." He looked again at the poster-sized enlargement of *GhoulBane*'s twenty-fifth cover, a full color fold-out depicting GhoulBane devouring a barely dressed, gun-wielding bimbette whole.

Bailey examined the print like an art critic at a gallery opening. "Nice job, and congrats on the expanded cover. You've really nailed the detail work on Ghoulie's veins."

Sean gave his mother a bright smile, then entered the living room. "Thanks. Those books you loaned me helped, especially the one on endocrinology." Pastor Bailey's youngest daughter was a third year med student at University of Iowa and had the best anatomy books Sean had ever seen. And she was a Ghoulie fan.

Bailey turned and offered his hand. "Always glad to help," he said as they shook hands. He leaned forward to say, "Sorry about this, but someone was rather frantic."

Helene froze in the archway with her arms crossed as if touching anything would taint her. "The police were here and you were missing again! What was I supposed to think?"

"That I'm not a kid anymore?" Sean sighed. His mother had been overprotective and over-reactive since he was twelve. After what had happened to him back then she'd become over-protective, paranoid, and terrified of grime. Getting mad at her wouldn't change that. "I'm fine, it's just…" *Aw, hell.* "Some, uh, *odd* people wandered into the yard. They were naked and lost, Nicole called the sheriff…" He shrugged. "After everyone left, I took a walk."

He paused, uncertain what else he should include. "Dad's brother… Uncle Paul…"

The corners of Helene's mouth tightened. "What about him?"

Sean glanced at Pastor Bailey then took a single hesitant step toward his mother. "A guy who looked a lot like him walked out of the tree farm this morning."

She blinked, the color leaving her face. "Your Uncle Paul's corpse was in the trees?"

Great. This will make her even more neurotic. "No, not his corpse," Sean said. "Him. Or at least a guy who looked like him, said he was him. Other people, too, who had died."

Helene shook her head and flinched. "*Dead people?* Here? Why would you say such…" She swallowed, gaze darting about as if rotting corpses reached for her. "Such an awful thing?"

"I know it sounds crazy, but they came out of the tree farm. They were naked, had no idea where they were or what was going on. The cops were here because Nic called them. But these people, they all claimed to be folks who'd *died*."

Bailey closed his mouth, settled himself, and said, "Sean, I know you've illustrated some pretty strange things, but you're scaring your mother."

Her? I'm scaring myself! "This isn't a comic, this happened. Today. Here." Sean turned again to his mother. "Mindy Howard died a couple of years ago out on the highway. She was here in my kitchen this morning. Evelyn Fischer. I'd never met her but she said she knew you."

"Not Evie." Helene scoured her arms with her palms. "No. You were a baby when she got hit by that snowplow."

Sean pressed on. "That Dunders kid who got run over was here too. And so was Uncle Paul. They're all at the hospital now. Go check, if you don't believe me."

"It's not possible," Helene muttered through clenched teeth.

"The cops said they're running some scam, but I can't figure out why. What leverage could a woman who's been dead thirty years possibly use to swindle someone? And a little kid con artist? It makes no sense. And if it's some joke or hoax, why so many cops? And a *helicopter*? Seems like overkill, if you ask me." Sean glanced at Pastor Bailey before turning back to his mother. "And why'd they walk up naked? Why'd they all stink of mold?"

"What are you saying?" Pastor Bailey asked.

Sean took a breath. "The cemetery's right across the tree farm. Its driveway leads to Juniper Road. Maybe those people *were* dead, but aren't anymore."

"No," Helene spat out, as if that was the final word on the matter. "Paul's dead. I saw him dead, saw him buried."

Then she stomped out of the house, headlong into a perky young woman on the stoop with a microphone and a cameraman.

The young woman tried to ask Helene a question, but Helene dodged aside and continued down the steps, pulling a bottle of hand sanitizer out of her purse as she stomped to the car.

The newswoman's smile stiffened, then she saw Sean and Pastor Bailey in the living room.

"My cue to go. Good luck, son." Pastor Bailey patted Sean on the shoulder then ducked out of the house and hurried to his car.

The newswoman was young, early twenties, and over-dressed for the heat; an eager newbie sent out to cover a Sunday morning fluff story. "Guess it's just you and me," she said, her eyes imploring Sean not to slam the door in her face.

"Guess so." Sean sighed, feeling sorry for her. He stuffed his hands into his pockets as the camera clicked on.

Deep breath, he thought as the woman asked her first question. *Don't spill your guts and sound like a lunatic. Try to plug the comic. Free advertising and all that crap.*

He took a breath and made himself smile. *And don't screw this up,* he reminded himself as he told her how the people had walked out of the trees.

GhoulBane fell forward, floundering to the edge of a gravel road. His flesh lay in oozing tatters, exposed bone coated with mud and dog shit, and he struggled to get his feet beneath him again so he could stand. Struggled and failed.

Road grit dug into his tortured flesh as he crawled, the shards tearing and burning, grinding raw bone to dust. Freshly fallen gold and crimson leaves swirled across the gravel, urging him on. Just a little farther, just a little more. He collapsed, his breath leaving flecks of bloody bubbles in the grit and dust. "Have to," he choked out, reaching forward, pushing with feet so pained he wondered how they still existed. "Have to get across."

Clover and foxtail, summer green on the far side of the road, trembled and cowered away, turning brown, brittle, and ashen in the wake of a Minotaur's furious screams. Still Ghoulie crawled, each movement fire and agony, each breath a choking clog of blood and foam.

The Minotaur bellowed its rage and frustration over GhoulBane's escape, heavy footsteps shuddering the world as it came closer, closer, a low, ripping growl following alongside. GhoulBane clawed toward the scorched and tortured grass, his panic a living, screaming monster of its own, but the growl grew louder, becoming a thundering tear in Ghoulie's brain. He wailed when hot breath and dog-spittle fell upon on his torn and bloody hands, wet himself at the teeth bared and snarling in his face. Minotaur behind and its hellhound ahead, Ghoulbane's desperate flight to the far side of the road was over.

"Go, girl," the Minotaur commanded and GhoulBane screamed his soul away as Peaches lunged, ripping, tearing, devouring, while the Minotaur—

Bap! Bap! Bap! "Sean! Open the door!"

Startled, Sean shoved away from the fading scent of Peaches' rancid breath, flipping over his stool and crashing to the floor in a frenzied panic. Sketches fluttered down like autumn leaves, following the busted-twig clatter of mechanical pencils and tech-pens. *Bones, Sean, they sound like dried old bones. Remember that sound?* He scrambled away and pressed his back against the wall.

My studio. It's just my studio, just another bad dream, he thought, his heart threatening to erupt from behind his ribs, his mouth as dry and gritty as the dust from the road. He raised his hands, wincing at a smear of spit and blood-red ink. The remembered ghost of road grit scratched his palms. He scrubbed them furiously on his jeans and left a sticky mess behind.

Thud! Thud! Bang! "Sean! You in there?"

He drew in one frantic breath after another and pushed to his feet. "Coming!" he called out as he stood. He wavered, taking a moment to glance down and confirm that his feet were still there—not gone, not eaten, right where they're supposed to be, by God!—then stumbled to the hall and the living room.

Hands shaking, he unlocked the deadbolt. He opened the door and stepped aside to let Mare in.

She huffed past with a load of groceries. "What a day! The AC was out on my ward again so everyone was super-cranky, the store was too fucking crowded, and I *finally* get to come home only to find Juniper Road's blocked. I had to go clear around to Pilot Mound and come in the back way, and it's hotter than hell out there."

Mare was sturdily built and curvy in all the right places, gorgeous to his eyes, but the day's heat had taken its toll. Her hair had clung to her plump, damp cheeks in dark curls, her bright, kitten-print scrubs had wilted to loose, saggy wrinkles, and she smelled faintly of sweat. "Why'd you lock the door? We never lock the door."

"Got tired of being pestered by news crews," Sean said, heading out to the sweltering afternoon. Driveway cement scorching his bare feet, he dove into the backseat of Mare's rusty Buick for the twelve-packs of pop and a huge bag of charcoal.

"Did you say *news crews?*" she asked, her hand resting cozily on his backside as he stood and kissed her.

"Yep. Let's talk about it inside, okay?" They'd been together a decade and he still loved to stroke the narrowing of her waist, but, with both hands full, he settled for a second kiss. Charcoal slung over his shoulder, he returned to the house.

She followed, carrying the last of the groceries. "Did Ghoulie finally break out? Some big star call for another album cover or movie poster? Des Moines or Ames commission a batch of community propaganda?"

I wish. "No. Afraid not." Sean set aside the charcoal and slid the pop into the fridge.

Mare handed him a gallon jug of milk. "What, then?" She tilted her head, giving him a sideways glance. "What'd you do?"

"Me? Nothing. I just helped some naked people that came out of the tree farm. They—"

"Naked people?" She sniffed, grimacing, as she handed him a carton of eggs and a bag of produce. "Let me guess. Transient streakers who haven't showered since last September?"

"Close, but no." Perishables put away, he wrapped his arms around her waist and tried not to sound like a lunatic. "Naked dead people. Ten of 'em."

She frowned, nodding as if it made perfect sense, then placed the back of her hand on his forehead. "You have a sunburn. Did you push-mow the backyard again? Without a hat?"

He kissed her and pulled away. "Nope. I ought to tell you they dirtied every sheet in the house, even the embroidered ones we got from your grandma. The first batch is in the dryer."

She stood frozen in place, her mouth working for a moment, before following him toward the living room. "Sean, wait. You're not making any sense. Tell me what happened."

He stopped in the archway and turned to face her as he tried to explain. Judging from her expression, he didn't do a very good job, but she listened, nodding in the right places, until he finished.

"Sean. Babe," she said before taking a breath. "This isn't possible."

"I know. But it happened."

"And *how many* news crews came?"

"All of them. Well, Eight, Five, and Thirteen, and a few newspapers. Fox hasn't shown up yet, but CNN called for a quote. Apparently no one else will talk to them at all."

He shrugged. "I got sick of the interviews and finally locked them out and unplugged the phone so I could get back to Ghoulie's new issue. Murph's sent a stack of emails wondering why I haven't shown him at least the prelims."

He let out a harsh breath and met Mare's gaze. "He's been called to a meeting with our publisher in the morning. Our sales are so crappy he's worried they might use any excuse to cancel us, especially if we miss deadline again. I can't tell him I'm late because of what's happening with the…the tree people." He turned away and headed toward his workroom. "What if he hires another artist? Ghoulie doesn't make much, but I can't—"

"Sean…" she said, reaching for him. "Forget Ghoulie. Forget the money. Are you sure you didn't hit your head or something?"

"Wish I had. The news crews' cards and a sheet from the sheriff are on the counter."

He shrugged again, knowing he sounded like a nutter. "I'd better get back to work."

He'd just righted his stool and gathered his pens and sketches when Mare walked into the little bedroom they used as a studio and office. She stared at her handful of papers and cards. "How? Why?" She blinked, shaking the documents at him. "I went to high school with Mindy Howard! Her funeral! This can't be real."

"I know, hon. It should be all over the TV news sites, maybe their teasers. Might even show one of my interviews."

She nodded, dazed. "Were they rotting? Like zombies?"

"No. Just scared, confused people. They looked perfectly normal, not scary at all."

She let out a nervous laugh as she read the sheriff's sheet again. "Ten confused zombie scam artists. In my house. Yaaay." She folded the paper and stuffed the business cards inside.

"You okay?" he asked.

"Think so." She forced a smile and took a breath, her color improving. "How're the layouts coming?"

"Okay, I guess. Finally started working on them 'round noon thirty so I'm way behind."

"Better you for a change than everyone else," Mare muttered. "At least you'll catch up. Murph is the procrastinator. Surely Black Pawn knows that." She looked past him to the drawing table. "Who's the kid? Thought you were doing Ghoulie."

Kid? What kid? Sean turned and took an immediate step back, crunching Mare's feet as he stared at a ghostly image in the blackened full-page illustration. A naked child screamed from within the darkness and clawed bloody streaks on a cinderblock wall. His feet were sawed off at the ankles, the exposed ends of his fibula and tibia coated with bright blood and dark filth.

Chapter Five

Her poor bare feet scorched and bleeding, and her legs aching and quivery from the long cross-country trudge, Mindy wiped sweat from her sunburned brow as she limped toward her mother's acreage in the northern county.

I hope Mom's there, that she hasn't moved, too.

Since it was only a few blocks from the hospital, she'd walked to her house first, expecting to find Jeff busy fiddling with his stocks online like he did most Sunday afternoons, but two middle-aged women lived there. They had been rather suspicious of a barefoot woman in scrubs asking for the previous owner.

She'd left before they could call the cops.

In town, few paid any notice to her but out in the county it seemed like every car slowed down to assess her intent. A farmer who had to be seventy suggested a bodily-fluid exchange for a ride, and a teenage kid in a rusted out Honda offered to give her a lift, no strings attached. She declined both.

Tattered feet or not, the long walk gave her plenty of time to think.

She'd seen desk calendars and newspapers before leaving the hospital. All agreed it was Sunday July 19, 2015, not Friday November 23rd, 2012. Even if she could explain away the heat, humidity, and green fields—which she couldn't—all of those calendars left little room for doubt.

She'd lost almost three years. She had no idea where she or the time had gone, only a normal sequence of memories, then blinking awake in Sean's backyard.

In her previous memory, it had been nearly dusk and spitting sleet after a long day of Black Friday sales at the mall. She had stopped at the Git-N-Go in Madrid for gas, then turned north again on Highway 17. All that was clear.

Did I make it to Luther? To Highway 30? she wondered as the curvy, paved road she walked on turned north. Instead of following the pavement, she walked straight into the muddy ditch. She limped across a meadow to the far side and entered the thin strip of woods separating the paved street from the twisting gravel road her mother lived on. She'd used the same shortcut countless times as a kid, and the well-worn path comforted her feet like an old friend. *Maybe Luther,* she thought, ducking under a low branch. *Maybe. But, no. I didn't cross—*

She stopped, heart hammering, as a mud-flecked Boone County Sheriff's car sped north on the gravel road ahead of her. She ducked, crouching behind a tree, but it had already passed. She heard the cruiser leave the gravel to pull onto the paved road. Still crouching, she turned to track its journey. Lights on but without a siren blaring, it sped away, heading toward Boone.

Were they looking for me? Did they come to warn Mom about me?

Mindy let her heart rate settle before she crept forward, then crouched again near the edge of the woods to watch her mother's house. Her mom's familiar SUV sat in the drive, and the house looked the same, but Mom had planted red and white petunias out front instead of her usual peach colored impatiens.

Tears stung Mindy's eyes. *Oh, Mom, you know those are my favorite! You never stopped hoping I'd come back!*

Another car approached, and Mindy ducked behind a scraggly bush. The car pulled in the drive and stopped, tires skidding on gravel. Her younger sister, Danielle, scrambled out. Dani was pregnant, her dark hair cut short, and she ran to the house.

She eased back to sit on her heels, her mind churning. *Dani. Pregnant. At Thanksgiving she thought Mikey was about to ask her to marry him. Maybe a Christmas engagement. Maybe*

Valentine's day. But soon. They were so cute together, so happy.

Mindy stood. *Almost three years is a long time. I don't know what happened to me, where I was, but I've missed so much.*

She smiled and limped out of the woods onto her mother's front lawn. She expected to see their aging golden retriever wander around from the backyard, slow but happy to see her. Instead, a small dog barked from inside of the house.

Three years too long, she thought, feeling a tight pang of sadness at the absence. *What was I thinking? He would have been twelve, almost thirteen. Far too old for a large dog.*

Mindy had not yet reached the deck when her mother yanked the front door open. She'd been crying, her haggard face blotchy and red, and her rich brown hair had become white with flecks of steely gray. She was emaciated, a mere husk of her soft self, and leaned on a cane like an old crone. Mom. Who'd been a laughing and vibrant fifty at Thanksgiving.

"Get off my property before I call the sheriff!" Mom screamed. "They were just here, and they told me all about you! Swindler! Cheat! Trying to ruin the memory of my Mindy!"

Mindy winced at the decaying shell her mother had become. "Mom, please," she said, tears welling in her eyes as she grasped the stair rail. "I'm so scared, I don't know—"

"You're not my daughter, and don't you try to trick me!" her mother screeched. "My Mindy died! She DIED and you're a filthy bitch for even thinking you can—"

Dani tugged on their mom's arm. "Come on back in the house."

I died? Mindy thought, knees threatening to buckle even as she reached toward her mother, still so far away. *I really died? Oh, Mom! Please don't leave me here alone!*

Dani said, "I'll take care of this, okay, Mom? Your heart… You know what the doctors—"

Mom wrenched her arm free and snarled, "You get off of my property right this minute, or I'm calling the sheriff. You hear?" She stomped into the house, leaving Dani staring down at Mindy.

"You better go." Dani crossed her arms over her chest. "I'll drag you to the end of the driveway myself if I have to. She's sick. She doesn't need this stress."

Mindy wiped away tears and met her sister's gaze. *I'm not dead or missing, I'm right here. Dani's my baby sister. She has to believe me, she HAS to.* "I… I know this is going to sound crazy, but I really am me."

Dani closed the door, cutting off their mother's wails and took an angry step toward Mindy. "No, you're not. I had to identify her body because her asshole husband didn't have the balls. She's dead. My big sister's *dead.* And you're some sick—"

What? No! Jeff! What's happening? Mindy steadied herself before she crumpled to the ground. "How'd I die?" she asked, her voice quaking. "Where's Jeff? Why is—"

"My sister died in a car accident, but you surely knew that before you came here, just like you know her husband's name."

Mindy searched her memory for a detail, any detail, which might confirm her identity. "I also know you played flute but gave it up your junior year, despite being the best in band. You said it wasn't a challenge anymore, but you really quit because you had a crush on Trent Sparks and he thought band kids were stupid."

When Dani's eyes grew wide, Mindy said, "You got your first period while we were at our cousin's house. He kept teasing you about being on the rag and Mom yelled at him then took us home. You like caramel on ice cream, but won't eat it in candy."

Dani paled and grasped the deck railing. "How did you know—"

What else? There has to be something that'll convince her. "Your first date with Mikey was to see *Twilight*. You hated the movie but said 'he's a keeper'. Last I knew, he still was."

"Still is," Dani said, nodding.

Mindy managed to smile despite her trembling lower lip. "Christmas engagement?"

Dani took a step down the deck stairs. "No, actually, it was while we were planning your funeral. He said he didn't want to wait anymore, didn't want to lose one moment we might have together." Tears poured down her cheeks. "We were married by Christmas, pregnant with our daughter by Easter. We named her Melinda, after you." She wiped the tears away. "Oh, God, how can you be here? This can't be—"

"I was driving home in sleet, I remember it like it was just a few hours ago, then next I knew, I'm in some guy's yard. Standing there. This morning. Almost three years later, in July."

"This has to be a lie," Dani said. "It *has* to. What you're saying is impossible. Dead people don't come back."

"It's the truth. It happened. You have to believe me."

Dani pursed her lips and shook her head. "You do look like her, sound like her, but Mindy's dead." She took a deep breath and let it out. "Mom can't take this, all right? Mindy's death and all the legal shit broke her heart, broke *her*, and she's been sinking ever since. I'm just thankful she's still with us. If you give her false hope that some miracle happened, and it's a lie, it'll kill her. I can't let you do that."

What? "What's wrong with Mom? What do you mean 'all the legal shi… What legal stuff?"

"Your calcu…, no, *Mindy's* calculating shit of a husband had insured her for over a million dollars before the accident. Grieving husband, my ass. We caught him fucking her best friend at the visitation. He ran off and married the tramp before my sister was cold in her grave."

Mindy took a step back, shaking her head. "He *what*?"

"You heard me. Big shot banker cheating bastard son of a bitch. Bad enough he treated Mindy like stale bread, but Mom blew her savings suing him. Turned out the brakes were bad in Mindy's car and the airbag malfunctioned. Wonder how *that* happened?"

"No, my Prius was fine! It had to be! Jeff just bought it for me, brand new, in October."

"Yep. Mindy picked out her car three days after he bought the insurance policy. The dealership had proof all parts were new, but the crash investigator said Mindy's brake hoses were old and cracked. Was only a matter of time before they went bad, and on a highway, on ice, with a malfunctioning airbag…" She shrugged. "He sued Toyota and won, then insurance paid up. Was quite a windfall."

Mindy's paced, her mind churning. *Jeff would sue whoever was responsible, definitely, but what Dani's suggesting is nuts. He wouldn't kill me, he loved me!*

Dani sighed. "Mom tried to prove it was his fault, but the court decided she was being greedy, him being a grieving widower and all. He danced off scot-free *and* a millionaire. So instead of trying to talk my dying mother out of her last few bucks, why don't you swindle the cold-hearted fucktard my sister married? Least he's loaded."

"That's not fair. I know Jeff can be a controlling jerk, but he does love me."

Dani rolled her eyes. "Yeah. And denial isn't just a river in Egypt."

Mindy pursed her lips at the familiar phrase and stared out to the driveway. She'd considered leaving him a few weeks before Thanksgiving, had even contacted a lawyer, but Jeff controlled the money, her friends, her freedom, and any possibility of escape. "Where is he?" she asked. "A couple of lesbians are living in my house and I have no idea—"

"Got promoted more than a year ago. Took the skank and moved to Minneapolis. I hear they spend a lot of time at a time share in Barbados."

Minneapolis might as well be the moon, if I have to walk there. Mindy let her breath out in a huff and sat on the bottom step. "Any more bad news?"

Dani descended the stairs, lowering her pregnant bulk to sit beside her. "Isn't that enough?"

I guess it is. Mindy looked out to the dirt road curving into the woods. "Mom pretty bad?"

"Yeah. Heart, blood pressure, some scary digestive issues." Dani paused to chew her lip. "They just did a biopsy last week. Might be colon cancer, might not. We'll know in a week or so."

Jeff. The dog. Mom. Me. Mindy clasped her hands between her thighs. "What a mess." She sighed and stood. "I should just go. Thanks for telling me the truth."

She took two steps then Dani said, "Your feet look like shit."

"Walking barefoot from the hospital kinda does that."

"You don't have any shoes?"

Mindy turned to face her sister and managed to meet her gaze. "I don't have *anything." Not a husband, not a family, and certainly not any stupid shoes.* She plucked at her scrubs. "I stole these when I escaped from the hospital. They're the total of my worldly possessions, and they're not even mine."

"Dammit, dammit, dammit. I must be crazy." Dani shook her head. "I can give you a couple of bucks to—"

Mindy turned toward the driveway again. "It's okay," she said over her shoulder. "I'll manage. Take care of Mom."

"Wait." Dani stood and walked toward her. "I have some of your old stuff. I picked it up when Jeff was throwing it out. You can have that. And when's the last time you ate?"

"I haven't. Not since—"

Dani held up a hand to stop her. "Get in the car. I'll get Mom settled then we'll get you something to eat, and decent shoes. I can do that much at least."

Chapter Six

Thankful for the worn familiarity of Dani and Mikey's dinky apartment, Mindy sat on their couch while they argued in the kitchen just a few feet away.

"I don't care who or what she is," Mikey grumbled, his voice low. "She can't stay."

"But what if she *really is* Mindy?" Dani asked him. Again. "We can't just put my sister out on the—"

"Mindy's dead. You know it, I know it, *everyone* knows it!" Mikey snapped. He blew out a tight breath and paced beside the fridge, head bent and work-worn hands balled. "She's obviously given you some drug to believe this nonsense."

"Gonna use the bathroom," Mindy said, standing. Without glancing at the pair huddled by the fridge, she walked to the bathroom and closed herself in.

Of course he doubts me, she thought, catching her reflection in the mirror. *I'd doubt me, too.*

Her own grimy face stared back and she leaned close, examining every pore and freckle. The thin scar above her eyebrow was gone, as was the little pucker along the edge of her upper lip. No acne scars, and her ear piercings had disappeared. *Weird.*

Same eyes though, mahogany brown with flecks of gold around the edges of the iris. Same slightly crooked nose. Same faint cleft in her chin. Same unruly mop of hair. She pulled her lips back to see her teeth then frowned before leaning forward to examine them again. Her right eyetooth, chipped by the softball that had split her lip, was intact. "Shit," she whispered before opening her mouth to look deeper inside. No fillings.

How much weirder can this get?

Using the mirror, Mindy examined the rest of her body. No scar on the back of her elbow from her fall down the porch stairs. No sunburn scarring on her shoulders. No marks from the stitches that had closed the arch of her foot after stepping on glass barefoot. Her birth control implant was no longer in her upper arm. And the mole by her belly button she'd removed because Jeff didn't like it was right back where it had once been.

It's like I'm all new. Newly Minted Mindy.

Smiling slightly, she sat on the toilet. The bathroom looked the same as always, other than the baby stuff in a net suction-cupped to the back of the shower surround. The same faded blue rug. The same iPod player on the same brass shelf behind the toilet. Same cheesy picture of butterflies on the wall over the towel bar. Same Pantene conditioner on the tub edge.

Nope. Not quite the same, she thought, standing. *The label design is a little different. More blue, less gold. And the bottle's flatter. The same, but still different.*

She gazed into the shower with longing. *Soap. Warm water. A good scrub. Be clean, feel clean. Not so grimy and sticky.*

Someone rapped on the door. "You okay in there?" Dani asked.

"Yep, almost done." Mindy closed her eyes and released a tired sigh as she pulled up her stolen pants. *Not pink, not pink,* she thought before looking down.

Normal golden urine tinted the water in the toilet bowl.

She glanced at the ceiling and muttered, "Thank you," before flushing it away. After washing her hands, she opened the door.

Dani stood in the hall and held a couple of plastic store bags stuffed with clothes. "I… I have these. If you want them," she said, thrusting them toward Mindy.

Mindy recognized her own clothes. Jeans. Sweaters. The lacy undies she'd bought for Valentine's Day in the hope he'd notice her. She couldn't hide her flinch. *Jeff. How could you?*

A baby fussed from the spare bedroom and Mikey brushed past without looking at either of them. Dani flinched when he slammed the door. He looked tired and smelled of manure and sweat. Probably from helping his dad on the farm or something.

"He's not himself," Dani said. "Things are tough at work. He's worried that…" She shrugged and lowered her gaze.

"It's tough everywhere," Mindy said, gently taking the bags from her sister's hands. "Lots of folks are out of work."

Dani met Mindy's gaze. "Not so much now. The economy's on the mend, especially in Ag products. Lots of guys are bolting for better paying jobs. His team's lost two people this month, and he got a call this afternoon asking for references for a third guy." She shrugged. "If he goes too, that'll just leave Mikey and Nate to do the work of five. He's kinda cranky."

"It's okay. I know I'm being a pain. Complicating everything."

Dani's face turned blotchy. "You look so much like her, sound like her," she said, voice cracking. "But this can't be real."

"I know, but it is," Mindy sighed. She chewed her lip for a moment, hesitating. "Can I… Can I ask a favor?"

Suspicion darkened her sister's gaze, and Dani shifted to lean back, one hand covering her rounded belly. "What kind of favor?" she asked, voice tentative.

Mindy willed herself not to cry. Now even Dani doubted her. "I'm filthy. Can I take a shower? Just a shower, then I'll go."

It broke her heart to see Dani's gaze turn calculating, as if gauging what valuables and precious trinkets Mindy might steal. "Okay," she said at last. "The towels are—"

"In the linen closet, here in the hall, I *know*," Mindy sighed as she walked to the door and opened it. Bed and bath linens filled the shelves, with a hamper and vacuum beneath, along with a tangled pile of winter boots. Mindy pulled a towel from the shelf and turned to face Dani. "I helped you move here. Helped you unpack. Remember? I bought you that vacuum as a housewarming gift." She wiped at her eyes with the back of her hand as she slipped past her sister to the bathroom. "I'll be quick. Tell Mikey I said you can check all my pockets before I go."

Before Dani could respond, Mindy locked herself in. She leaned against the door and let herself cry.

Sean crumpled up yet another sheet of paper. *I've never had a drawing blockage like this,* he thought, letting the paper fall to the kitchen floor.

Mare stood at the sink, sorting dishes. "You want to go to the cemetery? You sure?" She tested running water with one hand and squirted dish soap with the other. "What about the sheriff?"

"Those folks came to our house," Sean muttered, his hands clenching into his hair at his temples as he tried not to look at the microwave clock or the scattered wads of paper. Out of all of the loose sketches he'd drawn since locking out the news crews, only two featured Ghoulie. The rest were children, and most were detailed drawings of the same scared boy. None, not even the Ghoulie sketches, had anything what-so-ever to do with the script. Forcing himself to sit down and draw anyway, even with his zone-out-and-create music blaring on the iPod, garnered him no useful progress. Just the boy, other kids, then the boy again and again and again. *And the dog, don't forget the fucking dog,* he thought, pounding his fists against the side of his head. He'd worked for nearly six hours and had nothing useful to send to Murphy or Black Pawn, only a splitting headache and hand cramps.

Mare washed dishes awhile, head nodding to Sean's music. "Our house or not, you're not responsible for those people, hon, or where they came from. The six o'clock news showed the cemetery driveway blocked off and patrolled, with scads of people shaking protest signs. Looked like a madhouse."

"They also edited me to look like a raving, zombie-spouting lunatic," Sean muttered. "Just 'cause it was on the news doesn't make it true."

He tried again to draw Ghoulie facing down a mob of zombie construction workers, as per instructions. "Something happened to bring those folks back," he said, barely aware of his own voice as his pencil drew a young face around Ghoulie's world-weary eyes, "and whether I can get in or not, whether anyone believes me or not, I still have to try. Maybe figure out what's going on and why it won't let me draw Ghoulie!" He muttered a curse and wadded up the page, tossing it onto the pile with the others.

"You okay?" Mare asked, drying her sudsy hands.

"Not really." He tried to smile at her as she rubbed his shoulders. "It's just something I have to do. I'm thinking pretty late. Maybe midnight, ish. You can come along, if you want."

She grinned and perched on his lap. "I haven't been arrested since the street riots my freshman year." She kissed him soundly and handed him his bottle of Excedrin. "Might be fun."

Siren blaring, Deputy Todd Anderson pulled into the GetGoin' parking lot, first on the scene at less than one minute after the missing kid call came through. He checked in and exited the vehicle to sweltering midday heat and assessed the spectators and location, a block off Highway 30 and moments away from escape in any direction.

He hoped this was just a pissed off kid playing a scary trick on his folks, but his gut insisted it was a helluva lot worse.

The crowd parted, opening a path to the store, and he used every inch and pound of his towering bulk to appear imposing. A quick head count gave him eight individuals and, in the distance, he heard Boone Police approaching. "Everyone stay here, all right? In case we have questions."

The people nodded, some swallowing and looking incredibly worried, not that he could blame them. Child abductions were terrible on everyone. The not-knowing, the endless slavering fear, the guilt of 'if only I'd done this or been over there' that might have prevented the horror in the first place.

"Whatever we can do," an elderly woman said, her crone hands crushing her purse into a rag.

"Eight on site," Todd muttered into his shoulder radio. "Notify local they've agreed to be questioned."

The dispatcher squawked her affirmative as he opened the gas station's door.

The chilled air and darkness assaulted him, along with the familiar scent of fountain pop and hot dogs. A nervous clerk stood aside while a young family huddled together beside the counter in the otherwise vacant store. The infant slept, apparently oblivious to the upheaval, while Mom and Dad soaked their pullover shirts and short khakis with sweat and terrified tears.

Already grieving, already thinking he's dead or molested.

The GetGoin' employee wrung his hands and let out a sigh of relief as Todd walked in. "That was quick!" he said.

"Was just passing the Ford dealership on the highway when I got the call," Todd replied as both parents looked up, startled.

"Bought our minivan there," the father said, chin quivering.

"It's a good shop. Can you tell me what happened?"

"Justin's gone!" the mother wailed, turning red as she slumped against her husband.

"We'll do everything possible to find him," he said, knowing that while most kids come home, sometimes they never resurface, at least not alive. "Let's start with your names?"

Brent and Jill Lansing. Baby Eva. Justin, the missing boy, was eleven. Todd wrote down Justin's description and immediately called it in, only to hear his dispatcher re-broadcast the information to every police department, country sheriff, and state trooper in Iowa. The dad produced a couple of photos from his wallet. *Skinny, regular-looking kid.*

Todd couldn't tell if the Lansings were reassured or alarmed by the urgent chatter on his radio as he tucked the photos into his notebook. "What brought you to GetGoin' today?"

"Needed gas." The dad pointed to the north. "We live a few blocks from here. We're here all the time. I pump, Justin pays."

"He's right," the clerk said. "The kid's in here every day or two for pop, chips, whatever. Kid knows how to use the ATM card."

"Was that the wrong thing to do?" the mom asked, clutching the infant tighter. "Giving him the card? Sending him in alone?"

Not supposed to be wrong in small town Iowa but the world's a hard place sometimes. Least we're finally taking these calls seriously and not waiting. Might save a few more kids, Todd thought as he noted the information. After getting the mother's ATM card, he asked, "Did you see him enter the store?"

"Oh, he entered," the clerk blurted. "Even paid. I've got it all on tape."

"We'll need to have that." Todd relayed the presence of a surveillance video to dispatch. "What happened after he paid?"

"Went to use the restroom," the clerk said.

Both parents nodded. "He told us he needed to pee." The dad embraced the mom who folded right in. "I told him to hurry, we're supposed to be in Des Moines by four thirty. Family picnic thing."

Least they're not blaming each other, Todd thought as he nodded and wrote. *So many folks do.*

"I told him he should have gone before he left the house," the mom wailed. "But kids, they never plan ahead, do they?"

"Not usually, ma'am." Todd had used the GetGoin' restroom several times and he glanced down the short hall to confirm his memory. The men's room was right by the back door. "Is there a camera back there?" he asked the clerk.

"No. It's locked from the outside. We just have cameras on the counter."

"Did you see him enter the bathroom?"

"No, but I did see him waiting to use it. We got busy, and I lost track of him. He rides his bike up here most afternoons. I didn't think nothing of him standing back there by himself."

Todd managed to not purse his lips. He wouldn't let his daughter Hailey ride her bike beyond the end of the driveway without supervision. "Did anyone go around back to look for him?"

"I did," the dad said. "There's just a dumpster and a field. I yelled but couldn't find him. It'd been ten minutes, maybe, since I seen him. So I ran in and we called you."

So a possible opportunistic abduction, either from a customer in the store, or whoever was already in the bathroom. Or, hopefully, he snuck out with another kid and is whooping it up at a park or the movies.

"Need a forensic team, ASAP," Todd told dispatch as local police came in. "And put a track on the father's ATM card," Todd said before relaying the mom's banking information to the dispatcher.

"Did you go through the back door or walk around?" Todd asked.

The dad's face flushed. "Through. I've ruined evidence, haven't I?"

"Why are you questioning Brent? He was with me and Eva the whole time. You need to be looking for Justin! He went in here and didn't come back out!" she cried, trembling. "Please. You have to find my son."

"We'll do everything we can," Todd assured her then took the two policemen aside to bring them up to speed.

"I can get you something to eat." Dani waited for a pair of police cruisers to scream past before she pulled onto Story Street.

"It's okay. I've already bothered you too much." Mindy watched the cops barrel toward the highway as she clenched her precious bags of clothing tighter. She felt naked and exposed in jeans and a lacy cami that was technically underwear. It was too damn hot for a wool sweater, but the cami was better than nudity.

"I promised to feed you," Dani said. "And, really, we can stop at WalMart and get you a pair of shoes. You don't need to—"

"Your old flip-flops are fine," Mindy said, staring out the window. Boone looked the same, yet different. New restaurants. A new bank. Same old law firms and real estate agents.

"I am sorry about Mikey. I don't want to be…" Dani shrugged and, coasting to a stop in front of a taco place, flicked her turning signal on. "I don't want to be unkind."

That's dirty pool. She knows I love Mexican food. Mindy scowled at her sister as they entered the drive thru lane. "Mikey's fine. You're fine. Truly," she said, staring out the window again. "I'm the one who's messed up. You really don't have to feed me."

"Too bad. Baby's hungry and mommy is too." Dani ordered and handed Mindy her usual double tacos and cheesy 'taters, then she pulled into a parking space and turned off the car. "Eat," she said, unwrapping her own burrito. "I know you're hungry."

Yeah. I haven't eaten anything in almost three years, Mindy thought as she took her first bite. They sat in silence, eating and watching Sunday evening traffic. She wanted to ask Dani a hundred questions about her daughter and the baby on the way, about Jeff, about three years of changes to the world, but instead she ate her potato nuggets and tried to figure out what to do.

"Is there somewhere I can take you?" Dani asked, breaking the silence. "A shelter? A friend?"

Mindy shook her head and silently ate her potatoes. *What do I do? How can I survive with nothing but a couple of bags of clothes? I don't even exist anymore.*

"Hey," Dani turned to face her. "I can take you to Ames, to Des Moines, hell, I'll drive to Chicago if it'll help."

"I have nowhere to go. I don't know anyone anymore." Mindy stuffed her meal refuse in the paper sack. She glanced at Dani and managed a smile before reaching for the door latch. "Thank you for your help. I won't bother you—"

"No. Wait," Dani said, grasping Mindy's arm. "You have to understand. This is *impossible.* We… We have kids and can't take the chance that you might not be… Be my Mindy."

This smile came easier. "I know. It's okay. Really."

Dani still held her arm. "But if you are her, if by some miracle my sister's back, I cannot, *will not,* let her wander the streets homeless and alone. I *won't,* okay?" She moistened her lips and added, "There has to be someone, somewhere, who knows what's going on. Someone who can help."

"I haven't seen anyone but folks at the hospital, and the deputies who took us there."

"I'm not going to turn you over to the cops," Dani said, chewing her lip. "What about those other people you saw? Did any of them seem aware of what was going on?"

"No. They were all confused, too. And they're still at the hospital, as far as I know."

"Okay," Dani said, chewing her lip again. "What about where the cops found you? Was there a person in charge or anything?"

"No. I just woke up in some guy's backyard in Pinell. He seemed as confus…"

Perplexed at Dani's mortified expression, Mindy asked, "Are you all right? Did I say something wrong?"

Dani shook her head and turned on the ignition. "We buried you in a little cemetery east of Pinell." She backed out and drove to the exit. "Jesus Christ," she muttered as she turned onto the road, heading west. "What the hell's going on?"

Chapter Seven

After Mare suggested going back to basics and trying a grid-based layout instead of his usual freeform style, Sean managed to scrape out a few sketches. None would win any composition awards, but at least they weren't dark drawings of tortured children. And they featured Ghoulie, or rather a nebulous shape resembling Ghoulie. Maybe. If he squinted.

Eight spreads done. Not my best work, but it'll get to Murph before the meeting. Sean taped a fresh sheet to his drawing board. *God, I hate this stiff, structured shit.*

Mare tidied up the worst of his ratty lines on page six before scanning them into the Mac. "Looking better," she said.

"Yeah, better than dog shit on my shoes," Sean muttered, using a ruler to draw story cells on a blank page. "I haven't had to use layout blocking since I was in high school."

That scan done, Mare slid in the next. "Your lines are getting better. They're not so smudgy."

"Maybe I should just draw stick figures and be done with it," Sean muttered as he roughed in the next scene. Cursing, he reached for his eraser and scrubbed the page with it. *Bigger, bigger, you idiot. Ghoulie's full grown, not the size of a kid.*

Mare took a breath to speak, but someone knocked on the front door. "I got it," she said, bolting from the room.

Sean tried again to draw Ghoulie leaping onto a rushing semi. *Better not be another news crew,* he thought, pencil finding the familiar twisting line of Ghoulie's back and arm.

He heard Mare open the door and a quiet chorus of female voices, then Mare peeked into the studio. "I think you need to come out here."

"'Kay." Sean stretched and walked to her. "Who is it this time? The Drudge Report? The Onion? Another teenage blogger with an undead fetish ready to make fun of how I'm an idiot who screwed up zombie canon?"

Mare stared down the hall toward the living room and whispered, "No, nothing like that."

Sean grasped her hand. "You okay?"

Mare kept staring down the hall. "Think so." She leaned against him. "Just never thought I'd see what I'm pretty sure I just saw."

Still holding her hand, he led her to the living room then stopped. Mindy Howard and a pregnant woman lingered near the front door. The pregnant woman looked around as if she couldn't believe her eyes.

"Did something happen?" Sean asked them, wondering what was so mind boggling about his shabby living room. "I thought you were taken to the hospital."

"I was," Mindy said, nodding. "But I left. My sister Dani brought me here, hoping we could find some answers." She took a steadying breath then asked, "Do you have any idea what's going on? Did the cops say *anything*? Is there something, *anything* you can tell me?" She swallowed and her hands shook. "I'm totally lost here. I've lost more than two years of my life. Somehow."

Still holding his hand, Mare slumped to sit on the couch. "We took Home Ec together in high school. I went to your funeral. How can you be here?" she asked Mindy, her voice awed and terrified.

"I don't know. I was driving home then suddenly standing in his backyard."

"*Our* backyard," Sean said. It drove Mare batty when his mother referred to everything as his. He wasn't about to let a stranger do it, too. "It's our house."

"Okay," Mindy said, nodding. "But *how did I get here?*"

Sean admitted, "I have no idea. I woke this morning to find you and the others walking into our yard."

"So you don't know either," Mindy sighed. "This was just a waste of time."

"Not a total waste," her companion said. "Where'd you get such a great poster of GhoulBane? And the resin figurine? My husband would kill for such cool stuff like that."

Sean felt himself blush, but Mare said, "He's a Ghoulie Fan?"

"Oh my God, yes! Has every issue, some of them signed by the artist. He gave a talk on line drawing composition at the Ames comic shop last year, and Mikey was *thuh-rilled* to meet him. Was all he talked about for weeks."

"Oh, cool, I bet that was fun," Mare said, glancing at Sean who had long ago learned to keep his mouth shut. Better to say nothing than deny and be caught lying or fess up and be called arrogant. Since the stalker incident of '11, Mare had little patience for Ghoulie fans showing up at the house.

Despite Mare's stiff smile, Dani walked close to examine the poster. "Yeah, he said it was awesome and he thought the guy's from Iowa somewhere. You should totally get this signed. It'd probably triple the value."

"We'll look into that," Mare said.

All the while, Mindy stood near the door, watching Sean, fear and sorrow fighting to control her face. "Was that one guy first, just standing there in the trees," he said to her. "I thought he was trouble, so I went out to confront him, then you stumbled out. You were naked. You all were. I sent you inside to get a towel or something. Everyone else followed you."

He pointed east, toward the kitchen. "Everyone came from the tree farm. The cemetery's on the other side."

"Where I was buried," Mindy said, her voice soft. "What happened in the cemetery?"

"I don't know," Sean said. "I tried to find out this morning, but there were too many cops. We're gonna try again in a couple of hours." He glanced at Mare. "Did you want to..."

The women looked at each other and Mindy shook her head. "I... I'm not ready for that, I don't think. To see my grave." She shuddered. "Can I just wait here?"

Mare approached Mindy and took her hand, voice soft and coaxing, like she used with her patients. "Of course you can. I can't imagine how awful this must be. Let's get you something to drink."

Dani watched Mare lead Mindy to the kitchen. She hefted her purse higher onto her shoulder and said to Sean, "I really appreciate you guys doing this."

"Doing what?" He squinted at her. "You're not sticking around, are you?"

"No," the woman said, her gaze on the floor. "I can't. My husband won't understand."

She released a sigh and managed to look Sean in the eye. "I don't understand this either. My sister died almost three years ago. She… She's someone else. She has to be."

Before Sean could respond, Dani turned and opened the door. "Tell her…" she said, glancing over her shoulder, "tell her I'm sorry."

Sorry for dumping her on strangers? he thought, but did nothing to stop her. He heard her car door slam, saw the reflection of her lights as she backed out of the driveway and onto the road. When she pulled away, he stuffed his hands into his pockets and walked to the kitchen.

Mare and Mindy sat at the table, each clutching a glass of pop. Mindy's eyes were red and puffy. "Dani left, didn't she?"

"Yeah," Sean said. "Can I talk to Mare a minute?"

Mindy took a shaky breath and stared at her hands clenched together on the table.

Mare stood. "I'll be right back, okay?" she said, touching Mindy's shoulder. "I promise. Everything will be all right."

Mindy nodded and took a deep breath before raising her head as if facing certain retribution. "Sure. Sure it will."

They walked to his studio and closed the door. Whispering, head close to his, Mare said, "We can't just kick her out."

"We don't know her."

"I kind of do. She was one of the sweetest girls in school."

"So you already believe they're who they say they are?" Sean asked, running a hand over his head as he looked at the bedroom door. "Me having crazy thoughts is one thing, but you're supposed to be the sane one."

Mare pursed her lips then pressed on, undaunted. "I went to school with Mindy Robean. I *know* her, all right? And crazy though it may be, I have no doubt the woman out there is Mindy Robean Howard. Her family's already turned her away. That was her *sister* for God's sake. Where else can she go? She doesn't have anybody else."

Sean ran a hand through his hair. "Fuck."

"Hey, you're the one who found her. I seem to remember someone who tried to help these tree people."

"Yeah, but I didn't intend to open a homeless shelter for them. We don't have money, and we don't have *room*."

She nodded. "Maybe so, but we can't just toss her out, either. It's just…wrong."

"We don't even know what she is or what she might do to us." Sean paced. "I draw the undead, I don't live with them."

Mare shrugged. "She seems perfectly alive, perfectly sane, just like I remember her but a bit more timid. Who can blame her? And the Mindy I know wouldn't take anything, not that we have anything worth stealing." She paused to catch his gaze. "Think of how many folks have crashed on our couch for a few days, how many charities we've donated to. We've never turned anyone away before."

"You're right, babe. But how can she stay here? Where will she sleep?" He let his head roll back as he thought, *How can we afford to feed her? We can barely feed ourselves.* He sighed and muttered, "I guess there's the couch."

"There's a twin-sized bed in Jam's old room," Mare reminded him, her voice cracking.

He winced, his heart clenching. *Jam. God.* "Yeah, buried behind a ton of boxes and books."

Mare shrugged. "So? We excavate." She squeezed his hand. "She's just a scared young woman with nowhere to go. We should help her. All we can offer is some shelter, so that's what we do. At least until she figures something out."

We must be nuts. Or suckers, he thought, letting his breath out in a heavy sigh. "Okay. You go ahead and tell her. I'll start hauling boxes to the basement."

A storm front pushed its way across the sky after eleven, obliterating the moon and crackling with flashes of lightning in the northwest. Sean pointed his flashlight at the mud ahead of his feet and led Mare across the field as he grumbled over his late-night news segment. He'd sounded like an idiot, again. But at least much of the newscast had focused on a missing kid, not the tree people. Far behind them, Peaches barked and snarled, informing the neighborhood that someone was in the trees. Or maybe she was just barking to hear herself bark. Sean had always avoided dogs and didn't know the difference.

He glanced back toward the house. Mindy had looked about ready to shatter when they left, not that he could blame her.

"I think we're going to get wetter," Mare said, squeezing Sean's hand. "At least it'll break the heat for a while."

"And shut up the dog," Sean muttered, hoping Peaches remained securely trapped inside the invisible fence.

The looming rows of evergreens stood whispering in shifting wind, backlit by diffuse, untrustworthy light from far ahead. As he and Mare crept among the slippery shadows and snagging branches, they ran across more and more broken trees, as if someone had crashed against them instead of walking between. Sean squatted and took photos of a ruined row of saplings. *Did the police break them during patrols? Did the tree people damage them in their confusion?*

Flashlight turned off, they reached the cemetery a few steps after the first raindrops fell. Police tape stretched across a broken section of fence, and the air stank of the same musty funk Sean had smelled in the house. Across the cemetery, more police tape marked a creek that curled around the north and eastern sides of the gentle slope before plunging to Juniper Road and the Des Moines River not far beyond. A pair of sheriff's vehicles blocked the main entrance along the southern fence, their headlights on and shining onto the road.

Three deputies stood by the cars, facing a tangle of wild growth trees on the steep slope west of the cemetery but south of Sean and Mare. A flashlight flickered there, partially hidden by brush, then another moved up to join the first.

So it's not just us, he thought. *If we're quiet, maybe we won't be noticed.* He turned to assess the rest of the cemetery. The fence lay shattered before him, but to his left it ran unbroken to the north and across, barely visible beyond the glowing tarps near the curve of the creek.

Four rings of blue plastic tarps hung from tall frames standing in the creek's cleft. Light shone from within three of them like giant paper lanterns. The glowing tarps and occasional lightning illuminated the cemetery enough for Sean to make out the graves; all appeared undisturbed. He took a breath and looked to the south. The fence rose up again a few feet to his right and continued on unbroken past the woods to the gate near the cops.

No wonder the tree people walked into my yard, he thought. *If the gates were shut, this was the only way out of the cemetery. Still is the only way out. But the cops are a few hundred feet away at most. Maybe far enough that we can get a look at what's going on out here.*

He returned his attention to the closest glowing tarp-ring. *Can we do this? Can we get in, maybe take a few pictures, and get out without being noticed? Or at least quick enough hide in the tree farm before we're caught?* A third flashlight joined the previous pair in the woods downhill, and two deputies moved to intercept them.

Sean turned on his camera and took a breath. *We can do this.*

"What's going on out here?" Mare whispered, pointing. "Why hang all those tarps in the creek? And there, on that one grave. There's a weird, twisty thing on the grass. See?"

Screeewaaaawk!! "You, in the woods. Back up immediately," someone said over a megaphone. "This is a restricted area."

Nervous silence, then "We have a right to know!" a girl's voice screeched, echoing in the rain.

"You can't hide the truth for—" another teenager hollered, the last of his statement lost to thunder.

This is our chance, let's go! Sean lifted the police tape and held it up for Mare to duck under. She hesitated then slipped past. He followed and picked his way into the cemetery. Kneeling behind the closest tall gravestone, he took a picture of the twisted mass at his feet and hoped the stone hid him and the flash.

The flash-enhanced image glowed on the view screen. A convoluted network of whitish veins sprawled near the headstone. Were they plasma filaments? A root system? He paused to take another picture, a close-up, to better see the fluffed up, slimy texture. Then he looked around.

Each grave had its own odd, threaded shroud.

Mare grimaced at the image on the camera screen. "It looks like someone stretched a lumpy, veiny hunk of skin on the ground."

"I don't know what it is," Sean whispered, one hand reaching down to touch the tangled membrane. He found it warm and slick, slimy like snot, and he felt a faint pulse of fluid flowing within. "Whatever it is, it's warmer than the ground. And it's pulsating." He tried to fling it off his fingers, but the gunk stuck to him. "Sticky." He wiped his hand on his jeans and took another picture.

"Oh my God," Mare muttered, gaze darting around. "That's… It's…" She swallowed as Sean took a third picture. "I think we ought to go home," she said at last, her voice small in the rain. "It stinks out here and what if the stuff is dangerous? A terrorist biohazard or something? We're not even wearing gloves."

Just a few more, then we can go. Sean leaned forward to get another close up of the weird veiny membrane, making sure to get the gravestone in the shot. "None of the cops are wearing facemasks or protective suits, and none of the people today were sick. I'm willing to bet it's not toxic."

"Always the optimist," she muttered, crouching beside him. "So what do we do?"

"Get a few more pics," he said, motioning to a large gravestone close to the nearest tarp. "If nothing else, I can use these for inspiration for Ghoulie."

The cops and kids in the woods grew louder.

"Yeah, Ghoulie covered with snot strands. That'd be fun. Like I don't see enough of that at work," Mare said, barely audible over the warning squawk of the megaphone. Sean counted to three then they bolted, bent low, slimy strings shifting beneath their feet. They reached the next large gravestone and crouched behind it. "Make it quick, okay?" Mare said, wiping rainwater from her eyes.

"Sure." Sean shifted to take a photograph of the smear in front of him. "Just a couple more then we can—"

"Sean!" she gasped, pointing up the creek. "Did you hear that?"

"Hear what?" he whispered, gaze darting around. *Shit! Did a deputy spot us?*

"That!" she said, standing. "Something splashed in the water way over there. Something *big*."

He rose to look backwards over the gravestone to the cops and kids. Eight or nine damp, grimy teenagers clumped together, defiant and screaming. Two pointed up the hill, toward them, and Sean crouched again. "Mare. Get down. They're going to see—"

Lightning arched across the sky, bringing an immediate crack of thunder. Mare had walked toward the glowing tarps, still pointing. Past her, within the farthest, fluid splashed up to speckle the inside of the plastic.

"Hey!" the megaphone screeched. "You! Up the hill! This is a restricted—" The rest of the warning was lost to another peal of thunder. Sean bolted for Mare, swearing under his breath. He dragged her down to the ground as lightning crackled again.

Sean sneezed at the choking stink of mold. Beside him, Mare covered her nose with her hand.

"God, it stinks," Mare said.

Teenagers and cops yelled at each other down the hill, and one cop climbed the hill toward him and Mare. Not much time left. "I'm going to reach under the closest tarp and take a picture, then toss you the camera," he said, getting his feet beneath him. "You stay put. I'll run, get their attention, and once they're chasing me, you head back home. Get those pics downloaded and put on a disk, okay? Or the cloud. Somewhere we can get them back."

"What? Are you nuts? You'll get arrested!"

"Better than both us of getting arrested and losing the pictures," he said. Finger on the shutter button, he jumped down into the creek.

Teeth clenched, he faced into the wind and rain, and lifted the bottom of the plastic, pointing the camera toward the water while watching the deputy approach. Lightning crackled to the west as he pushed the button. Before the image finished processing, he tossed the camera to Mare and bolted out of the creek and toward the tallest gravestones near the crest of the hill.

"Stop!" the deputy yelled, but Sean skirted a knee-high gravestone and kept running. "You can't escape!"

Escape isn't my plan, Sean thought, taking a zigzag route to the eastern bend of the creek and the splashed tarp. Someone down the hill hollered in pain as Sean leapt into the water and ripped the tarp half off its ring. Struggling to catch his balance in the mud and current, he scrambled aside before falling face-first onto a thrashing wad of white, foamy slime or knocking over the floodlight that shown down upon it. As large as a beanbag chair and releasing strings of delicate bubbles, the mass quivered and splashed about under the water's surface like a fish caught on a line.

The burbling slime-mass roiled, dousing Sean with water and foam as it flipped. Bits of it slid off and floated away, leaving a purple-tinted swirl in their wake. *What the hell's happening here?*

The deputy jumped down into the creek, hand on his gun, his uniform drenched and muddy. He was maybe twenty and looked terrified.

Despite his own fear, Sean smiled at him. "Hey," he said, gesturing at the thrashing mass as a human foot burst out, flecking them both with purple slime. "Whatcha got here?"

"Nothing you need to see. You're gonna come with me."

"Fucker maced me!" a young man's voice screeched from the dark. "Fucking bastard asshole!" The deputy turned with a lurch toward the noise.

A gun went off with a loud high pop that echoed through the storm. Out there, somewhere, a woman screamed.

Be a warning shot for the kids. Let Mare be all right! Sean froze, heart slamming, while, before him, the slimy thing fizzed and fell apart, exposing an arm, a torso, the back of someone's head. The deputy cursed and clambered out of the creek, leaving Sean alone. He crouched in the water and tried to help free the thrashing person from the muck.

The kids continued to scream at the cops, and he heard a crash and sounds of fighting. *It's toward the gate,* he told himself, as he glanced where the deputy had recently stood. *Not toward Mare.*

"Filthy goddamn pigs! You're breaking my fucking arm! Do you know who my dad is? I'll have your fu—" The rest was lost to the storm.

A woman burst up beneath Sean's hands, gasping and coughing up water, as the remaining frothy mass floated away and dissolved into a purple swirl.

She slumped sideways and collapsed into the water, but tried again to crawl up the bank, looking up at him with fearful eyes, dark and gleaming. She dripped with purple mucus and white foam, and she slipped again as she cowered away from him. Her scream sounded like a trapped rodent. Despite his apprehension, Sean approached her and held out his hand.

"It's all right," he coaxed, heart hammering. "Come on. I'll help you."

How can this be happening? he thought as he examined her young face, surely no older than mid twenties. *So human, so impossible.* "Can you stand? Can you talk?"

She opened her mouth and squeaked at him, and she barely resisted as he grasped her hand and drew her to her knees. The whites of her eyes shimmered lilac in the floodlight, the irises deep violet. Her skin was cold and clammy, goose pimpled, and she shivered.

"Gonna get you out of here," he said, drawing her toward the bank. "Get you dried off, covered up." Her knees buckled and she collapsed in the creek again as she blinked dumbly up at him. The brilliant purples in her eyes had already faded. She smiled, but it was mindless, like a child's doll. Whatever she was, she was no threat. It was like looking into the eyes of a newborn. "Aaah gah?"

"Yep, ah gah. C'mon," he said. "You can do it. On your feet, now."

The deputy returned and, reaching for the radio at his shoulder, barked, "What do you think you're doing?"

"Helping this poor woman stand." Sean draped one of her arms over his shoulder and got his strength beneath her. "I could use a hand here, or didn't they teach you to help people back in Deputy Academy or whatever the hell it's called?"

The young deputy's cheeks turned red. He stammered then said, "You're under arrest for interfering—"

"Fine. Arrest me," Sean said, struggling not to slip on the remaining mucus. "But help *her*. She's freezing out here!"

Together they managed to drag the young woman, stumbling, out of the creek and down the hill. A row of teenagers lay face down on the ground near the police cars, their hands secured behind them and a deputy standing guard. The third deputy carried a blanket toward Sean and the young deputy, huffing as he dragged his heft up the hill.

"Great, just great," Todd muttered as he approached. "You were supposed to call for backup."

"He was trying to help her," the young deputy replied, voice sounding whiny. "And he didn't seem—"

"Didn't seem could get your ass killed," Todd said. He stopped and sighed at Sean. "What are you doing here?"

Sean smiled. "Guess I'm a bad penny."

Todd wrapped the woman in the blanket and sent her down the hill with the young deputy. He glared at Sean. "Bad, no. Too damn curious for your own good, yes." He sighed and looked Sean over. "I saw flashes. Where's your camera?"

"Dropped it in the chase," Sean lied.

"Uh huh. A cheapskate like you? I don't believe that."

Sean held his arms wide. "You can pat me down. Check my pockets…"

Todd's shoulders slumped. "I don't have time for your crap. Not after the day I've had." He grabbed Sean's upper arm and turned him toward the northwest. "Go home. Forget whatever you saw."

"You know I can't—"

"Yes, you damn well can," Todd snapped. "We have backup on the way, but, for right now, I've got two rookies down there who will keep their yaps shut if I tell them to. I'm already in enough shit without having to drag your sorry ass in for a bullshit charge of trespassing on public property just so you can show up in arraignment and spill your guts to the judge and a hundred cameras tomorrow morning. No. Those kids are bad enough but they didn't see anything. You... You'll get me fired for starting a media shitstorm."

"What happened?" Sean asked as Todd pushed him toward the hole in the fence. "Why are these people—"

"Shut up and go home or you're going to jail. And those pictures had better not show up on the internet." Todd glared at Sean. "We're friends, remember? I've always trusted you. Don't fuck me over now."

Todd turned and walked away, huffing back down the hill. A million questions dancing in his mind, Sean watched him go.

Part Two
Growth

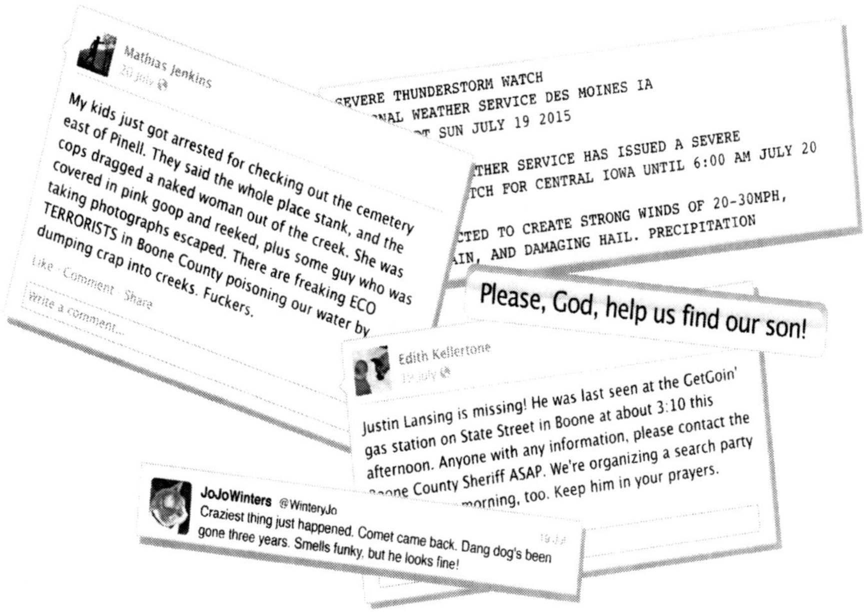

Chapter Eight

Rain pattered against the window. Mindy sat on her saggy borrowed bed, rocking herself with her arms wrapped around her legs. Her mind raced over the same few worries: Jeff, her family, being dead, having no provable identity or money, and being taken in by strangers.

I'm stuck, right and proper, she thought, face pressed against her knees as another peal of thunder rumbled outside. *What can I do?*

Sighing, she raised her head and looked out to her room. It was small, with scuffed mint green walls and worn Berber carpet with an orange stain—likely Kool-Aid or juice—just inside the doorway. A battered dresser leaned against one wall, its drawer fronts decorated with Transformers stickers shooting monsters scribbled in marker. The closet doors were gone but the track remained, and a cracked plastic shade covered the lone window.

Mare had given her a tour of the house. Other than the GhoulBane artwork, everything looked second hand or, at best, bought on sale at a discount store years ago. *They can't afford to let me stay here long,* she thought, resting her head on her knees again. *I'll cost them more food, more electricity, more water, more everything. I don't want to be a burden to anyone. I just want my life back. But I can't, because Jeff—*

The back door opened and she sat straight, breath caught in her throat. *What'd they find? Oh, God, do I really want to know?*

Mare and Sean came in the back door and talked in the kitchen, their voices sounding excited as they moved toward the living room, then the hall. Mindy stood, listening, her stomach tying itself into knots as they went into Sean's studio, the room next to her.

"Did it get too wet?" Mare asked. "I tried to keep it dry, but the rain…"

"I don't know yet," Sean said. "Where's the USB cable?"

"Top left… Here, I'll get it," Mare said.

Mindy stepped into the hall and braved a glance into the studio. Sean sat at a black and silver Mac, toweling his face and dripping wet hair while his feet tapped with hurried frustration. Mare, also drenched, rifled through a desk drawer. Sean saw Mindy and smiled. "C'mon in," he said, waving her into the room. "We took some pics."

"Found it!" Mare proudly displayed a white cable and plugged it in. She snapped the other end into the camera and stepped aside to dry herself as Sean clicked the mouse again.

"Why such a rush?" Mindy asked. "Surely it'll wait until you're dry."

"Maybe not," Sean said, flicking something on the camera. "I got caught by a deputy. He knows me and saw the camera. Gotta get the pics off it and onto a disk before he gets here."

"Oh." Mindy stood by Mare, pressing her forearms against her stomach to quiet the terrified glurgle. *Is it because of the photos, or because I might get in trouble for leaving the hospital?*

"Aw, shit," Sean muttered as the status bar filled and disappeared. "They're loading too quick. Looks like I forgot to put the camera on hi-res."

"Dammit," Mare muttered, scrunching her hair in the towel. "Hopefully they'll be okay."

"Should be," Sean said, leaning forward as shiny veins on a grave filled the screen. "960 by 1280. Not great, but it'll do," he said. "It's not like we'll be printing them."

"What are the veins?" Mindy asked.

"Not sure. Some kind of mold, judging by the smell," Sean said, moving on to the next picture, a close-up of the slime. Again, Sean's few clicks brightened and enhanced the photograph. Mindy could see raindrops beading on the translucent surface. "Is that what I came from?" she asked, grimacing.

"No," Sean said, clicking a few times as another puddle flickered on the screen then disappeared again. "I'm pretty sure you came from one of these."

The new picture showed a puffy ball in a creek, partially hidden beneath a fallen branch and spewing countless fragile tendrils of slime and foam.

Mindy thought it looked like a slimy version of the fizzy tablets people dissolve in water for cold medicine or denture cleaning. "That's it, isn't it? The thing that made me."

"I helped another woman come out of one," he said. "She was slimy, like you were when you first came here. All the goop just floats away."

Mindy's hands clenched against her belly as someone knocked on the door. *The sheriff!*

"Shit, shit, shit," Mare muttered, tossing her towel in the corner before hurrying from the room.

"Stall them, if you can." Sean leaned forward, chewing his lower lip, as he typed. A screen popped up, with another status bar, then first picture disappeared. He moved onto the next.

"Is there anything I can do?" Mindy asked as the next picture saved and closed.

"Are the cops looking for you?" Sean pulled a stack of CDs out of a drawer as the third photograph saved.

Mindy winced. "Probably. I kinda escaped quarantine at the hospital."

He kept saving files. "Hide in the bathroom. But be quiet."

"Go ahead. Let him in." Sean walked into the living room, camera in hand. "No reason to keep him standing in the rain."

Mare continued to face the barely open door. "He doesn't have a warrant."

Outside, on the stoop, Todd sighed and said, "C'mon, Mare. I told you I'm not here as a deputy, I'm here as a friend, okay? Just give me the memory card and I'll get out of your hair."

"Friend or not, you're still a cop. You want to take my private property, you'd better have a warrant."

Sean laid a hand upon Mare's shoulder and drew her away from the door. "Mare, babe, it's okay. Let him in."

Todd entered, his bulk diminished under a rain slicker, and nodded his thanks. "Look, I know and you know what you saw, but right now is not a good time. I'd really appreciate it if you could just give me the memory card—"

"I told you," Mare said, "not without a warrant! Friends still have rights, you know."

Todd frowned. "Give it to me, and I will keep you out of this shit that's about to hit the fan."

Sean held out the camera. "Here. It shorted out anyway, but I'd appreciate a receipt at least."

"Don't need to make any more paper trail than we already have." Todd opened the side of the camera. "Corroded batteries, that's a nice touch," he muttered as he slid the memory card loose. He held it like a coin between his fingertips. "This the right one, or have you substituted a fake?"

"It's the only one I have. The pics are on it. Or were."

Todd dropped the card onto the floor and crunched it beneath his boot. "The correct answer is 'no comment', or 'I'll have to ask my lawyer'. Anyone else comes to talk to you about what happened tonight, that's all you say." He tossed the camera back to Sean. "Got it?"

Sean caught it and watched Todd pick up the pieces of memory card. "Yeah, I got it." *Rather have gotten the receipt.* Curious, but reminding himself that Mindy was hiding down the hall, Sean asked, "Why are you doing this? Destroying evidence?"

Todd sighed and stood. "Because there's too much weird shit happening today and you haven't done anything but try to help these people. Or whatever they are. I don—"

Sean took a step forward. "They're *miracles.* I saw—"

"I know what you saw," Todd sighed. "I've seen it, too. It's been a shitty ass day, okay? I've had to explain to these scared fungaloids that every person they used to know and love has moved, died, remarried, or thinks this is all a cruel joke. I've been spit on, yelled at, hit, kicked, and threatened. That part's pretty normal, but being the first on the scene after a kidnapping and having to question terrified parents was pretty awful. Plus I've been up for almost twenty-four hours, the last five in the rain. I'm tired. No, I'm *exhausted* and my ass is already in enough trouble. I just want to file my report and sleep for about four days."

He sighed and turned to go. "I don't think the recruit knew who you were. But if he talks, if *anyone* shows up to question you, remember what I said."

"Dammit, Todd. What'd you do?" Mare asked, her voice soft.

Todd sagged. "Some of the fungaloids disappeared from the hospital. I was lead man there, so it's my ass. I'll be damned if I let this evidence leak."

Sean frowned. *He keeps calling them fungaloids. Is that stuff in the cemetery a fungus? It certainly would explain the smell.*

"I'm not going to ask you if you have copies of the pics—I know you do—but have you put them online, anywhere? Email? Twitter? The cloud?"

"No," Sean said, holding Todd's gaze. "Personal use only. I swear. Inspiration for Ghoulie and all." He wanted to ask more questions, about the mucus balls, the people, and the why of it all, but instead he held his tongue.

The men stood there, gauging each other, until Todd nodded. "All right. Once the news breaks, and it will, do whatever you want with them. Put up billboards alongside the interstate or sell them to *The National Enquirer* for all I care. But if your photos hit the web first, I'll lose my job. I can't afford to lose my job."

"We'd never do anything to hurt you or Hailey. The pics won't go anywhere. I promise."

Todd nodded and held out his hand. Sean shook it and Todd grinned. "Good to see you. Sorry it's under such squirrelly circumstances. We should get together for a drink or something some time."

Sean grinned back. "I bartend at Hap's Place Wednesday nights. Stop by and I'll get you a burger and a beer, on the house."

"It's a deal." Todd wished them a good night and left.

Mare closed the door behind him and turned to smile at Sean. "It's been a long time since we last saw Todd."

"Yeah," he said, shrugging. They'd been friends since they were kids, playing video games and getting into trouble together. Todd had been the one to suggest Sean go to art school instead of the military and had encouraged him to ask Mare out. But after Todd's wife had entered the picture, they'd drifted apart. "Kim broke his heart, I think." He grasped Mare's hand. "Maybe he'll start coming around more."

Mare squeezed his fingers. "Hope so. He's a good guy."

"He's gone?" Mindy asked, peeking around the corner.

Sean removed his hand from Mare's. "Yep. Just left."

Mindy smiled, relieved. "So, um, what happened out there? In the cemetery?" she asked, fidgeting. "Why am I here when I should be dead?"

Sean gestured toward the hall. "I don't know. But something in the pictures might help explain it."

Mindy listened to their tale and examined the pictures on Sean's computer. "It's not possible," she said, staring at the whitish veins sprawling in front of Evelyn Fischer's gravestone. Evelyn, the disoriented woman who'd kept sneezing at the back of the van. Born February 1942, died December 1985, and apparently back again July 2015. As a fungus. That cop had said so. And the doctors had found fungus in her blood.

Mindy clasped her hands between her thighs and stared at the photo. *Did I really come from one of those globs? How can this be real?*

"You okay?" Mare asked, squeezing Mindy's shoulder.

"I don't know," Mindy sighed. "Other than I'm just a fungus."

"You're not a fungus," Sean said from behind her. "Yeah, you smelled musty when I first met you, but you don't now."

Oh gee, thanks, Mindy thought, glancing up at him.

Mare frowned and nudged him aside. "Didn't you say that you were urinating pink, but you're not anymore?"

"Yes, but—"

"You're obviously not sick, you're not showing signs of skin lesions or systemic infection, and Sean's right. You smell just fine." Mare shrugged. "I work with sick people all day every day and I've seen a *lot* of fungal infections. I'm no doctor, but you're not showing a single symptom. You're not a fungus."

"But the doctors said we were infected, that it was all through our bodies, our cells."

"Maybe you've fought it off," Sean said, shrugging. "That woman I helped out of the creek… I saw her change. As she stood, her eyes stopped being purple."

"Just like my urine did," Mindy said. "So maybe the infection goes away?"

"I don't see why not," Mare said. "And I really don't think you're contagious. Someone would have come to take us to the hospital by now, or we would've been notified. Not all fungus is bad, after all."

"Right. Like mushrooms," Sean said. "Besides, none of the cops were wearing protective gear. Just regular uniforms. They didn't seem worried about infection."

"'Kay," Mindy sighed, warily eyeing the photo of Evelyn's grave. She still felt like a freak. A fungaloid freak.

An awkward silence settled over them. Mare said, "It's been a long day. I'm heading to bed." She squeezed Mindy's shoulder again and said, "Try to get some rest."

"I'll try."

Sean watched Mare go, and said, "You can look at them all you want. Or whatever. Just don't delete or save over anything, okay?"

"So I can, like, check my Facebook?" Mindy asked, hopeful. Jeff almost never let her check Facebook, if he let her use his computer at all. Heck, if he let her do anything at but take care of his needs, his wants, his demands.

Sean shrugged. "Sure. Why not? I have work files on there I don't want to lose. As long as you don't screw them up, you can do whatever you want."

Mindy managed a smile. "I won't. Promise."

Sean turned to go, but paused in the doorway to smile at her. "And no porn site viruses. My Mac's too innocent for that stuff." He winked. "Look at anything else you want, but stay away from the porn."

She laughed. "No porn. Got it."

They bade each other good night and, hand shaking, Mindy opened a browser window and went to Facebook.

Her page still existed, and she had 41 new messages waiting, all condolences for her family about her death. Despite insisting on full access to her account, Jeff not only hadn't bothered to open or respond to any of them, he hadn't posted anything about the accident in her timeline. Jeff had actually encouraged her last post, an excited, pre-dawn note about driving to Des Moines to shop. That brief post, which normally might have gotten a couple of thumbs-up, gathered more than twenty grieving comments. None of them received responses from Jeff, but Dani, her mother, and Mikey each had commented about the funeral arrangements and where to send donations.

Mindy took a breath and located her best friend's avatar. Just as Dani had said, Stace lived in Minnesota with her hubby, Jeff Howard. Not only did they have new lives in a new state, their pictures showed them fawning over their young son. Jeff had insisted he never wanted kids. Ever. Under any circumstances. But apparently he'd only refused to have children with *her*.

"Rotten bastard." She closed the browser window and was faced, again, with the weird goop on Evelyn's grave and the fizzy ball in the creek. She examined both photos for a long time and tried to ignore the faint sounds trickling through from Sean and Mare's bedroom. They sounded so happy.

She lowered her head. Had she and Jeff ever giggled while having sex? Ever enjoyed each other? Not that she could recall. Not even in the early days of their marriage, or their one drunken encounter that had started it all.

Eventually the house fell quiet again. Mindy couldn't help but imagine her hosts entwined and breathless, whispering and caressing one another. If Jeff had ever reached for her, he'd only been interested in getting it done, leaving his mess, then rolling over and going to sleep. She allowed herself one harsh moment of frustration and regret, then took a breath and reminded herself she wasn't done yet. By God, she wasn't going to screw up her second chance.

Lips pursed, she opened another window and visited news sites, reading everything she could about the day's odd happenings. Most seemed to blame an Ag chemical spill making people crazy. Or drugs. Or a cult. The only comments about anyone coming back from the dead were limited to angry posts accusing Sean of scaring people to sell his stupid comic, or because he was too drunk or stoned to tell fantasy from reality.

But on one message board, a little boy wanted to know if he came to Iowa if his dog would come back, like the man on TV said. He missed her so much.

"Aw, maan," Mindy said, her eyes stinging. She knew how a kid could love their dog, and how it hurt to lose them.

But I came back. Other people came back. What's to keep a dog from coming back, too? If whatever had brought her back was in the water, maybe it wasn't limited to people already buried in the cemetery.

She looked over her shoulder toward Sean and Mare's room, now silent. *He helped me, helped everyone. Would he help the kid?*

Deciding he would, Mindy took a breath, and responded.

Chapter Nine

"No no no no no!" Ghoulie said, lurching away and slamming on his side onto hard dirt floor. He kicked out, finding nothing but more pain from his missing feet, and screamed, "I can't! I can't!"

"Sean!" Mare yelled, shaking him. "For God's sake! Wake up!"

Scream still ripping out of his throat, Sean rolled away from Mare and landed, naked and gasping for breath, on the floor beside the bed. *I'm home,* he told himself, gaze darting about the room illuminated by the always-on light shining from behind the half-open bathroom door. *Everything's okay.* He winced then braved a glance at his feet, toes splayed and digging into the threadbare carpet. *Still there, still whole.* Sean leaned his head back to bonk against the nightstand and blew out a relieved breath.

Mare crouched on the bed, watching him with a worried smile. "Babe. It's just a dream," she soothed. "A bad one, sure, but just a dream."

He nodded, not trusting his voice, and took a moment to collect himself. He hadn't had a scream-himself-awake dream in months, maybe years, even though they'd been common after his abduction. Standing, he took a breath and muttered, "I'm too old for this shit."

He'd taken a single stumbling step toward the bathroom when a knock sounded on their door. "You guys okay?" Mindy asked.

Mare leaned over the side of the bed and reached for a T-shirt. "Yeah, we're fine," she said, thrusting her arms through the sleeves. "Just a bad dream."

That's right. We have a houseguest. Grumbling, Sean snatched his jeans and boxers off the floor before walking nude to the bathroom.

Better be some left, or it's gonna be a long night, he thought, snatching open the medicine cabinet with a shaking hand. He found his old prescription meds behind the sunblock and antibiotic ointment. When reaching for the pills, he knocked most of the shelf contents into the sink, but he didn't care. Four Prazosin tablets rattled in the bottom of the bottle. Six months expired, but oh well.

He managed to fish one loose without dropping any down the drain and dry swallowed it while screwing the cap back on. He pulled on his clothes, tidied up, and gulped a couple of palmfuls of water. He met his own gaze in the mirror and decided he looked more tired than crazy.

Mindy jumped and Mare nodded hello when he opened the bathroom door.

"I didn't mean to intrude," Mindy said, retreating to the kitchen. "I just didn't know—"

"No intrusion. I do crap like this all the time. Since I'm already awake, I'm gonna try to work."

Once his nerves settled enough to create a good line, drawing came easier than it had the day before. He even managed to sketch a couple of spreads without layout blocking.

He heard Mindy return to bed, but he kept drawing, only occasionally having to toss desperate sketches of footless children pleading from the dark.

It's 3:17 in the goddamn morning, Todd thought as he staggered out of his SUV. *Missing kid, dead people oozing out of slime balls, and now this. Jesus, I'm exhausted.*

He was the third officer to arrive at the crime scene but at least there were few spectators in the way. He staggered past vehicles flashing red and blue lights on the back of apartments and shops to the city cops kneeling near a dead woman.

Blood from her mashed head had spattered nearby dumpsters and walls. Other than massive cranial trauma, she appeared uninjured, but until the Division of Criminal Investigation finished their job, there was no telling what she'd endured. The flattened mass of her skull beside the otherwise normal-looking body reminded him of roadkill on the highway, and her teeth had scattered across the alley like dice tossed in a crooked game of craps.

Gawkers peered down from windows and a young black woman lurked near a stairway leading to apartments above a real estate office. She smoked a cigarette and eyed all three cops warily.

"That the witness?" he asked the men documenting the body.

"Yep," the nearer officer said without looking up. He bent and photographed a bloody cast-iron skillet. "She's all yours."

Skillet. That's different. Lover's quarrel, maybe? Todd thought, trying to not remember the mess of his own marriage as he took a wide path around the deceased. He introduced himself to the witness and took her information. "What'd you see?"

The woman took a drag on her cigarette. "Not a goddamn thing," she said, not meeting his gaze. "Heard screams, heard a fight, saw her lying there, and called you assholes."

"So you didn't see who flattened her head with that frying pan?"

She blew out the smoke. "Nope."

"What did you see, LaTonya? You wouldn't be standing here if you didn't have something to tell us."

She glanced at the other officers. "It's bullshit, man," she said, dropping the cigarette and crushing it under her sandals. "Makes no fucking sense."

Todd offered her a patient smile. "Try me."

"I didn't see anyone, okay? I didn't. But I heard them. Kept crying, bawling like a baby, with 'I'm sorry, I'm sorry, I don't have a choice,' every time they fucking hit her. Even after she'd finally died."

LaTonya hacked up a wad of phlegm and spat beside the stairs. "She ain't got a head anymore for God's sake. That takes some work, some effort, ya know? To really pound someone flat like that." She fished another cigarette out of her pocket and lit it. "What kind of asshole goes to that much trouble and apologizes while doing it? It's just fucked up."

Todd had to agree, but he'd seen crazier things. "You recognize the victim?"

"Nah," LaTonya said as she took a drag. "Don't know who she pissed off, neither. Just glad they weren't pissed at me."

"Sean? Sweetie?" Mare's voice coaxed from the soft, cozy dimness of sleep. "I think you need to get up."

He rolled onto his back, one arm covering his eyes before the morning burned them to ash. His mouth tasted like old spit and stale coffee. "Unngh. What time is it?"

"Quarter after eight. I know you didn't get to bed until almost dawn, but there's a reporter outside. She's asking for you and says she's not leaving."

Sean groaned as he rolled out of bed and staggered to the bathroom to piss. "Why does she want to talk to *me*?" He kicked the door closed behind him.

"Because of what happened yesterday. And last night. And something about Ghoulie. I tried to answer her questions, but apparently I'm not photogenic enough or something. She just turned off the cameras and asked where you were." She paused then said, "Mindy's scared half to death they're looking for her. She's hiding in the linen closet."

Probably the pushy girl from yesterday. "Okay, okay. Can you grab me some clean clothes?" he asked around his toothbrush.

"Already have. And there's more."

He spit and rinsed. "Good more, or bad more?"

"It's not good more," Mare sighed. "Murph emailed about an hour ago. They didn't even look at the sketches before telling him this will be Ghoulie's last issue. They're not renewing the regular contract and they've refused another mini-series, too. Three years was long enough. Ghoulie's done."

Figures. "Even if, by some miracle, we have decent sales this time?" Sean asked, leaving the bathroom. Mare had laid a clean pair of jeans and his one and only collared shirt across the bottom of the bed, along with socks and his good shoes.

She leaned beside the bathroom door, arms crossed over her belly. "Even if sales increase. Least that's what the email said. After two failed series and returns on the minis, Black Pawn's done with you and Murph both." She approached him as he pulled on the jeans. "Do you want a printout?"

"Nah. Frankly I'm surprised we lasted this long." He reached for the shirt. "Maybe if I don't come off as a loony, this interview will help? If not Ghoulie, maybe another contract? Another comic publisher? Shit, a couple of band posters or a matchbook cover?" He kissed her and looked into her hopeful eyes. *Anything to keep the full financial load off you.*

She smoothed his bed-mussed hair. "Couldn't hurt, babe."

The same pesky reporter stood on the stoop and Sean sighed as the cameraman adjusted the camera and light. "You guys do know I'm just a dude who draws comics, right?" he asked as he closed his front door behind him. "I'm not an expert on anything except maybe converting pencil drawings to vector graphics. I honestly don't know why you're talking to me again, especially after I came off as such a crackpot last time."

The reporter shrugged as she smoothed her blouse and hair. "Boss seems to think you're as good a face as any on this tainted water story." She checked her teeth in a reflection on the camera lens and added, "Besides, with the sheriff, CDC, and hospital all denying anything's happened at all, you're all we've got." Plastic smile back on and the microphone poised, she said, "Ready?"

"Guess so." Sean flinched as neighbors across the street came out to watch.

The reporter filmed her intro then turned to Sean, asking if he'd seen any more people lurking around the tree farm.

"No, I haven't."

A thin line appeared between her eyebrows. "Mr. Casey, access has been severely restricted to the Juniper Road area and local hospitals. Something's going on right near your property." She paused, then continued, hopeful. "Did you see something else? Maybe something you're not supposed to talk about? Did you witness the sabotage to our local water supply?"

Water sabotage? What the hell? "I don't know anything about any of that," Sean said. "Look, I'm on a deadline. For my comic. GhoulBane."

"Yeah, yeah, comic." She gestured and the cameraman stopped recording as her plastic smile faded. "You're the only person we've met who has the slightest idea what's happening out here. Well, other than the sheriff and doctors who either deny everything, or say 'no comment' then sic lawyers on us."

"I don't know anything about water sabotage. I just saw…" He paused, trying to figure out how to explain the tree people without getting Todd in trouble.

The reporter spread her hands wide. "Please, Mr. Casey. People have a right to know who's responsible." As if sensing a weakening in his resolve, she gestured at her cameraman and he lifted the camera and resumed recording. "What did you see?"

"It's not really something I can put into words. I'm an illustrator, not a poet, but I do know it's a… *What the hell am I doing? Even if Todd doesn't get pissed at me, everyone will believe I'm nuts.* He sighed, the camera catching every breath. "There's nothing to be afraid of."

"You're telling our viewers not to fear toxic—"

"Nothing's toxic." The camera rolled on as he took a breath and added, "That's all I can say, and I shouldn't have said that much."

The reporter blinked for a moment, then gathered herself. "Yesterday you told us the dead have risen and today you're insisting waterborne Anthrax isn't toxic?"

Sean shook his head, confused. "What? Anthrax? Who said anything about Anthrax?"

"The CDC is investigating and we have confirmed reports of positive tests. So you're denying the presence of Anthrax in our local water?"

"There isn't any Anthrax in the water! It's just a harmless, slimy—" *Shit.* Sean took a cleansing breath. "I'm an illustrator. That's it. Not a scientist, not a theologian. An illustrator who helped some people yesterday. Why are you asking me these stupid questions?"

The reporter pushed the microphone closer to his face. "So, Mr. Casey, you're telling us waterborne Anthrax is safe?"

Sean clenched his mouth and glared at her. *Fuck it. I'm screwed either way.* "Why are you harassing me over bullshit lies instead of trying to help these people?"

The cameraman muttered, "Dude, you're ratings gold!"

The reporter smiled. "So instead of accepting the truth of Anthrax tainted water, you're still insisting the dead have risen?"

"No. I'm saying you're an opportunistic bitch and your station is a shitty TV tabloid."

Without so much as a flinch, her smile turned into a concerned frown. "You obviously need psychological help, Mr. Casey. Can you tell us more about these dead people you've imagined?"

"Get off my porch." He turned to stomp into the house and slammed the door in her face.

Mare and Mindy had wandered next door for iced tea and gossip when Sean turned on his computer about an hour later. Despite the sinking feeling in his gut, he read Murph's emails. At first angry and frustrated, by the most recent email Murph had become resigned to their fate, and their failure. *And why not,* Sean thought, opening Chrome and locating the first bookmarked job search site. *He has a regular job.*

"Ooh. Someone needs line drawings of faucets for a farm plumbing catalog. Faucets *and* hydrants. Be still my heart," Sean muttered as he clicked to apply.

Web design, animation, more web, he thought, working through the postings. *Doesn't anyone need print graphics anymore?* He'd found two potential jobs by the end of the listing queue and closed the window to see a popup ad. *Damp basement getting you down? Call us to clean mold and mildew so you can breathe easier!*

He opened a fresh window. *All this rain, I bet lots of folks have wet basements. Our sump's working almost constantly, and it's a wonder we haven't had any mold—*

Sean stopped, finger over the mouse button. *Mold. The spore people in the creek. It had to start somewhere.*

A few minutes of Googling later, he found a topographical map of Boone County and zoomed in to just east of Pinell. Juniper Creek meandered past the cemetery and he traced it upstream to its source northeast of town. *Over by the chicken farm,* he thought, opening a new window. This time, he searched for water table information then saved both images and a satellite view to his hard drive.

He brought all three into PhotoShop, each on a separate layer, and adjusted their sizes until various points lined up, especially the curves in Juniper Road. He frowned at the screen as he flicked through the layers, his gaze drawn again and again to the chicken farm north of town. *Upstream from the cemetery. On high ground. And chickens can create a lot of toxic gunk.*

He scowled at the image and let out a harsh sigh. *All this rain, there's no telling how much it's spread.* He stood and, deciding he must be crazy after all, went to find his shoes.

Chapter Ten

Nicole grimaced and unplugged the radio, cutting off a report about a woman found beaten to death behind a pizza joint, which had followed an equally grim update on the missing local boy.

Mindy sighed, thankful for the break from bad news. Endless dreams of wintry car accidents had been awful enough for one day.

Nicole grabbed the pitcher of tea then returned to her kitchen table. As she reached for Mindy's glass, she said without looking at Mindy, "So. What'd you do for a living?"

"I am...*was*...a housewife." Mindy ignored the clench in Nic's hand as it poured the iced tea. "Mostly."

Mare, relaxed and comfortable in Nicole's tidy kitchen, held up her own glass for a refill while rubbing her lower belly with her other hand. "You didn't have to work?"

Mindy wished Nicole wasn't so nervous and twitchy around her. She managed a thank-you smile as Nic returned her glass. "I've always wanted to bake for a living, or at least the joy of it. Cookies, cakes, that kinda thing. Jeff won't let me, so I volunteer at fundraisers for the Kiwanis and the Chamber of Commerce. Pancake feeds, raffles, stuff like that. When Jeff says it's all right." She let out an exasperated breath. "Used to. Sorry. This time jump stuff is still unreal."

Nic blinked. "You're kidding."

Mindy glanced at Mare, who had begun to stare.

"Um. No, not kidding," Mindy said, shifting in her seat. "I lost almost three years. It's seriously weird."

"That's not what I meant." Nicole put the tea into the fridge then grabbed a dishtowel off the oven door handle to sop up the mess. "Your husband *let you* take raffle tickets?"

Mindy swallowed and sipped her tea, hoping they didn't notice her shaking hand. Jeff's ambition allowed no disobedience, no distraction, no possible impediment to his goals. He'd even, on occasion, bashed in headlights, altered records, or left dead animals as gruesome messages for his rivals, anything to ensure his plans would succeed. Nothing else mattered. Nothing. If she didn't fall in line and help him, she was an obstacle, which simply was not tolerated.

She set her glass down and managed to squeak out, "He has to keep up appearances with his job, and me taking care of him, making sure he has everything he needs all of the time, is a big part of that. If I have spare time, I can volunteer. If the charity is suitable."

Mare seemed to be struggling to find her voice, but at last she said, "You're actually joking. Right?"

"No," Mindy said, shaking her head. She remembered when she had been nominated for Kiwanis Secretary. Jeff had been furious. How dare she be nominated to be an officer before he was? How dare she have a goal or dream? How dare she upstage him? Did she sleep with the nominating committee? If that's all it took to get a nomination, why didn't she do it to get *him* on the ballot?

He'd struck her then, the first and only time he'd escalated from verbal to physical abuse. She'd called a lawyer the next day, but it had been so expensive, thousands of dollars for a retainer. And Jeff never let her have more than twenty bucks at once. She was trapped, and he liked it that way.

Mindy took a breath and said, "Jeff, he wants, arrgh, *wanted* to move up at the bank and part of that's participating in community activities. Being noticed. Ya know? And I had to help him. It's really not a big deal."

Nicole tossed the towel on the counter and sat. She started to speak, then stopped herself and shook her head.

Mare said, "I honestly don't know what to say."

"Me either," Nic mumbled, looking away as she sipped her tea. "Aaron knows I'd kick his freaking butt if he tried to tell me what I could or couldn't do."

"Not supposed to cuss, Mom!" Nic's daughter hollered from the living room.

"I didn't," Nic hollered back.

Mindy took a breath. "I'm guessing your husband loves you. Jeff… I thought I'd won the luck lottery when he came along, yet look what he did to me."

She held Nic's distrustful gaze and her voice cracked as she said, "I think it's his fault I'm dead. Was dead. Shit." *And now I'm cursing. Way to go, Mindy.* She scrunched her eyes closed for a moment. "Whatever you call this—"

The little girl, Steffie, bounced in with a blue mason jar in hand. It was partially filled with change. "You said the S word. It costs a quarter," she said, grinning as she thrust the jar toward Mindy.

Mare covered a chuckle with her hand while Nicole gaped. "Stefanie Cheyenne! We don't know her well enough to make her pay the cuss jar!"

"But, Mama, you said that *everyone* had to pay when they cuss. Isn't she everyone? That repairman had to pay last week when he said the S word after hurting his finger. Why him and not her?"

"Well, yes, but," Nic blustered, pointing. "Go on back in the living room with your brother."

"I'd happily pay, but I don't have a quarter," Mindy murmured before Steffie could turn to go. *I don't have anything.*

"I got it," Mare said, rummaging in her pocket. "I think." She produced a dime, two nickels, and some pennies. "Twenty-three cents," she said, dropping them into the jar. "Close enough?"

"You can get me the two other cents later." Grinning, Steffie bounced back to the living room.

"How old is she?" Mindy asked, watching her go.

"Four and a half," Nicole sighed. "Going on thirty."

Mindy smiled. "She's good at math."

"It's that jar," Nicole said. "Aaron started it when he was home for Christmas, to keep himself from swearing too much around the kids. When he asked Steffie what to do with the money, she said she wanted an American Girl doll, of all things." Nicole sipped her tea. "More than a hundred bucks, but we're saving up for one. And Steffie keeps track of every penny."

"Good for her," Mindy said. "She's obviously a smart kid."

"Heh," Nicole said. "Determined is more like it."

Mare stretched and popped her neck. "Oh yes, we've all seen pictures of the doll and the outfits she needs to have for it. She was up to twenty six dollars in the jar, last I knew."

"Almost thirty now," Nicole said. "Aaron promised to take her to the Mall of America to pick it out in person." She gazed toward the living room and sighed. "I hope he's home before she hits the hundred bucks."

"I'm sure he will be," Mare said, touching the back of Nicole's hand.

Silence settled around them and Mindy considered asking about where Aaron was stationed, but sipped her tea instead.

Nicole let out another sigh then turned to Mindy. "So. What are you going to do about your husband?"

Mindy raised her head and blinked, startled by the question. "I don't know. I haven't really thought about it."

"Oh, I'd be thinking about it," Nicole said. "I'd go after his ass— Assets, that's for sure."

Mindy sighed. "Not sure how. He has a new wife, a new job, even a new state. And I don't really exist, not legally anyway."

Something thumped and Pip, the little boy, screeched from the living room. Nicole stood. "There has to be a way around that. A way to remind that controlling jerk that paybacks are a bitch."

"Mom! You said the B word!"

Nicole continued on to the living room. "Grab my purse while I see what your brother got into."

Mindy watched her leave and, as she returned her attention to the table, noticed that Mare was looking at her intently. Mindy blushed and lowered her eyes. "What? Did I say something wrong?"

"Nope," Mare said. "But you shouldn't let anyone control you like that. Ever."

Braving the oppressive weather, Sean walked up a dirt road north of town, his gaze downward and his mind churning over his lack of employment. *I should contact city tourism boards and chambers of commerce,* he thought as he trudged along. *See if anyone needs illustrations or logos for craft fairs or corn feeds, maybe a Character Counts promotion for school—*

An MSNBC truck sped past, splattering him with mud. He looked up, surprised to see a long line of news vehicles parked a few hundred yards ahead.

Barronsen Poultry's gates had been closed—*first time I've ever seen that,* Sean thought—and the press milled in the road. Sean noted the chain link fence encircling the property. He turned, jumping across a flooded ditch to a tree line separating the farm's fence from a field of soybeans.

The beans weren't much taller than knee high, giving him no cover from vehicles approaching from the south, and the thin strand of trees and brush weren't any better at hiding him from the north. He felt exposed as he walked toward the back of the chicken farm.

A sheriff's SUV sped up the road, lights and siren on. Sean ducked and watched the SUV drive toward the reporters, but the farm's long pre-fab buildings blocked the rest of the view.

If I can't see them, they can't see me, he decided, walking along the edge of the tangle as he let his gaze drift over the poultry farm.

The place was tidy, modern, and mowed, emitting only a mild ammonia stink to the air, even from the containment ponds not far past the fence. He saw massive feeding bins and ventilation fans alongside the nearest poultry barn. A row of livestock transport trailers and an end loader stood between a pair of towering corn cribs about midway to the far corner. A tabby cat sunned itself on the upper slope of the end loader's bucket, utterly unconcerned with whatever was happening near the road.

Sean reached the corner of the property and climbed through blackberry bushes to reach the chain link fence. He saw more of the same. Eight poultry barns parallel to one another. Massive grain bins. A storage shed with a garbage dumpster alongside. Long swaths of mown grass contained by pristine chain link that separated the farm from the wild tangle behind and the bean field beyond. Nothing at all out of the ordinary, and the ordinary was clean and in good repair, except that the storage shed could use a coat of paint. *Maybe I was wrong,* he thought, sighing as he turned toward the road again. *The containment ponds don't even reek. I can't see how this place is putting—*

He turned back. The tangle of undergrowth and trash trees he stood in thickened as it rounded the corner of the poultry farm, and continued beyond the fence, gaining more trees on its course down to the creek. Sean took a breath and walked deeper into the brush along the back of the farm. Broken furniture and rusted appliances soon littered the bramble and the deepening trench. He'd passed all but two of the poultry barns when he started smelling the familiar, moldy funk coming from the ditch. His heart quickened and he stepped down the slope, skirting around a marshy sea of garbage and junk, typical refuse illegally dumped in so many isolated ditches. A scrawny young frog swam bored circles in a plastic peanut butter jar just beyond Sean's feet; it had probably jumped in but couldn't climb back out.

Sean dumped the frog into the marshy mess and tossed the jar aside.

As the musty stink thickened, he continued downhill, tripping over rusted, half-buried barrels, tractor parts, and tires. Decayed machinery he couldn't identify rotted among the trees.

He paused, eyes widening. A miniature slime mass quivered in a stretch of trickling water. He crouched to examine it. Not much larger than a golf ball, it was a diminutive version of the foamy wad that had produced a woman the night before. He touched its fluffy, slimy surface and a shuddering ripple of blue-violet circled the mass, flowing outward from his fingertip across the surface of the water.

As he stood, he noticed more frothy spheres peeking from the water, partially hidden by foliage but obvious once he'd seen the first. Some were the size of melons, but most were miniscule. He saw bits of clear slime, too, caught upon submerged grasses and twigs.

Well ahead, an apple-sized wad released streaks of bubbles and he splashed to it, kneeling on a mossy scrap of plastic to keep his knees dry.

Wish I brought my camera, he thought, then shook his head. Todd had destroyed his memory card, making the camera useless. Silent and enthralled, Sean watched the sphere fall apart, finally dissolving to expose a thirteen-lined ground squirrel—a squinney—taking a desperate gasp of air. The little rodent shuddered, tail floating in the water, and blinked at him with violet eyes, unafraid.

"Hey, little guy," Sean said, grinning as the squinney climbed out on quivering legs. It chattered at him, and he stroked the top of its head. "Aren't you an amazing thing?" he whispered.

It blinked, eyes darkening, and it backed away. Another blink and its eyes had darkened again to shiny black. Moments later, it bustled up the ditch and disappeared into the bramble.

I don't care if they think I'm crazy, it's still a miracle. The refuse beneath Sean shifted as he stood. He propellered his arms for balance but fell on his ass in the muddy water anyway.

He stood again, cursing and scraping off the worst of the gunk. A cracked shard of fiberglass had flipped into the water. It had once been part of a sign, painted maroon with white letters and most of a flower. Although quite faded and crusty, he could make out *Lotus Lab* over *Parkin* before the broken edges cut off the remaining type. He looked where the hunk of sign had lain. A spongy fungal mesh spread over the filthy refuse the sign had covered. Sean reached into nearby rotten leaves and grasses, peeling them away to expose more of the mesh, which sent tendrils into the water.

Is this where it started? he thought, *looking around. Looks right, smells right.* He picked up the scrap of fiberglass and frowned at it. *Lotus Lab. Makes a lot more sense than chickens or regular ditch crap.* Sign in hand, he climbed out of the ditch and headed for home.

"Is there anything I can do to help?" Mindy asked, ducking out of the way.

Mare rubbed her lower belly as she hurried through the kitchen. The nursing home had called, asking her to arrive early because another aide was sick. Although she'd muttered about her own stomach pain, she'd agreed.

"Um. You can rotate laundry for me, I guess." Mare sat to put on socks and shoes. "Sean can fold it when he gets home."

"Laundry. Got it," Mindy said. "What about cleaning? Supper?"

"Sean usually does that since he's home all day." Mare stood, her hand still rubbing her lower belly. "Maybe I should just stay here. Screw the job—"

Why the sudden change of heart? Mindy wondered. *At Nicole's you practically prayed for more hours.* "You said you'd go in."

"Yeah, but what if…" Mare shook her head, her eyes worried. "Sean's not home yet. I should wait for him."

"I can tell him his mother called. I'll rotate laundry. I'll even thaw something for supper. It'll be fine."

Mare sighed, nodding, but didn't seem convinced. She rummaged through her purse. "Godammit, where'd I put my keys?"

"By the microwave?" Mindy suggested, pointing.

Mare snatched them up and took a breath to speak, but someone knocked on the door. Both women stopped to stare toward the living room. Mindy released a scared groan as her belly clenched. She took an involuntary step back, against the counter, and felt her heart thud. *Not the cops again. Please.*

Mare licked her lips and took a breath before she patted Mindy's arm. "I'll see who it is."

Mindy moved across the room, out of sight but able to listen as Mare opened the door.

"Um," a woman's quavering voice said, "this is gonna sound totally crazy, but homebaker115 said the guy who lives here could help me. Are *you* homebaker115?"

Mindy's hand covered her mouth. "Oh God."

"Excuse me?" Mare said.

"My… My son," the woman said, followed by a child's nervous 'hey', "after the guy talking about dead people… He was on TV. Last night?"

Mindy peeked around the corner as Mare leaned back, crossing her arms over her chest. "I'd rather not talk about that."

"Yes, of course," the woman said, nodding. "I know it's crazy. My son, he…" She swallowed, eyes brimming. "Our dog…"

"You came to tell me about your dog?"

"Never mind. I knew this was crazy." The woman lowered her head and took a step back. "Sorry to bother you."

"But what about Betsy?!" The kid tugged on her arm. "You promised!"

Mindy steeled herself and stepped into the living room. "I'm homebaker115."

The woman took a breath and managed a stiff smile. "Was it real? What you'd posted last night? The crazy guy we saw on the news?" Before Mindy could respond, the woman caressed the back of her son's head and said, "We've had Betsy since she was a puppy and she's just amazing. Sweet, friendly, but protective, ya know? Last year, even, she saved Joey from what we think might have been a kidnapper. We *love* that dog."

"But she got hit by a car," Mindy said, approaching them.

"Last night. Killed right in front of our house when we let her out to pee." The little boy wrapped his arms around his mother's hips. "We'd just seen the news, with that guy who said the dead people came back. Sean Casey? He lives in this house, right?"

Mare and Mindy nodded.

"Anyway, after the news, Joey was convinced that Betsy could come back, too. He wouldn't let it go, you know how kids are. So he, well, *we*, got online to see if there was more information. It didn't look good, but when we got up this morning homebaker115 had commented that she didn't understand it, but it really happened. It was possible. And she had proof."

Mare turned, gaping. "You what?"

"She sounded so upset, so worried about her son," Mindy said, flinching and wishing she could crawl away. "I had to say something."

The woman took a breath and looked at Mindy and Mare. "So we found where Sean Casey lived, and thought we'd start with him." She wiped at the corner of her eye and said, "Can you help us? Is there any possible way we can get our Betsy ba—"

She turned as Sean walked up the sidewalk. He was splattered with mud and greenish gunk, and he carried a filthy shard of plastic. The woman took a startled step. "It's really you! The zombie guy! You're finally here!"

Sean paused, then continued up the steps. "Yeah," he said, trying to slip past. "But they're not zombies, they're just people given a second chance. Excuse me, okay? Can I get into my own house, please?"

The woman stepped aside, nodding. "Sure. Absolutely."

"Where have you been and what'd you fall into?" Mare asked. "Your note said you were taking a walk, not a slog through a swamp."

Despite the muck, he kissed her, leaning forward to avoid staining her scrubs. "I'll tell you in the other room."

He took a step toward the kitchen the woman called out, "Wait! So this really is real? You can save our dog?"

Sean stopped, head tilting, and turned to ask, "Your dog?"

"Betsy. I was just telling these ladies that she got hit by a car last night, and that one there," she said, pointing at Mindy, "commented online to my son that maybe Betsy could be saved, could be brought back to us."

"I don't have any control over this," Sean said. "It's a miracle, sure, but it's not my miracle."

"But you're the miracle guy!" the woman said, her voice rising in grief and desperation. "Please. For my son, for our family, can't we just try to give Betsy a chance to come back?"

Mare scowled and Mindy tried to shrink, become invisible, but Sean stood there, staring at the woman. At last he nodded. "Bury her in a wet spot," he told her. "The closer to the water the better. Okay? I don't know what will happen, but that's your best chance."

While the woman gushed her thanks and dragged her son to their car, Sean motioned for Mare to follow him.

Mindy stood in the living room for a moment, then rushed out to help wrestle a stiff German Shepherd from the woman's trunk.

Chapter Eleven

The dog stank. Not the full-throated gassy reek of a three-day-dead raccoon, but a soft decay with a promise to deliver a choking aroma. And maggots. Soon.

At least it's wrapped in a sheet, Mindy thought. *And at least I'm carrying the butt end.* She didn't look at the weird, tire-wide dent midway up the dog's chest that left the corpse flattened and oddly bent. Nor did she look at the dried blood on the sheet or the flies crawling all over it. Or even consider that once, not all that long ago, she was in a similar state.

She swallowed down bile. *Uh uh, no way. Not gonna think about any of that.*

Joey, the little boy, cried as he gamely carried a shovel at least a foot taller than he was. Every time he tripped over it, Mindy winced. "Can you balance it on your shoulder?" she suggested.

Joey tried, only to drop it and fall to his knees, bawling.

"It's okay, sweetie," his mother, Donna, coaxed, shifting her grip on their burden. The sheet, although tied and taped, shifted, and Mindy saw what looked like a snout poking Donna in the belly. The stink seemed to increase, but surely that was her imagination.

They managed to reach the backyard without dropping the dog. Mindy and Donna lowered it to the grass. "So. Near the water," Mindy said, desperate to rub her hands on her jeans, but unwilling to put dead dog cooties on them.

Donna nodded, eyes brimming with tears. "I can't tell you how appreciative I am," she said, meandering toward the tree farm while her son knelt and petted the bundle's head. "Doing so much to help a total stranger, even though it's likely crazy anyway."

Mindy nodded toward the house. "That's kind of their thing." The ground felt especially squooshy on the house-side of the shed and she called Donna over for a second opinion.

"It'll do, I think," Donna said. She and Mindy returned to the dog and lifted it again, Joey trailing behind with his shovel.

"Do you think Sean will help us dig the hole?"

Mindy glanced at the house. "No idea. He seemed pretty intent on talking to his girlfriend."

Donna nodded and managed a sad smile. "It's okay. My job, anyway." She accepted the shovel from her son and began digging, the shovel sliding easily into the wet ground. Each scoop seemed heavier, weighted down with wet earth. After a dozen shovelfuls or so, Mindy offered to take a turn and she leaned into it. It felt good to work, to stretch, to lift.

"Wow, you look like you could do this forever," Donna said.

"Nah, I'm already getting tired," Mindy lied. She'd helped her dad dig a few post holes as a teenager and had found it exhausting. This, though, was easy. Too easy. After a few more shovelfuls, she faked a light quaver in her arms, then another with the next scoop before panting and handing the shovel back to Donna. As the other woman pressed the shovel into the ground, Mindy swallowed, seeing how far she'd dug. Water seeped into the hole and they were nearly deep enough to fully bury the dog.

How'd I do that? she thought, reminding herself to pant and wipe her brow. *I never could have dug that much without taking a break before.* Across the yard, past the rhubarb, the rude guy from the paddy wagon splashed out of the trees and strode toward the neighbor's house with a heavy-looking duffle bag slung over his shoulder. Mindy nodded hello when he glanced at her, but he merely glared in response before he went inside.

Jerk.

Joey crouched, still petting Betsy's head. Donna glanced at Mindy and asked, "About last night. Your answer to my post?"

"Yeah?" Mindy accepted the shovel after Donna managed six or seven scoops. She stepped into the hole and resumed working. Water stood in the hole, just an inch or so, but she dug anyway. Wanted to bury Betsy plenty deep.

Donna watched her work. "You said that you had proof." She paused as Mindy scooped up a dripping mound of black dirt with a corroded Frostie Root Beer bottle cap in it. "Do you really? Have proof, I mean?"

Mindy smirked at the bottle cap and shook her head. *Never heard of Frostie, but I guess you never know what you might find while digging up someone's backyard.* "Yeah, kind of," she said, dumping the dirt onto the pile before going in for another. "I guess I'm the proof." Water seepage and suction made the scooping harder, but still not too difficult. A few shovelfuls later, the water covered her feet and she felt around with the shovel for high places to scrape out. *Should be plenty deep, plenty wet.*

"You?" Donna's eyes grew wide. "You're not saying—"

"Yeah," Mindy admitted. She stepped out of the hole and leaned the shovel against the shed. "I died in a car accident almost three years ago, then I walked into this very yard yesterday morning. I don't know what's happening out here, but it's definitely real."

"Seriously?"

"Yeah. Seriously. But don't say anything, okay? It's weird enough to think about without everyone knowing." Mindy managed a smile then said, "Now let's see if this works."

"I've never heard of Lotus Lab," Sean said. He turned on the shower and removed his shirt.

Mare paced in the bathroom, rubbing her belly as if it ached. "Me either. The chicken farm's been there as far back as I can remember." She sighed harshly and muttered, "What the hell do we do now?"

"I don't know," Sean admitted, wondering what had Mare so agitated. "I'll Google it and go from there, I guess. But it's affecting animals, too. I saw a squinney spore out of one of those slimy ball things."

"Great," Mare said as she sagged against the vanity. "We'll all be overrun by vermin."

"I kinda doubt that. Surely the predators will spore too. The wild animals will probably end up a wash." He gave Mare a hopeful smile. "Not sure about the folks with dead dogs, though."

Mare blew out an exasperated breath. "Not sure how I feel about that. I'm happy to help people, sure…"

"But letting them dig up our yard to plant their dead is something else entirely. I know." He bent to peel off his wet jeans. "Sorry, babe. Shouldn't have said okay without talking to you first."

Mare shrugged. "It's all right. I probably would've let her, too, once the shock of it wore off. Takes balls to ask to bury your dog in a stranger's yard, but after seeing that poor kid... I'd have caved. I know I would've. You were just quicker to decide."

Stripped to his boxers, Sean held Mare's face in his hands and kissed her. "What's wrong, then? If it's not that woman with the dead dog, what's going on?"

She paused, chewing her lip. "The phone was ringing when we got back from Nic's—just my stupid job—but there were four messages on the machine. One was your mother. She wants you to fix a light switch or something, and she has a loose—"

Sean rolled his eyes and reached into the shower to check the water temperature. "That stupid basement switch? Again? I don't know crap about wiring and I keep telling her she needs to—"

"The other three calls were threats," Mare interrupted, grimacing as he turned to look at her. "They were pretty nasty and I'm just glad Mindy had gone off to pee by then so she didn't hear. I don't know if I could've handled her freaking out. I had enough trouble all by myself."

Sean met her worried gaze. "What kind of threats?"

"Started with hallelujah you're the antichrist and you and your dead friends should be sacrificed so Jesus can hurry up and save the rest of us," she said. "Then it was you should be gutted like the sick necrophiliac fuck that you are, and, um, the last was since you're responsible for the zombie apocalypse you should be the first to get his brains eaten, preferably by someone throwing your decapitated head at the encroaching horde."

So now I'm not just crazy, I'm a sick freak, too. Still in his boxers, Sean sat on the toilet and stared at her. "What do we do?"

Mare sagged and sat on the floor, facing him. "Call the cops? Lock the doors? I don't know. I'm just thankful almost no one believes you." She took a breath and raised her head. "Maybe I should stay home. I know we need the money, but—"

Sean flinched. *If the nice lady with a dead dog can find us, the crazy assholes can, too. And they've already found our phone number.* "Go," he said, standing. "You'll be safe there, at least. I'll get ahold of Todd, maybe. Take Mindy with me to Mom's..." He gave Mare a tight smile and reached for her hand to help her up. "Go. Work. Try not to worry. I'll figure something out. Just email me before you head home, okay? A text from a friend's phone... Something besides a phone call."

"Sean, you know I can't—"

"Screw the rules," he snapped. "If your fuckwad boss doesn't like it, we'll worry about his meltdown later. If I don't respond within five minutes, go to a friend's and call the cops. *Do not* come home unless I say it's okay."

"But... What about you? Mindy? What if these people actually show up? You've never done anything to hurt anybody. Why would these people want to kill you?"

"I don't know, but it'll be okay," he said, hugging her. "I promise. It'll be okay."

Mindy and Donna had returned about half of the dirt to the hole when Sean walked up to them, his hands stuffed in his pockets and his face pale. Mindy gave him a worried smile as she scooped up another shovelful.

"Afternoon, ladies," he said. "How's it coming out here?"

"Better," Donna said, wiping beneath her eyes with the back of her wrist and adding another muddy smear to her face. "Thanks again for letting us do this."

"No problem," Sean said with a nod and a smile, neither of which looked genuine to Mindy. He pulled a green Post-it pad and pen from his pocket. "Can I get your name and number? In case your dog comes back?"

"Betsy," little Joey said. "She's Betsy."

"Betsy. Right," Sean said, handing over the pen and paper. "Whatever happens, I'll keep you informed."

Donna wrote her information and Mindy let Sean take over the shovel. He made quick work of moving the remaining dirt and tamped it down. The others helped him press in the hunks of sod.

Mindy stood back and nodded to herself. A fresh grave was never a pretty thing, but they'd managed not to mangle it too badly. At least the moist dirt compacted well.

"We need to talk," Sean said as he waved goodbye to Donna.

Mindy looked at him, and tried to ignore the worried twist in her belly. *Oh no! Have I screwed this up, too?* "Talk? About what?"

"Some crazies called making threats," he said, walking with her toward the house.

"Threats? Good God, why?"

"Not sure yet," Sean held the back door open for her. "But the sheriff's on his way."

She swallowed. "I can hide in my room, if it would—"

He locked the door behind them. "I think you need to talk to them. The sheriff, I mean."

"No," she said, shaking her head. "They'll take me away, lock me up in a lab or something."

Sean sat at the kitchen table and motioned for her to sit as well. "I don't think so. I called Todd, the deputy who was here last night, to ask him what I should do about the threats. I also asked about the people I'd helped yesterday. He told me there never was a quarantine."

"Really?" She sagged in relief. "That's good news."

"There's more. When I asked if all of them had places to go, he admitted some were missing. That five had fled the hospital." He paused to meet her worried gaze. "Apparently you weren't the only one. But, anyway, the feds have arrived with a team of grief psychologists and social workers who are supposed to help with housing and jobs and adjusting to technology changes. Get you spore folks back into the groove of society again."

"Spore folk *what*?" she asked, confused.

"The stuff you came from is a fungus, as far as I can tell, and fungi reproduce by sending their spores out into the world to create more fungi." He shrugged. "Seemed like as good a name for the process as any, and a whole lot less creepy than non-zombies."

"Okay. Spores." She took a breath. "But the cops. You're sure they're not looking to lock us up or run tests on us?"

"No," he sighed, "I'm not sure. All this happy-crappy seems like B.S. to me, especially if the feds are involved, but Todd also said the local cops are trying to keep tabs on the spore people because they might be in danger."

"What? Why?" she asked, looking over her shoulder as car doors slammed outside and someone yelled.

Sean took a shaky breath then stood and laid a gentle hand on Mindy's shoulder. "Because a woman was found this morning with her head bashed in. She had no ID and might be one of the spores who escaped. They'd like to make sure you, and the others, are all right. They're just trying to get a head count."

The yelling turned into a chant and Mindy stood, the sick twist in her belly tightening. "So they won't try to take me away and lock me up? You're sure?"

"I'm not sure of anything right now, but I won't let them take you," Sean said as he walked to the laundry room and came out with an aluminum bat. "Not without a warrant or court order. I'll call a lawyer, whatever it takes. Okay? You can stay here as long as you think you need to. I promise."

Mindy nodded and moistened her lips. "Okay."

She followed him to the living room and they both stopped, gaping, as five people paraded on the sidewalk in front of the house. They carried signs about surviving the zombie apocalypse and they chanted, "Not eating my brains!" over and over.

Sean pressed Mindy behind him and muttered, "What a mess."

A skinny, bearded guy with a shaved head had a rifle slung over his shoulder. His sign read, "Kill Shot," and showed a slavering zombie with crosshairs centered on its forehead. A short, hairy guy had an axe strapped to his back and his sign suggested zombie decapitation equaled human survival. The other three were women, one with pistols on each hip, the other two with a gun and a knife.

A police siren yelped nearby, one loud warning tone, and the five picketers froze for a moment before clenching their signs closer to their chests. The sheriff's cruiser pulled up, lights flashing, and a large deputy got out.

It's that cop from yesterday. The grouchy one who kept treating me like a psychotic thief. Mindy took a mincing step toward the hall as Sean flinched. "I'll go wait in the other room," she said.

Sean grimaced and stuffed the bat under the couch. "Probably a good idea."

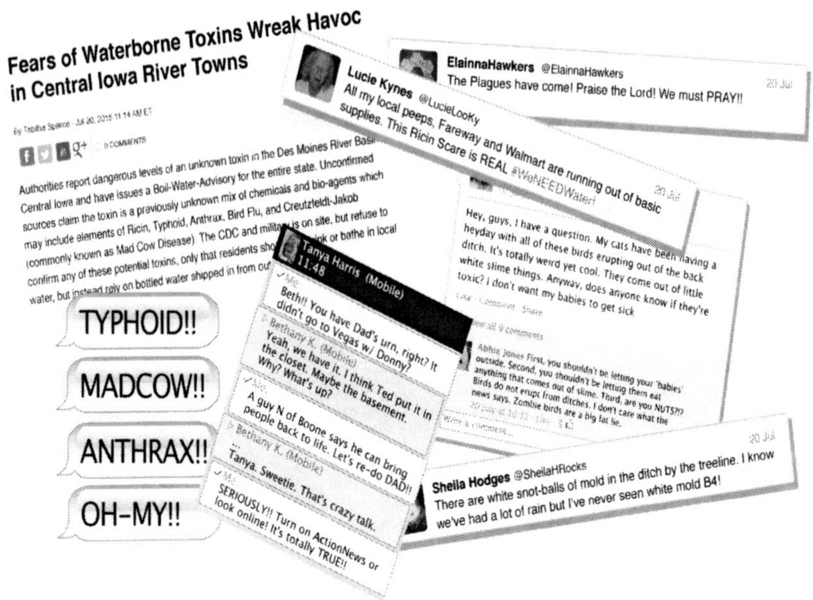

Chapter Twelve

"That's enough," Deputy Hendrix said, raising a hand to stop Sean from playing the messages. "Since you don't have caller ID, and the callers did not identify themselves, there's little I can do without the rigmarole of a court order, Mr. Casey. Since there were no direct threats, only their preferences as to what they'd like to see happen, I suggest that perhaps you should ignore the taunts. Or change your phone number."

Sean stood there, fuming, while Hendrix wrote in his little notebook. "Aren't you going to do something? They threatened to kill me and my family."

"No, they stated what *should* happen, not what *will* happen, so there technically was no threat."

"This is bullshit!"

Hendrix looked up, one eyebrow raised. "Do you have a family?"

"A girlfriend, yes, but I don't see—"

"Are you the antichrist or a zombie?"

Sean glowered but said nothing.

Hendrix tore off a sheet of paper and handed it to Sean. "Good day, Mr. Casey." He turned to go.

Sean glanced at the paper which informed him that his complaint had been addressed and no further action was warranted. "What the hell?" he muttered, following Hendrix to the living room. "No further action? There are armed people in my front yard! On my property!"

"No, they're on the sidewalk, a public avenue, and only one of the women is actually armed. She has a permit to carry. The others are carrying dummy weapons." Hendrix gestured to a resin sculpture of Ghoulie with a machine gun that stood on the TV cabinet. "Like for costumes at that freak convention out in California weirdos like you go to."

Sean glanced out the window and wondered which woman's guns were real. "This isn't ComicCon, it's my home."

Hendrix sighed and turned to face him. "Yes, a home that you opened to freaks just yesterday morning. Then you blabbed about it to every news station in the state. Do you know what's happened since you began this journey, Mr. Casey?"

Other than a dead dog buried in my yard, phoned threats, and five people picketing my house? Sean crossed his arms over his chest. "No. Enlighten me."

"You should watch the news more, and talk to reporters less," Hendrix said. "Since you 'rescued' those fungaloid freaks, not only have mobs of ag protesters sucked up our time and resources, we've had a kid go missing and a woman murdered. Here. In Boone County where a stolen car or domestic assault is a busy investigative week. Now we're dealing with four massive crises in less than twenty-four hours and it all started with those damn fungaloids you keep blabbering about."

"Oh come on!" Sean snapped. "First you accuse them of being frauds, now you're blaming them for kidnapping and a murder? That's nuts and you know it."

"Nuts? What's nuts is that there are real crimes to pursue and I'm here, yet again, dealing with you over a matter that you brought onto yourself." Glaring, he took a step toward Sean, but Sean held his ground. "Since you're suddenly such an outspoken critic of our office, which strikes you as a better use of our time? Angry mobs? Missing boy? Murdered woman? Or coming all the way out here to listen to you complain about grumpy phone messages and innocent citizens exercising their right to protest?"

"I'd definitely label the kid as the most important," Sean said, seething, "but I'm a citizen too. I pay taxes. I vote. Don't all citizens deserve service and protection?"

"Of course they do," Hendrix said as he walked to the door. "If any of those costumed folks threatens you with a real weapon or one of your telephone friends says they're actually coming to hurt you, give us a call. Until then, try to stay off the news."

"Thanks for taking me with you," Mindy said, looking over her shoulder toward Pinell as Sean turned his wheezy, rusted out Chevy onto the highway. She'd planned to do more online research about Jeff, but, real weapons or not, the protesters worried her.

"Let's just hope we get in and out before my mother comes home from work," Sean said. "I don't suppose you know anything about light switches or loose door hinges?"

"My dad fixed that stuff, but never taught me. And Jeff..." She shrugged and swallowed the bitter lump in her throat. "He always called a repair person. Said that kind of thing was beneath him. We didn't even own a screwdriver or hammer."

Sean glanced at her but said nothing.

"Jeff was an ass. I get it, I do, all right?" Mindy muttered.

"I don't know if you really do," Sean said as they stopped at a four-way. "Maybe I'm wrong, but you don't seem like the kind of person who'd be swayed simply by money. How'd you end up with someone like him, anyway?"

"College," Mindy said, shrugging. "We met at a party. He was in a frat, and I was a dumb, naive freshman who got caught up in the drinking and a cute, popular guy paying all kinds of attention to me." She felt shame flare on her cheeks and she chewed her lip before admitting, "I felt so special, and he was so sweet, telling me how amazing I was. Before I knew it, I was drunk, naked..." She flinched and looked away. "Only I got pregnant."

"I'm so sorry."

"Yeah, well, it's the bed I made, right? After he, we..." She took a breath and let it out. "He promised to call, after the party. Of course he didn't. When I missed my period and got the pregnancy test back, I found him and told him. He tried to deny it, to get out of it, but he was the only guy I'd been with. There wasn't any doubt, at least to me."

"I'm sorry."

She shrugged off Sean's concern. Back then she was eighteen, broke, and barely into her first semester at college. Her father had been livid. Ashamed. He'd left her no choice, marry the guy or take her shame and never come back. And Jeff... He'd become sweet again once he learned the baby was his. Said he wanted the baby. Said he loved her. She didn't trust the nice Jeff, but what else could she do?

"Even though I'd figured out by then he was a jerk, my dad was Catholic and insisted I marry him. His folks insisted on a paternity test first. So they stuck a needle in me and, not long after, we got married. The baby died about a month before she was due. That was… Awful." She shrugged, not wanting to relive those details. "It kinda went downhill from there."

Sean glanced at her, frowning. "How could it not? You married your rapist. I thought they only made women do that shit in third world countries."

"That's not what happened. Just because I didn't mean to—"

"I know exactly what happened. A guy got a girl he just met drunk and coerced her to have sex with him. Last I heard, that's rape."

"I was *pregnant*," Mindy said, hating the bitter taste of it in her mouth. "My parents insisted. What was I supposed to do?"

"File charges? Sue for child support? Cut his balls off?"

Mindy fidgeted, her eyes downcast. "Those weren't options."

Sean remained quiet for a mile or so. At last he said, "You definitely deserve better than him *or* your dad. A *lot* better."

She thought of Sean and Mare's playfulness, their passing caresses, their comfortable silences. "How about you and Mare? How'd you two end up so happy?"

"A lot of luck, I think." Sean smiled. "We met in college, too. In class, not a party. We became friends, started dating, and never looked back. We just…mesh," he said. "She's happy with me how I am, and I'm happy with her how she is. All in all, it's been pretty great. We have our grumpy moments, especially when money's impossibly tight, but mostly we're really good together."

"But no kids?"

"Want 'em, can't have 'em," Sean said, shrugging. "It's a medical thing."

She'd wanted another baby but Jeff had said trapping him once was bad enough. Mindy stared at her hands, still clasped between her thighs. "I'm sorry."

"Me, too. It's been a tough hurdle for us. We can't afford to adopt, so we tried fostering a little boy. He was four when he came to us, and we had him almost a full year. God, we loved that kid. They told us he was messed up, a neglected drug baby, but we thought he was simply awesome."

Sean sighed and turned onto a residential street. "When they sent him back to his birth mother, it was the worst pain I've ever felt. Mare bawled for weeks. Was awful to be so helpless, so hurt, loving a kid we couldn't have. Everyone thought it'd tear us apart, but facing the grief together made us stronger, I think. We decided we didn't want to endure that pain again, so it's just us, no kids. But that's okay. We're happy."

Mindy nodded, wishing she could offer some comfort. Then she blinked and raised her head. "Am I staying in his room?"

"Yeah." Sean pulled into a driveway beside an immaculate bungalow and turned off the car. "It's actually kind of nice to have someone in there again."

"What was his name?"

Sean opened the car door. "Jamaal. But don't tell Mare I told you. Every time she hears his name, she starts crying."

As Mindy exited the car, a tidy, graying-haired woman hurried down the steps, beaming and oblivious to Sean's exasperated sigh. She wore a sleek teal blouse and tailored khakis, but cheap, scuffed loafers. *Maybe she's been gardening?* Mindy thought. Jeff would have sent her back into the house for stepping outside without proper footwear. *And here I am in second-hand flip flops. He'd surely bust a gasket over that.*

"I see you got my message!" the woman said as Sean ducked into the back seat for the toolbox.

"Yeah, Ma." Sean slammed the car door. "Same light switch?"

"And the bathroom door hinge," she said, beaming at Mindy. "I'm Helene, Sean's mother. Aren't you a pretty little thing. Has Sean finally come to his senses and chosen a nicer girlfriend?"

"Uh, um… No?" Mindy said, confused.

Sean stomped past with the toolbox. "Still with Mare, Ma. Mindy's just a friend of ours."

"Why can't you pick someone who'll take better care of you?"

Sean stopped, shoulders sagging, before he turned. "We've been through this. Like it or not, I love Mare and she's not going anywhere. Mindy's split from her husband and needs a place to stay so she's in Jam's old room. Do you have a problem with that, too?"

Embarrassed, Mindy took a step backwards, her spine against the car, as Helene ran an appraising eye over her. "She's cute. You should keep her and ditch the other one."

Sean continued into the house. "Not gonna happen, Ma."

"A mother can hope," Helene sighed before following. She stopped at the foot of the steps and motioned Mindy to her. "Come on now. We can look through my scrapbook while he works."

Oh, yay, Mindy thought, meekly following. *Maybe I should have stayed with the zombie gang.*

"I don't give a shit how pissed off drivers get," Todd said, looming over the relief deputy as a semi sped past without slowing. "Divert traffic to the next road south. Now."

They all had been working nearly non-stop since the fungaloids had erupted the morning before and, between various panics, thefts, a murder, and a kidnapping, the department had been forced to rely on functional idiots to fill low priority positions. Only this functional idiot had become the first responder to a totally fucked-up scene: a child's body found nude and mangled in a ditch along highway E26 south of Fraser. After less than four hours of sleep since the previous morning, Todd had long since run out of bullshit tolerance and this guy had picked a bad day to fuck up.

Ignoring the queasy-sick twist in his gut, Todd couldn't stop thinking, *It could be Hailey down there. Thank God it isn't.*

The relief deputy glared back. "It's my crime scene, my—"

"Yeah, a crime scene you walked and puked all over before the investigator got here. Have any idea how much trouble that makes for DCI? For us?"

A kid lay in the ditch, not a measly stolen apple. Todd ground his teeth to keep from screaming. "You're not certified for crime scene investigation, so you can either divert the fucking traffic so professionals who know how to do their jobs won't get run over by rubber-necking motorists, or you can hand me your resignation right goddamn now and go the fuck home." Todd took a breath and loomed closer to the much smaller man. "Pick one and get out of the way."

He didn't wait for a response before taking a few steps up the breakdown gravel and descending into the ditch. Brad Jorst, county investigator, was kneeling on the cornfield side of the remains, taking pictures.

Brad's face was drawn and exhausted. After collecting cemetery and creek bed samples all day yesterday, plus two dead bodies in the last twelve hours, he'd had an impossible couple of days, too.

"What do you need me to do?" Todd asked, sticking to the beaten-grass path Brad had broken to the body. He struggled not to flinch. *It's a kid, just a poor, defenseless kid.*

"Rewind the whole damn planet to day before yesterday." Brad yawned as he took a photograph of the boy's open and emptied belly. "And remove us of idiot newbies, while you're at it."

"I wish." Todd remained outside the circle of police tape Brad had set up. The less footprints and stray hairs left behind, the better.

The boy that had once been Justin Lansing lay nude on his side in the weedy ditch, his skinny-kid body bruised and his feet gone. Wind ruffled his ginger-red hair and his eyes, once blue but now a milky gray, stared at Brad's knee and the relief deputy's pile of puke congealing beside it.

Brad's path down was simple, straightforward, a clear but non-damaging trek through the abundant vegetation. Idiot newbie's tracks, however, peppered the whole scene and mangled the nearby weeds. There was no way to tell what fiber or trace evidence might have been lost under his clumsy feet. At least it was muddy enough to cast and disregard his excess prints, but they never should have happened in the first place.

Brad shifted and nudged aside a sprig of goldenrod to take another photograph. "Backup coming?"

"Supposed to be," Todd said, scowling as the relief deputy paced along the edge of the road, obviously following neither of the instructions demanded of him. Sirens blared from far, far away, their urgent wail fading and strengthening in the wind.

A lime green Honda full of gawking college kids pulled up behind Todd's SUV. Two got out and started down the ditch. The idiot in uniform did nothing but pace.

"Fuck," Todd muttered, rushing back up. "Get your asses back in the vehicle now," he barked, stopping the kids in their tracks. "This is a crime scene. You're contaminating it. One more step and I'm hauling the lot of you to jail."

They stopped, muttering at each other, while Todd continued his climb. Idiot newbie stopped his pacing only to stand there slack jawed and worthless.

"Fuck this shit," Todd muttered. He reached the road and pushed past idiot newbie to the jittery college kids. "In the car and on your way or you're going to jail," he said. "We'll call your parents for you."

One kid glared, defiant, but the rest retreated to the car. "C'mon, Kyle," a tall blond kid said. "We saw it. Let's go."

"Got your badge number, asshole," Kyle said. "Next I'll have your job." Then he turned and stomped to the car.

Take it, it's yours. See how well you like all the fucking paperwork, let alone dragging a dead kid from a muddy ditch or peeling a woman out of an alley. Todd watched the car pull away, then he strode over to the idiot newbie, who stood rigid and snarling by the SUV like a chained dog defending his territory.

Todd thundered past again, reaching out to pluck the badge from idiot newbie's chest. "Forget the resignation," he said. "You're fired."

Sean kept a homeowner how-to manual in the tool box and he consulted the dog-eared page about basic wiring before shining a penlight into the electrical box and poking about with one finger. "Ground looks good, and the white's snug in the nut. Black wire's tight in the top terminal," he muttered, "but the bottom…"

The terminal screw's missing. And it's been vacuumed out: no cobwebs, no dust, not even the scrap of wire insulation I left in there on purpose last time. You really are cleaning outlets and switches. Goddammit.

Muttering, he set down the light and rummaged through the tool box for a screwdriver and a screw. "Mom!"

"Yes, sweetie?" She appeared at his elbow with a glass of cola and a ham sandwich, cold and stuffed with lettuce and onion instead of her customary grilled ham and cheese. Over the usual scent of disinfectant cleansers filling the house, he caught a faint waft of smoke as she approached.

"How did you lose a screw inside the switch?" He sniffed. *Definitely smoke, but from where?*

"I… I don't know," she said, beaming as she held out her offerings. "You've been working so hard and Rosemary's obviously not feeding you right. Why don't you take a break?"

Are you kidding? I want to finish this and get the hell out of here before you start in on Mare again, he thought, but said, "I just got here and I ate before I left the house."

He found a packet of screws and an appropriate screwdriver. Kneeling before the switch with a flashlight in his mouth, he muttered around it, "If you want me to come over, ask. Don't sabotage your electrical as an excuse, okay?" Screw started, he slipped the loose wire beneath and tightened. "And don't clean in here, either. You could get electrocuted or cause a fire."

Shit. The wiring. He sniffed the switch, wondering if that's where the smoky scent was coming from. Nope. Smelled like wires, lumber, and air-freshener. Only his mother would have lily-scented wiring.

"Oh, I didn't clean anything," she said. "But it is nice of you to come help me."

Uh huh. That's why the switch boxes in my house are dusty and yours are sparkling and perfumed. "Yeah, well, screws don't fall out on their own. Is something burning in the kitchen? I keep smelling smoke."

"Oh, that's probably me!" she said, blushing. "Last night's storm knocked down some branches. Decided to burn them." She nudged his arm and leaned close. "Your new young lady is really sweet. Quiet. Very respectful. I think she's a keeper."

Goddammit. He gave her a sideways glare then looked away. "Mare's a keeper, and if you weren't so nasty to her, maybe we'd both come over more often."

"Not only is Rosemary's greatest ambition to wipe asses for a living, she's crude, mouthy, and unwilling to listen to reason. Have you talked to that girl?" Helene said, nodding toward the dining room. "She's the sweetest—"

Fuck. Sean spat out the flashlight and caught it in his hand. "That's enough, Ma. Okay? I love Mare and she's not going anywhere. So drop it."

Helene scowled at the floor but said nothing as Sean reattached the switch plate.

As he slapped his tools into the toolbox, she said, "I saw you on the news last night.

I wish you weren't talking about such horrid things, though. Dead people! I don't know why Rosemary encourages such nonsense, after all the time and money we spent on your therapy."

"Don't blame her," he snapped. "I'm the one who found them. I'm the one trying to convince the press it's all real."

"Of course, dear. Whatever you say, but a mother knows better. You're a good boy and didn't come up with such creepy ideas on your own."

Sean clenched his teeth and let out an aggravated growl. *Yeah. And I illustrate horror because it's joyful fun.*

"You looked *very* handsome on TV, but a little sloppy. I can give you a proper haircut, since Rosemary is oblivious."

She's not oblivious, we're just broke, and you know it. "Goddammit, Ma," he said aloud as he snatched up the toolbox and marched toward the bathroom, trying not to cough at the oppressive stink of bleach. "I am so sick of this shit."

"It's an older house," she said, trotting to keep up. "It occasionally needs repairs."

"It's not the fucking house," he muttered, flinging the toolbox beside his feet. He wiped a crusty, brownish smear off the doorknob before he tried to close the bathroom door. It bound up immediately and, as he squinted at the hinge, he saw the top plate hanging loose from the door, missing both screws.

He sighed. *Always with the damned screws. Are they removed on purpose or do you vacuum them up when you're on one of your cleaning sprees? Surely you'd have to loosen them first.*

"If you don't want ham, just say so. I might have some chicken salad in the fridge or—"

"I told you, I don't want a sandwich," he muttered, rooting through for a hammer and pry bar. "I want you to stop taking screws out of things, okay?" It took a couple of taps to pop out the top hinge pin and he stuffed it into his pocket. "Stop breaking hinges and ruining plugs, drawer pulls, or switches. Please. But even more than that, I want you to *stop badgering me about Mare.* It's getting old, Ma, and it's pissing me off."

She leaned back, frowning. "So now it's okay for local news curiosities to curse at their mothers?"

Jesus goddamn Christ, let it fucking go! Sean took a breath and let it out before yanking out the lower hinge pin. "I love Mare. She loves me. You've had more than a decade to accept that but you just can't, can you?"

"You can do so much better!" Helene moaned. "You're my son! Surely you can find someone who's worthy of your talent and brilliance, not a...woman with no ambition or respect."

Sean wrestled the door loose and turned it onto its edge. "I'm a college dropout who can't keep a regular job," he muttered, slapping the loose hinge in place. "You keep forgetting that." *Shit, I can't even keep a comic in print.*

Helene nudged his arm. "It's not you, sweetheart. Rosemary's dragging you down. We were doing just fine until she came along."

Sean started to line up a screw, but the hinge slipped so he shoved it into place again. *Yeah, just fine. Dad left you because you scrub everything in sight as if you can scour away what happened to me, and I spent most of my childhood in therapy for the nightmares I still have.* "Mare's about the only 'fine' thing in my life, and I'm damn lucky she hasn't left me."

"Oh, sweetie, that's so untrue. You're special. Someday you'll see I'm right," Helene said, soothing.

He grunted and glowered. *Not likely.*

Helene shifted, opening her mouth to speak, but Sean interrupted her. "Have you heard from Uncle Paul?"

His mother blanched and blinked, eyes wide and startled. "Of course not," she said as if indulging an imbecile. "He's dead, and good riddance for that! Really, Sean, you need to start listening to your mother instead of Rosemary."

Goddammit.

Glowering, Sean worked in silence a few moments while his mother watched and fussed over him. He brushed off her attention and asked, "You've lived here your whole life, right?" in a vain attempt to change the subject away from Mare. Somehow.

"You know I have." She massaged his shoulders. "You're too tense. She's working you too hard."

"Ma, quit fussing," he said, shrugging off her touch. "Ever hear of a place called Lotus Lab? Somewhere near Pinell, maybe?"

"No. Can't say that I have." She paused, head tilting. "Can you manage without me for a moment? I think I hear Mindy. Why can't you make your mama happy and snatch her up before someone else does?"

Before he could reply, she scurried away, calling out, "I'm coming!" and taking his sandwich and cola with her.

She always gets me pissed off then leaves me festering. Muttering to himself, Sean shook his head and finished setting the hinge screws.

The house was still standing when Sean and Mindy returned, but Sean hesitated before pulling into the driveway. Eight zombie hunters shook their signs at his car and, cowering behind them, three women in skirts and blouses sang a hymn and held a banner rejoicing in Jesus's arrival. The protesters remained on the sidewalk, likely because a sheriff cruiser with two deputies was parked at the curb, but a group of regular-looking folks milled about in Sean's driveway.

A deputy opened the cruiser's passenger side door and stood, barking for the people in the driveway to make room. They moved.

"Stay here," Sean told Mindy as he parked the car and slipped out, doing his best to ignore the various masses of people lunging at him. He shrugged off the grip of an eager woman with a funeral urn and approached the cruiser.

"Hey," he said as the deputy rolled down his window. "Thanks for being here. This is all a bit nuts."

"Thank your neighbors for so many complaints," the deputy muttered, peering up at Sean. "You the homeowner? The guy who talked to the press yesterday?"

At Sean's nod, he muttered, "At least almost no one believed you, otherwise we'd have a madhouse out here."

The cop shifted to look in his rearview mirror, and reached for his radio as a little blue car crept by, the passenger taking pictures. The deputy picked up the mic and told the dispatcher that the homeowner had returned but a blue Civic had driven by three times. He gave the dispatcher the license plate number and a description of the driver, then put the mic back in its stand.

Sean watched the car turn the corner. *Drive-bys too?*

"Mr. Casey?" the deputy said, drawing Sean's attention. "We're out here if you need us."

Sean nodded his thanks even as he glanced at the zombie gang and their ready weaponry. He swallowed. Up close, the blades and guns were obviously replicas, other than a single pistol on the hip of a fat woman with a long braid. Her hip holster, and the gun inside it, looked no nonsense. The three Jesus ladies seemed intimidated by the zombie gang, and the group in the driveway just watched him with wide, desperate eyes.

"While I really appreciate you being here, what about that missing kid?" Sean asked, turning back to the deputy. "Isn't finding him more of a priority than me and a few protesters?"

"He was," the deputy said while the other picked up the mic to answer a question the dispatcher had asked. "Now we're stuck with you."

Sean took a deep breath and walked toward Mindy, still waiting in the car, but stopped when a tall guy with a resin rifle blocked his path.

"Dude," he said, holding out his hand. "You're fucking awesome, man, and this is a goddamn fucking pleasure!"

Sean blinked and accepted the handshake. "Excuse me?"

"You faced walking death and lived!" His companions gathered close. "Not only that, you're telling the world!"

Confused, Sean struggled to find his voice. The woman with the real gun slapped him on the back. "We've been waiting for this. It's incredible. Right here in Iowa."

Sean withdrew his hand. "I don't think you guys understand. They're not zombies, okay? They're just people who've been—"

The woman with the braid nodded. "Reborn and given a second chance to lose the shackles of consumerism. We know!"

"It's spreading like a fire all over YouTube," the tall guy said. "You're telling folks it's time to climb from the crypt of moral decay and believe in the miracle of independence. Riveting stuff, man!"

The group raised their weapons and cheered, "Fuck corporations! They ain't eatin' our brains!"

Sean looked at the various members of the group and swallowed. "Is this what all of the zombiephiles want? A break from consumerism?"

The woman shook her head. "Most are just stupid kids, but some want to dance while the world burns." She patted the holster at her hip. "We don't get along with anarchists."

Blushing, she paused and leaned close to whisper, "Are you really GhoulBane's illustrator?"

Sean hesitated then nodded with a sigh. *Zombie hunter fan. In my yard. With a gun. Fuck.*

She wrung her hands and blinked at him, blushing, then mumbled, "Can I get you to sign an issue, just one? Maybe tomorrow? I don't want to be a bother."

Like picketing in front of my house and scaring me and my neighbors isn't? "Sure. One issue. Sure. Okay. Just please stop scaring us and the neighbors, okay?"

She nodded so he backed away and turned to walk right into the church ladies' sign. As he excused himself, one touched his arm and said with grave sadness, "We're praying for you."

"Um. Thanks," he said before hurrying toward the car. The mass of people watched him, each carrying a grim offering.

One woman thrust a brass urn toward Sean. "Save my dad!"

"No, my Sprinkles!" another woman said, nudging the first aside. She held a photograph of a very fat, very fluffy cat. "I need my Sprinkles Baby back! Please!"

"My dad outranks your flea bitten cat!"

A shoving match started and Sean skirted around them to let Mindy out of the car. “Go. Save yourself,” he said, pressing the house keys into her hand even as the throng of desperate mourners surrounded him.

Chapter Thirteen

Happily pooped after playing with the neighbor kids, Mindy wandered into Sean's studio and watched him draw what looked like a rotting corpse leaping through a breaking window.

She waited until he lifted his pencil and asked, "Can I use the computer again?"

"Sure," he said, shrugging as he put that pencil in a cup and grabbed a different one.

She sat and took a breath before opening Chrome.

A quick search in Google confirmed what Dani had said. Jeff had sued Toyota for the faulty Prius and collected not only millions in damages from the car company, but from insurance as well.

Mindy sat staring at Jeff's smug face on the screen, her hands pressed between her thighs. At first she wanted to run across the hall and vomit, but anger took root, making her huff out one furious breath after another.

He didn't love me, loathed touching me, and treated me like a dog, but I was worth insuring for one point eight million dollars.

You think I'm gonna let that pass, Jeffy?

Oh hell no.

Phone still off, Sean cycled through the messages on the machine as he cooked supper. Any mention of a threat, plea, or request for an interview earned a press of the delete button. Only one message remained, from Deputy Todd.

Hey, Sean. Just wanted to touch base and let you know that some fuzzy cell-phone pics of the slime hit Tumblr this afternoon. We're hoping no one will believe it's real, but you know how these internet things go. Anyway, you're off the hook.

Sean returned to sautéing chicken and peppers. *Finally some good news, not that I had any intention of sharing the pics.*

Movement caught the corner of his eye and he muttered a curse. Someone was in the backyard. Again.

"Mindy!" he called as he walked to the back door. "Can you keep an eye on supper?"

He didn't wait for her reply, but walked outside, blinking away sudden sweat. "Hey!" he barked at a crisp young couple who looked like they'd walked out of a JCrew ad, if those ads included skulking around with a shiny spade. "Just what the hell do you think you're doing?"

"I, um," the girl said, clutching a gilded urn to her chest, while the boy merely narrowed his eyes and clenched the spade, its blue Lowe's price tag fluttering in the slight breeze.

"This is private property," Sean said, walking straight toward them. "You do not have permission to dig here."

"It's my mom," the girl said, cringing. "We heard you bring people back, and we just thought—"

"You just thought you'd trespass and vandalize my yard?" Sean snapped, looming over them. "I can't bring your mom back, okay? And even if I could—which I can't—whatever's going on didn't happen here, but at the cemetery," he said, pointing. "It's over there, on the other side of the tree farm."

The young man glared at him, defiant. "We've been there. Cops are guarding nothing but mud, tombstones, and flowers. Here, though," he said, pointing with the spade, "are several fresh holes."

Sean took in his yard and cringed. Lots of holes. Some big, some small, most scattered near the edge of the puddle at the back edge of his property. *Thanks, Mindy, for giving folks this idea.*

"I didn't give permission for them, or for you," he said, not without pity. "Besides, if she's cremated I don't think it'll work anyway."

"What? Why?" the girl asked, cradling the urn as if to soothe it.

"I think you need a body, not ashes." Sean pointed toward his driveway. "Now go on. Go home."

"You *think*?" the boy snapped, looking Sean over top to bottom. "Who are you to make a decision based upon a mere thought? You're just a long-haired, low-rent freak."

"Actually, I'm the long-haired, low-rent freak who owns this yard and I'm not going to allow snotty assholes to dig it up without at least a please and thank you. As far as I'm concerned, you're trespassing. Want me to ask the cops out front if they agree?"

"It's a shitty ass yard," the boy muttered as he stomped off, the girl trotting to keep up.

Beyond the rhubarb, Earl Simmons stood in his own back yard with his vile mutt, Peaches, panting beside him. Earl clapped slowly until Sean turned to glare at the portly old puke. "He's right. It is a shitty ass yard."

Sean flipped him the bird and trudged back to the house. *And you're a shitty ass human being.*

"We've started a petition!" Earl yelled. "Get you and your sign-carrying freaks kicked the hell out of this neighborhood."

"At this point, I don't give a fuck," Sean muttered to himself, "as long as I get the comic done." Without looking at Simmons or his awful dog, Sean walked into the house to find Mindy humming at the stove and two more messages on the machine.

While Mindy called her sister from the kitchen, Sean grasped the chance to get online. He dug several pages into Google but found no mention of an American company called Lotus Lab.

He stared at the screen, thinking. *Does that mean they pre-date the internet? If so, they closed before 1995.* He held the sign fragment, turning it in his hands. *It's definitely old,* he thought, thumb running along one cracked and chipped edge.

More searching brought him few options for fungus labs in Iowa, other than the ag testing center in Ames. Close to Pinell, but likely too far away to pollute their creeks. Another dead end.

He scowled and leaned back, fingertips tapping on the mouse. *How about the property?* he thought, then brought up the county assessor's site.

Barronsen's Poultry was bought by cash transaction in June, 1998, and the barns were built, appraised, and properly tax-filed in 1998 and 1999. The property had been previously seized in a 1996 foreclosure, after being passed between family members several times from 1991 to 1994. The online records stopped there.

He Googled every name on that short list of real estate transactions and found only a poultry farmer with several farms scattered across three counties, two old women who'd already died, and a man arrested three times since 1994 for tax evasion, swindling, or money laundering. He was serving out his current sentence in Newton.

That's a couple of hours drive, Sean thought, glancing at the clock. *Maybe he'd know who owned Lotus Lab. Or maybe it's just another dead end. Since whatever I'm looking for is obviously pre-internet, maybe I'd have better luck with newspaper archives?*

Mindy walked past, sniffling. Sean asked, "You all right?"

"I guess so. My sister barely talked to me. She just said Jeff kept or destroyed all my other stuff. If I want my license or whatever so I could maybe get a job, if I want to know what happened in court, if I want to know *anything*, I should talk to Jeff, not bother her because between mom and her kid and her marriage, she could not deal with having an undead sister. Then she hung up. My own sister hung up on me." She gave Sean a pitiful glance then continued to Jam's room, closing the door behind her.

He winced, uncertain what to do. *Do I try to comfort her or would that be too intrusive? Too forward? Would someone like Mindy think I was trying to make a pass at her? But if I do nothing, is that too cold and uncaring? Is—*

Someone pounded on the front door.

Saved by a stranger, Sean thought, standing. He rapped lightly on Mindy's door. "I gotta answer that," he said, "but are you okay?"

"Yeah. I'm fine."

She didn't sound fine, but Sean said, "Okay," and went to see who waited on the stoop this time.

Another reporter stood there, with a cameraman busily filming the various protestors, now spilling onto the street. Several mourners in the driveway clamored for his attention, and zombie hunters posed for the camera.

The reporter waited expectantly.

"I'm not answering any more questions," Sean said. "It's a miracle, and that's all I'm going to say." He held the reporter's gaze as Mindy walked past, muttering on her way to the kitchen. "Please leave."

"But Mr. Casey, surely you have an opinion on the toxins the chicken farm spilled in the creek east of your home. Could they be the cause of your unorthodox opinions?"

Sean rolled his eyes and slammed the door in the reporter's face.

Sean slouched at the computer as eleven PM rolled around, clicking on 'get mail' while scanning in the day's drawings. Seven pages of detailed pencils, done and ready to send to Murph for any changes before inking. Sean put another stiff illustration bristol sheet into the scanner and stretched. *Fifteen pages to go, but plenty of time to get them done before deadline. Another eight or so tomorrow and, with luck, the rest on Wednesday. Hopefully Murph will get his notes and corrections back before this weekend. So I can get 'em inked, colored, and out the door.*

11:03, still no email from Mare.

Behind him, Mindy flipped through a box of drawings and pulled one out every now and then to examine it closer. "Wow," she said, squinting at the original black and white inked illustration for a center spread. "This is amazing. How'd you get so good?"

Sean pulled out the bristol for page five and put in the next. "Been drawing almost my whole life as a way to deal with the nightmares after I was kidnapped," he said, hitting the scan button before checking email again. 11:05. Nothing.

"You were kidnapped?" Mindy asked.

"Yeah, when I was a kid," Sean said, shrugging. It was so long ago and he had long tired of rehashing the few memories he had. "I was gone a couple of weeks and came back not remembering much of anything about it, no matter how the cops and psychologists tried to pry details out of me."

"Oh my God! I'm glad you're all right!"

"Yeah, well, that's questionable some days," he said with a wry chuckle. "My therapist finally decided I had Post Traumatic Stress Disorder and one of the ways she had me cope was to draw or paint out my anger and fear. Turned out I liked it, and was pretty good at it, so I took all the art classes I could at school, even some summer program things."

Still no email and the phone, with the battery reinstalled, remained silent. "I took illustration and graphic design in college, then an online course thing for pro comic art…" He switched out the illustration again to the day's final scan. "That's really about it. Drawing's all I know how to do." 11:06. Still nothing. *Goddammit, Mare. Where are you?*

"This is seriously cool. Making comic books."

The scan finished and Sean pulled the bristol out and set it on the stack before squinting at the images in PhotoShop. They looked all right, straight and intact with adequate detail, so he sent his pre-set adjustment filters to tweak polished pencil drawings. While the image auto-processed, he checked email again.

Mare! Just a short note asking how things were at home, but Sean grinned as he replied, *Crazy, but all good. Come on home. Love you!*

After processing, the first scan looked awesome, a nice, crisp pencil sketch. He was about to process the next image when Mindy said from close behind, "What about these?"

Sean turned to see her holding his discarded drawings of terrified children. The rumpled vellum made them more pitiful, more horrifying, more desperate to escape their fate in the dark.

"They're nothing," he said. "Just a bad dream."

Chapter Fourteen

Mindy flew forward, tumbling, while Jeff whispered, “This is all your fault, Minders,” as if his voice alone flung her into the ether. She spun through the swirling haze like a ball thrown into a frigid wind.

Helpless. Cold. Toppling forever without end.

Trap me, Minders? Serves you right. Serves you fucking right!

Her eyes bolted open and she lay in bed, gasping, sweat icy on her skin as she raised a hand to her throat. She smelled snow and frost and a car heater, heard the rush of her blood in her ears and her own desperate breath. Heart hammering, she pushed herself up to sit.

Just a dream, she told herself, closing her eyes and opening them again. *I'm okay. It's just a dream.* She took a deep breath, then another, forcing herself to calm.

Movement caught her attention, maybe a breath, more felt than heard or seen. She turned her head to see a man standing in the open doorway, an inky shadow against the dark hall.

I closed that door, I know I did, she thought, gasping as thunder rumbled from far away and sudden rain splattered against the window. *Sean went to bed with Mare, right after she came home. Why would he be here, watching me?* Mindy's heart slammed hard, terrified, and she choked out, "Sean?"

Her door still stood open, but the shadow was gone.

Ghoulie woke to darkness, his skinny-kid arms bound behind him and something tight around his face. Despite agony pounding from his feet, he managed to roll to his side and sit. *I'm in a cellar,* he thought as he felt cool dirt under his knuckles. *It stinks. Something died down here.*

He heard movement in the dark, low, almost silent, a rustle of grit to the left. Ghoulie turned, sucking in deep, scared breaths. "Who's there?" he called out, voice cracking.

No answer, but, as he strained to hear, the floor-level grit shifted again and, much higher, he heard a soft scrape. Something breathed, something big, its movement lost behind a peal of thunder and a woman's sudden shriek.

Startled, Sean bolted upright and out of bed, blinking and naked, while Mare screeched and scrambled back against the headboard.

"What happened?" he asked, ready to pounce, to rend, to shred. Mare had never woken up screaming before, not once in their years together.

She pointed toward the corner, and Sean saw it. A man. Lurking in a shadow beside the open bedroom door.

Sean lunged, growling, and the shadow shifted but Sean hit him anyway, shoulder into the guy's gut. The man let out a huff of air, but didn't fall. They grappled, wrestling into the kitchen, and Sean barely heard Mindy's startled gasp from the archway as the man flung him onto the floor.

"I wasn't doing nothing, but you had to start a fight," the shadow muttered, edges of his body gilded by the light from the open bathroom door beyond the bed, but his features lost to the dark. He knelt and pulled back for a punch, mountainous rises of his knuckles gleaming.

Aw, shit, Sean thought, ready to turn his head aside so his nose wouldn't get shattered.

Then as another shadow blocked the bathroom light and extinguished his attacker's glow, Sean heard a loud click.

"Okay, fuckface," Mare said. "You're gonna put your hands on your head right now, or I'm gonna blow a big goddamn hole in it. And don't even try to think you can get the drop on me. Your cranium will be hamburger before you turn halfway around."

The man remained motionless as Sean crawled to his feet.

The shadow's head nudged forward as Mare shoved the gun against it. "Hands on your head, asshole. Right fucking now. Or you're a splatter."

He complied.

"On your knees," Mare said as Sean staggered to the kitchen light.

He fumbled for the switch and flicked it on to see Mare, nude and furious, holding their .38 to the back of his Uncle Paul's head as Paul settled onto his knees.

Sean gaped. *What the fucking hell?!*

Paul looked at Sean with a shrug and an aw-shucks grin. "So. Naked fighting and guns, eh? I musta crashed a helluva party."

"It's the middle of the night and we were asleep!" Sean snapped as Mare gave him a confused frown. Head swimming, he took a step forward to spit blood into the sink. "And what the hell are you doing breaking into our house?"

"I want to know who this asshole is!" Mare said, gun still pointed at Paul's head.

Sean stared into Paul's eyes, so like the ones he saw in the mirror every morning. "My Uncle Paul. He spored about the same time as Mindy."

"He's *family*? Aw, piss." Mare fled to their bedroom and slammed the door.

Paul stood, grinning. "Dude. You fight like a pussy, but you married a bad ass bitch."

"What are you doing here?" Sean asked, his heart rate easing closer to normal.

"My buddies couldn't let me keep crashing at their place, so I thought I'd just come home."

Sean crossed his arms over his chest. "This isn't your home."

"Used to be, though," Paul said, holding Sean's gaze, just a regular-looking guy in a muddy workshirt and faded jeans. "And you still keep the back door key under that same paver."

"What key and what paver?" Sean asked, confused. They'd never needed to lock the back door until the news crews and picketers arrived. "We've never had a key for that door."

Eyebrow raised, Paul pulled a key and fob from his pocket and jiggled it at Sean. "This one. I obviously know a lot more about your house than you do."

Sean narrowed his eyes and glared as his hands clenched beside his armpits. *Don't you dare try to take my house. Don't you fucking dare.*

Mare opened the bedroom door fully dressed and took a breath before walking through to the kitchen. She held Sean's jeans and a pair of boxers. "Mindy, can you give us a moment?"

Mindy, her face bright and flushed, nodded once then bolted.

Paul grinned at Mare. "See? You like me too!"

"Shut up," she snapped, then tossed the clothes to Sean. "Babe, you wanna take care of that?"

Oh, Christ. Mindy, Sean thought, eyes closing as embarrassment crawled down his body. But he was already yanking on the jeans and wondering why his uncle had decided to cause trouble on a rainy night.

"After I split at the hospital, I went right to my buddy's place, just a couple of blocks away," Paul said, gripping a glass of water. "He was sitting on his front porch and recognized me right off, said he couldn't believe his eyes." Paul took a drink and sighed, apparently unaware that Sean was staring at his forearm as if cockroaches swarmed over it instead of a dark, lumpy mole. "He's pushing sixty now and has liver cancer. Terminal. He's so doped up on OxyContin it's a wonder he saw me at all. Maybe he thought I was a spirit or hallucination."

Sean squeezed Mare's hand before she could start yelling again. She usually had the patience of a boulder, but between the spores, the picketers, and Paul's violent entrance, fury had edged into her eyes and voice.

Sean managed to hold his temper tight in his throat. "Sorry about your friend, but it still doesn't explain why you came here, in the middle of the goddamn night, and broke in."

"He wasn't the only friend," Paul sighed, rubbing his mole as if it itched. "I tried several. One's dead, another's in jail for kiddy porn, a couple have moved who knows where, and one's wife ran me off with a shotgun."

Glancing at Mare, he muttered, "You'd like her."

Mare started to speak, then rolled her eyes and looked away.

Silence hung awkward in the air as Paul rotated the glass in his hands. Sean hid his grimace, wondering why the simple action made his belly lurch as if his uncle were twisting the head off a bunny instead of merely toying with a glass of water.

"The last…" Paul said, "Well, let's just say after spending one night listening to him talk to his imaginary friends about beasts rising from the depths to serve their awakening tentacled master, I got the hell outta there."

"Ah, a Cthulhu-ite," Sean said, relishing his horror geekdom. "They're an interesting bunch. I drew a series, oh, two years ago, about—"

"Let's skip that for now, babe," Mare grumbled, glancing at Mindy. "Maybe when it's daylight."

"Sure," Sean said. That three-parter had been especially creepy and Mindy already appeared flustered and pale.

"Right, Ass-a-thought-something." Paul shuddered. "I dunno, whatever it was, it was creepy as hell. He was the last one I could find. Everything's gone or dead or rotted away. There's a froo-froo coffee shop where Smokey's garage used to be, and, shit, the guys I did find are all old men."

"It has been twenty years." *For both of us.* Sean felt his palms sweat as the nightmare flickered in his mind.

"No, it hasn't," Paul said, staring him in the eye. "It's been two damned days. That's it. Two days. Now all of my surviving friends are beat to hell or batshit crazy." He sighed and sipped his water. "Or both."

Mindy nodded and stared at her hands. "Yeah. It's all changed. They've moved on without us."

"Look, I have nowhere else to go," Paul pled, shifting his gaze to Mare. "I wandered around awhile, looking at this or that, hungry as hell, bored out of my mind, and I finally decided I just wanted to go *home*." He leaned forward and touched Mare's hand. "Can't you understand that? Wanting to go home?"

Mare held firm, she didn't speak or pull her hand away, but she tensed beside Sean.

Paul drew back his hand. "I'm sorry I scared you. The front door was locked, so I came around back, checked the paver and, right there, the key, you know? So I let myself in. I figured Sean would have the big bedroom I expanded off the kitchen, so I tried the little ones first and hoped one would have a spare bed or cot or something. No luck. Artsy crap in one, and she was in the other," he said, nodding toward Mindy.

"So I walked into your bedroom and scared you. I didn't mean to, just wanted to ask Sean if I could crash here. I didn't expect anyone else to be in there."

"What about the couch?" Mare asked, her voice tight. "It's right there in the living room, and it's empty. Don't you think finding you sleeping on the couch might have been less of a hassle than you scaring the shit out of us in the middle of the night?"

"I didn't, I didn't think..."

"Yeah, you didn't think," Mare muttered. "Fucking asshole."

Paul frowned but said nothing, and Sean wondered if he remained silent to accept guilt and appease Mare, or to merely keep his true thoughts to himself.

Mare still held Sean's hand and glowered with constrained fury but, beside her, Mindy had curled into herself and stared silently at her clasped hands.

"I think the three of us need to talk," Sean said, hating the coppery taste of the lie.

As far as he was concerned, no discussion was needed. "We'll decide what to do with you, if anything."

"Fair enough," Paul said, standing. He took a breath then sighed it out again before saying to Mare, "I am sorry I woke you, sorry I scared you." Then he turned and walked to the living room.

Breathing easier once Paul had left, Sean nodded toward their door and whispered, "Come on to the bedroom with us, Mindy."

Mindy looked up, surprised, as Mare stood. "Me? Why me?"

"Cause you're part of this, too." Sean stepped aside to let Mindy pass then he followed the women into the bedroom and closed the door.

Mare sat on the edge of the bed. "I don't trust him. His friends got old, and his life evaporated. Whoopty fucking hoo."

"Yeah, cry me a river," Sean said, wanting Paul out of the house and as far away as possible. Just looking at his uncle made his belly clench. "That still doesn't explain why he didn't knock, or call out, or just come by during the day. Why scare the crap out of us like that?"

"Exactly," Mare said, looking up at Mindy who'd remained quiet and withdrawn over by the dresser. "Do you have any comments? Any concerns?"

Mindy raised her gaze to them and shrugged. "Kind of. I guess. When he was here with the rest of us that morning, he didn't hardly speak at all. Just sat on the couch and frowned at everyone. But when we were all in the van…" She shrugged again.

"What happened in the van?" Sean asked. *Give me an excuse, any excuse, to toss him out on his ass.*

"Doesn't matter," Mindy said. "He just wasn't very friendly. But I wasn't friendly either, I guess. I was scared and confused. We all were. I wonder if, maybe, that's part of this, part of the fungal infection that brought us back. How we're not really ourselves at first, but as we get better, we become ourselves? I dunno. That probably doesn't make any sense."

"Sure it does," Mare said. "I see it every day. The nicest people can be real pissy if they're sick or in pain. Once it gets properly managed, they're themselves again."

"Right," Mindy said, then she took a breath and raised her head. "I didn't like him then and honestly, I don't know if I like him now, but I do know what he means, what he's going through. And, since you want my honest opinion, I guess I have to say it doesn't seem right or fair to take me in like you did, but cast him, family, out into the rain."

She paused to chew her lip. "I know what that's like, and it sucks. My own sister did it to me. She threw me away. I can't step back and just let it happen to someone else, even if I don't like him much. It's not right."

Sean and Mare stared at each other until Sean muttered, "Fuck," under his breath. *Family was family, and fair was fair. Goddamn it and our principles all to hell.*

"You're right," Mare said, shoulders sagging with begrudging acceptance. "I guess he could have the basement or something. But only 'til he can find another place." She took a breath and sat a little straighter. "He needs to find another place. Soon."

"Piss. Okay. Guess I get to tell him then," Sean said, reaching for the door with a sweaty hand. *Don't, don't do it,* his mind whispered, but he opened the door anyway and entered the kitchen. As he walked to the living room he cursed himself for agreeing to let his uncle stay.

Mindy watched Mare after Sean walked away and she said, "Can I ask a favor?"

"Sure, anything," Mare said, smiling patiently at her.

"I need something to do. I need underwear. My own shampoo. Maybe a magazine to read. I need *money*. I'm never gonna make Jeff pay for what he did to me without money." She took a breath and straightened her shoulders. "Do you know of anyplace that might hire someone without identification?"

Mare stood, her brow furrowing. "Actually, I do. The nursing home I work at has several, um, undocumented workers in housekeeping and the kitchen. Pretty sure they get paid cash, under the table, but I've never asked."

Cash would mean no tax records, but it's a start. "I can clean or cook, sure. Plenty of experience in that. Do you think they'd hire me?"

"Maybe. With all the folks calling in sick lately, they're pretty desperate for warm bodies. I can run you over there tomorrow, if you want, and talk to HR."

Mindy thanked her and dodged past as Sean returned. Hopeful, she returned to her room and lay in bed a long time (door locked, just in case), staring at the ceiling as Sean and Mare quietly argued, then made up, then made love, the sounds muffled by the thin walls. She thought about the past two days, and how neither Mare nor Sean had said one word to anyone about her being a fungaloid.

Or a spore, she thought, rubbing goose-pimples off her arms. *Sean calls us spores. And Paul didn't seem to recognize me, but I sure recognized him.*

She thought of the others in the police van, the other spores. All had been dead far longer than her; the closest was the old farmer who last remembered the harvest of 2009. Ten years back, fifteen, twenty for Sean's uncle, more than thirty for Evelyn. Would they even comprehend the new phones? The computers? iPads? Twitter? Facebook? All of the ways people didn't communicate back in the eighties, or, hell, any time during the twentieth century. Who could rightfully speak for them?

She tried to sleep but couldn't. Her mind kept gnawing on the same nugget in the back recesses of her brain.

Modern communication equals technology. Spores are being treated as freaks, and they have no grasp of technology, no way to get their word out. Who will speak for them?

Sean's trying, but he doesn't really know how bad it is being a non-person, she thought, sitting up. *He just thinks we're second-chance miracles.*

"But I can speak," she whispered aloud. "I can tweet. And tumblr. And blog. Whatever." She took a breath and stood. *If I don't know it, I can learn it, because I'm still new, still modern. I still know the technology.*

Mouth set tight, she walked to Sean's studio and turned on the Mac.

This time, instead of merely reading her own Facebook page, she posted. And tweeted.

Then she started a blog.

Chapter Fifteen

Sean hurried across town on a sweltering Wednesday afternoon, a week later. Much of the media attention had faded as worries over tainted water moved downstream, but a few picketers and desperate people with their urns and dead pets remained. Betsy the smooshed dog had spored, slimy but otherwise fine, much to the delight of her grieving family. A few other animals had spored as well, but Sean didn't understand why anyone would bury their pets in a stranger's yard without permission or leaving a way to contact the owners. Some of the anonymous pets had run into the tree farm and disappeared, but he'd taken others to the humane society. Mindy had become infatuated with a spored cat, a slinky black purring thing, so three spores now lived in the house.

Sean took a deep breath and waved at a neighbor mowing his yard. His nightmares had been horrid of course, endless tortures of missing feet and devoured entrails, but he'd completed the drawings for Ghoulie's last issue. Only the publisher's sign off, some inking, and all of the digital coloring remained. Easy peasy. Plus, with Paul installing siding and shacking up most nights with random women he'd dug up somewhere—complete with disgusting play-by-play replays when he came home—the whole household had settled into a crowded routine.

Their tight finances had eased since Mindy had taken a job in the nursing home kitchen, working the same shift as Mare. It paid less than minimum wage in cash, but every night she gave Mare a few bucks to help cover room, board, and transportation. The three of them had even picked up a RedBox movie and a take-and-bake pizza Friday night to celebrate Ghoulie's pencils being finished. If not for his increasingly vicious nightmares, life would be pretty grand.

As Sean walked up the sidewalk to Hap's Place, he smiled. All in all, it had been a good week. Hectic, yes, and sleep-deprived, but manageable. Paul was rarely home, Mare was getting used to living in a crowded house, and Ghoulie was on schedule!

"Hey, Sean," Phyllis, the elderly daytime barkeep, said as he entered. "Still have the crazies at your house, I see."

"Getting used to it," he replied as he went into the kitchen to clock in. He took a quick glance in the fridge—ham, chicken salad, sandwich veggies, condiments, and white or wheat bread, easy enough to make—then returned to the bar as the juke switched over to Roy Orbison.

Phyllis had dragged cases of canned beer and pop behind the bar to stock the fridge and was just settling herself onto her knees. "I can do that," Sean said, reaching out to help her stand.

She batted away his hand. "I'm not so old I can't fill a danged fridge."

"You're seventy-two!" a regular muttered from the table in the corner. If they weren't planting or harvesting, ten or twelve men spent their afternoons slowly pickling their livers and playing cribbage. A few, most bachelors, sometimes stayed 'til well after dark.

"You got room to talk, you old fart," Phyllis replied as she opened the fridge door and started stuffing in Pepsi cans.

Sean checked the kegs, noting Miller Lite was getting low, and that the well was about to run out of vodka. "Stubby? You drinking gin sevens or screwdrivers today?" he asked.

Stubby raised his glass, the clear liquid easily seen from beyond his mangled and chopped-off fingers. "Sours in honor of Willard. Passed away last night. Cancer got him."

"Sorry to hear that," Sean said. "Thought he was in remission?"

"Apparently not," Stubby said, returning to his game.

"I already put a bottle of Monarch over by the cash register," Phyllis said, standing easily. "Same for the Jack. Only a shot or so left in the bottle, but don't worry about it. These bozos are just wells and beer. Doubt we'll get any big spenders." She bent at the waist and plucked the empty pop cases from the floor as if her back and knees had never pained her at all.

"Thanks." Sean watched her scurry to the kitchen. She never scurried anywhere, usually preferring a slow, steady shuffle.

One of the card-playing regulars brought up his empty glass and Sean refilled it with Michelob, stepping aside so the tap wouldn't splatter him. "Bag of those Frito-bandito chips, too?" Ol' Mort asked, usually milky eyes twinkling.

Sean obliged and, as he handed it over, asked, "You finally get those cataracts taken care of?"

"No, why?" Ol' Mort glanced over his shoulder to make sure no one was touching his peg.

Sean shrugged and added the beer and chips to Mort's tab. "The eyes're just looking good today."

Mort rubbed the left one as if it itched. "Yeah, I can just 'bout see clear again. It's all Catherine's fault," he said, leaning close to whisper. "She started on some new vitamins or something, and she's 'bout wearing me out, almost like we was still newlyweds." He winked. "Think I should tell the doc 'bout her miracle cure?"

Sean definitely approved of Mare's miracle cure. He chuckled and stepped aside as Phyllis huffed by with a rack of beer glasses. "Couldn't hurt."

Mort laughed at that and said, "If it hurts, you're doing it wrong, kiddo," then strode back to his game.

Sean blinked. Mort used a cane, had for years. Hip injury.

The front door opened and a massive man blocked the encroaching sunlight. Phyllis looked over and, frowning, grabbed a bar towel and stepped closer to Sean.

The cribbage players kept playing, but a few nodded hello.

"Fellas," the guy said as the door swung closed.

"Howdy," someone at the table nearest to the door replied. Stubby glanced over and scrubbed his mangled fingers on his shirt as if scratching an itch he couldn't quite reach.

"What can I get you?" Phyllis asked as Todd Anderson, in civilian attire, settled his heft onto a barstool.

Smiling, Todd took in the bar. "Kitchen still open?"

Phyllis rattled off their short sandwich and snack food menu. Todd ordered and, as Phyllis scurried to make his sandwich, Sean filled a glass with ice and plucked a Coke out of the fridge.

"I don't think I've ever been in here before," Todd said, fishing out his wallet. "Not a bad little place."

"Your basic small town bar." Sean filled Todd's glass. "Beer, sandwiches, guys playing cards. We even clean the bathrooms." He pushed the cash back toward Todd. "My treat. I told you if you came in I'd buy you a sandwich and a drink."

"Yeah, but I kinda need a receipt today." Todd pushed the cash toward Sean. "Just in case the boss asks why I was here. Stopping here for a quick supper is one thing. Stopping for a quick conversation is something else."

Great. Sean scooped up the cash and rang Todd's order. "I'm guessing you're not here to talk to Phyllis."

She returned with Todd's food—a sandwich, pickle, and heaping handful of potato chips—and set it before him.

"As much as I'd love to converse with such a delightful young lady—"

"Oh, save it for someone your own age." Phyllis untied her apron and wadded it in her hand. "You flirts are all alike."

Todd raised his sandwich and grinned at her. "Who said I was flirting?"

"Been tending bar almost fifty years. I know a flirt when I see one." Still clutching her apron, Phyllis waved good night to Sean and the regulars before scooting out the door.

"Why's she in such a hurry?" Todd asked before taking a bite of his sandwich.

"No idea," Sean lied as he filled another beer for a regular. Todd did not need to know that Phyllis's heroin-addicted son lived at home, and she could smell a cop blindfolded from halfway across town.

Todd chewed and contemplated Sean, finally shrugging before taking a sip of his Coke. "This is off the record. Okay?" he said, barely loud enough for Sean to hear over Willie Nelson.

Sean leaned his forearms on the bar and gave a single nod.

"Your friend Melinda Howard is causing a bit of a problem."

"I have no idea what you're talking about."

"Uh huh," Todd said around another bite of sandwich. "Her blog's sign-on IP has been traced to your house and she's been positively identified by those same deputies who sit out front to keep your fans from fighting each other. Heck, I've seen her twice myself. We know she's there."

Sean said nothing.

"It's a helluva blog and it's pushing some really powerful buttons. Banking. Insurance. Civil rights. We're getting pressure from the governor to bring her in and question her. But the attorney general is balking because there's no precedent on how to legally approach the fungaloid issue. Especially when the fungaloid in question is a young, pretty, articulate white woman hollering about fraud, civil rights, and murder."

"Spores. Fungaloid's like nigger. It's degrading."

"Fine. Spores. But she's demanding reinstatement of full citizenship, as well as reversals of judgments surrounding her death and prosecuting her ex for attempted murder. The governor isn't happy about that, lemme tell you, especially now that she's getting a legion of pissed off online followers. They're making a helluva stink in the statehouse."

He grinned as he sipped his cola. "As much as I hate to admit it, she's too pretty and feisty for her own good."

And you've always been a sucker for that combination. Sean refilled another beer. "So her blog's not protected under free speech?"

"That's the rub," Todd said around another bite. "Is she a citizen or is she not? No one knows what to do with her."

"Why are you telling me this?" Sean asked.

"Because it's not just her. We have seventeen funga…*spores* that we know about. Three were murder victims, kids missing from twenty some years ago who walked out of a strip of woods near Fraser a few days back, and at least one of your spores has been killed since coming back. Several have been assaulted, and one… He disappeared yesterday and no one's seen him since. With all that's been happening lately, we're…concerned."

"Again," Sean said, "Why are you telling me all this?"

"I know, I know," Todd said, his voice lowering further. "Why am I talking to you? Because you're the face of this phenomenon, the truth of it anyway. And, frankly, you're not threatening my job if I don't round up all the funga-spore-whatever-they-ares and put them someplace dark and quiet."

"Is that what you're intending to do?" Sean asked, hands balling as he stood straight. "Lock them up?"

"Not me," Todd said, holding Sean's gaze. "I think you're right. They're people. Weird, freaky people who have no logical reason to be here, but people just the same."

"What changed your mind?" Sean asked.

Todd set down his sandwich. "Evelyn Fischer."

"Her? Why?" Sean asked, perplexed.

"She was murdered the night after you'd found her, before anyone knew about your spores. It took us until yesterday to figure out who she was. She had no identification, no money, no anything, just a dead woman in an alley. Her DNA had no hits in the database, nothing on her fingerprints. A real Jane Doe."

"I don't understand," Sean said. "How does her death—"

"She, and your friend Melinda, were the last two women we hadn't found and I had a hunch, okay? Just check their dental records against our Jane Doe. Sure enough, same lower jaw, same everything, except this Evelyn had perfect teeth, not a single filling in her head.

"Her autopsy and DNA came back completely human, nothing weird or out of the ordinary at all other than she was in apparently *perfect* health. No calcifications, no scars, nothing but an utterly healthy forty-two-year-old woman with her skull bashed almost flat. We've already taken a swab sample from her brother and I'd bet my house it'll show they're siblings."

He paused. "You're right. They're the same people who died, just like you said, every one a victim of an accident or injury, none from disease. The exact same people, right down to their DNA, memories, and fingerprints. But I'm a county deputy, a government employee. If I speak up publicly, if I refuse to follow orders, I'll lose my job, maybe go to jail, which won't do anyone any good. You, though, and your friend Melinda, have the attention of the media and internet."

"I don't know how I can be any clearer than I already am and they already think I'm crazy," Sean said. "I don't know what more I can do."

"You have to find a way, because it's spreading," Todd whispered. "There are reports of weird fungi in streams and ponds as far south as Quincy, and fish and bird populations are exploding all over the river basin. I can't talk about what's happening in cemeteries, but I know you've seen it first hand."

He paused to take a slow breath. "Think about it, Sean. The Des Moines River empties into the Mississippi and DNR tests show the fungus isn't diluting as it flows south. People and critters will keep sporing all the way down to the gulf, and no telling what will happen when this crap hits the ocean or leaves our local water table. Before we know it, we'll be up to our elbows in spores. I took an oath to protect lives. I can't let scared politicians round them all up like cattle for slaughter or start pointing fingers and making them enemies of the state. Which is exactly what will happen if the politicians aren't stopped. Soon."

Todd removed a business card from his wallet and tucked it under his plate. "My sister's become a trial lawyer," he said, tapping the card twice, "a damn good one, in Des Moines. She does pro-bono work and knows how to manipulate a sound bite. Call her. Cover your ass, and do what you can to help these poor people."

Sean eyed the card but didn't pick it up. He wasn't sure he'd need a lawyer, but Mindy might. "Has anyone figured out what's causing this?"

"Yeah. Toxic spill from some chemical manufacturer, back in the seventies or eighties. We found unmarked barrels, more than one, buried in a gully north of town. Most were corroded and leaking. Our problem is, six or seven companies used the facilities out there. One would go bankrupt and close shop, then another would move in to make their own potions or solvents. We don't even know who made what since most of the records are just gone."

He munched a few chips. "EPA regulations weren't as stringent back then and there's no telling what crap just got dumped or discarded before anyone knew any better. I don't know what they found, but I do know it's a chemical mess up there. Maybe that's what did it. A little of this solvent, a little of that chemical… It could have mutated a common fungus, which then went nuts and made your spores. We really don't know yet."

"I was there, last week," Sean admitted. He looked up as a regular approached, empty glass in hand. Sean excused himself to get the fellow his refill.

"See anything interesting?" Todd asked when Sean returned.

"I saw a squinney spore. That was pretty cool. And I found a busted hunk of sign for some place called Lotus Lab."

"Ah, them," Todd said around a sip of pop. "Blooming Lotus Research Laboratories, from back in the early eighties. Property transfer records indicate the Chief Operating Officer was Egyptian, we think, but everyone else was local. There's a barely legible photocopy of his passport, international tax ID and work visa, anyway, with addresses in Cairo, Luxor, and Al Masid. We thought they were a pretty good fit for the spill, but every record we've found states they were cross pollinating hybrid flowers for international suppliers. Still are, even though they moved their operation back to Egypt. They're a dead end."

"You sure?"

"Yup." Todd chewed the last of his sandwich and swallowed. "The C.O.O. guy has Alzheimer's now, so there's no use talking to him about anything, but his son's a big-shot in the import/export flower business. Nice fella. Tried to sell us orchids."

After Todd left, Sean picked up the card and wrote *Blooming Lotus Research Laboratories* on the back before slipping it into his wallet. Orchids or not, it was the best lead he had.

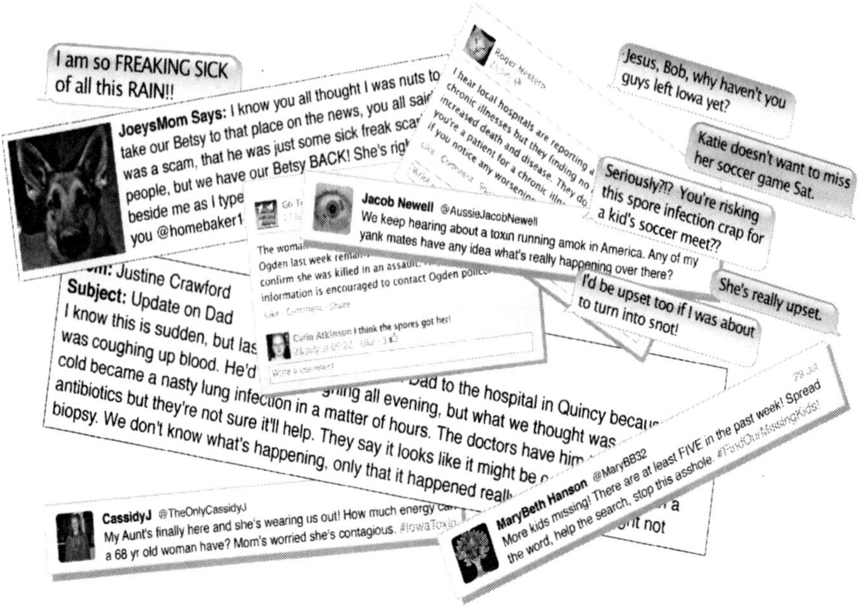

Chapter Sixteen

"Do you have a minute?" Sean swallowed a yawn as he rapped softly on Pastor Bailey's office doorframe. Between a late night at the bar and a full banquet of horrific nightmares, he felt exhausted.

"Sean! Our local celebrity!" Bailey said, standing. "Come on in!" His desk was awash with papers and hymnals, and the window behind him illuminated the book-filled office with warm light.

"More like local crackpot, according to the news," Sean said, entering Bailey's office for the first time in nearly twenty years. He reached out to shake the pastor's offered hand. "How's life, family, and soul saving?"

"Could be better, could be worse." Bailey smiled as he motioned for the chair in front of his desk. "Always more to be done on all fronts. How about your life, girlfriend, and Ghoulie?"

"About the same," Sean said as he sat. "Mare's the best of that set, by far."

"Same with my family," Bailey said, sitting. He pondered Sean for a moment before asking, "You're not here to make small talk, are you?"

"No, afraid not," Sean said, covering a yawn with his fist. "I have some questions, if you have some time."

"If you're going through half of what I imagine after seeing you on the news, I'd expect you to have a lot of concerns." Bailey grasped his coffee and leaned back. "Since I'm confident you're not a crackpot, let's hear those questions."

Sean chewed his lip, uncertain where to begin. "Why don't we start with the elephant in the room," he said. "The spores."

"What do you think?" Bailey asked. "Not the obviously edited sound bites I see on TV, but what you feel in your heart."

"To me, they're a miracle, a sign of hope that we can have another chance to do things right. A lot of people disagree, though. I've recently been told the spores might be rounded up, might be imprisoned or killed if I can't help them."

"Fear drives most people," Bailey said, nodding. "Change. Uncertainty. When known rhythms suddenly shift, it knocks a lot of beliefs out of whack and makes people doubt their faith and beliefs. This is a very unusual time. A frightening time."

"I have a group in front of my house this very minute with signs calling to burn the spores alive because they're abominations to be cleansed. There's another group demanding we all kneel before them like they're gods." Sean sighed and lowered his head. "They're neither of those things. What happened to them is a miracle, but they're just people."

"People who've been resurrected," Bailey gently corrected. "Brought back from the dead."

"But that doesn't make them any less human. They're not to be idolized or feared."

"Okay, how about this," Bailey said. "Most everyone knows of Christ rising from his crypt, right?"

Sean nodded. "Sure."

"Well, you'd remember from Sunday school that Jesus also raised Lazarus? Another miracle. But some believe that Lazarus was killed, murdered by a fearful mob, after his resurrection." Bailey paused to give Sean a sad smile. "Fear and worship often run hand in hand. Never forget that, Sean. It's how so much evil has polluted the teachings of Christ, how so many churches have lost their way and now preach hate instead of help."

Sean stared at his knees, his thoughts churning. "What am I supposed to *do*?" he asked, raising his head. "I want to help, to keep them safe, like I've been asked to…"

"But you're afraid."

"Yes. But there's no one else to speak for them. If I don't find a way to save them, they could all be tortured or killed. But if I do stand for them, I could be arrested. Or killed. Or my house burned down, or who knows what. Some of those people picketing my house are crazy *and* furious. That's a scary combination."

"I can't make that choice for you, Sean. Even if you were still a member of my congregation, I couldn't. This burden is yours and yours alone."

I know, Sean thought, staring at his knees again. *But I'd hoped you'd have more guidance than this.*

"Okay," Bailey said, leaning forward and setting aside his coffee mug. "When you look at yourself in the mirror, when you look into your own eyes, your own soul, does that soul want to step aside or defend them?"

"You're asking if I'm weak or strong."

"No, I'm asking what you, deep down, believe. There's no right or wrong answer, only *your* answer."

"I believe I'm one bounced check away from not being able to buy groceries next week," Sean sighed. "I believe politicians are crooks, the sun will rise tomorrow, and that I'll love Mare 'til the day I die."

Bailey smiled. "Those are all honest, reasonable convictions. What about your spores? What convictions do you have about them?"

"They're human," Sean said, his voice firm as he met Bailey's gentle gaze. "No different from you or me."

"Then stop looking at them as miracles. If you don't deify them, maybe others will stop demonizing them."

Sean smiled. "Thank you. That helped."

"You're welcome, but you'd have gotten there on your own eventually. What else have you got?"

"Nothing. Just wanted your take on how to handle this whole resurrection mess. Thought you might have some insight, it being your bread and butter and all."

"That's it?" Bailey asked, leaning forward. "A little nudge to an answer you'd have found on your own?"

"Pretty much, yeah. Just some help past the uncertainty." Sean shrugged. "Out of curiosity, if you were me, what would you do about the spores?"

Bailey walked around his desk. "I'd hope they had good lungs. We're a little short in the choir."

Sean chuckled. As he stood to go, Bailey said, "I don't think I'm quite done with you yet."

Sean paused and faced the pastor. "Did your daughter want another Ghoulie poster or a couple of comi—"

"Sit," Bailey said, gesturing toward Sean's chair. His tone was not to be disobeyed.

Sean sat, worry gnawing at his belly. "Is something up with my mom?" he asked as the pastor sat at the edge of his desk.

"She's fine as far as I know," Bailey said, leaning forward, his hands gripping his thighs. "I want to talk about you."

"Me?" Sean sat back, blinking. "I haven't done anything worth—"

"Sean," Bailey said softly. "When's the last time you slept?"

"I... I slept last night."

"Uh huh. For how long?"

"Well, um," Sean felt his cheeks get hot as he tried to figure out a way to dodge the question.

Bailey pressed, "In one stretch, without waking, how long did you sleep last night?"

Great, he had to be specific. Sean shrugged and stared at Bailey's knees. "Twenty, twenty-five minutes at a time. Maybe. Off and on all night." *I've spent more time awake than asleep, lately.* He took a breath and raised his gaze again. "I don't watch the clock. It's too depressing."

"Most people don't dream if they sleep in twenty minute bursts. Do they?"

Despite fidgeting, there was no avoiding the question. "No."

"But you do. Still?"

"Sometimes," Sean admitted. "Usually I wake myself up before-hand. But not always."

Bailey nodded and released a tired sigh. "Still having nightmares, then?"

Again, there was no avoiding the question, but Sean grimaced and looked away. "Yeah, they never really stopped."

Silence lingered between them for a few moments, like a bag of snakes struggling to break loose. Snakes Sean did not want to look at, ever, ever again.

"Have they increased because of the recent child abductions and murders?"

"Maybe. Probably." Sean shrugged and let out a heavy sigh. "I don't know, but they're worse. Yes."

"Are they still the same dreams as after your abduction?"

Sean flinched, shaking his head, and gripped the chair arms tight enough to make his fingers ache. "Let's not talk about that, okay?"

"No, it's not okay," Bailey said, stepping toward Sean. He knelt and touched the younger man's hand. "I know you left youth group, left the church because of the nightmares—"

"And the harassment, let's not forget that," Sean snapped.

"Children can be cruel, yes," Bailey said. "But you're not a child anymore, you've grown to be a good, caring man, but you still carry the trauma—"

"I don't think about it," Sean said. "I don't. I can't, okay? It's just a big empty hole in my mind. A couple of weeks of nothing at all. And if I do try to think, to remember, the hole just sucks me in. I can't live my life, I can't do my job, I can't do anything. I don't want to waste all of my time looking for something that's not there, to wallow in the darkness—"

"Sean," Bailey interrupted, "you're incredibly talented and you could have become a successful artist or designer—"

"But instead I just draw a crappy ass horror comic, is that what you're saying?"

"No, I'm saying that you insist on drawing horror because your subconscious is still coming to terms with what happened when you were a child. Your conscious mind may have blocked it out, but deep, deep down in your brain, in your memories, in your soul, you're still screaming and terrified. Kids are being taken, like you were, and, like you, your spores were gone a long time then came back. I think the combination has triggered something in your head. While I understand and applaud your desire to be the spore's champion, I don't think they're helping you."

"I told you," Sean said, cutting his gaze away from Bailey's patient stare, "they're just people."

"I believe you. But I saw you the morning they first came. You were relaxed. You looked rested, better than I'd seen you since losing your foster son, and while the situation was crazy, you were handling it just fine."

Sean glared at Bailey. "So now I'm not?"

"I think you're holding up as best you can," Bailey said. "But, as your friend, I worry about what all of this is doing to your psyche."

"I'm fine," Sean said. "Just a little stressed."

Bailey nodded, his gaze grave. "Anyone would be stressed, but most people would still manage more than twenty minutes of sleep, out of utter exhaustion if nothing else."

Sean glowered but said nothing.

"So the dreams are the same? A Minotaur looming in the dark? A dog eating you alive?"

"Yeah," Sean admitted. "Sometimes I'm chased, sometimes I'm tied, but yeah, it's the same stuff. Before the spores came, I might go a week or so with some other kind of nightmare if I dreamt at all—falling, being crushed, being lost, normal stuff—but, sooner or later, I'd be back in the dark with the Minotaur and his damned dog."

Bailey nodded. "Are they worse now? Since the kidnappings and the spores?"

"Been waking up screaming again," Sean admitted with a shrug.

"I thought you hadn't done that since you were thirteen."

"I hadn't. Well, once in almost forever I would, but now it's nearly every night."

"If you allow yourself to dream," Bailey said.

Sean nodded. "Yeah. I've even put myself back on the meds, and they're not helping."

"So what's changed in the dreams? Since this started, what's made the Minotaur and his dog more frightening?"

Sean took a breath and forced his hands to unclench the chair arm. "Ghoulie, well, me… My feet are gone. Cut off, eaten, I don't know why, but they're gone. When I realize that, I wake up screaming." He looked away and thought, *that dream's always made me scream. It just used to be a rarity, not every fucking night.*

"So your subconscious is connecting your memories to these new crimes?"

"What?" Sean leaned forward, perplexed. "Nothing's changed, not really. They're just bigger, bloodier, and more frequent."

Bailey shook his head, his eyes growing wide. "You haven't been watching the news?"

"Not if I can help it. I saw myself on TV once. That was enough, thanks anyway."

Bailey rounded his desk and dragged out a waste bin stashed beneath, then fished out a tidily folded newspaper. He tossed it to Sean. "It's yesterday's *Tribune*. Look at it."

Sean unfolded the paper and, as he read the headline, darkness flowed over his vision.

It read, THIRD FOOTLESS CHILD FOUND DEAD.

Mindy held steady in the middle of the kitchen as her boss yelled at her for screwing up the evening dessert menu. Camille's voice seemed to rise with every syllable. "I told you use leftover frosting on the sheet cake, not make…*confections*."

"Yes, ma'am," Mindy sighed. "I just thought the residents might like something pretty."

"We're not here to provide pretty. We're here to feed them quickly and cheaply before they croak. That's frosted sheet cake cut into squares. I don't have time for this. If you can't follow simple instructions, you can find another job."

Without a social security card or ID? Not likely. I need this job to pay a lawyer to go after Jeff so I can get my life back. Lowering her gaze, Mindy nodded and said, "Yes, ma'am. Sheet cake. I won't mess it up again."

"You'd better not. At the rate the patients are dying off, those cupcakes will last longer than this nursing home will." Camille muttered an expletive and stomped off to holler at the woman peeling potatoes at the sink.

"Don't let her get to you," Juanita whispered as she huffed past with a huge pot of water. "I think they're beautiful."

"Thanks," Mindy whispered back. She finished icing the last few and looked up to see the elderly dishwasher, a nearly silent woman named Ramonna, watching her. "I'm just about done with this bowl," Mindy said, assuming Ramonna wanted to wash it.

"*Cuánto*... No, ah... How costo? How cost?" Ramonna asked, gesturing toward the tray of cupcakes. "*Dos docenas el sábado*, ah... Saturdo?"

Juanita returned and laid a gentle hand on Ramonna's narrow shoulder. "She wants to know how much two dozen would cost if you were to make them by Saturday."

"For this?" Mindy asked, confused. "Spruced up cake with a little ganache?"

Juanita spoke to Ramonna who replied in rapid Spanish. "Her granddaughter turns nine this weekend and she would rather pay you for such pretty little cakes made with love than purchase plain ones at the store."

"Oh. Um... I don't know," Mindy said, thinking. *A couple of bucks for the cakes, another couple, maybe, for the ganache, something for sprinkles. But I don't know if Mare has cupcake cups or food coloring or anything, so I might have to buy supplies.* "Ten dollars?" she suggested. "I'll have to buy the paper cups and all, at least."

Juanita translated and Ramonna beamed. "*Diez dólares, sí. Gracias amable señora*," she said, nodding eagerly. "*Gracias*."

"You're welcome," Mindy said, smiling as the old woman returned to her washing. She met Juanita's cheery gaze and asked, "Was that too cheap?"

"Maybe a little," Juanita admitted. "But they are very pretty, and you were very kind to agree to make them."

Mindy twirled the last cupcake in the ganache. "I love baking and I'm happy to make a couple of dozen for her granddaughter."

"You are a good soul," Juanita said, ducking back to her station as Camille barked at them to stop talking.

After taking a moment to confirm the townhome's address on his slip of paper, Sean pulled in behind the sheriff's SUV and turned off the ignition. A woman walking a fluffy little dog eyed him warily and he couldn't blame her. His wheezy Chevy stood out in the neighborhood of matching townhomes, immaculate lawns, and pristine import cars.

He gave the woman a reassuring smile and nod, then snatched up Bailey's newspaper.

Feeling exposed and out of place, he walked to a cheery porch of concrete and brick, the mirror image of the one next door. He rang the doorbell. Nothing. So he rang it again and confirmed the address one more time. *I'm at the right place, but everything looks the same. With curvy roads and matching houses, how do people not get lost around here?*

Another woman, this one pushing a stroller, narrowed her eyes at him as she pushed her little darling past. Sean pulled open the storm door to pound on the entry door behind. "I know you're home!" he hollered into the jamb. "I need to talk to you!"

He heard heavy thumps from within and a deadbolt release, then the door was snatched open and Todd stood there, glowering in a bathrobe and pointing a pistol at Sean's head. "Oh, goddammit, it's you," he muttered, turning to shuffle away while his free hand rubbed his face. "With all the complaints and threats we've received, you're lucky you didn't get shot."

Sean took a steadying breath then followed. "Why didn't you tell me?" he asked, shaking the newspaper.

Todd let loose a sputtering fart as he continued shuffling toward the kitchen. "Tell you what?" he asked.

"About the dead kids," Sean said, stopping just inside the kitchen doorway.

"I don't want to hear about any dead kids. It's too damn early." Todd opened the fridge and rummaged inside, finally producing a can of diet cola. He popped the top and took a long drink. Then he burped. "There, that's better."

Sean crushed fury between his grinding teeth. "Don't you think after what happened to me all those years ago, that I might want to know about more dead freaking kids?!?"

Todd took another deep drink and muttered, "Didn't know you were on the investigative team. Musta missed that memo."

"Oh now you're being a smartass," Sean said. "Thanks. Thanks for that. Again. Fuck you, Anderson." He turned and headed toward the front door.

"Sean, wait," Todd said, following. "Why are you so upset about those kids?"

Sean spun on his heel to glare at Todd.

Todd took another deep drink, emptying the can. "In any way other than most anyone should be upset about dead kids, I mean."

"Is this the real reason you talked to me last night at Haps?" Sean asked, thrusting the newspaper toward Todd, who barely glanced at it. "You know about the bad shit that happened to me when I was a kid, when there was some murdering pervert on the loose. I've heard how you cops look for patterns, connections—"

"Considering all the similarities, you were a potential person of interest, yes," Todd said, lobbing the empty can into a waste basket in the corner. "The only known survivor of the Boone County Creeper and now this similar M.O. back here in your home turf? Honestly, Sean, since about half of child molesters were molested as kids, most any time a kid in Boone, Story, or Webster County goes missing, a cop drives by your place, just to be sure you're home."

"Fuck you," Sean spat, approaching the massive deputy. "I'm not a danger to anyone. The state crawled up my ass with a microscope when we went through the foster parent program and they knew kids would be safe with me. I was a damn good dad and I'd rather cut off my right arm than hurt any kid. You of all people should know that."

"I was your friend back then too, remember? I know how fucked up you were."

"Yeah. Right. Your mom wouldn't even let us in the same class because she was convinced I'd hurt you."

"Actually, it was because you'd suddenly got into horror novels and comics and slasher films and shit. I was twice your size. *No one* thought you could hurt me. Not even my mom. She was just weirded out."

"So if I'm so goddamned creepy and a perennial suspect, why hasn't anyone questioned me about these kids?"

"For starters, you have a deputy planted outside your door and your hermit schedule is utterly predictable. You're home most of the time, or working at the bar, or, rarely, buying cheap shit at WalMart or the office supply store. You live a very exciting life, Seanny my boy."

Sean started to speak but Todd added, "Plus another little boy went missing yesterday about the same time I left the bar. After playing with a neighbor, he called home to say he was on the way, but never made it the two blocks. Unless you can teleport twenty miles in less than ten minutes, you didn't snatch him."

Sean felt his knees weaken and he slumped against the wall. "So there's more than three?"

"Five, actually. Six if you count the one they're labeling a runaway," Todd said, motioning for Sean to follow. "You want a pop?"

"Sure, okay," Sean said, staggering behind. *Six kids. Good God, what's happening?*

"How much do you know about the kidnappings back in the nineties?" Todd asked as he dipped into the fridge again for two diet colas and a pizza box.

"Not much," Sean admitted. "I vaguely remember hearing about it before I disappeared, but, shit, I was twelve. Invincible."

Todd tossed him the pop. "Yeah, we all were at that age. And afterward… I still remember how freaked out your mom was, how she barely let you out of her sight for two seconds."

"Yeah. I finally got away when I went to college. Like everything else, she decided to scrub my abduction clean and never speak of it again. I never did learn what really happened. There's not much of anything online."

Todd contemplated him for a moment. "It's ugly. Sure you want to know?"

"Yeah," Sean said. "Especially if what's happening now is connected to what happened to me back then."

"Okay." Todd dropped the pizza and his pop on the kitchen table then yawned his way to a cupboard for paper plates. "Eleven kids disappeared from ninety two to ninety seven," he said as he walked back. "I've dug through all the old files this past week. Boys, girls, black, white, ages from four to fourteen. No rhyme or reason to any of it, other than all were fine one moment, then gone the next."

Sean accepted the plate and, at Todd's urging, sat. "Were they all taken from outside like I was? Sidewalks, parks…"

"Nope," Todd said as he sat and opened the pizza box. "Two were taken from stores and one was listed as a probable runaway. The fourteen-year-old, back in ninety-four. She'd been having trouble at school and her mom said she was upset over bullying classmates when she'd gone to her room, but was there, sleeping, around eleven." He coaxed out a slice and slid it onto his plate.

"But gone in the morning?" Sean asked, grabbing one himself.

"Yeah. Want me to nuke that up for you?"

Sean shook his head as Todd continued.

"Everyone really thought she was a runaway. But she walked out of the woods near Fraser a couple of days ago, fine as could be. She said there was a guy with a dog, and they'd hurt her. Bad. That's all she knew. Said she was blindfolded and tied up."

Just like me, Sean thought, nodding. *Just like the nightmares.*

Todd swallowed a mouthful of pizza. "The other kid coming out of Fraser was a seven-year-old boy. Same story. Man, dog, the dark. A lot of pain. We found his folks, though. They're supposed to fly in from Seattle today. So that's something. Won't they be surprised he's still seven instead of almost thirty?"

"And the girl?" Sean asked around a bite of cold sausage pizza. "You find her family?"

"No father, and her mother committed suicide a year or so after the girl disappeared. Poor woman knew her daughter'd been taken, but we didn't believe her."

Todd tossed his pizza back onto his plate. "Of course I wasn't on the force then just a kid, but I feel guilty for how that poor woman was treated. Missing teenage girls were often considered runaways unless there was evidence suggesting otherwise. Still are, sometimes. Makes me wonder how many of them are actually kidnap victims or sold into human trafficking."

He leaned back and belched. "It's a goddamn mess out there and we're all running our asses off. Feds are all over the place but don't seem to care about missing kids or your spores, they're too busy taking water samples. Fuckers. The cyberjunkies have decided the feds are covering their asses over a terrorist event, probably anthrax. Or mutant pesticides. Or some other 'we're all gonna die!' thing. So that's put a run on the hospitals."

"Seriously?"

"Seriously. Do you have any idea how hard it is to convince a doddering old woman that her pet kitty isn't gonna die from drinking tap water?"

"Probably not easy."

"Two words. Fucking. Impossible. And people *are* dying. There's been a definite increase in deaths from terminal illnesses, especially for the elderly, but it's been a hot, wet summer. It happens."

Sean nodded, unsure. Mare'd lost several patients the past couple of weeks. More than usual, even for summer.

Undaunted, Todd continued with his rant. "But the media! God, they're the worst pain in the ass, always getting in the way and using any little rumor to spin the story and stir up more panic. I am so sick of reporters."

Tell me about it. At least mine have mostly faded away. As Todd grumbled out a sigh and finished munching his piece of pizza, Sean pointed at the newspaper headline. "The kids from the nineties… Were they missing feet, too?"

"They only found two of them," Todd said, taking a sip of pop. "The third and sixth victims. It never made the news, but, yeah. Their feet had been cut off and cauterized."

"Not gnawed?" Sean asked, watching Todd's eyes.

Todd stared intently at Sean's face. "You remembering something after all these years?"

"No. It's a nightmare I never really stopped having."

Chapter Seventeen

"You've always had these nightmares?" Todd asked around a slurp of pop.

Sean hesitated, uncertain if Todd was asking as a friend or investigator, then he nodded. "I don't have any memories of when I was missing, just the dreams."

"So the dog gnaws off your feet?"

God, I hate that dog! Sean stood and paced near the table. "No. He gnaws the stumps. The feet are already gone."

"We haven't released that detail," Todd said, watching Sean. "The press knew about the missing feet, but not the tooth marks after being cut and cauterized. And the news only found out about the feet missing because of a leak."

"It's one of the spores killing these kids, isn't it?" Sean asked, wincing at Todd.

"Nope," Todd said, shaking his head. "The theory of spore involvement did come up since so many kids disappeared right after they returned, but, no, it's not one of them."

"You're sure?" Sean asked, leaning over the table. "If it all started after they spored—"

"The earlier dates don't match," Todd said. "None of them died close to when the disappearances stopped in ninety-seven. Some before, and a few well after, but none near. And those who died after… Women? Children? Old men? They simply don't fit the profile. At all."

"But, the timing… There has to be a connection."

"Not necessarily," Todd said. "I've been in this job long enough to know that just because two events happen at the same time and geographic vicinity does not mean they have to be related. There's an armed robbery at a convenience store and, while on that call, a gay kid gets beat up at a honky tonk bar the next block over. Same time, same area of town, totally unrelated events."

"But, my dreams, they've gotten worse since the spores came."

"Another coincidence." Todd shrugged. "Maybe it's just because they, like you, came back from something terrible and it jarred something loose?"

Sean acquiesced. Bailey had said the same thing and it made as much sense as anything, he supposed. Dreams weren't real evidence, just replays of his own fears.

"They're all having nightmares too, as far as we can tell. Sometimes hallucinations. Mostly replaying their deaths in their heads over and over again. The poor bastards."

Sean nodded. "Horrific flashbacks are common in PTSD, awake and asleep. God knows my head's been shrunk enough about it. Be sure to let the families know the kids sporing back after the Creeper are going to be a mess."

Todd said, "The Boone County Creeper never really stopped. Yeah, eleven local kids disappeared twenty some years ago, but other kids have been found all around the country since then eviscerated and missing their feet. We're pretty sure whoever was doing it left the area in ninety-seven. Maybe he traveled for a job that expanded his hunting grounds, maybe he moved around a lot, but, for some reason, he's back now because something changed. It's no longer an occasional snatch, it's become a compulsion."

"Okay, so it's not a spore," Sean said, sitting again. "Do you guys have any idea why he's back or why it's now a compulsion?"

"Yeah, we have a theory," Todd said as he tossed his pizza crust onto his plate. "The cops guessed the creeper to be in his thirties back then—which fits with what the kids who came back from the woods told us—so now he'd be in his fifties. His parents would be in their seventies, maybe eighties. Coming home to take care of mommy or daddy while they're sick and dying, or recently dead and dealing with their estate, would upset anyone's psychological applecart. Only our creeper's already short a wheel and axle so he keeps grabbing kids to cope."

Todd paused, then stood to gather up their mess. "There are a lot of fifty-year-old men with dying relatives. Unless we get a good lead, it's going to be a bitch to narrow down the suspect pool. So far, we have nothing but dead kids and dog spit."

Sean returned home around five. He ducked past the various groups in front of his house, but was blocked by a reporter. *Not now, not after today,* he thought. "Please move," he said, but the reporter just pressed her microphone closer.

Dammit, I'm done with this shit.

Before she could begin her endless repetitive questions about his crackpot theories, Sean pushed past her to stand on his stoop and address the madness. "Listen up, everyone!" he called out as the camera's red light flicked on and the reporter held out her microphone. "It's time for a paradigm shift, all right? Yes, some people came back from the dead. They did. I don't know why, and I sure don't know why they picked my house to come back to, but they're here and we all have to figure out how to help them."

"Help them?" a woman with a *Burn the Filth* sign screeched. "We need to burn the sin outta them before they corrupt our children!" Her companions cheered and shook their signs.

Sean stared at them. "You'd say that to parents who lost their child in an accident and feel blessed to get them back, or a man who's thankful to hold his beloved wife again?"

"The abominations must burn!"

He stepped down from the porch. "Seriously? You're calling to murder someone, burn them alive, simply because of your misplaced fear?"

"The dead rising is a sign of the end, of the degradation of America," the woman spat. "I'm trying to save the world, save our children, while you want to watch it burn!"

"Funny, I'm not calling to burn anything, let alone innocent people," Sean said. "You are. And, need I remind you, your precious Christ rose from the dead. You want to burn him, too? That makes you a murderous hypocrite, doesn't it?"

The woman pulled back, but Sean turned away before she could speak and faced the group carrying a banner demanding the spores use their magic to lead them to power and riches. "And you! Wanting to turn regular people into something to worship and exploit for your own gain? You should be ashamed."

Sean stood in the middle of his own yard. "You all should take a few moments and think, really think about what you're demanding of these people. That's right, people. Living, breathing, human beings, no different from any of us."

He turned and pointed at one of the Jesus ladies. "You," he said as the woman he pointed at flinched. "Has anyone you loved ever died? Wouldn't you give anything to have them back, even for just one day? Just one chance to see them again? Some folks have had their prayers granted, yet you've stood on my sidewalk for more than a week deeming it a sin you yourself have surely desired. How dare you, a sinner no better than any of us here, presume to know the will of God?"

He turned again. "And you!" he said, pointing at a college-aged zombiephile covered in fake wounds and blood, "You think it's so cool to paint yourself up like a corpse and cheer about eating someone's brains even though right now, this very moment, there are children missing from right here in Boone County. Kids who will quite likely be tortured and killed while you stand in my front yard cheering death and mayhem. What if your little brother was missing and a bunch of self-centered assholes were celebrating death, huh? Have some compassion and pull your head out of your ass. This isn't a game, it's people's lives!

"Every last one of you, if you can't stand with me and demand these folks get their rights and lives back like they deserve, then you can get the fuck off my property right goddamn now. They're people. Just people. If you can't accept that, then fuck off. I'm done dealing with you arrogant assholes."

Two groups, the original zombie hunters and mommies carrying signs demanding to *Let the Missing Kids Spore!* clapped. Everyone else glared and muttered amongst themselves.

"Write down their license plate numbers," Sean said to the zombie hunters, loud enough for everyone else to hear. "Anyone with a nasty sign who's still on my property in five minutes is getting sued for trespassing, harassment, property damage, and whatever else my lawyer can come up with. I'm thinking big cash plus jail time."

"You got it, boss," the bearded zombie hunter with the rifle said, nodding eagerly.

"I'm not anyone's boss," Sean sighed. "I'm just done being pushed around by fear mongers and idiots." He turned then to the mommies and their desperate plea to save the kids. "Any of you know the missing kids?"

A woman with her red hair pulled back into a ponytail nodded, her eyes bright and damp. "Yes, a little girl in my son's third grade class disappeared two days ago. Such a sweet, peppy kid. She doesn't deserve this."

"No one does." Sean grasped her hand and looked into her terrified eyes. "This is going to be hard, but, if the worst happens, you tell her parents she can come back. Tell them don't cremate her, and to bury her as close to water as possible. She'll come back. They all will, God willing. Can you do that?"

The woman nodded, tears welling in her eyes. "Yes, I can tell them. Thank you. Thank you so much."

Sean nodded and, when he turned toward the house, the reporter watched, still recording.

"And you," he said, striding directly toward the camera. "There is no reason these people should be persecuted. They've suffered enough. So quit promoting the hate and let them resume their lives. All of you viewers out there know this: They're *people.* Human beings. Start treating them like it. Help them. Reunite them with their families. Offer housing. Maybe a job. Clothing. Teach them how to use cell phones or the internet or ATM cards so they can rejoin modern society. They have nothing but memories and we can't stand aside..."

He took a breath and let it out. "If you can't find compassion for them, if you can't bring yourself to do more than blindly hate, blindly fear, then keep it to yourself. Some of us are actually trying to do the right thing."

Mindy yawned as she followed Mare into the house. Camille had ridden their asses until every crumb, smear, and speck of salt had been scrubbed, sanitized, or put away. Which was fine—she, too, was a firm believer in a sparkling kitchen—but surely there was a better way to manage the work and mess than screaming. It only made everyone jittery and prone to more mistakes.

Maybe she likes to see us upset, Mindy thought, giving Paul a polite but disinterested nod as she trudged through the living room. He was flicking back and forth between two old basketball games on ESPN. Again.

Mare went into Sean's studio but Mindy continued on to her room. After gathering her comfy clothes, she headed to the shower to get the stink of cafeteria cooking out of her skin and hair. Paul had left his fart-streaked underwear and filthy jeans on the floor. *Eeyuck. Always leaving his nasty crap lying around for me to trip over.* Mindy grimaced and kicked the clothes aside. *Rotten lazy puke.*

She showered quickly in case Mare also wanted to scrub her job away, then dressed but damp, she left the bathroom and walked across the hall to Sean's studio.

He was frowning at a printed piece of paper and looked from it, to the pencil drawing taped to his board, then back to the paper again. He did not appear to be pleased.

"Can I use the computer?" she asked, picking up her cat, who'd been begging for attention. "For the blog?"

"Yep," he replied without glancing at her. "Just going to re-do this two-page spread's new layout sketch then get to bed. Black Pawn wanted new layouts for five spreads. I'm exhausted. It's been a *long* day."

"I hear ya," Mindy said as she woke the Mac. A click on her bookmark sent her to the blog and, kitty dozing on her lap, she began a new entry, talking about the fun and excitement of being a cash worker in a kitchen. She wrote about cupcakes and ganache and working for a boss who cared more for conflict than efficiency. She proofread the entry and uploaded it, then sorted through comments awaiting approval from her earlier posts. More followers, more questions she tried to answer, more encouragement, more jerks telling her she was a lying sack of shit. Same as usual.

Just gonna delete those creeps. She paused, hand trembling over a comment from *HiFiJH.*

Oh shit. Jeff. She swallowed the bad taste in the back of her mouth and clicked view.

I don't know who you are or what stunt you're trying to pull, but it won't work. Break into my dead wife's online accounts and steal her identity? That's bad enough, but then you decided to slander me? Oh, buddy, you're messing with the wrong guy. Cease and desist or I'll sue your ass for every penny you'll ever make. This will be your only warning.

"Jerk," Mindy mumbled. "Is there a camera on this thing?" she asked Sean. "Like for video chatting? I kinda need a picture of myself."

"Yeah, there's one at the top of the screen, but I usually have it turned off. You might try PhotoBooth? I think it takes pics. Or iChat."

"Thanks," Mindy said as she searched for the app. A few moments and one mouse click later, she had taken a craptastic photo of herself. Undaunted, she turned her head for better lighting, sat a little straighter, and tried again. *Much better.*

She returned to her blog and sent HiFiJH a private message, cc'd to her own email at an account Jeff had never heard of as well as her brand new lawyer, courtesy of Sean's cop friend.

Jeff! Darling! The word you're looking for is libel—check a dictionary if you doubt me—and it's only libel if it isn't true. So sorry your petty threats are meaningless. By the way, it is me. See? Took this pic just now, special just for you.

Go fuck yourself.

Minders

She attached the picture, complete with her chipper smile and damp hair, and hit send. Then she laughed. It was great to be alive again.

Chapter Eighteen

A scream caught in his throat, Sean woke well before dawn. He lay still and quivering, staring at the bathroom light until his heart rate slowed to a more reasonable rhythm. As he calmed, he rubbed his toes against Mare's calves to confirm his feet were still there, and of course they were. Tonight's dream had been a doozy: watching the dog eat his severed foot out of his scuffed sneaker while the Minotaur shoved him face down onto the cellar's dirt floor and forcibly stripped him naked.

But he wasn't a child anymore. He wasn't bound and helpless, wasn't maimed, naked, or about to be raped. It was just a dream.

He took a cleansing breath and rolled to spoon against Mare's back. She made appreciative noises and pressed closer. As always, she smelled like home, and he breathed her in.

Arm around her, he reached again for sleep, reminding his brain to wake him before the next glimpse of madness began. But his mind's eye remembered the dog working a foot out far enough to gnaw on it, and the terrifying pile of bloody, half-chewed kids' shoes in the shadows beyond.

No rest for the wicked. Sean kissed Mare's back and sighed before drawing away.

She followed, rolling to snuggle against his chest, her hand gently tracing the faint line of his appendix scar. "You okay?"

"Right as rain."

Her hand quested lower to fondle him. Once his cock was delightfully cradled in her cupped hand, she muttered, "Liar."

He chuckled despite himself and kissed her. One good grope of his personal barometer always told her the truth of his mood. "Was just another bad dream. Go on back to sleep."

She moved one electrifying finger to caress behind his testicles and soon had to shift her hand aside to give him room while adding the base of her palm to the enticement. As he sighed happily and basked in her attention, she asked, "What if I don't want to go to sleep?"

Grinning, he reached for her. "I dunno. Have any ideas?"

"Maybe," she giggled and, kissing, they played, gently coaxing until the need for each other became too great to ignore. They made love, both sighing happily as he eased inside, each dragging the other to the comfort of the abyss. After, he slumped sweaty and spent beside her and she twitched, sated, in his arms. He nuzzled his face into her skin and sought sleep.

The edges of his mind had grown foggy and dim when his bladder insisted he needed to get up anyway.

"Dammit," he muttered as he untangled himself from Mare's legs and the wad of sheet that had encircled them.

"Everything okay?" she asked, her voice drowsy.

He leaned over for a kiss. "Just gotta piss. Be right back."

"'Kay." She hugged his pillow and buried her face into it.

Sean staggered to the bathroom to relieve his inconvenient bladder. As he rubbed his face and stumbled back toward bed, movement in the mirror caught his eye.

He glanced over without thinking, his sex-and-sleep-hazed brain expecting to glimpse the familiar reflection of himself, but instead a towering Minotaur glared at him from within the shower, one horn distorted by a crack across the mirror's corner.

Sean yelped, scrambling to face the beast, his spine and buttocks crushed against the vanity, but the shower stood empty except for the bottle of store-brand shampoo, a washcloth, and a bar of soap.

What the hell? He leaned toward the shower without leaving the steady assurance of the vanity, and yanked the curtain aside. Empty.

"Babe?" Mare asked from the bedroom, their bed creaking as she moved. "What's wrong?"

"Nothing." He sagged and rubbed his eyes. He pulled his hand away and braved another glance into the shower, then let out a sigh of relief. Same old boring fiberglass stall as always. "Just thought I saw something."

He heard Mare flump back upon the bed. "Maybe you need another one of those pills so we both can get some sleep."

"Maybe." He peered around the narrow accordion of curtain but saw nothing but shower. Nothing in the linen cabinet or near the toilet, either. Sighing and cursing his overly creative imagination, he turned around to open the medicine cabinet, then swallowed a scream.

The Minotaur loomed where he had been before, grinning, his head tilted forward to make room for his horns while a slow dribble of drool leaked from his horrid jaws. "Missed you," the beast grumbled, its thick, pointed tongue licking blood from bovine lips. "I'd almost forgotten how tasty children are."

"It's not real," Sean whispered, opening the cabinet and snatching the bottle of pills off the shelf. "Not real."

He heard the Minotaur's bellowing breath and smelled his vile animal stink. Despite the tremor in his hands, Sean managed to shake out a single pill. He dry swallowed it and put the bottle back into the cabinet. Then he slammed the door and jumped.

"Still here, Sean," the Minotaur's reflection assured him. His horns had gouged wounds into the shower ceiling until bright plaster salted the shaggy mess of his topknot and shoulders.

Sean met the beast's fiery gaze. "I'm not afraid of my imagination," he said, hands balling on the counter's edge.

The Minotaur chuckled, the movement dusting fresh plaster flecks upon him. He reached out and Sean froze, too terrified to move, as the Minotaur caressed the back of his head then dragged one hard claw down his spine to the cleft between his buttocks. "I think you're lying to me, Sean. Last time you lied to me, I fed pieces of your belly to my Lulu." He gripped Sean's buttock, much like Mare had minutes earlier. "Maybe this time I'll give her different meat."

"You're a dream," Sean said, skittering toward the toilet and away from the cold bite of nails on his ass. "A filthy, fucked-up dream. No one cut open my belly, no dog ate my feet. Ever. Get out of my head. You're just a goddamn dream."

"Sean?" Mare eased the door open. "Everything all right?"

The shower was empty, as it should have been, and he nodded. "Yeah. I'm okay," he said, closing his eyes as he brushed past her. He dared not glance in the mirror.

She followed. "You don't look okay. What happened? Is it the feet thing again? Just because it's really happening doesn't mean your dreams are doing it."

"I know," he said as he dragged on his undershorts then his jeans. "It's nothing. Just shit in my head."

"Sean, babe, talk to me," she said, reaching for him.

"Nothing to talk about," he said, quickly kissing her. "Go on back to bed. I'm wide awake and gonna try to sketch another panel or two. Maybe Black Pawn'll like them better this time."

She searched his eyes, but at last she nodded. "Okay. Wake me if you need anything," she said, holding his face in her hands. "Anything."

"I will. Promise." Before she could delay him any longer, he left her standing alone in their bedroom, her hands still reaching for his skin.

Despite wretched children pleading from the dark depths of his sketch pad, Sean managed another full pencil spread before the rest of the house woke and began their morning. He chuckled at Paul and Mindy arguing like siblings over the bathroom, and gratefully accepted a fresh cup of coffee and a kiss from Mare.

She draped an arm over his shoulder and sighed as she examined the new layout. "Was pretty crappy of them to insist on a revamp after you finished the inks."

"Yeah, but it's the last issue," he said, erasing an errant smudge. "Might as well give 'em what they really want."

Mare huffed and took a sip of her coffee. "I say give 'em what *you* want. It's not like they can fire you again."

Sean laid a crisp new line and glanced up to wink at her. "Don't think I didn't consider it. But my early sketches were so craptastic, I'd rather Ghoulie went out on a decent looking issue, even if I have to redo half of it."

"I guess you're right." She kissed the top of his head. "You might want to take a break pretty quick, though. Mindy's making pancakes. Your uncle's on his third helping. He'll eat 'em all if you don't hurry."

"Tell her I'll be right there," Sean said as his belly made hopeful, glurgly noises. Mindy sure could cook.

He finalized the illustration, taking care to ensure Ghoulie's outstretched arm didn't obscure the next frame's base sketch, then he popped his spine before heading to the kitchen.

Paul blabbered about the house he'd been working on and how one of the other crewmen pissed on the last wall's sheeting every day before finally hanging the siding on top. "Don't matter how much she cleans, that bedroom will always smell like piss." Paul laughed, voice muffled by a mouthful of food. "Is that funny or what?"

"Is that part of your company's value added service?" Mare poured syrup on her pancakes and grinned as Sean walked into the kitchen. "Right on time!" she said, giving Sean a kiss and a discreet grope as Mindy slid a second steaming pancake onto an otherwise pristine plate.

"How do you like your eggs?" Mindy asked as she poured a fresh scoop of batter onto the griddle.

"Cooked." Sean reached for the butter and syrup as Mare squeezed around to the far side of the kitchen table. Across from her, Paul shoveled in the last of his plateful as if he'd never tasted anything so grand.

Mindy laughed, a fine, tinkling sound, and cracked a couple of eggs into a skillet. "Cooked. No problem."

Sean had just sat when Nicole knocked on the back door, her kids in tow.

"Come on in!" Mare called out then asked Mindy, "Have enough for more?"

"Absolutely!" she said as she flipped the next pancake.

"Smells good in here," Nic said as she ushered in Pip and Steffie. Both kids squealed and ran to Mindy. Nic's smile stiffened as the kids embraced Mindy's legs and she nodded a familiar hello to everyone but Paul. "Um, hi. Have we met before?"

Paul scrambled to his feet and offered his hand. "Paul Casey, pretty lady. I'm Sean's uncle, and, um, one of them."

"Oh, yeah, I remember you now," Nicole said as she cautiously accepted the greeting. "I'm Nicole. And married. From next door."

"You staying for breakfast?" Mindy asked. Kids hanging on for the ride, she took the couple of steps to slide hot eggs onto Sean's plate. Once the skillet was back on the stove she knelt to hug them both.

"I actually just came over to ask Sean a favor," Nic said, withdrawing her hand from Paul's grip. She gave him a suspicious glance. "But I guess we could eat. Sure."

Sean swallowed his mouthful of pancake. "What's the favor?"

"Sink drain's backed up," she said, smiling easier as she turned to face him. "Can you clear it out?"

Sean was about to agree, but Paul bowed slightly and said, "Let the boy eat his breakfast. I'd be honored to clear out your drains." Before Nic could respond, he turned to the kids and bent to their level as he clapped his hands. "You kids wanna learn how to pull ucky gunk from a drain so you can help your mommy?" When the kids eyed him and clung to Mindy, Paul reached out, his sprawling mole flexing along with his forearm, to cup the back of Pip's head.

Staring at the mole and Paul's hand on Pip, Sean exploded to his feet, his hands clenching at the unexpected rush of fury over the similarity of the Minotaur's caress on his own head. Instinct demanded he break Paul's arm, or at least scream, *Get your fucking hands off him!* but instead he said, "I'll take care of the drain, Nic. And leave the kids alone, okay, Paul?"

Paul stood, eyes narrowing. "I was just being nice to—"

Despite irrational fear tickling the edges of his mind, Sean held steady while Mare and Mindy watched him with wide, startled eyes. "Things have changed. Folks don't touch other people's kids anymore." *Especially Steffie and Pip. Keep your filthy hands off him, or so help me, you'll regret it.*

"I didn't do one damn thing to hurt him."

"Mister?" Steffie said. "That's a quar—"

"Not now, sweetie," Mindy said as she flicked off the stove then grasped the kids' hands. "I'm sure Mare will keep good track for you. Let's go see what's on TV, okay?"

Silence reigned as she dragged the kids to the living room. While Paul turned to blink at the departing children, Sean closed his eyes for a moment and saw piles of bloody kids' shoes without feet. The dog, chewing... *What the hell's wrong with me today?*

His fists unclenched then clenched, fingers curled as if crushing a larynx while the Minotaur's low laughter echoed behind his ears. He opened his eyes and stared at Paul's forearm. *It's that mole. Just seeing it makes my skin crawl. Why do I detest it, and him, so much? I barely knew him as a kid.*

He took a breath and raised his gaze to his uncle's face. His voice was calm but rigid and allowed no rebuttal. "Never said you'd hurt him. I said to leave him alone."

"What bug crawled up your ass?" Paul snapped at Sean before the TV could drown him out. "I try to be friendly—"

"Friendly's fine." Sean pushed Paul aside to fetch the drain snake from the bathroom. "Just don't touch kids you don't know."

Mare chimed in, "He's right. Folks don't do that anymore. Too many child molesters and kidnappings." She paused then added, "Puts people on edge. Especially now."

"Yeah, keep your big-ass hands off my kids," Nicole said.

Don't look at the mirror, Sean reminded himself as he bent to pull the snake from the vanity, but damn if he couldn't smell the Minotaur's stink and feel his hot breath.

"You have got to be fucking kidding me," Paul said. "I hop forward twenty years and it's illegal to talk to kids with their mom standing right there?"

"Talk all you want," Nic said, "just don't touch them. You're one of them spore things. Nasty abominations, the lot of you. If the kids weren't so attached to Mindy, I wouldn't let her near them, either."

"That's not fair," Mare said. "Mindy's been great. It's not her fault she's a spore."

"Maybe so, but… She was *dead*."

"Forget her. I don't get why I can't talk to a kid in my own kitchen!"

My kitchen. Sean found the snake and let out a sigh of relief as he left the bathroom and strode past the bed to the kitchen. "Times change, Paul. Kids are off limits now. Deal with it."

"No VHS, computerized cars, nothing's fried anymore, and you can't be nice to a fucking kid? Hell, I don't even have my tats! The future is bullshit." Paul snatched up his Chicago Bulls cap. "My luck I'll be late for work."

Sean followed to see him jam the hat onto his head as he stomped across the living room and out the front door.

"You might want to clean off the steps, asshole," Paul hollered as he gave Sean the finger. Mindy, who sat with the kids watching PBS, flinched when the door slammed behind him.

Sean blew out his tension with a long, tired breath and said to Nicole, "Let's go get that drain cleared out."

Mindy washed breakfast dishes and tried not to listen to Sean and Mare discussing the morning's argument in their bedroom. Apparently Mare was embarrassed over the scene, but Sean remained insistent that no one, not even his own uncle, should be allowed to touch someone else's child.

"What the hell, Sean! Nicole was right there! It's those damned nightmares, isn't it?" Mare asked, her voice rising. "I don't know how much more I can take. It's infecting your sleep, your artwork, your—"

Mindy turned on the faucet to drown out the discussion and rinsed off her hands. Water off, she grabbed a clean dishtowel out of the drawer as she left the kitchen and continued on to Sean's studio and the computer.

She opened Facebook only to jerk back, staring, while sick terror twisted her gut. Her message queue and post comments were flooded with threats posted from total strangers.

Die bitch.

Shoulda stayed dead.

Rape you.

Gut you.

Greedy cunt. Didn't learn your lesson the first time.

I'll cut U up N wait til U re-gro so I can do it again.

I'm coming and you can't hide.

I'll kill you slowly. Strangle you maybe. Fuck you for sure. Then wait for you to spore again and my buddy will cut you up while he fucks you up the ass. Then we'll kill you, maybe make you bleed out, naked and strapped down. Then wait for you to come back, only we'll make sure you spore full of nails. We'll keep hurting you and killing you until me and my buddies are bored. Sounds fun, don't it, bitch?

Do spore bitches scream?

"Guys?" she called out, her hands shaking.

She heard no break in their argument, so she stood and backed away from the computer. She wanted to close the browser window, to delete and block all of the horrid posts, but instead she left them there, glaring on the screen.

Is Twitter the same? she thought. *G+? The blog? What do I do?*

Mindy paused when she reached the kitchen. On the other side of the door, Mare yelled, "It's been twenty damn years of this nonsense and it's only getting worse. Jesus! You have to fix this, Sean, before it kills us both."

Aw, shit, Mindy thought, but she steeled herself and called out, "Guys?"

"What?" Sean snapped as he snatched the bedroom door open and scowled at her. Mare sat on the bed. She'd been crying and it looked like Sean had, too.

Mindy flinched. "I don't mean to interrupt, but I got some really nasty threats and I don't know what to do."

Mare pushed herself to her feet. "I'll look," she said, squeezing past Sean. "No chance it'll freak me out." She wiped at her nose as she walked past Mindy and on to the studio.

"You guys okay?" Mindy asked Sean, cowering.

"I don't know. I hope so." He took a step forward and grasped the back of a kitchen chair before falling into it. He stared straight ahead as if he saw something he couldn't bear to see, yet he dare not look away. "I'm so fucked up, Mindy. These nightmares. I don't know how she puts up with me."

Mindy glanced over her shoulder, seeing nothing but a tidy, white laundry room and its door with a full length mirror hanging on it. Nothing new or different at all.

When she looked back, Sean flinched. "Sorry I was such an ass earlier."

She sat, slowly, without removing her gaze from his. "Was it because of your nightmares?"

"Partly," he admitted. "I just... Aaron asked me..." He swallowed. "I have to protect them. I'm not good for much, but, damn it, I can do that. I can keep his kids safe."

Mare returned, her face pale. "Call Todd," she said to Sean.

He stood. "What happened? What about the cop out front?"

"No one's there," Mare said. "But someone painted 'Die bitch, die!' on the front of our house." She swallowed back a grimace. "And there's a dead cat, gutted on the stoop. Looks like that big, friendly tabby from down the block."

Mindy nodded and clenched her hands between her thighs. Jeff had gutted cats before, left them as warnings against competitors and a woman who'd dared to accuse him of harassment at work. He never did the deed on his own, of course—he'd never dirty his hands with cat blood or a busted out windshield—but he had a knack for finding scum who'd be happy to deliver a terrifying message for a couple of hundred bucks. Or a bottle of cheap booze. Whatever it took to show he was in charge.

"It's my husband," she whispered, raising her gaze to Mare as Sean paced the kitchen and talked into the phone. "I'm so sorry you got dragged into this."

"Right back atcha," Mare said, hugging her.

Chapter Nineteen

Mindy sat silent in the living room as Deputy Anderson took pictures of the house and dead cat then searched the computer.

It's all my fault, she thought, blinking at the ceiling. *How did I ever think I could confront Jeff? How could I risk hurting these nice people?*

Todd talked to Sean first, then came out to sit across from Mindy.

His questions were direct but kind, and Mindy did her best to answer them. Questions about her contact with Jeff since her sporing, questions about their marriage, about the ways Jeff sought to outflank anyone who dared to oppose his ambition. And questions about her death.

"I'll check the court filings, rulings, and the coroner's report from your accident," he said. "I don't know why it wasn't treated as a suspicious death."

"It wasn't?" she asked, perplexed. "But my sister said they took him to court." She flinched as Sean trudged by with a steaming bucket that smelled of pine cleaner, while Mare followed with brushes, sponges, and a big bottle of fingernail polish remover. *Dammit, Jeff. You just had to be an ass and make messes for other people to clean up. What'd they ever do to you?*

"Civil court, most likely," Todd said. "They rule on money and fault, not if it was actually a crime."

"Doesn't matter. Dani said Jeff won both times." Mindy sighed. "He always wins."

"If we can prove he tampered with your car, that's murder. He won't win unless he's already been tried for it."

He definitely murdered me, probably because the insurance was worth more to him. Mindy flinched and stared at her hands. "My sister said just insurance and mom suing him."

"I'll check," he assured her, "and I'll let you know what I find. To the best of your knowledge, has he ever harmed anyone before? Physical assault? Attempted murder?"

She chewed her lip. "He'd rant about it sometimes, but he never did anything himself," she said. "Usually he hires things done. Bribes, mostly. Intimidation. Sabotage. Whatever it takes to get his way or shore up his self image." She took a shaky breath and said, "Now he's coming after me, and hurting Mare and Sean to do it."

"Everything's going to be fine." Todd stood. "You might want to get a restraining order, though."

"He won't care about that," Mindy said, looking up at him. "To him it's just a piece of paper." *And papers can be bought.*

"It starts the legal protection process. Starts the criminal paper trail. Also, if you file a legal complaint first, he'll have to come here, whereas if he decides to sue you for libel, you'll have to defend yourself wherever he is."

"Minnesota," she said, standing. "Nothing I said was a lie."

"He still might sue. Get that restraining order filed. Start the legal dance here, in Boone County, on your home turf, okay?"

"Okay," she said, nodding. "I've already talked with the lawyer you told Sean about."

Todd smiled. "Then do exactly what she says. She's good."

"Um, why would a cop recommend a lawyer?" she asked as she walked with him to the door.

He laughed, and she found it a warm, friendly sound, the laugh of a good man enduring a tough job. "Because she's my little sister and she can out-argue most anyone in a courtroom." He winked. "Or anywhere else."

He paused to shake her hand, his massive paw comforting and firm around hers. Their eyes locked for a long moment then he left, waving goodbye to Sean and Mare.

Red paint. Great. Thankful to be free of protestors for a change, Sean climbed into the spirea bushes beside the porch and accepted a drippy scrub-sponge from Mare. "I am sorry about all this," he said as he scrubbed tacky spray paint and tried to ignore the branches scratching his skin. At first, it looked like he was smearing more than cleaning, but the sponge rapidly became coated with paint and he handed it back to Mare.

"I really don't think this is your fault," she said, switching out his red-tinged sponge for a fresh one.

"Not this specifically," he said, sopping up pink drips before they got out of reach. "I meant this in general. My nightmares, picketers, dead animals in our backyard, news crews…" He shrugged. "The whole spore mess."

She frowned and swapped out the sponge again, rinsing the dirty one in the bucket. "If, two weeks ago, you knew it'd be like this, would you have refused to help them?"

He paused to let out a slow breath, his head hanging. "No," he said at last. "I'd still help them."

"Of course you would." She offered a consoling smile. "Yes, your nightmares worry me and God knows living with a starving artist isn't the easiest gig in town. But no matter how crazy or tough it gets," she accepted the sponge and handed him the scrub brush, "I never, ever worry that you'll ever be anyone but the same principled guy I fell in love with."

Their fingers touched as he accepted the brush and she blushed, pinkness rising in her cheeks. "You will always stand for what's just. What's fair. Even if it goes against your own best interests. And frankly, babe, that's damn hot."

He smiled, holding her gaze. "Thank you. And I know you'll always keep me sane. Plus you let me see your boobs."

She laughed at that, deep and happy. "You do more than see them," she said, winking.

"True, true," he said, leaning over to kiss her despite the twigs digging into his side. "I slather 'em with peanut butter and slide my face around in the sticky peanutty awesomeness."

Giggling, she swatted him with a fresh sponge. "Just that once!"

"Twice," he reminded her. "Only the second time it wasn't peanut butter."

"You're a lech, Mr. Casey," she said, grinning as he kissed her. "And a pervert of the highest order."

"I should clean up my act then," he said against her lips. He would have caressed her too, but his hands were a mess and he didn't want to ruin her shirt.

"Don't you dare." She chuckled and ran a hand through his hair before taking another kiss.

Footsteps rumbled on the porch and Sean drew away as Todd left the house. "Get a room," Todd teased, then glanced back to the house before continuing to his SUV.

Mindy walked onto the porch, her hands wringing together, and she paused at the steps. "I am so, so sorry about all this," she said, her eyes downcast. "I never meant for him to—"

"It's just paint," Mare assured her. "I'm more upset about the poor cat than our house."

"I should go tell them," Mindy said, gazing down the street to watch Todd drive away. "Apologize."

Sean scrubbed at paint embedded in the siding's texture and wished they knew someone with a power scrubber. "Don't bother. Gonna bury him in the backyard once I'm done with this, and he'll surely spore in three or four days. Be right back to chasing rabbits and taunting dogs before you know it. They'll just think he'd been out tomcatting. No reason to upset them."

"You're right," Mindy said, turning away. "I'll go start the hole."

She'd just stepped into the house when a blue Jeep pulled up and a short woman in jeans and a button-up shirt climbed out with a clipboard and an envelope.

"This 938 Hobson?"

Mare stood. "Yes. Can I help you?"

"Are you Melinda Howard?"

Mare glanced at Sean. "Uh, no. She's busy. Can I help you?"

The woman pulled a business card out of her pocket and held it out for Mare. "I need to speak to Melinda Howard. Please."

Mare accepted the card and her face turned pale. "A process server? Why? What'd she do?"

"No idea, ma'am. But I need to speak to her."

Mare glanced at Sean, who shrugged. No one had ever served papers on them before.

"I, uh… I'll go get her," Mare said.

Sean climbed out of the bushes while Mare fetched Mindy. The process server lingered near the steps. An awkward moment stretched long enough for their neighbor, the always delightful Earl Simmons, to come out and take a few pics of the graffiti on the house.

"Fighting with your old lady, Casey, or trying a new mode of artistic expression?"

he asked, grinning.

"Neither," Sean replied as he tossed the scrub brush into the bucket. "Those kids you stiffed last Halloween meant to get your house but wrote down the address wrong. I set 'em straight so they're off getting more paint and TP."

"Uh huh. Anyone called my wife Ruby a bitch I'd shoot him," Earl said. "Then I'd make him clean up the mess."

Sean knelt to rinse his hands in the bucket and muttered, "Wouldn't make her any less of a bitch."

Mindy hustled out the front door and down the steps to the server. She'd been crying. "Mare said you needed to talk to me?"

"You're Melinda Howard?" the server asked. "Formerly married to a Jeffrey Howard of Maple Grove, Minnesota?"

"If that's where he is, then yeah, it's me." Mindy signed the clipboard before receiving an envelope, then the process server wished her a good day and left.

Hands shaking, Mindy tore open the envelope while Mare gently rubbed her shoulder and murmured words of encouragement.

"It's not Jeff," Mindy said, sagging as she flipped through the multi-page document. "It's the insurance company. They've decided to sue him for submitting a fraudulent claim and have listed me as a co-complainant."

"Really? That's good, right?" Sean asked.

"Maybe." Mindy handed Mare the papers. "They're asking for two and a half million in damages. Jeff won't like that."

The zombie hunters had resumed their cheerful picketing, and Mare and Mindy had left for work, when Sean settled in front of the computer. Google still held nothing for Blooming Lotus Research Laboratories, but additional keywords began to glean results. He read about various corpse funguses and how a particular strain tended to infect Egyptian mummies. Some even speculated the 'Mummy's Curse' which led many tomb robbers to a quick, unexplained death, was in fact a virulent fungal infection.

I wonder if that explains why Old Willard and some of Mare's patients are suddenly dying, he thought. *Can the same fungus that makes the spores also make people sick? Even kill them?*

He stared at the screen. *But they all had cancer or some other chronic disease. Least all I've heard about.*

Curious, he checked local obituaries in the Boone paper. They usually listed maybe ten or so obituaries in a given week, usually for the very elderly and infirm, but their online listing showed nearly thirty, just for the past four days.

I'd call that an affirmative for my theory, he thought, skimming the obits. Cancer, lots of cancer. Kidney failure. Heart disease. Parkinson's. Emphysema. Diabetes. Most of the obituaries said they'd died suddenly, or that their chronic condition had taken an unexpected bad turn. The one news article he found on the excessive deaths concluded that they were likely due to extreme heat and humidity, so free fans and ice were available at fire and police stations across the county.

But, as he clicked through other articles in Local News, he found several reports of rapidly healing broken bones, folks bouncing back from surgery faster than expected, even one farmer who woke up to find his long-amputated hand had returned. "It'd itched like a bastard for a few days," the fellow said. "But when I got up this morning to take my whiz, I had 'em both!" The article included a photograph of the man holding up both hands. One looked normal, the other sort of roundish with short finger-stumps, but still definitely a hand.

Stubby's fingers seemed to itch the other night, and Mort's cataract had turned clear, Sean thought, returning to Google and Bing. *It all has to be connected.*

Encouraged, he dug deeper, twenty, thirty pages into the search results, seeking anything tangible about Lotus Labs.

In Bing, on the thirty-second page of links and sites, he found an archived news article, from 1983, written for a magazine he'd never heard of. *Small Town Iowa Company to Create Growth Medium for Medical Testing and Research.* The short article—complete with grainy photographs—mainly dealt with the business opportunity of custom culture media, but in one section, the owner and visionary for Lotus Blossom Lab Supplies (formerly Blooming Lotus Research Laboratories) stated:

We hope someday our mediums will do more than grow bacteria cultures. We've discovered a new composition that shows great promise for growing clusters of living cells, perhaps entire organs. We are quite excited at the revolutionary prospects for stem cell research, not only for modern medical uses but also organ transplant technology. Our goal is to make replacement organs safe and affordable for every patient by using their own cells to start the process.

Sean printed the article and muttered, "Stem cells? You got 'em to grow, but didn't stop at replicating organs, did you?"

Sean glanced at three grainy black and white images printed below the article. One showed a squat concrete building, the next a bespectacled Middle Eastern fellow with a cheery disco-era mustache, and the third a group of male technicians and female office workers. *Todd said he employed locals. Maybe some are still alive.*

Sean stood and turned away from the computer, but his email dinged. He sighed then leaned over to open the newest email from Murphy.

Sean! Just got off the phone w/ B.P. They need this revamped all-spore issue ASAP (scans attached). Burn the midnight oil, drink pots of coffee, I don't care, but get inks turned in by tomorrow. They want to go to press immediately and hit while our fire's burning hot! Stores are clamoring for our back issues—apparently everything's sold out these past couple of days. I'm not talking just a few shops. It's GLOBAL, dude! As of the phone call, three copies of last month's issue were somewhere in Australia, and a couple of singles from April and May were still at stores in the States. Otherwise every fucking issue on the planet has SOLD!!

They'd never seen anything like it, even the back issues and discount bargain crap is gone. The Pawn Forums are screaming for Ghoulie. We're a hit! A huge fucking hit! So bite that spore shit and let's ride this wave, buddy! They're going back to press for more copies of this month's issue to meet demands, tripling next month's run, and are talking about re-issuing the back stuff in special collectors editions. Can you believe it?!? One guy even mentioned bound books or a graphic novel!!

And, oh, they offered to renew our contract, but I told them we'll have to think about it. Let the bastards sweat a while. Maybe it'll bring us more money? It'd better. They've paid us peanuts and we all know it, but we've hit, we've finally HIT!!

Holy fucking shit, Sean, get drawing!!

While the email and updated script printed, Sean sighed and turned to frown at his drafting table. He clenched his hands into his hair and muttered, "Fuck." The previous revamped sketches remained unfinished and untouched since Mare'd interrupted him for breakfast. *All that work, now useless. I am so sick of this issue,* he thought, sagging. *Maybe even sick of Ghoulie.*

Muttering to himself to suck it up because they needed the money, Sean retrieved a glass of ice water and a couple of Mindy's amazing cupcakes from the kitchen while hollering at teenagers burying something in his backyard.

Frustrated and grumbly—*Goddammit. Can't they at least ask first?*—he drew the shades and cranked his hardcore tunes into a screaming frenzy before forcing himself to work. Murph's notes had been restructured, crossed out, rearranged, and scribbled over, leaving the narrative a confused and clambering mess.

Panel by panel, page by page, Sean ignored the random knocks on the door as he made sense of the madness and blocked out the story in loose-sketched thumbnails. That done, he began his full-size pencil roughs for character and dialogue placement, thankful for the lack of mental intrusion from footless children in the dark.

Afternoon gave way to evening and he focused in, muttering along with lyrics screaming from his iPod as the story took shape under his hand. Three spreads fully sketched, he stood and stretched then shuffled across the hall to piss, mind lost to the comic and his voice mumbling along with Killswitch as if it were a Zen prayer.

The bathroom door was closed so he opened it, his brain focused on Ghoulie and getting page seven to flow smoothly. Habit had long since burned into his brain that he and Mare lived alone and she was at work. His home, his castle, his spare bathroom.

He'd already pushed the door open when the gears in his mind locked at the sight of Paul standing naked at the vanity, shaving, a red and black horror sprawled over his right forearm. The Minotaur lingered in the mirror as he had all day, but instead of taunting Sean, he drew a razor over his hairy cheeks.

"Crawled out of your cave, eh?" Paul asked, glancing over. "Bad enough I have to cross a gauntlet of crazies to enter my own house, but you playing that screaming shit you call music 'bout pushes me over the edge." He shook his razor under running water and resumed his task while cold terror flooded over Sean.

The brutish head of the Chicago Bulls tainted Paul's pink, enflamed skin, a massive tat that covered the full width of his forearm and incorporated his mole into the bull's brow and nose.

Head swimming, Sean took a quick step back. *The tattoo, the reflection! It's him. Has to be. Oh, God. What do I do?*

"You can quit staring any time now," Paul muttered as he tidied up the edge of his sideburns. In the mirror, the Minotaur glared at Sean, then resumed shaving. "In my day, we kicked the shit out of gay guys, so quit your fucking gawking. 'Kay?"

"You...you got a tattoo," Sean managed to choke out despite his bowels clenching. *Oh fuck, oh God. He's in my house!*

"Yeah," Paul said, rotating his arm to show the new artwork. "Not as good as the one I had before, but it'll do." He gave Sean a suspicious glance. "Didn't think you liked basketball."

"I don't," Sean said. "Just had to piss. Sorry to bother you." He backed away and closed the door.

He wanted to flee; his feet demanded he grab his car keys, bolt for safety, and never return, but he forced himself to walk calmly to his own bathroom instead.

No Minotaur watched him from that mirror. He urinated, hearing Paul shower beyond the wall to the left of his elbow.

I have to act like everything's fine, he thought while cold sweat trickled down the back of his neck. He flushed without thinking, then hollered, "Sorry, habit!" after Paul thumped the wall in protest.

The house thrummed with his music as he stuffed the .38 into his jeans and walked quickly from the bathroom to the laundry. Mare's aluminum bat lay on the floor beside the dryer. He grabbed it and continued on to his studio, barely able to hear the shower over Five Finger Death Punch.

Bat tucked hidden yet handy behind his file cabinet and gun in his waistband but under his shirt, Sean sat again at his drawing board. He held the pencil poised and trembling over the page, his ears struggling to hear the bathroom over the familiar blare of death metal.

The shower stopped and the bathroom door opened a few moments later. Sean hunched over his drawing and laid down a series of crappy lines as he heard Paul walk into the hall.

"Can't you turn that shit down for ten fucking minutes?" Paul asked from the studio doorway.

Sean jumped and turned, pencil clutched like a weapon in his hand. "Oh, sure, sorry," he said. He plucked up the iPod remote and adjusted the music to a saner level. "Better?"

"Much," Paul said as he turned away. "I thought Nirvana sucked ass, but that shit's awful."

Sean tossed aside the pencil and stood. *Could a .38 easily kill in one shot?* Memories of skeletons and muscles from Life Drawing flashed in his mind, suggesting openings to vital organs and quick death.

I could do it, Sean thought. *Kidneys, lungs, back of his fucking head. Hell, grab the bat and bash his brains in. Make him pay for what he did to me, to all those other—*

He blinked, his throat tight and his skin clammy, as he stood taut beside his chair. *But Todd said it wasn't him, couldn't be him. My dreams are just that. Dreams. A dog never ate my guts. I have both my feet. It's just me being paranoid again.*

He took a shaky breath, his heart thudding fast and loud. *I could leave Mare alone. Ruin her future. For what could be no more than coincidence and paranoia. I have to be sure.*

Instinct demanded he kill the fucker right now. Instead he sat, pistol gouging into his belly while he listened to Paul rattle around the basement, then climb the stairs. A few more footsteps, then the front door banged closed and he was gone.

Sean jolted off his chair and ran to the kitchen for the phone.

Chapter Twenty

Todd left the briefing with the others, his ears still ringing from the ass chewing they'd received over the lack of leads. They'd made no progress on the kidnapped and murdered kids, or Evelyn Fischer's murder. Petty crimes had gone unsolved with almost all of their focus on the kids and murders, while the federal authorities in the area showed little interest in anything beyond the spore fungus in ground and river water. Their lack of assistance only increased the sheriff's frustration and fury.

"Anderson, wait," he heard from behind and stepped aside to let other deputies pass. The sergeant nodded his head toward the meeting room and Todd returned, closing the door behind him.

"I sent your notes on the Melinda Howard case up the line this afternoon. The attorney general and the Iowa Insurance Division have both been in a froth over the lawsuit, and their breath is only getting hotter on my ass since the death threats and vandalism."

"Yes, sir," Todd said, thankful the higher-ups had noticed. "If he'll hire someone to kill a cat, he'll hire someone to kill her."

"Exactly," the sergeant said. "And you're going to make sure it doesn't happen twice."

Todd swallowed his surprise. "Sarge?"

"You're assigned to her case, full time, at least until the insurance fraud case is resolved. I don't care what it takes, you make sure she gets to testify at the trial." He gave Todd a single nod then turned to leave the room.

"But, Sarge! Kids are getting killed. You can't just put me on guard duty like this." *Someone else, okay, but not her. That smile, those eyes. Shit.*

"I damn well can," the sergeant said, glaring. "The governor's mentioned replacing our entire staff if we don't make headway somewhere, immediately. The attorney general called the sheriff not an hour ago to tell him if that girl gets hurt, he'll be replaced. That moved her to the top of our priority list. Since you've interviewed Mrs. Howard twice now, it's your case. Focus on it above everything else."

Which means I'll be cooped up with a woman I'm already attracted to. Great. "Yes, sir," Todd said, feeling anything but agreeable as he accepted the file from his superior.

The sergeant left the briefing room and Todd followed, silently fuming as he flipped through the folder. Other than a couple of printed emails from the attorney general and the insurance division, he'd written everything in it.

Not starting with much, he thought, sighing. He left the briefing room and walked to archives to request a copy of the original accident file for her death, any notes from her autopsy and inquest, plus whatever else a legal records search of her and her ex husband's names dug up. The archive clerk promised to get him the paperwork as quickly as possible, hopefully by morning.

Momentarily appeased, he walked to the parking lot and called his mother to tell her he was on his way.

"She's still up," his mother said. "We've been watching movies and eating brownies."

Todd grinned. "Save a couple for me, willya?" Then his phone beeped. *Sean. Shit.* "Got a call, Mom. If you don't hear back from me right away, I'm on my way there."

He clicked over to the other call. "Hey, Sean. What's up?" he asked as he unlocked his SUV. Damned thing still smelled like puke from the drunk driver he'd dragged in around seven thirty.

Sean sounded panicked. "It's him! My Uncle Paul! He's snatching and killing those kids! You have to stop him!"

Todd nodded good night to another deputy and entered the vehicle. "I told you, it can't be him. He died in ninety-five but the kidnappings didn't stop."

"You don't understand!" Sean said, voice rising. "He got a tattoo! I just saw it! Chicago Bulls, right on his arm."

Todd started his truck. "Sean. Relax. It's just a tattoo."

"No. He's the Minotaur! He has to be, can't you see? He's the one who hurt me back when I was a kid!"

Todd let out a tired breath and rubbed his eyes. *I do not need this madness right now.* "No, he's not. He died before you went missing."

"No he didn't," Sean snapped. "My mom always told me I was gone when he got killed. So maybe I found a way to escape his lair or wherever he'd hidden me, and now he's back hurting more kids."

Todd rubbed his tired eyes. *I just want to go home. See my daughter.* Despite fatigue and frustration, he managed to keep his voice level and reassuring. "I checked the dates after our talk yesterday. Paul Allen Casey was found dead on the side of the road, a victim of a hit and run, on October 13th, 1995. Your parents reported you missing on the 16th, three days later. He couldn't have kidnapped you. He was already dead."

Silence filled the phone.

"Sean?"

"That's not possible," Sean said, sounding deflated. "I know my mom said it was a horrific couple of weeks. I was gone then her brother-in-law killed. It's why Dad started drinking. It's why their marriage fell apart. Me *then* Paul."

"Maybe she just got the order mixed up," Todd suggested as he pulled out of the lot. "It happens, especially if she was dealing with a drunk, too."

"But the tattoo! The Minotaur!"

"Sean, buddy, it was a fucked-up time for you, we all know that. But calendars don't lie. Our records don't lie. Your uncle died then you disappeared. Other kids were taken after you. There's no way it was him. It's not possible, okay?"

"Fine. Sorry to bother you," Sean said, then the call disconnected.

"I see the zombie folks are back," Mare said when she finally came home.

"Yep. Least it's just them."

She leaned over to kiss his brow and examine the day's work, her hand stiffening on the back of his neck. "These aren't the same layouts as this morning."

"Nope."

She pulled away and sighed. "What the hell? *More* changes?"

"Email's on the desk." Sean tightened the line for Ghoulie's lower back and thigh as he wrestled a child kidnapper out of a black SUV. *Only three pages to go. Might get the base pencil art done tonight after all. If Murph thinks I can turn out a full issue of drawings and inks in one day, he's been smoking crack.*

Mare read, slumping onto the chair. "Wow. Every issue? This can't be real."

Sean erased out the scraggly bits and moved on to the next cell. "Apparently it is."

She stood and walked to him. "You don't sound happy."

"Not sure what I am," he said, glancing up at her. "I don't know whether to be excited or pissed over this issue. Shit, this is my fourth freaking batch of pencils, every set rush-rush, only to have me toss them two days later and do something entirely different. Yeah, it means more money, but I'm so sick of it, I just want to walk away from the whole thing, ya know?"

"I know," she sighed. "But Ghoulie's your baby."

"Was my baby," he corrected. "Murph has him acting more like an undead super hero than a troubled ghoul seeking revenge, and I can't do shit about it. Big issue! Just draw it! Rush, rush!"

She gave him a commiserating nod, but said nothing.

He flung his pencil onto the table. "And Paul. Fucking goddamn Paul."

She grimaced and rolled her eyes. "What'd he do now?"

"Got a tattoo."

"A tattoo?"

"Yeah," Sean said, then tried to explain how the Bulls tat made him certain Paul had been his abuser. "It all adds up, ya know? How I've been messed up since first meeting him in the backyard, and it's gotten worse since he moved in. The nightmares, hallucinations, and why I keep fixating on his fucking mole, a mole that's now a bull, like my Minotaur's head."

"Sean, babe…" Mare soothed, running her fingers through his hair.

"But it's not him. It can't be," Sean sighed, looking up at her. "Was about to just shoot him and be done with it, but I found some sense and called Todd instead. He said Paul died a few days before I was taken." Sean huffed out an aggravated breath. "I almost killed the guy, for nothing. Nothing but my stupid fears."

"He is an ass," she reminded him. "And he keeps bitching that we haven't kept his house up like we should."

Yeah, some days he can't take two steps without reminding us about missing bathroom molding or the crack in the kitchen ceiling. Sean chuckled and shook his head. "I don't think being an ass about home maintenance is a killing offense."

She sat on his lap and draped her arms over his shoulders. "I think he's just one of those people who rub folks like us the wrong way. Mindy fits in fine, he doesn't, and we're all tiptoeing around him because he makes us edgy. Family or not, he needs to go."

She smiled into Sean's eyes and kissed him. "So who gets to tell him? You or me?"

"I'll do it," Sean sighed as Mare slid off his lap. "Soon as he gets home."

"He out on another pub crawl for poontang?"

Sean stood and stretched. "Didn't say. Just showed off his tattoo, showered, bitched about my music, and left."

"You nasty puke!" Mindy snapped. "Why? *Why!?* Arrgh!"

Sean and Mare glanced at each other and shrugged as the bathroom door was flung open and Mindy marched through.

"I don't want to be a…a *bitch*," she muttered, lowering her voice at the last word, "but I cannot see one single reason to have three—*three!*—filthy piles of clothes lying on the floor for me to trip over when I'm taking a shower. I just can't."

She huffed, arms crossing over her chest, and glared at Sean. "He leaves his nasty stuff just lying there. Stinky socks, muddy jeans, grimy shirts, you name it, but his underwear is freaking disgusting. You need to talk to him."

"Okay," Sean said, shrugging.

"Okay? Just okay?" Mindy asked, leaning forward. "Have you seen what he leaves lying around? Skid-marked underwear! It looks like he lives on gas station burritos and beer and never wipes his ass. Ever. Except by scratching himself through his undies. It's gross and I'm sick of walking on it."

"I don't blame you," Mare said.

Mindy took a breath and continued. "Twice now I've gathered up his nasties and washed them, but he's supposedly an adult and I'm not doing it anymore." She took a breath and stood a little taller. "I'm not even *touching* it anymore. It's just too dang gross."

"I'll get it out of there," Sean sighed, ducking toward the bathroom.

With his attention riveted on the mole, he hadn't noticed the mess on the floor, but Mindy was right. Filthy clothes lay all over, including skid-marked Jockeys. Sean grimaced. *I wouldn't want to walk over that, either.*

He retrieved a laundry basket from the laundry room—no Minotaur in the mirror—and returned to gather up the mess. Mare had remained in the studio, scowling at Murph's tangle of notes.

"So they're exploiting you and the spores because 'drawn by famous, crazy artist' sells more comics?"

"Basically," Sean said, tossing sticky, stinky clothing into the basket. "And he's added some of my neuroses. Check Murph's notes for page eleven through fourteen. Kidnapped kids ravaged by a dog. I never should've told him how I came up with Ghoulie."

Mare flipped to the next page and grimaced. "Lousy fucker. That's low, even for Murph." She tossed aside the pages and picked up his article about Lotus Labs. "You need a different writer."

"Starting to wonder that myself. Be nice to not have to scramble all the time, at least," he said, gingerly picking up a particularly disgusting pair of briefs. Bloody smears of shit stained a swath that ran nearly to the opening in front. *Urgh. That's some severe digestive issues.* Sean grimaced and flung them into the basket. *It must run right through him. No wonder he eats like a horse.*

"Wow, this does sound like the place, doesn't it?" Mare said, pointing to the article about the lab.

Sean stood and hefted the basket. "That's what I thought. Maybe I'll be able to track down some of the people in the employee pic. Surely a lot of them are still around."

Mare stared at him, one incredulous eyebrow raised. "You could start with your mother," she said, pointing at the last image. "Pretty sure that's her."

Sean dropped the basket in the hall and stepped over it. "What?"

"Look at it, Sherlock." As Sean pored over the picture, she said, "Do you remember back, waaay back, when she still liked me and you took me over there for supper that first time?"

"Yeah," he said, squinting. *Might be her. Looks like her, but it's awful grainy.* "We'd only been dating a month or so and she was thrilled I wasn't gay. With all the paranoia and crap, I'd barely left the house except for school."

"Yeah, that's the time. Well, while you were off doing whatever it was she sent you to do so we could have our 'special girl talk', she showed me a scrapbook she'd made."

He handed the paper back to Mare and rolled his eyes. "Gak, that fugly flower-fabric thing with the puffy heart on the front?" *Last time I looked through it, I was four, maybe five, but she showed it to everyone. Was always awkward as hell.*

"Cheap fabric, hot glue, pillow fluff, and buttons? That's the one. Anyway, I got to sit through her childhood pictures, school pictures, and wedding pictures. *And* tales of her life as a secretary, then being pregnant with you…"

"My condolences," he said, returning to the basket in the hall. "No one should be forced to sit through all that."

"Yeah, well, before she got to your kindergarten award for coloring inside the lines, she flipped past a color copy of that same article, least I think it was, with barely a comment. I don't remember the headline, but I know I've seen that picture of everyone standing in the lab before. It's her, I know it is."

Sean carried the basket toward the living room. "I dunno. When I asked her if she'd heard of the lab. She said no."

Mare followed. "Can you blame her, with all the hubbub? She is the queen of denial."

"That's true," Sean said, hesitating in the archway. *Do I wash his filthy clothes or leave them for him?* One glance down at the bloody-feces briefs, and he flipped on the light for the basement stairs. "I'll take the article to her and ask her again."

"Cool," Mare said, remaining on the landing as he descended. "I'm sure she'll love to see her Seanny Buttercup without having to sabotage her house first." Her laughter and kissy sounds followed him down the stairs.

"Urgh. Don't start in on that," he groaned as he reached the bottom and flicked on the basement light. He paused, gaping, as Mare's kissy noises faded. *Holy crap, he's a pig.*

She started down. "Problem?"

"Go ahead and stay up there," he called up. "Our favorite houseguest has left a mess. You don't need to see—"

"Like hell I don't," she said, hurrying to stand beside him.

Both remained silent for a few moments as they took in the chaos of nudie mags, junk food wrappers, beer bottles, and second-hand Michael Jordan paraphernalia scattered amongst filthy clothes and even filthier bed linen. It stank of beer, semen, tortilla chips, and pot. Despite the room being nearly as big as the entire upstairs, Sean could see only brief glimpses of the linoleum floor.

He closed his mouth. *How is this possible? He hasn't been here two weeks yet. And if he can afford all this crap, why isn't he paying rent?*

"Condoms?!?" Mare said, stomping into the mess and pointing to one crusty sample hanging off the edge of an empty KFC box. "He's brought *women* here?" She turned, gesturing to the filth. "Women who'd put out in this?!?"

"Apparently so." No woman he'd ever met would consider kissing a guy in something like this, let alone more. He felt his gorge rise and he swallowed it down. *Urgh. Don't even think about him having sex in the dungeon of filth! Guess I know why he's always so glad to send me off to work on Wednesdays.*

"He has to go," Mare said, gingerly picking her way back to him. "This mess has tossed him over the bar and out the door." She reached the clear floor at the bottom of the stairs. "I don't give a shit who he balls, but this…" she said, gesturing to the room. "This shows a total disregard for our home and health. It'll draw bugs, if nothing else. And he has the balls to bitch because we're not maintaining home repairs to his standards? What the fuck?"

"You're absolutely right," Sean said, upending the laundry basket onto the mess since the additional clothing would make little difference. He took a breath and sighed it out while Mare pointed at something smeared on the wall over the couch—nacho cheese sauce, perhaps?—and congealed pizza on a milk crate before moving on to other disgusting points in the chaos.

Sean, however, noticed paneling stripped off the eastern wall to expose a gaping hole that led to the space under their bedroom addition. *Why rip off the paneling?* he wondered, reluctant to step into the filth in his bare feet. He had put in an extra sump and boarded it up years ago. *It's just studs and dirt back there, a little wiring.*

His thoughts lurched to a stop as his eyes widened. *Most of Paul's clothes are muddy. Could he have buried something?*

"Shit," he muttered before turning to trot up the stairs. "Be right back."

"What's wrong? What did you see?" Mare asked, following.

"Not sure yet," he said as he retrieved his tennis shoes and pulled them on. "The flashlight got decent batteries?"

Mare found it in the junk drawer and flicked it on. "Seems to."

Sean held out his hand and she tossed it to him. They returned to the basement and Sean stumbled across the filth.

A chair stood beneath the hole, its seat speckled with fresh dirt, and Sean climbed up to shine his light in.

"Smells," he said, glancing at Mare. "Musty. But I don't see anything from here but mud."

She covered her mouth with her hand. "Oh God, what's he done?"

Sean hefted his upper body into the hole, leaving his lower half sticking out.

He shone the light around, making sure to illuminate every corner, every lump and divot. Along the western wall, at the corners to his left and right, two puddles quivered in fairly large holes and the sump pump had been disconnected and removed from its pit in the far corner. He lifted the flashlight and saw a glimmering reflection of water where the sump used to be.

Sean's heart slammed and he eased himself out again. "We better call Todd," he said, meeting Mare's terrified gaze. "The sump pit's flooded and there are two more holes, both full of water." He swallowed and stepped down from the chair. "They're all about the same size as the slime that dog, Betsy, spored out of."

Mare nodded, her face ashen. "He might be growing dogs."

Sean flicked off the flashlight. "Or two of those missing kids."

Chapter Twenty-One

While Sean and Mare fiddled around in the basement and her cat batted at a scrap of crumpled paper, Mindy updated her blog and checked comments and email. If she hadn't stepped in Paul's slimy clothes, it would have been a near perfect evening. Camille calling in sick granted them a happy shift in the kitchen, and not only had Ramonna *adored* the cupcakes, another food worker and two nurses had placed orders, too.

So Mindy cheerfully blogged about starting a small in-home baking business and decided not to mention the morning's paint or dead cat on the stoop. Since Jeff obviously read the blog, she saw no good reason for him to know she'd been frazzled. Especially since that nice Deputy Anderson had promised to look into what had really happened with her and the accident.

She thought about his sweet face, how kind he'd been, how safe she'd felt, then she shook her head. *Don't go there, Mindy. It's just his job to be that way.*

She flagged but didn't delete the threats and taunts Jeff had surely paid for. *Gonna leave those for my deputy,* she thought, smiling slightly, as she opened her email.

Mostly junk, a couple of Facebook notifications, and a message from the insurance company's legal department. They apologized for the short notice, but, due to the Attorney General and State Insurance Examiner's interest in the matter, she needed to arrive at their main office in Des Moines at ten A.M. to be interviewed, submit to DNA confirmation, and give a deposition regarding legal matters pertaining to her accident so they could proceed with the lawsuit against her husband.

Oh, wow. On a Saturday? They're not screwing around. Mindy chewed her lip. *That means leaving by eight thirty, maybe nine in the morning. That's not short notice, that's almost no notice at all. And I can't drive myself.*

She heard Sean and Mare return from the basement, so she hurried to the kitchen to intercept them. "I need a huge, massive favor," she said, pausing as she saw Mare pacing and Sean punching a number into the phone.

Something happened, Mindy thought, glancing down the dark cavern of the basement stairs. She swallowed and wondered what Paul'd been up to down there.

"Yeah, Todd?" Sean said, phone crushed against his ear. "Yeah, I know it's late, but about my uncle…"

While Sean talked, Mare took a cleansing breath before putting on a smile for Mindy. "You said you needed a favor?"

Mindy glanced past Mare to Sean fretting on the phone. "Just got an email saying I needed to be in Des Moines tomorrow morning, but I can see you're having enough trouble for one night. I'll just tell them I have to reschedule." She paused, then asked, "What happened? Why's Sean calling the deputy? It's almost midnight."

"Looks like something's sporing in the basement. Back under our bedroom. We're… concerned."

Mindy swallowed and nodded. *I would be too.*

"What do you mean you're going to be here in the morning anyway?" Sean turned to face the women. "You're *what*? Why?"

He shook his head and covered the receiver. "Mindy, did you know anything about Todd being here in the morning?"

Mindy grinned. *He's asking about me?* "No, why? Is he driving me to Des Moines?"

"She thinks you're driving her to Des Moines tomorrow," he said into the phone. "Shit if I know. Here, you ask her."

He thrust the phone into Mindy's hand and paced alongside the kitchen counter.

"What's this about Des Moines?" Todd asked her, yawning. "I was told you were likely to be home all day tomorrow."

She frowned, confused. *Why would he care where I am?* "I was, but I have to give a deposition to the Attorney General in the morning."

She heard a muttered curse. "Great," he said. "Nobody told me that." He sighed, heavy and grumbling. "When are you leaving?"

"Supposed to be there at ten, so, uh, eight thirty? Nine? Ish? If Sean or Mare can drive me. I really haven't had a chance to ask them yet."

"Don't bother. I'll drive you. It'll make things simpler, anyway." Another tired sigh, then he asked to talk to Sean.

Sean stood quietly for a moment, nodding. "Sure, I can be up by eight, no problem. Thanks, man. See you then."

I guess I'm going, Mindy thought, feeling nervous tickles in her belly. *The state and Attorney General are involved! Won't that tick off Jeff?*

Hours later, Mindy lay in the dark, heart slamming from her latest vision of falling endlessly through black snow, and she tried to settle herself enough to get back to sleep. She'd just sunk into the shadows of her mind, body heavy and drowsy, almost there, when she heard heavy footsteps in the hall. Her cat, usually quiet and cuddly, hissed and jumped off the bed. *Dang Paul,* she thought, covering her head with the pillow. *It's two forty-two in the freaking morning. I hope he's not so drunk he'll sing old country crap in the shower again.*

She tried to reach for sleep, but her eyes bolted open when she heard her doorknob jiggle.

I locked it, she thought, staring at the door. *You scared the crap outta me once—*

She yelped and scrambled to sit as her door exploded open and two men burst through. One carried a tire iron and the other rushed the bed, snarling, "Got a message from your ex."

Mindy flung herself off the foot of the bed in a vain attempt to evade them, but the second guy blocked her escape. She cowered, stepping backward one slow step, her gaze darting between the two. *What do I do? Where can I go?*

She cried out as the first guy grabbed her by the hair while his partner swung the tire iron, hitting her across the back near her shoulder blades. Something cracked, a high, sharp sound. She screeched, knees buckling from the pain, then the guy who held her hair twisted her face upward to punch it. She saw bright flickers and tasted blood. The pain was enormous, expanding in twirling waves.

He let her go and she collapsed to the floor, struggling to push herself upright until one of them kicked her in the gut and knocked her against the bed.

A woman screamed and Sean bolted upright a heartbeat before Mare gasped awake beside him. *Mindy?* he thought the same time Mare said, "That's Mindy!"

Sean clenched his teeth and reached over Mare for the gun. Thankful he'd slept in his shorts, he scrambled out of bed and sprinted to the hall. Mare followed.

Two shadows moved in the dark near the foot of her bed, their bodies silhouetted by the window as they hit and kicked her. Sean grabbed the nearest one by the arm and yanked him aside to tumble toward the hall. "Get away from her!" Sean screamed, ducking as the other swung a tire iron at him.

"Fuck you, freak," the guy with the tire iron said, pulling back for another swing.

Sean lunged forward and shoved the gun against the guy's throat, slamming him against the wall. "I said, get away from her."

The iron paused, quivering in the air, before dropping to the floor with a clatter. "Fuck, Dude. Calm down," he soothed. "No reason to shoot anybody."

Sean said nothing as he pulled back the hammer. The click echoed in the dark and, near his feet, Mindy whimpered and tried to crawl away.

"Gun or not, you shouldn't have turned your back on me," the other guy said from behind Sean. Before Sean could finish thinking, *Oh shit,* a loud, clanging thwapp filled the air, and the second guy grunted and fell to the floor.

"Shouldn't have left your legs splayed, asshole," Mare snapped. She whapped him with the bat across the belly.

"Okay, okay," he gasped, hands held up to ward off another swing. "You win. Damn, bitch, we didn't know you had bodyguards."

"I don't," Mindy mumbled, managing to teeter to her feet. She wiped at her mouth with the back of her hand and muttered, "Just friends," before she quavered and fell loose and unconscious to the floor.

"Sure you don't want us to take you to the hospital?" the nameless deputy asked Mindy for the third time.

"I'm sure," she said, sitting on the wingback chair while holding the ice-pack tighter against the throbbing agony of her cheek. Knowing Jeff had become desperate enough to send goons was worse than the bruises. Trembling, she blinked at the open door, the drips of her blood on the carpet, and at Sean and Mare talking with the deputies. *More trouble for them, once again, all because of Jeff. He's serious. They could have killed me.*

She flinched. *What are you thinking, Mindy? He did kill you. He ruined your car and*

KILLED you. You were an obstacle between him and millions, so he removed you. When are you going to make him pay for that?

The deputy who tended her shrugged. His partner accepted Sean and Mare's signatures then returned their gun to them. Both of the attackers sat handcuffed on the couch. Neither looked like upstanding citizens with their baggy jeans, homemade tattoos, and plastic ear gauges. Tire-iron had blubbered about being hired by some guy on Craigslist, but the other guy had stated he wanted a lawyer and would say no more. He, too, clutched an ice-pack, but not on his face.

Sean held the door for the deputies while Mare knelt before Mindy. "Let me see it," she coaxed as the goons were taken away.

Mindy relented and let Mare probe her throbbing cheek.

"Don't think the bone's broken, but it's gonna bruise like a bitch," she said. "And his ring cut you pretty good."

Mindy moistened her lips and tried not to cry. Jeff had always said her face was the one good thing about her. "Will it need stitches?"

"I don't think so," Mare said. "It's just the skin, no meat, and it's already stopped bleeding. Let's get some antibiotic ointment on it and a bandage."

"'Kay," Mindy said as Mare drew her to her feet and led her to the bathroom. She sat on the toilet and let Mare gently clean her face and tend the wound that wasn't much more than an angry-looking scratch.

Mare daubed ointment on the gash. "It's going to be okay."

Mindy nodded and pressed her clasped hands together between her thighs, but said nothing.

"Hey." Mare lifted Mindy's chin and looked into her eyes. "Nobody's gonna hurt you again. Todd'll be here first thing in the morning. He's going to be guarding you until this is over and I really don't think your ex will want to mess with us anymore, let alone the county sheriff."

"Jeff doesn't care," Mindy said. "Not when money's at stake."

Mare lifted Mindy's hands and squeezed them. "Then he's gonna have a hard lesson to learn. I'll bust his fucking kneecaps before we let him hurt you again."

Todd drank a Diet Coke and munched on a microwaved breakfast burrito while opening copies of numerous reports the records clerk had emailed him overnight. He'd barely had time to send them all to print when his phone rang. The Sarge. He swallowed and answered.

"Yes, sir?"

"There's a file on my desk about a home invasion at that house in Pinell you've been assigned to. Two suspects broke in and assaulted Melinda Howard around quarter to three this morning."

That bastard. Todd stomped out of his home office and closed the door to block the printer's invasive hum. "She all right?"

"A little battered, but fine. She refused medical treatment. Both suspects are in custody, but they've lawyered up. We're checking their residences now."

Todd requested a copy of the report. "Where was Hendrix? He was assigned to watch the house all night so I could sleep."

"Don't know. He didn't report in after his shift." Sarge paused then said, "We're sending a patrol to his house."

"Keep me informed, sir. And can you send me the incident report?"

"Of course. I have a meeting with the sheriff at seven. I'll email it right after."

Todd thanked him and closed the call. 6:54. *Shit. Gotta go!*

Sean had not encountered Paul or any other troublemakers when Todd arrived at seven-twenty, wearing a sport coat and khakis instead of his usual uniform. After giving Todd a replay of Mindy's assault, Sean blinked blearily and escorted him to the basement. He and Mare had been up until nearly four with Mindy, and the remaining night's dreams had been brutal. He sighed and rubbed his face. *Virtually no sleep once again.*

"You haven't touched anything?" Todd asked after he assessed the chaos.

"I dumped a load of dirty clothes he'd left in the bathroom right about here," Sean said, pointing. "Mare and I both walked through the mess once each. Otherwise, just the chair I climbed on to look under the addition, that's it. Oh, and the light switch. Neither of us touched anything else. Pointed a lot, but didn't touch." He covered a yawn with his hand and remained at the foot of the stairs holding Todd's coat while Todd worked his way across the mess to the hole leading to the cellar.

The chair creaked as Todd climbed up, and the hole was a tight fit, but he eased out a few moments later and picked his way back across the mess, scowling. "Yeah, I see some slime in the closest hole," he said, straightening his shoulder holster before donning his coat. "But scanning equipment isn't going to fit in there, and if I remove them, it'll kill whatever's growing. I'm not willing to take that chance if it may be a kid."

"Okay," Sean said, stuffing his hands into his pockets. He wouldn't either. "So what do we do?"

"Leave 'em," Todd said, shrugging. "It'll just be another day or two. They're safe where they are, for now at least." He looked around the trashed basement again and asked,

"Where's your uncle?"

"No idea," Sean said. "He comes and goes."

They walked up the stairs. "It's suspicious, I'll give you that, but he might be a really sloppy guy and those holes might have been dug by groundhogs or something that crawled under your house and later died."

Sean rolled his eyes. "Groundhogs? Seriously? Does that mean we're gonna have six more weeks of winter?"

"Something, okay? Doesn't mean they're the missing kids."

"Doesn't mean they're not," Sean reminded him.

Todd gave him a sideways glare. "I need proof, Sean. Not wild imaginings and hunches, unless you want me to call in a forensics team to cordon off the house and dismantle half your basement just because you're afraid of your uncle's mole."

Goddammit. "I know I'm a mess, okay? You don't have to keep reminding me. But he's given me the creeps since the moment I saw him standing in the trees out back. I don't want him in my house, I don't want him anywhere near me or Mare."

They reached the top. Todd asked, "Why is he living here?"

"Mindy. She didn't think it was fair to welcome her but turn him away. Hard to fight that logic, especially when I'm low on sleep."

"Yeah, conscientious, forgiving women get us all into trouble someti—," he said, falling silent as Mindy bustled out of her bedroom barefoot in a summery dress, her hair a gamboling torrent of curls. The gash on her face had scabbed over, but the bruising had barely begun.

Sean cut his gaze to Todd who stood gaping for a moment before slamming his mouth shut. Sean grinned. *You dog!*

"Oh, no! You're here!" Her eyes grew wide and her cat meandered around her legs as if trying to trip her with adoration. "Am I late?"

"No, ma'am," Todd said, his voice catching. "I'm early."

"Did you want to look at the nasty messages now?" Mindy said, blushing. "Or question me about last night?"

Todd smiled and shook his head. "We can talk about it on the road, and I'll look at the comments after we get back."

Mindy tossed her cat into the bedroom before hurrying to the bathroom. Todd cleared his throat. "He doesn't fit the dates, but I'll get a deputy, a decent one, out front to watch the house. Just in case. Soon as I leave, you get new locks for both doors and replace them. Today. Buy ones with good deadbolts."

Sean yawned, wondering how they were going to afford locks. "Okay. Sure."

Mindy returned with her hair corralled and a little makeup on her face to obscure the scab. "Ready!"

Sean tried not to smirk as Todd glanced at his watch, fidgeting and nervous as if heading to prom. "Then let's get this boat on the road."

Sean locked the door behind them and shoved a chair under the doorknob. Once it was good and wedged in, he balanced an empty metal can on the seat and dropped a couple of teaspoons inside. *That'll make a good clatter,* he thought, then checked the back door again. Blockaded by cinder blocks, it was as locked as it'd ever be and they'd hear someone shattering the glass.

Assured he had done all he could, he stripped and crawled back into bed beside Mare. The .38 lay freshly loaded on her nightstand. Sean stared at the tidy circles of rimmed bullet bases gleaming in light reflected from the bathroom.

After a time they faded and he fell asleep.

Mindy kept her hands folded in her lap from nervousness over the upcoming deposition and her resolve not to touch anything.

Todd's SUV was computerized, digitized, and a shotgun stood pointing upward in a clamp on the center hump. Another gun, this one with a cord running to a digital box, was strapped to the dashboard. She saw mirrors and cameras, two radios, unidentifiable gadgets, and more flip-switches than she could count.

"Can you fly this thing?" she asked, braving a glance at him. "Looks like there ought to be an 'extend wings' button somewhere."

"No, it doesn't fly," he said, laughing. "But it does great over bean fields. Maybe I'll show you sometime."

They chatted as he drove east on Highway 30, mostly about her job, the interview, and maybe visiting his lawyer sister about her case, until his phone rang. He said, "Yes, sir," before hanging up and pocketing the phone again.

He glanced at Mindy. "There's a report I need that's been sent to the house. Can we take a short detour so I can grab it?"

"Sure." She shrugged. "We're ahead of schedule anyway."

He apologized as they drove through Boone and into a nice neighborhood of newer townhomes. He pulled into the driveway of a brick two-story and turned off the vehicle. "Why don't you come on in?" he said as he opened the door.

"Sure." She followed him to the walkway. "You have a cute house."

"Thanks. I picked it up for a good price during the housing mess a few years back."

He plucked up a newspaper as he stepped onto the porch and unlocked the door before beckoning her inside. A hallway ran straight ahead flanked by a sunny sitting room on the left and stairs going up on the right. Everything looked bright and welcoming, with hardwood flooring and walls painted cheerful shades. "Make yourself at home," he said as he trotted up the stairs. "I'll be right back."

Mindy wandered down the hall, past a bathroom to a kitchen that opened to a cozy living room. Two Disney Princess DVDs lay on the floor in front of the TV beside a coloring book. The leather couch held a scattering of manila folders and the naked bottom half of a Barbie stuffed between the cushions.

"Thanks for waiting," Todd said as he walked down the hall with another folder.

Mindy smiled at the naked Barbie legs poking upward, ready to dance on the ceiling if the couch wasn't holding them down. "You have a daughter?"

"Yeah," Todd said as he gathered up his folders and walked to the kitchen. "She, like her father, leaves things lying around."

Mindy rescued the doll from the cushions and followed him to the kitchen. Marker makeup embellished the nude Barbie's factory-tinted face, and someone had drawn on rings and bracelets as well. "You being in law enforcement and all, am I allowed to ask your daughter's name, or how old she is?"

He smiled at her, and she saw a brightening of color on his cheeks as he unlocked a black briefcase. "You can ask me anything. No guarantees that I'll answer."

"Fair enough." She pondered her question for a moment then walking the doll across the edge of the kitchen table, asked, "Does Scribble Face Barbie spend a lot of her spare time naked in your couch? I thought cops were kind of against public nudity."

Todd laughed and tossed the folders into the briefcase. "She's been naked pretty much constantly since she came to live with us a few months ago. The tramp." He shrugged. "She's usually on the stairs though. I've stepped on her at least twice."

"You're a floozy," Mindy said to the doll, "throwing your naked self out where unsuspecting men will walk over you."

Todd contemplated Mindy. "Maybe I should arrest her for being a public nuisance?"

Mindy laughed and set the doll aside. "Maybe," she agreed. "But I don't think it'll do any good."

He plucked the doll from the table and smoothed its hair. "You're right. Hailey has four or five others just like her. A plague of 'em. Toss one and someone gives her three more to take its place."

Mindy watched his eyes. "You love her a lot, don't you?"

"Of course I do. She's all I have."

"Widowed?" Mindy asked when she saw a shadow of pain cross his eyes.

"Divorced. Kim was…" he shrugged. "She was always a wild thing. Wanting to go out, to get looked at, to court trouble. She loved danger, excitement, and cops." He sighed and tossed the doll onto the counter next to the coffee pot.

"She was a badge bunny, and stupid me fell for her, but she refused to settle down. Hailey was a baby when she…" He clenched his hands then opened them. "Last I heard, she was dancing at some strip club in Reno."

"I'm sorry."

"Eh, it's ancient history now." He took a breath and met Mindy's gaze. "She wanted out, I wanted Hailey. Wasn't much else to argue about."

"That's… Wow." Mindy dropped her gaze. She couldn't imagine a mother abandoning her child like that.

"So, anyway, I kind of know what you're going through with that ass you married. Kim never tried to kill me, but…"

"Yeah. It was all about her, never you or your daughter."

"Pretty much."

"I'm better off, too," Mindy said. "Sean and Mare are great, and the baking might go somewhere. I'm starting to save a little money. If I can just get past this mess, things'll be golden."

"I hope so," Todd said. "You deserve a little golden. How about bad dreams? Are you suffering with them like the other spores are?"

She was about to whine about falling through black snow when he exploded forward. The front door banged open; he pulled his gun and motioned for her to stay behind him.

"Just us!" a woman called out as steps bounded down the hall.

Todd sagged, the breath rushing out of him as he put the gun away and strode to the hall. "Mom! How many times have I told you to knock before just walking in?" He paused, his voice softening as he said, "How's my squirrel girl?"

Mindy saw Todd bend then stand again, sunburned kid arms hugging his neck. "Dad! Look! We found a Space Princess backpack and matching notebooks and folders. Even a lunchbox!"

"Can't beat WalMart early in the morning. Nothing's picked over," the woman said, followed by an exasperated sigh. "Sorry to just barge in. I wanted to drop off the haul, and she was so excited you're home. We haven't seen you for days."

"I'm not home, not really. Supposed to be on the way to Des Moines," Todd said as an obese older woman walked past him into the kitchen, her plump arms weighed down by plastic shopping bags.

The woman stopped, her eyes and mouth growing wide. "Oh!" she said, blinking at

Mindy. "I didn't expect you to have company!"

"Hi, I'm Mindy," she said, offering to take some of the bags. "You must be Todd's mom."

"Deb," she said, nodding hello as she handed over part of her burden. "Todd said he was guarding you, but I never expected it to be here."

"It's not quite like that, Mom." Todd walked up to them, a little red-haired girl in his arms. She pressed her face against her father's neck and watched Mindy with one nervous brown eye.

Deb plunked her bags onto the counter while, beside her, Mindy did the same. "Oh?" she asked her son, looking Mindy over before turning to him. "What is it then? I thought you said you wouldn't be off work until maybe tonight. Here it is, twenty after eight in the morning."

Mindy said, "We're just here to pick up some reports, ma'am."

Deb sighed and faced Mindy. "And you bought that line of crap? Girl, you have no idea who you're dealing with."

Deb leaned close and lowered her voice to almost a whisper. "You have to understand my son," she said, glancing over her shoulder at him. "He's a charmer. A babe magnet, we used to call them, so you be careful, you hear?"

Todd carried his daughter to the living room. "Oh, yeah, Mom, that's me. All us massive head thumpers are super charming," he said as he lowered Hailey to her feet. A slender girl with scabbed knees and a short, wavy blaze of hair, she peered around her father then ducked out of sight again.

Todd strode back to the kitchen and towered over his mom like a grizzly looming over a rotund raccoon. Smiling, he shook his head and started to unpack the bags. "Babe magnet, that's actually a good one."

"I try," Deb said, still observing Mindy. "So what do you do?" she asked. "When people aren't threatening you, anyway."

Todd walked past with a lunchbox and stack of snack foods. "Mom! You don't need to pester her."

"No, it's okay," Mindy said, smiling at Hailey who crept closer. "I work in a nursing home kitchen, and I've started to sell baked goods on the side."

Deb nodded. "I saw your blog. If half of it's true, your ex is a creep."

"It's all true," Mindy sighed. "And, yes, he is."

"Then you're better off without him." She patted Mindy on the arm. "Pay attention to what he says," she said, nodding toward Todd as he put away the cookies and chips. "He knows his job."

"Yes, ma'am. I will."

Deb lingered a few moments longer then stepped aside, nearly tripping over Hailey, who stared at Mindy with wide, curious eyes. "Are you dating my dad?" she asked, her voice small and tentative.

"No, sweetie," Mindy said, kneeling to be face-to-face with her. "He's just keeping me safe."

"He's good at that," Hailey said, giving Mindy a hesitant smile. She touched Mindy's scabbed cheek. "You got hurt?"

Mindy nodded. "Bad men broke into the house and hurt me."

Hailey started to pull up her tank top, and Deb reached out to stop her, but Todd grabbed Deb's arm and shook his head.

Hailey, her gaze locked on Mindy's, bared her belly. "My mom hurt me, too. So we're the same, right?"

A wrinkled collection of dime-sized circles peppered the left side of Hailey's chest and belly. They lay next to one another, overlapping, and spelled *cunt.*

Mindy blinked back her shock. "Yes, sweetie, we are," she said, reaching out to lower the little girl's hand and shirt. "Your dad won't let anyone hurt you like that ever again."

"I know," Hailey said, smiling, then she gave Mindy a quick hug. "Nobody'll hurt you, either."

Deb grasped Hailey's hand and said, "C'mon now, we have more errands to run before all the lazy folks are out of bed. Let's let your daddy work."

Mindy stood as Deb led Hailey away and she watched Todd lower his head and stuff his hands into his jacket pockets. "Her mom did that?" she asked after Deb and Hailey had gone outside and closed the door behind them.

"Yeah." He managed to meet her gaze. "She was teething. Crying a lot. I was working and Kim couldn't sleep, so…"

"So she took it out on her daughter." Mindy shook her head and her voice cracked as she said, "What the hell?"

"I offered to keep the DA from prosecuting if she'd give me Hailey, leave, and never come back. She agreed. She signed the divorce and custody papers before she left the interrogation room. Was the last time I laid eyes on her."

"Your daughter's adorable, but your ex… Jesus, what a shit."

"So was yours. My mom, she…" He swallowed and shook his head. "I haven't dated at all since Kim. Not once. Hailey's too precious to take a chance with, but she keeps reminding me everybody else has a mom, you know? That's hard. My mom doesn't like to see me raise Hailey alone. So, together, they hoped we were…" he shrugged.

"It's okay," Mindy assured him, breaking the awkward silence. "I understand. Truly."

"Guess I'd better double check to make sure I don't forget anything then get you to that interview. Don't want to be late."

"No, we don't," Mindy whispered as he left to lumber down the hall and up the stairs again. Smiling at the girly space unicorns on the folders, she finished unpacking Hailey's school supplies.

Chapter Twenty-Two

Sean bought new locks and an alarm at Lowe's—*so much for meat this week*—and nearly had the front lock installed when a middle-aged couple walked up.

"You're the spore guy, right?" the man asked, reaching for the woman's hand. "Sean something?"

"Afraid I am," Sean sighed as he held the lock pieces together so he could thread the first screw. He held the second between his lips and mumbled, "What can I do for you?"

"We'd like to buy a plot," the man replied. "I… I did some checking and this area's cemetery plots usually run about five hundred dollars, give or take." He paused to glance at his companion. "We're willing to offer three times that. Cash."

Sean dropped the screws and stood. "You're what?"

The woman trembled, but stared Sean in the eye. "We have the money. We, we just need to borrow your yard for a while."

"I, I..." Sean shook his head and tried to make sense of it. "*What?*"

The man said, "Our son. Taylor. They found him two days ago, discarded like garbage behind a bar in Ames. You might have seen it on the news."

Sean shook his head. He'd avoided the news.

The man took a breath and straightened his spine. "We've learned that local cemeteries are refusing to bury accident and murder victims. They'll only take them if they've been cremated. If we do that, he'll be gone forever. But, you, you've been helping with these spore things. Helping to bring people back."

"He was nine," the woman said, thrusting a picture toward Sean of a plump, dark-haired boy laughing while riding a bumper car. "Please. We just want our son back. You're our only hope."

"Fuck," Sean muttered under his breath. He cut his gaze to the deputy sitting in the cruiser and the zombie gang sitting on the curb reading comics. "You do know it's illegal to bury bodies anywhere but a cemetery, right? So what happens when we all go to jail?"

"We'll pay for your lawyer too," the man said.

When his wife whispered, "Kurt, you know we've maxed out—" he hushed her.

"We'll sell our house if we have to. Our cars. Have a bake sale. I don't know. We just want Taylor back."

"I have a lawyer," Sean sighed. "And money isn't the issue." He ran a hand through his hair and cursed again. "Just a minute, okay? Wait right here."

The couple nodded and he left the door standing open as he went in for Mare.

She sat at the computer scanning in yesterday's pencil layouts. "Murph's having convulsions," she said without looking up at him. "Needs those inks now."

Sean rolled his eyes. *Fuck Murph.* "Yeah, well, I have something a bit more pressing," he said, then explained the couple on the porch.

Mare stood, her face pale. "They want to bury their *kid*? Here?" When Sean nodded, she whispered, "We might already have two in the basement!"

Sean sagged, nodding. "I know, I know."

Mare paced. "Crap, crap, crap. We can't let folks bury people here. Pets are one thing, but... *People*?!"

"But we can't just let a kid be dead, either. Fuck." Muttering, he tore a scrap of sketch paper off the pad and wrote on it before handing it to Mare. "Sound reasonable?" he asked.

She read quickly and nodded. "Think they'll go for it?"

"Shit if I know," he said, leaving the studio. "But at least a nine-year-old can tell us who to call."

The couple stood on the porch, fretting as they waited, and they watched him with hopeful, terrified eyes.

"I can't," he said, thrusting the paper toward them so no one else could see, despite two of the zombie gang craning their necks. "It's illegal, and in case you haven't noticed, there's a deputy parked out front all the time who will surely arrest me if I allowed it. While I truly believe the spores are people who deserve the same rights as everybody else, I can't afford to go to jail. I understand your pain and am truly sorry, but I can't help you."

The couple read the note. Both nodded, their mouths dropping open.

Sean gave them a gentle smile. "Do you understand?"

The woman looked up, blinking away tears. "Just this?" she whispered. "That's all we…you have to say?"

"Yes. Do you understand?"

"Yes, we do," the man said. "Yes. Thank you for your time." Then they left, his arm coming around her as they walked to their car, weeping.

I have a feeling this is going to become too common. Sean scowled and knelt to return to his lock, tucking the scrap into his pocket.

The first screw set easily, but the second fought him. He'd just got it to thread when he heard footsteps approach.

"Mr. Casey?" a man said. "I'm here from Life Progress dot com. I'm sure you're aware agricultural pesticides are to blame for the rise of dead people as far south as St. Louis and the panic it's causing. Can I get an interview for our site?"

Sean tried not to sigh as he finished setting the screw. "Let me finish this first, okay?"

"Of course, sir."

Sir. Ha! No one calls me sir. Shaking his head, Sean finished installing the lock and tossed his screwdriver into his toolbox. "Go ahead, but make it quick," he told the reporter as another weeping, desperate family pulled up in a minivan.

Mare sat in the passenger seat with her arms crossed over her chest. "I can't do this."

"Yes, you can."

She stared out the window. "And not shoot my mouth off? I dunno."

Sean glanced at her as they passed a slow-moving hay baler. "Maybe she doesn't know anything. Do you want to forget it? "

"No. She worked there. She knows *something*. I just really don't want to talk to your mother."

"I don't either. But you know I can't leave you at home alone. Not with all the crap that's happened lately. Besides, it gets us out of the house together. Think of it as a date."

Mare huffed. "Some date."

They drove in silence to Boone. As they approached his mother's house, Mare's hands clenched and unclenched and she continually shifted in her seat.

Sean pulled into the driveway and turned off the car. "It'll be okay. Once I ask my questions, we'll leave. Quick." He stepped out and Mare sighed as if facing dental surgery via chainsaw. She opened the door.

Helene, as usual, scampered out the front door to meet him, but her smile froze into a toothy rictus as she saw them. "Sean! So glad to see you! Such a marvelous surprise!" she said, waiting for them near the steps.

Can't even acknowledge her, can you, Ma? Sean grasped Mare's hand and squeezed it. She squeezed back.

Helene said, "Where's that nice girl you brought last week? She was adorable, even if she'd been dead."

"Delighted to see you too," Mare muttered under her breath.

Hang in there, babe. We'll get through it. Sean made himself smile at his mother. "She's in Des Moines. Had some spare time today, so I thought we'd stop by for a visit."

Helene held his face in dry, cleanser-scented palms and stretched up to kiss him. "Always happy to see my baby." She patted his cheek and let him go. "The comic doing well?"

"Great. It's great." He nodded toward the door and tried to lead Mare to the stairs, but his mother remained in the way. "Can we talk insi—"

Helene stepped in front of Mare, blocking her access to the steps. "Rosemary! There you are! I'd have missed you if it wasn't for your pretty manicure!"

Mare shrugged and glanced at her free hand. "Mindy brought home a bottle and did my—"

"It is a lovely Smuckers strawberry color, dear, but wouldn't a mocha be less likely to clash with the poop?"

Mare released Sean's hand and walked away. "That's it. I'm going back to the car."

"Babe, wait," Sean said, turning, but Mare kept walking.

"Oh, don't worry about her," Helene soothed, rubbing his shoulder. "She's just having one of her moods. You come on into the house; I'll make you something to eat."

Goddammit. Sean turned. "Stop treating her that way. Just *stop*."

Helene blinked, her eyes wide and innocent. "What way? I complimented her and she stomps off in a huff."

"That was no compliment," he snapped. "I thought you could be decent for ten damned minutes, but nope. Not you. Mare's job gets your uptight OCD germophobe panties in a twist so tight you can't help but be nasty."

Helene gave him a coaxing smile and patted his chest. "Now, sweetie, you know that's not true."

"Because you're not wearing panties today? Never took you for going commando," Mare said from behind Sean. Both he and his mother jumped.

Helene took a startled step back. "Of course I'm wearing panties!"

Mare stood beside Sean. "Then why are they twisted? That must be very uncomfortable and could cause chafing, which could lead to bed sores and infection. Perhaps a good sponge bath and a hospital gown would work better for you. I'd be happy to provide both."

Helene ground her teeth and balled her hands. "Don't start with me, Rosemary."

"It's Mare. And you started it a freaking decade ago."

"I did no such thing! Sean! Tell her I did no such thing."

"You did, Ma," Sean said, grasping Mare's hand.

"She had no right to touch…" Helene's face turned red and she spat out, "His *thing*!"

Mare stood her ground. "You sat for almost an hour with him in a shitty diaper. You wouldn't change him, so I did."

"You had no right to touch my husband's thing!"

"Ex-husband," Sean corrected, trying to help Mare. Both women turned to glare at him and he stepped away, hands up in warding. "I'll just referee from over here."

"It's not a 'thing', it's a penis," Mare said, returning her attention to Helene. "And when a man can't get up to use the pot, sometimes he'll get feces on his penis. I clean up sick old men all day, every day. Nasty old crones like you, too. People poop. Someone has to clean it up. Deal with it."

"You're filthy. Going through life with excrement all over your hands."

"Nah, I wash 'em about a zillion times a day and use sanitizer. My hands are cleaner than yours." She paused to smile. "Just think, *Hel*, someday someone just like me will be wiping shit out of your 'thing'. It'll get up in there, and she'll have to dig to get it all out. Won't that be *fun*?! It's a party for everyone! I'll take pictures, it'll be so grand."

"You do not have permission to clean my, my…" Helene cleared her throat then settled on, "My personals."

Mare stood nose to nose with Helene. "Oh, I won't clean you. I'll make you sit there in your own filth just like you made Pat. I'll let it get dried and crusty. Let it draw flies. Let it stink. Just like you did."

Sean turned his gaze to his mother and awaited the next bombardment in an oft-delayed but inevitable battle. They were hollering in the front yard on a Saturday, with kids biking by and folks doing lawn work. He smirked. *In Mom's neighborhood, no less.*

"I'd get you fired if you left me like that."

"No, you wouldn't. Because we'll stick you in the cheapest, crappiest, most understaffed nursing home we can find. You'll have some poor little immigrant wiping your ass and cleaning out your 'thing'. That'll make it even better!"

"You wouldn't dare."

"Might not have a choice. You know we don't have any money and can't afford quality accommodations. Geesh, Hel, even you should realize that!"

Helene drew in and huffed out a few breaths. "He was hard. The old pervert. You actually expected me to touch him, clean him, when he was like that?"

"Men get that way! Jesus!"

"I didn't touch it when we were married, and I damn sure wouldn't touch it when he was *nasty*."

Mare covered her mouth with her hand, but couldn't hide the laughter burbling out of her. "Oh my God. That's it, isn't it? I'm not afraid of some old dude's poopy dick, but you couldn't even bear to touch your husband's during your marriage?" She turned aside, nearly doubled over in mirth. "Holy mother of God, you'd have a heart attack if you knew what I did with your son's."

"Hey!" Sean said, sudden heat rising on his cheeks. "Don't drag me into this."

"Maybe that's why you were an only child," Mare giggled. "Your mom's penile-phobic! It makes so much more sense now. Oh, God. Did you even clean Sean's when he was a baby, or just wipe around it?"

Helene flushed and crossed her arms over her belly. "You have no right to talk to me that way, and you certainly have no right to touch my son!"

"Oh, please. We've been together since college. If you've heard of it, we've probably done it. A lot. How's that feel, Hel?"

Helene pressed her lips together, her breath coming slow and furious. "Is this why you came here? To insult me? To disgust me with how you've corrupted my son?"

Corrupted me? Heh. Most of the kinky stuff was my idea. Sean cleared his throat and tried to wish his embarrassment away as he segued into the reason for their visit. "Um, actually, we were talking about something in your scrapbook."

Helene narrowed her eyes at Mare. "My scrapbook?"

"Just had a question about one of your mementos, Ma. Can we take a look?"

Helene swallowed, her wary gaze darting between them. "I don't know. What memento?"

"Geesh, Ma, does it matter?"

Mare grasped Sean's hand and started to lead him away. "I told you she wouldn't let you look at it."

"Yeah, guess you were right." Sean waved and turned toward the car. "See you later, Ma."

"No, wait!" Helene called, following them. "Don't go. Just... Why now? You've never wanted to look at my scrapbook before. Even when you were little. Even when I asked you to."

She stood there, wringing her hands, her face an odd mix of pale terror and flushed cheeks, and a single bead of sweat rolled from her temple to her left ear. Sean felt pity for her, more than he imagined he could. "Why do you think, Ma?"

"Because of that dead girl you've befriended? And those things you said on the news?"

He nodded, but said nothing. Mare, too, remained silent.

Helene hesitated, tugging on her hands so hard she left welts. "Do you remember something? Something from when..."

"No, Ma. It's still mostly a big vat of nothing. Just found out last night that you worked there. At the lab."

Helene dropped Sean's gaze and nodded. "I don't know anything, but you can see what I have. It's not much. It can't help your friend, but I don't see the harm in letting you see it."

She wiped the sweat bead away with a shaking hand and climbed the steps to her front door. Sean and Mare followed her inside.

Todd lingered nearby as Mindy spoke with the insurance company rep and passed the time by reviewing the files about her accident.

He hadn't worked that day, nor seen the reports before, but they were sorely lacking details. Had she skidded before driving off the embankment onto the highway below, or had she barreled down without slowing? He found no photographs of skid marks, but plenty of the chipped concrete at the edge of the bridge. No photographs of her brakes or the interior of the car, only her body, mangled and spewed through the windshield. No witnesses other than the shaken college student who'd nearly got crushed by a flying car—despite the icy conditions, she'd swerved before being hit by Mindy's Prius—and an over the road truck driver who saw the flight and impact, not the initial takeoff. Todd found no mention of the lack of airbag deployment in the initial report, little about road conditions or traffic. Few details at all.

He flipped to the front page. Although the report was made by Collins, Hendrix had been the first responder and photographer. The same deputy who'd left his post and allowed Mindy to be attacked the night before. The same deputy with constant debt problems and who hadn't answered his phone that morning.

Todd called the office and requested his detail sergeant.

"Hear from Hendrix yet?" he asked as he scrutinized the few accident photographs again. Six, total, for a fatal accident: three were of the concrete embankment, one of the crumpled Prius taken from atop the bridge, and two of Mindy, bloody and dead. *What the hell? There should be four, five times as many pics. At least. With pertinent details.*

"Yeah," Sarge said, sounding distracted. "He just called from the hospital. Food poisoning. Guess he finally stopped puking and they're sending him home with electrolytes or something. Gonna take a couple of days off."

"Sorry to hear that," Todd said as he put the photos away. "But he should have called in for a replacement."

"I know, and I've already reamed his ass," Sarge said. "How's your little rabble rouser?"

"She's fine. Talking to the insurance company."

"Keep us informed," Sarge said, then the call went dead.

Todd resumed reading. Clayton Mechanic Specialists had checked over her car and discovered the failure in her brake line and mis-installed airbags. Again, the file contained far fewer photographs than he expected and virtually no details. *They went to court with this? No wonder the state lost.*

What the hell? he thought, squinting at the signature of the grease monkey who'd dismantled Mindy's car. Ryder Hendrix.

Deputy Hendrix had mentioned his brother once. Said his name was Rye and he was a gear head who worked on junkers in his backyard and pit crewed for a dirt racer to help make ends meet, just like Deputy Hendrix took on odd jobs and favors.

He watched Mindy shake hands with two pencil pushers in suits. *Wonder what beef the Hendrix boys had with her? It have anything to do with her rich ex and their empty wallets?*

His phone rang. Brad Jorst, the investigator heading the Creeper case.

"Anderson," Todd said, closing the folder and setting it aside to reach for a notebook and pen. *Maybe we caught a break. Brad never calls to chat.*

"Wanted to give you a heads up," Brad said, his voice partly obscured by a cacophony of chatter on the other side of the line. "We found that missing spore."

"The one who disappeared from a work detail Tuesday?"

"That's him," Brad said, the noise fading away as a screen door creaked then banged closed. He took a deep breath then let it out. "Those two jokers who assaulted your assignment last night? Couple of deputies checked out their residences on a warrant. They found a helluva mess."

Todd looked over his shoulder at Mindy, still discussing insurance. "What kind of mess?"

"Looks like they'd spent a few days torturing the spore. Busting him up, cutting him. They fucked the guy up. Even the weekend M.E. looked green. Gave us the same old bullshit about not specifying C.O.D. until after the autopsy, but we all could tell it was from decapitation. All the blood. But he did say the guy had layers of scar tissue. *Layers.* Said they probably waited for him to heal, then did something else. Jesus, Todd, his arms were broken in several places and bent around a row of hooks. We couldn't get them off because they healed that way, all twirled up like a snake. And his legs? Busted then twisted around backward and folded in half, mid thigh."

Todd ran a shaking hand over his face. "Fuck me."

"Yeah, you and me both. The bones healed that way, Todd. Not just broken, but healed into *solid, bent bone.* I heard these spore things are tough, but, shit, this is nuts."

Mindy gave him a concerned glance, the morning's scar no longer visible at all.

Her hair was a mass of glossy dark ringlets, her skin glowing and flawless. The dress she wore clung to her plump curves, begging to be caressed. He wondered what kind of man would ever harm someone like her.

Todd wanted to pull Mindy to her feet and inform her she was gorgeous, stunning, but instead gave her a thumbs up and turned aside. "Yeah, it's nuts," he said to Brad, wishing he'd let the call go to voicemail.

"So we're thinking he endured days of this. Getting cut up, bones busted and rearranged, then do it all again. They'd even cut off one hand and his dick, but they'd mostly grown back. What the hell? Not only that, the slice across this throat, the one we think killed him? It had started to seal up, too."

Brad paused and Todd heard him light a cigarette and take a deep drag despite having quit smoking two years ago. He coughed once, then said, "Shit, we're not even sure if he's really dead. For all we know, he might wake up and start dancing on the way to the morgue."

Todd watched Mindy ease out of her chair, watched her move as if no one had ever beat her with a crowbar or shredded her through a shattered windshield. She glanced at him and blushed, smiling, as the attorney general himself beckoned her into the next room.

Todd followed, phone cradled against his ear.

Brad took another drag then coughed again. "Just wanted you to know what kind of monsters you're dealing with. We're thinking this spore was just a warm up, and his real performance is yet to come. Keep an eye on her."

They reached the deposition room and Todd settled in beside the door. "Not letting her out of my sight."

"I can't believe you kept all this stuff," Sean said as he flipped through his mother's scrapbook. Mare remained silent as she leaned over to examine the old photographs, mementos, and clippings she'd been forbidden to touch. The scent of pine cleaner lay heavy in the air, cloying and thick, as if every surface had been repeatedly scoured smooth. Which they probably had.

"I really don't know why you want to see any of it," Helene said, her hands shaking as she sat across the table from them.

Sean forced himself to smile at his mother. "We found a copy of an article online. It had your picture in it, said you used to work at the lab."

"I did," she admitted, her eyes downcast. "Was there about seven years."

"Mom. I asked you the other day if you'd ever heard about them and you said no. Why would you do that?"

Helene shrugged. "I didn't think it mattered."

Sean snapped a page over. *Of course it matters, Mom. It's why we're here.*

"What'd you do? Your job, I mean?" Mare asked, her voice soft. Helene stiffened but said nothing.

Sean flipped further into the book, past her high school years and her wedding. "You can talk to Mare. It would be good if you talked to her."

Helene took a heavy breath and raised her gaze to Sean. "Sure you don't want something to eat?"

The wedding passed and photos shifted to blissful newlyweds. "Still not hungry. We ate at home."

"I could use a glass of water," Mare said. "Please?"

Helene flinched, but did not move. Mare sighed and slouched, her foot tapping beside Sean's.

"Goddammit." He turned a page to baby shower invitations and a photograph of a pink and blue cake. "We've been putting up with this crap for a freaking decade. Mare's not going anywhere, Mom. Why can't you be polite, at least? Why can't you let it go?"

"Some things you can't let go." Helene burst to her feet. She scurried to the kitchen as Sean returned his attention to the book. He didn't remember it being so massive and detailed.

Helene returned with a glass of iced tea that she set on a crystal coaster in front of Sean. He slid it to Mare who muttered, "Thank you," to his mother before braving a sip. Helene scowled at her and tsk-tsked.

Sean pointed at a picture of his father and Paul fishing. "I barely remember Uncle Paul from when I was a kid," Sean said, watching his mother. "What happened? He and Dad have a falling out?"

He saw a tremor in Helene's clasped hands as she jerked her gaze from the iced tea to him. "I guess they did. Your father never really said. Just, one day, they stopped talking."

Mare returned the glass to the coaster. "Surely you know why your husband stopped talking to his brother."

Don't push her too hard, Sean thought, glancing at his mother. *We want her to talk, not start another fight.*

Helene's voice was quavering and strained. "He never said, and I didn't ask."

Sean flipped a couple of pages deeper into the scrapbook. He reached preschool as a happy little boy with a big grin and bright eyes, and an unexpected pair of Nikes on his feet. "How did I ever get Nikes?"

Helene grinned and rushed to his side to caress the photo. "Oh, those! I'd gotten a bonus at work. We all did. New government contract. I wanted to get you something nice for school. At first your dad thought it was silly to spend so much on shoes you'd outgrow in a few weeks, but I found those on sale. Air Jordans? I think that's right. Your father was a big fan of Mr. Jordan and, in the end, he didn't mind so much. You really loved those shoes. They made you think you could fly."

She stroked his hair and sighed. "You were so cute, leaping into the air like you did."

Sean struggled to keep his voice level and calm. "Dad was a Bulls fan?"

"Oh, yes, both Casey boys were until…"

Her voice trailed off and she bustled toward the kitchen again. "I should get you some crumb cake. Made it yesterday, but it's still good."

Sean and Mare shared a glance, but said nothing. He flipped past pictures of a picnic, tickets to a Fleetwood Mac concert, and a wedding invitation for people he'd never heard of before, complete with flattened silk blossoms. He began to wonder how much of his mother's life had been a secret when he reached the page with the article about Lotus Labs.

The article had yellowed and faded, but his young and smiling mother stood with Evelyn Fischer and two other office-attired women behind several men in lab coats and a grinning Middle Eastern man.

Mare leaned over and whispered, "That's it."

Helene returned, plate of crumb cake in hand. She paused, then lurched forward with a stiff smile on her face. "Let's just forget all that."

Sean accepted the cake. "I don't remember you working there."

"Really, it was nothing. Part-time temp work." She reached forward to turn the page.

Yeah. Temp work. For seven years. At a job you're trying not to talk about. He politely took a bite. "It must have been interesting. Science and all that stuff."

"Just accounting, some bookkeeping. I didn't even know what they did."

"Really?" Mare leaned back and contemplated Helene. "The article mentioned stem cell research." Before Helene could reply, she grimaced and pushed away the glass of tea.

"The government had them doing experiments on embryos, didn't they, back before it was regulated? How could you work for such a place?"

Helene snatched up the glass, pinching it between her fingertips and thumb as if it was sticky. "It was a research facility. To help people."

"Right, it's always helpful to fiddle with stem cells in a secret government lab." Mare turned to Sean. "No wonder she doesn't want to talk about it."

Helene stomped to the kitchen and dumped the tea before tossing the glass into the trash. "I told you, Rosemary, they were researching ways to help people. They tested fungi, not embryos."

"What kind of fungus did they work with?" Sean sighed as Helene scoured her hands with three splurts of soap and a scrubby pad under steaming water. *You can't even bear to touch anything Mare's used. You need help, Ma. Serious help.*

"I have no idea. Something from Egypt, I think that's where the invoices came from. I don't really remember, just that they lost the big contract and went bankrupt." She dried her hands and returned to the dining room. "I don't know anything and none of this is my fault. I was a bookkeeping clerk, not a mycologist. We just did our jobs, not pester the mycologists with questions that were none of our business. Clerks weren't allowed in the lab."

"Was Evelyn a clerk too? Were you close?"

She leaned forward to yank the scrapbook out of Sean's grip. "I don't remember what she did. I barely remember her at all, other than she was hit by a snowplow and died."

So why did you get upset when I mentioned she walked out of the tree farm? Sean moistened his lips. "She came back, Ma, as a spore. Remember? Then someone killed her. Why would anyone kill Evelyn?"

Helene scowled. "How should I know?" She slapped the book closed and turned to walk away. "I've told you all I know. Now that that's settled, I don't feel well and I'm going to lie down. Please leave."

Cradling the scrapbook to her chest, she disappeared down the hall.

Mare jumped as the bedroom door slammed. "I guess we've been dismissed."

Chapter Twenty-Three

Driving up the interstate with Todd that afternoon, Mindy watched mushy cornfields blur past. Her mind was still reeling from meeting the attorney general and Todd's sister, the ball-busting lawyer. Both had been incredibly nice and taken gobs of notes about Jeff, their marriage, and the recent threats, and both kept insisting they weren't afraid of narcissistic shits and would stop him in his tracks. With a great lawyer and the state on her side, maybe things would turn out all right after all. Maybe, for once, Jeff's cheating wouldn't allow him to win.

She grinned. *Maybe he'll even go to jail!* "Was a pretty good interview, don't you think? I did all right?"

"You were great," Todd said, going around a minivan which had slowed to a snail's pace on the interstate as they approached. "The insurance investigator seemed especially pleased."

Mindy laughed. "He was just shocked I remembered so many details about what happened when we bought the car, but it was just a few weeks ago to me." She tilted her head as she heard his stomach grumble. They hadn't had a chance to eat lunch and she was hungry, too. *I'd really love to cook tonight,* she thought around a happy sigh. *Cook something intricate and special. A celebration supper.*

"I think it's great how you're standing up to your ex and taking control of your life," he said. "If you don't, who will?"

That's true, she thought, letting the concept stew in her mind as the miles rolled away behind them. *And no one's here to tell me I can't, or I'm not good enough. Not anymore.* "My whole life I've done what other people have told me to do," she explained, watching him. "This independence is… Strange."

"Okay," he said, "right now, of all the things in all the world, what do you want to do?"

Can't believe I'm considering this but he's such a nice guy. I have to thank him somehow. "I think I want to cook for you," she said softly as he turned to gawk at her and nearly steered the SUV onto the gravel beside the highway.

"What? *Me?*"

"Or you and Hailey and your mom, if that'd be better." She took a breath and moistened her lips. "Sean and Mare like my cooking all right, but you seem like a guy who appreciates a well cooked meal."

Despite his scowl, she pressed on. "It'd be nice to cook for someone who could recognize the difference between pesto and verde, for example. To them it's all yummy, but still just a green sauce. I bet you know how different they are. I noticed you have both in your kitchen cupboards."

He mumbled for a moment, his eyes rooted on the road ahead. "Pesto and verde? Yeah, sure, one's Mexican, one's Italian, but—"

"What's your favorite food?" she interrupted. "Of all of the meals you've ever had, what ranks at the top?"

"Um, I had some amazing chicken something once, years ago. I don't remember what it was called, but it was really lemony, and had these weird salty pea things that just…" He pulled one hand off the wheel, brought his fingertips together and snapped them wide apart. "Pow!"

"Capers," she said, nodding. "With pasta and a light sauce?"

He grinned and glanced at her. "Yes! You know the stuff?"

Definitely chicken piccata. She grinned back. "I do, yes."

"It was amazing," he said. "I could have eaten myself into a coma over that sauce."

She felt heat brighten her cheeks and flow down her throat. *You asked, so don't chicken out now.* "Can we stop at the grocery store on the way back and see if I can cook it as well as you remember?"

Both hands white-knuckled on the wheel, he stared ahead as they barreled down the interstate. "Okay," he said, glancing at her. "It's going to get me in a lot of trouble, but okay."

The house was still standing when Sean and Mare returned. Two zombie hunters sat on a car hood, drinking beer and eating tacos from a greasy fast food bag while they read GhoulBane back issues. Sean gave them a tired wave and they nodded back. The deputy spoke into his radio mic, but made no other indication he'd noticed their arrival. Otherwise, the yard was deserted.

Sean sighed and walked to the front steps. The lawn looked muddy, ratty, and overgrown. "I really need to mow."

"Maybe it'll be dry enough tomorrow?"

I doubt it. They climbed the steps and Sean unlocked the door. "I saw online this morning they've found spore slime near Memphis."

"Jesus," Mare said, shaking her head as she entered the house. "So far, so fast."

"It's been raining a lot. Rivers are swollen. It's going to spread quickly."

Mare tossed her purse onto the couch on her way to the kitchen. "Do you think they're picketing Elvis's house now?"

"Heh. Probably." Intending to resume inking spreads, he started toward the studio but paused, a cold sweat trickling down his spine. The bathroom door stood open and a grimy pair of jeans lay wadded on the floor just inside.

Paul was here. But we'd locked the doors. Fuck.

"Mare!" he called out, turning to rush to the kitchen.

She dropped the ice cube tray she was emptying and pressed a startled hand over her heart. "What? What's wrong?"

"He was here," Sean choked out. His mouth felt very, very dry. "Stay there. I'm gonna check the house."

She nodded, her eyes wide, and he walked past her to their bedroom. It had been ransacked, their dressers opened and dragged across the room, and the mattress flipped against the wall.

Sean's heart skittered and his hands clenched. *He was looking for something.*

"Babe?" he choked out as he returned to the kitchen. "Where'd you hide the gun?"

She opened the freezer and pulled out a box of diet fudge bars. She upended the box and the .38 slid into her hand, sealed in a zipper bag with the air squeezed out. She tossed it to Sean. "As much as he bitched about missing fat and sugar, I figured he wouldn't look in there."

He nodded. *Smart girl.*

Even in the bag, the gun was frigid cold yet a comforting weight in his hand. And it was loaded.

He returned it to Mare before pulling the flashlight from the drawer and stuffing it in his back pocket. "Watch the stairs. I'm going to check the studio and Mindy's room first."

Mare nodded and he grabbed the softball bat before continuing to the hall. No sign of Paul, but his spread for pages twelve and thirteen, a shadowy figure taunting terrified children in a dark alley, had been taped to the drawing board when they'd left the house. Only scraps of tape remained. *Goddammit. Now I have to do it again.*

"He took an inked spread," Sean said as he stomped to the stairs. "I swear, this comic will never get done."

"Fucker." Mare stood between the back door and the laundry room, her back to the corner and the gun pointed toward the floor. The metal had already begun to frost in the humidity.

Sean flicked on the stairwell light and thundered down. The mess looked diminished and rearranged, but Paul was nowhere to be seen, not even behind the furniture or under the stairs.

Muttering, he hoisted himself into the hole. Both puddles in the near corners held slime, and a third slime pocket had newly become visible in the back. The slime to the left had faint bubbles coming from its hazy surface. He'd seen the tiny bubbles before, when Betsy the dog and other animals spored in the back yard. In about ten, twelve hours the bubbles would turn to ooze and the slime would start to dissolve. The other nearby pocket remained fuzzy and bubble free.

He climbed out and glanced at his watch. *Maybe somewhere around three am for the first one. Whee.*

He checked the windows while he was in the basement and locked the two he found unlatched. He saw no obvious grit or footprints beneath.

Once upstairs, he checked other windows. All but the laundry room were already latched, as they should have been. The washing machine had mud and grit in its otherwise empty drum so he examined the window closer.

"He came in that way?" Mare asked.

"I think so," Sean replied, stretching to reach the latch. "Was the only one unlocked, but I know we locked it yesterday." He flicked the lever over and pressed past Mare. "Gonna try something."

Out in the backyard, he saw a few new critter-sized slimes but shrugged them off. No holes big enough to bury a person had yet been dug. *Probably tonight, then.* He strode the couple of steps to the laundry room window and tried to open it from the outside. A couple of jiggles later, the top frame bounced off the track, rendering the latch useless. "Tricky bastard," he muttered, before trying other windows. They all remained in place.

Despite her initial nervousness, Mindy managed in Todd's kitchen easily enough. He had a big skillet, a whisk, and adequate measuring tools. She had to pound the chicken with a can of baked beans and zest the lemon with a box grater, but she didn't mind. It was so nice to cook for someone special. Todd had changed into jeans and a polo shirt, and he hovered in the living room, basking in the aroma but never getting in her way or interrupting.

She hummed as she worked her way through the recipe in her head. She couldn't remember how much wine or lemon juice, so she modified the sauce by instinct until it tasted glorious.

"Can you get plates and silverware?" she asked as she carried the pot of pasta to the colander in the sink. "Maybe a couple of wine glasses?"

Todd leapt to be of service and took a deep, pleased breath as she arranged everything on a platter. "This is amazing," he said, following her to the table.

"I hope it tastes as good as you remember," she said as she placed a hearty portion on his plate. He poured the wine and insisted he was sure it would be ever better.

As they ate, she relished his blissful sighs and how he slowed down to savor and swoon over every bite. *Always nice to cook for a happy eater.*

"So what made you decide to do this?" he asked as he placed another cutlet on his plate.

"I love to cook and, well, you've just been so nice to me," she said, trying not to feel self conscious under his warm scrutiny. "Even that first day, when I came out of the trees, you were nice. I don't think anyone else that day was, other than Sean. There's not much I can do to say thanks for…for never treating me like a freak."

"You're not a freak. You're just a person out of her time."

She toyed with her pasta and sighed. "Yeah, I guess I am."

"Hey," he said, drawing her gaze to him. "It's going to be okay. We'll get your ex. Make him pay."

"It's not him, not really," she said. "It's more I've never really had a chance to do anything before. But now..." She blushed and lowered her eyes. "I met with some really important people today, and I didn't get nervous or screw up once. I have a couple hundred fans following me online. I've started my own business. All these things I never would have done, never could have done, if I hadn't died."

He reached for her hand and she let him grasp it as she met his quiet, concerned gaze. She felt tears sting. "I want Jeff to pay for being so rotten to my mother after my death. I want him to pay for the crap that's happened these past couple of days. But, in a weird way, killing me was a gift. I'm a new, better person because of it. I just want him to leave me alone to live my life. Is that too much to ask?"

"No. It's generous, actually. Considering." He squeezed her hand then let it go. "You have every right to be angry, you know."

"I was," she admitted after a sip of wine. "I was hurt. Furious. But then I realized he hadn't taken anything but time. I'm back. I'm still me. I still have my memories, my dreams. The only thing I don't have is him and that's just fine."

"What about your family? Your mother and sister?"

She set down her wine. "Mom died a few days ago. Her heart just quit. Dani sent an email, told me not to come to the funeral. Said it was my fault Mom died so quickly after I came back."

"I'm sorry."

"Me, too. Mare took me to the cemetery the day after the funeral to put flowers on her grave, so I got to say goodbye. I just hope Dani can forgive me."

"For what? For coming back? For being given another chance?"

She looked at him and shrugged.

"She should have been thrilled." Todd set aside his fork and stared into her eyes. "I understand fear. I do. I see it every day. But if I'd lost someone I loved like that, I can't imagine being mad at them for coming back. Fear passes. Family remains."

"It's not that simple. She has her own family and it's all over the news, the internet, that we're making some people sick."

"But, you're not. That's media hype," he insisted, his voice firm and unyielding. "I've dealt with hysteria since the beginning and can assure you that you're not the problem at all. It's the crap in the water. It makes things... *More*. If you're sick, you get sicker. If you're fast you get faster. It's made junkies more addicted and thugs angrier and assholes more assholier."

"Really?"

"Yes. Scientists and medical people have been crawling all over this stuff these past two weeks. They don't yet understand how, but it's a weird fungal enhancer. It grows healthy cells, improves them, streamlines them, makes them more efficient throughout the body. They say it enhances brain activity in the front lobe. Creativity. Focus. Energy. Personality. That all gets stronger, even in non-spores. But, if there's a problem, a mental dysfunction or a chronic disease, it's enhanced, too."

"So my mom's heart disease…"

"It got worse. Fast. Not because of you, but because this stuff's in the ground water, probably has been for a while. She'd been drinking it for weeks and, given this stuff's potency, her death was inevitable. It's not your fault. You're a victim of this too. A lucky one, yes, but still helpless to prevent it."

He took a sip of wine. "The CDC told us that's why only otherwise healthy accident victims spored. For anyone who died from disease, sporing caused the disease to explode in the fungal bodies, taking over the healthy cells and killing them again before they'd fully formed. It's a mixed bag. Some folks re-grew lost limbs, others dropped dead of a previously managed illness. Between all of the unexpected death calls, hyped up paranoia, and the missing kids, we're getting run ragged at work.

"People are scared. The reality is that the world's changing and sooner or later we'll all get heart disease or diabetes or cancer. When we do," he snapped his fingers, "that'll be the end of that."

Mindy nodded and reached out to touch his hand. She'd seen too many relatives die slowly and in great pain, weak and gasping for every desperate breath. "At least we won't suffer. Won't linger endlessly in agony anymore."

Todd lowered his gaze and picked at his plate.

"What?" she asked. "What don't you want to tell me?"

"Spores are different," he said, pausing before looking into her eyes again. "We've had a problem with…"

"With what?" she asked, worried.

"One of the spores…" He muttered a curse and drained his glass of wine before refilling it. "He disappeared a few days ago, kidnapped, and we found him tortured." He drained the second glass and pushed away his plate, his gaze pained. "He healed. You heal. That scratch on your face from this morning? It's already gone."

Mindy reached up to touch her cheek. She felt no welt, no pain. Even her beaten back had stopped hurting. "Oh boy."

"There are a lot of sick freaks out there. This stuff in the water might make them more vicious, and a spore, someone like you who heals rapidly, could last longer and endure more. There's a lot of play value in a victim who won't easily die. With millions at stake, there's no telling how far an ass like your ex might go, especially if he's amped up by the fungus."

"Don't," she said, pushing away from the table as she gathered up her dirty dishes.

He stood, following her to the sink. "I just need you to be careful. Extra careful."

The dishes clattered as she stacked them on the counter. Trembling, she turned to face him. He towered over her, a massive wall of muscle and intimidation, but Mindy felt no threat, no scorn, only the calm assurance of safety and fortitude.

She thought he might kiss her—and she was pretty sure she'd let him. She blushed and managed to smile. "Thanks."

He blinked, his mouth falling open for a moment. "Why are you thanking me?"

"For caring." She started toward the table to gather up the rest of the supper mess, but paused to kiss his cheek.

When she returned, hands full of plates and wine glasses, he stood where she'd left him, watching her, an astounded smile teasing his lips.

Mindy skirted past him, feeling his gaze on her. "Let me just get these washed up. Do you have a something I can put the leftovers in?"

"Yeah," he said, moving toward the cupboards in the corner. "Let me get you a—" His phone rang, and he glowered and muttered a curse before excusing himself to answer it, leaving Mindy to smile as she located the bowl herself.

Laundry room window nailed shut. Check. Doors locked and barricaded. Check. Deputy still outside. Check. Sean sat at the drawing board with a glass of iced tea and tried not to worry.

Mare turned on her music—a well loved Madonna CD—and he relaxed as she belted out *Nothing to forget, all the pain was worth it* while clanging around the kitchen.

That's my Mare. Nothing keeps you down for long. He practiced a few brush strokes to loosen his hand before returning to the latest cell, three children tied in the dark while spore slime bubbled behind them.

He had the kids brushed in, and the main shadows on and around the spores when Mare, singing *Good little girls never show it*, moved from the kitchen to the bathroom. He heard the faint clink of the toilet lid hitting the tank over her singing *Do you know? Do you know?*

Then Mare screamed.

Sean shot out of his studio and rushed to her, knocking aside a kitchen chair in his haste. She stood in the bathroom, pants wadded below her knees, screeching, her hands and thighs smeared with blood.

"Sean! Oh my God! Sean!" she wailed, reaching for him then drawing her hands back as if loath to touch him with her stained palms. "What's happening? Am I dying? Oh, Sean!"

Clots and dribbles of blood twirled in the toilet and her underwear was a gruesome mess. He swallowed. They'd both heard, hell, everyone had heard, how people were dropping dead from unexpected diseases. *Not Mare. Please, anyone but Mare.*

Despite the blood, he held her, shaking in his arms. "It'll be okay. You'll be fine. Let's get you to the hospital."

She nodded and whimpered as he cleaned her up, helped her put on fresh clothes. "I've been hurting for a couple of weeks now," she said as he found her shoes. "Belly cramps. I just thought it was a stomach bug or too much greasy food, not something…" She tugged at her hair and rocked like a child trying to soothe herself. "Not anything bad. I should have gone in right away. Should have had someone check."

He held her face in his hands and kissed her. "It's okay. You're going to be fine." Shoes on, he helped her up and held her close as they staggered to the front door, Madonna wailing about nothing equaling nothing. Sean struggled not to wail himself. Wailing would not help anyone. And, no matter the cost, no matter the task, he had to help Mare.

She clenched at him, her hands like talons against his arm. "My mom, my grandma, they died from cervical cancer."

"I know, babe, I know," he soothed as he helped her down the steps.

"I thought that, maybe, since all that stuff was removed when I was a kid I'd be okay. I wouldn't—"

They reached the car and he opened the door for her, eased her in. "It's not cancer," he assured her. "Shh. Let's get you to the hospital."

"It has to be!" she sobbed, her face in her hands as he hurried around and slid behind the wheel.

"Maybe we were too rambunctious last night," he suggested, backing out then speeding down the road. "Maybe it's just a burst blood vessel or something."

"People are dying! I see it every day at work. Just fine, then bam! They're dead. And now it's my turn. Oh, God, oh Sean. I'm only twenty-nine. It's too soon. I can't leave you!"

He grasped her hand and squeezed it. "Shh. You're not going to die. This is fixable. It has to be."

Traffic was uncooperative, too many hay mowers and weekend dawdlers on the road on this rare sunny day, but he managed to keep her coherent if not completely calm as he rushed her to the hospital in Boone.

A hospital worker stood at the emergency room door with a clipboard. "Accident, illness, or unknown?"

"Unknown," Sean said. "She just started bleeding."

The clerk asked their names and symptoms and Sean gave her the details. Once past the sentry, they entered to find the emergency room awash with people gasping for breath, looking pale, haggard, and terrified. He located a chair for Mare before he stood in line at the registration desk.

He often looked over his shoulder, terrified she too, would start fading. All around, people moaned in pain and fear.

The digital check-in requested insurance information, medical history, all the standard crap, so he knelt before Mare and hurried, asking her when he didn't know the answers.

They were almost done, checking off family history issues, when the middle-aged man beside Mare hitched a pained breath and fell forward, landing with a loose smack on the floor beside Sean.

Mare screamed and covered her mouth as she lurched toward the woman hacking and coughing on the other side. The old woman across the aisle from them whimpered and daubed at her oozing face with a grimy hankie, but the others sighed and looked away. Sean reached over to roll the man onto his back, but dead, unseeing eyes stared at him. No one seemed to care.

Mare silently rocked herself, her eyes closed.

"Look at me," Sean said and Mare did, her whole body quivering. "I am going to take this to the receptionist and be right back, all right?"

"Hurry. Don't leave me here to die alone."

He hurried. When he returned, he stepped over the dead guy to sit beside her, to hold and cradle her. No one came for the dead guy for almost half an hour and he was thrown onto a cart and pushed away like a load of dirty laundry. Sean saw four others fall dead to the floor while waiting to see a doctor, and he lost count of those who simply slumped unconscious against their neighbor. Three hours later, they called Mare's name. Other than crushing fear, she seemed unchanged, no worse, but no better. He tried to feel encouraged, but found it impossible in the sea of death and dying.

Blood smeared her chair when she stood, but he ushered her away from it, hoping she wouldn't see. Dark blood stained the crotch of her capris. No one seemed to notice them stagger past.

Haggard nurses helped her onto an examination table and asked many of the same questions he'd already answered on her digital check in. They requested he leave while they helped her undress. She protested, demanding he stay, but the nurses were insistent.

He remained in the hall outside her exam room, pacing and terrified, until they let him back in. Mare lay on the table in a hospital gown, her knees up under a thin blanket, a soaking pad beneath her, and she reached for him, both hands grasping until she clenched his shirt, his skin. Her pale, sweat-tacky face gleamed blotchy in the bright fluorescents, and, despite the heavy stink of antiseptic, he smelled death lingering in the air.

"She asked me if I was afraid of you," she muttered, glaring at the nurse who readied a tray of instruments and swabs. "If you'd ever hurt me."

He stroked her hair, one arm cradling her against his belly as if drawing her into him could erase their fear. "It's okay. It's just their job."

"I'm lying here bleeding and they ask insulting questions like that. I know it's their job, but, dammit!"

"It's okay, babe. Everything's okay." He leaned over to kiss her and tell her he loved her. *They can accuse me of anything they want, as long as you'll be all right.*

The nurse continued to lay out instruments without any sign she cared about Mare's rant. Another nurse bustled in with a clipboard and more questions about Mare's accident—she'd been impaled falling through a tree when she was eight—and the subsequent hysterectomy, about her family's history of cervical cancer, and about their sex life, complete with blunt questions about force, coercion, and violence which only served to further aggravate Mare.

Mare was still giving the nurse her opinion of those questions when a middle-aged woman entered, yawning. She introduced herself as Dr. Ledders, then skimmed the nurses' notes before looking into Mare's eyes and taking one of her hands. "Okay, Rosemary, we're going to figure out what we have going on, all right? Gonna start with a quick pelvic and have a look see. Just hang with me a little longer."

Mare nodded and clenched Sean's hand tighter. He took a breath and tried not to let his terror show.

Instruments in and poking around, Mare buried her face into Sean's belly as Dr. Ledders glanced up, frowning. "How complete was your hysterectomy?"

"They saved my left ovary and vagina," she said, voice muffled against his shirt. "Nothing else. Was just too damaged."

"Well, you have a cervix now. Going to take some samples." Ledders inserted a skinny probe-looking thing and it came out bloody. She handed it to a waiting nurse, then inserted yet another instrument, then a long swab. A few more probes, then she removed the last of the bloody instruments and reached into Mare with a gloved hand.

"Oh God." Mare scrunched her eyes closed and shook her head. "It can't be there. My mom and grandmother died from cervical cancer."

"I feel a mass," Ledders said, palpating Mare's belly. "Beside your left ovary."

No no no no no. Sean thought his knees would buckle, but he managed to remain standing even as Mare began to quietly weep.

Ledders poked and palpated then removed her hand and gloves. She stood and came to the side of the exam table and, once again, took Mare's hand. "We're going to get you prepped for an ultrasound. Get a good look at what's happening in there. All right?"

"Is it cancer?" Mare asked, her voice small and quavering.

"I don't know. We need to take a look, okay? If it is cancer, with luck, you came in quick enough we can give you another hysterectomy and clear it up. We've had a few patients we've managed to save. But we have to take it all out before it has a chance to metastasize. But ultrasound first. Then surgery right after, if needed. Okay?"

Mare nodded. "Okay. Can Sean stay with me?"

Ledders squeezed her hand. "Until you're being prepped for surgery. Just let me talk to him for a moment, all right?"

Mare nodded and Sean kissed her before following Ledders out the door on the far side of the exam room. Medical personnel rushed past, their faces drawn with fatigue.

Ledders regarded Sean with a cool stare. "I know who you are," she said. "We all do. You're that friendly guy on TV who keeps telling us this is a miracle. Does it look like a miracle now?"

An orderly pushed a gurney with two bodies piled upon it. One an old woman, the other a man in his twenties.

"No," Sean said, his belly twisting in shame and fear. "This isn't. I only meant—"

"Yeah, the people who've come back. They're the miracle. But their fungus is a plague. Thousands have died. Millions will before it's over. Your girlfriend will quite possibly become one of them." Ledders paused to watch him. "Still excited about this blessing?"

He swallowed the bitter taste of bile. "Mare's going to die?"

"I told her the truth, it all depends on what we find. With her history and the strange things we've seen lately, it could be anything. But if it *is* cervical or uterine cancer that's reached the bleeding point, the chances of her not already metastasizing are essentially nil. If it's that advanced, there's nothing we can do for her. But right now, we just don't know."

Sean felt his knees weaken and he stumbled backwards to lean against the wall. He let out a shuddering sob. *Oh, Mare. Oh, babe.*

Ledders took a step toward him, trapping him, forcing him to hear. "Not everything hits the news. This fungus you've been lauding has infiltrated rivers and ground water throughout the entire Mississippi river basin. Iowa is lost. Missouri. Most of Illinois, Arkansas, Tennessee… There are frantic reports coming in from Wisconsin and Minnesota.

Kentucky. They expect to start seeing mass deaths in Mississippi and Louisiana by the middle of next week. We've been carting bodies away in trucks for three days now. They die so quickly, we can't keep up."

"I didn't know," Sean choked out.

"Now you do. The CDC is warning Ohio for next weekend. The Dakotas. Kansas. Essentially every community, every state between the Appalachians and Rockies will be infected. We will lose perhaps a third of the Midwest's population. Millions will die, most didn't have to. They had treatment options before your little blessing arrived. We are helpless to stop it, to treat it. And no one knows what'll happen once it reaches the gulf. If sea water doesn't kill this fungus, it'll infect the entire planet in a matter of weeks. Nowhere will be safe."

She poked him in the chest with a single finger. "You've been celebrating a potential global epidemic. The unwarranted deaths of perhaps billions of people. Why don't you think about that the next time you have a little press conference. Show a little respect, okay? A little gravitas."

She gave him one more withering look then stomped away to confer with a nurse before continuing to the next exam room, the next doomed patient.

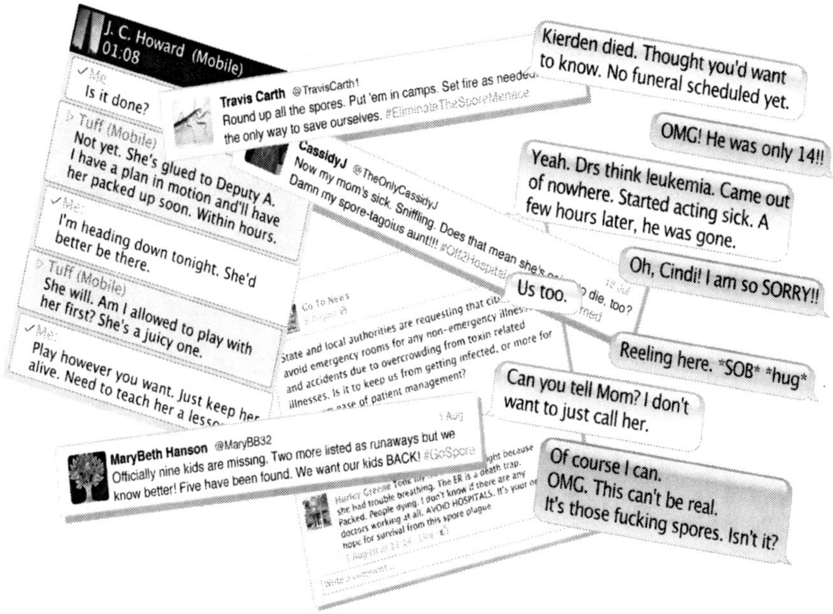

Chapter Twenty-Four

Todd held the phone away from his head to lessen the pain of screams pounding against his ear. "Mom. Calm down. What's wrong?"

"She's gone! Oh, Todd! I was right there and she's gone!"

Hailey?! He took a staggering step, then another, then fell, hard, to his knees. "What do you mean, gone?"

His mother sobbed her answers in staggering bursts. "We were doing lawn work. There in the front yard. I was raking up grass clippings. The mail came and she wanted to fetch it from the mailbox. She scampered off to it. I had my back to the road and when I turned to see what mail had come, she was gone. Just gone."

Mindy stood at the edge of the kitchen, watching him while terror and confusion struggled to control her face. She clutched a dishtowel and raised it to her mouth, when

Todd barked, "Hailey can't be GONE!!"

"I was right there! I swear!" his mother wailed. "Not ten feet away! I thought it was all right to let her fetch the mail. Oh, God, what have I done?"

He tottered to his feet, his head reeling. "And you didn't hear anything? See anything?"

"Just the mailman pulling up. When I turned around, he was opening a mailbox just two doors down the street. It had only been a few moments."

"Fuck fuck fuck fuck." Todd balled his hands at his temples. *My gun's upstairs. My badge.* He ran for the stairs, shaking the house as he thundered up. "Did you call the office? Local PD?"

"Yes. They're on their way."

He burst into his bedroom and yanked his badge and gun off the bedside table. "I'm on my way, too. Who's the mailman?"

"Evan something. Our regular Saturday guy. He was just really late today."

"I'll get someone to stop him." *How can I find her before he hurts her? Fuck!*

"I don't know how it happened. I was right there!"

It only takes a second. Fuck! Hailey! Daddy's coming! Todd thundered back down the stairs. "I'm on my way, Mom. Answer whatever questions they have. Maybe we can save her. Maybe there's still time."

Mindy stood near the door, lower lip quivering as he rushed down the stairs. "What can I do to help?"

Can't leave her unguarded, can't not look for Hailey. Fuck me and my fucking job!

"Get in the car." He shoved past her and out the door.

She followed without comment and was in the passenger seat, reaching for the seatbelt, as he shot the SUV out of the driveway and screamed it down the road, sirens blaring.

Mindy pressed herself against the door not because of fear, but because she wanted to remain out of his way. Todd drove like a crazed beast, whipping past cars while yelling into his radio mic. She bit her lip when he told the dispatcher she could fuck herself, it was his daughter who was missing, all while taking a corner at more than forty miles per hour one handed.

They reached the opposite side of Boone in what felt like moments, not minutes, barreling into a neighborhood of two-story craftsman homes with compact, well maintained yards. Five police and sheriff vehicles blocked the road and two cops frisked a terrified mailman against his delivery truck.

Todd flipped the SUV into park and was out the door and across the yard before

Mindy finished unbuckling her seatbelt.

She exited the SUV to see him push both local cops aside and flip the mailman around to face him. She heard him growl, saw him expand his already considerable bulk into a raging tower of fury.

"What the fuck did you see?" he snarled, bending to be nose to nose with the mailman. "Did you see her come for the mail? Did you speak to her at all?"

Mindy was stopped by a young deputy with his arms out to halt her. She stretched and craned her neck to see past him, unable to imagine what horror Todd was going through.

The poor mailman shook his head and she heard him blubber, "No. I didn't talk to her. The little girl waved as I pulled up, and she ran to talk to Mrs. Anderson," he said, pointing at Todd's mother bawling on the stoop. "I put the mail in the box and moved on to the next house, then the next. I didn't see anything else. We're timed. There's a schedule, and the mail was really late from Des Moines. I don't have time to even look behind when I'm—"

"I do not give a flying fuck about your schedule or late mail," Todd growled, shaking off the two cops who tried to drag him away. "Did you see any other vehicles? Any pedestrians who aren't normal for this neighborhood?"

"Um. A couple of cars, but there's always some different car somewhere. And folks walk dogs, push kids in strollers…" He ran a shaky hand over his head. "Crap. I don't pay much attention."

"I want full, complete descriptions of them. Now. Any people? Delivery trucks? Workmen?"

The mailman blinked, eyes widening. "There was a truck! Yes. Plumber, I think. Parked right there," he said, pointing toward Todd's SUV, sitting half on the road, half on the sidewalk in front of the neighbor's house. "I had to drive around it and nearly got creamed by some kids in a Nissan with a blown muffler."

Todd turned and barked at the deputy who blocked Mindy's approach. "Gunders! Find out which neighbor called a plumber today. Now. Ask, too, about some kid with a loud Nissan." He glanced at the mailman. "What color was the Nissan?"

"Black. Dented on the passenger side."

"Get that, Gunders?"

The deputy nodded. "Yessir. I'm on it, sir."

The deputy rushed to the neighbor's house and Mindy approached Todd's mother. Deb slumped on the front steps, bawling. Mindy sat beside her and whispered, "It'll be all right. He'll find her."

"It's my fault," Deb whimpered, leaning against Mindy's shoulder. "I should have gone with her, should have watched instead of raking."

Mindy drew her arm around Deb's plump shoulders and soothed her as best she could. The rake and leaf bag lay mid yard, a step or so to the right of the walkway leading from the public sidewalk to the house. They were, at most, fifteen feet from the mailbox. *A few steps. A scant few moments. So quick. So close. Whoever grabbed Hailey was waiting. Waiting for her.*

Todd walked up to them, fury on his face but fear in his eyes. "Talk to me, Mom," he whispered, kneeling before them.

Deb explained that she'd decided to mow because it finally was a sunny day, and how she made Hailey stay on the porch while she mowed. Hailey had held the bags while Deb filled them with clippings, like she always did. Then the mail came.

"I looked up when I heard that awful muffler. The Snyder kid, from a couple blocks down," she said. "And I saw the mailman nearly hit him. Hailey did, too. He was coming to deliver our mail and she asked if she could go get it. I held her hand, just like you told me to, and even though it was just Evan like every Saturday, I waited for him to finish with our mail and pull away, then I let her go get it. I raked, just a couple of strokes. That's all. Moments. And she was just gone."

"Check the mailbox," he said to the nearest deputy. The young man turned without comment. "Did you see a plumbing truck?" he asked his mother.

"No. No plumber. But there was a mechanic's van. It had been there most of the day."

"Mechanic?"

Deb nodded, sniffling, and pointed across the street. "Yeah. Two guys. I think. They were doing something at the Decker's garage. Back and forth since this morning."

"I'll check," a city cop said then jogged across the street.

Mindy met Todd's terrified gaze. She'd seen no work van of any kind.

"Mail's still here," the deputy called out. He wore a glove on his right hand and closed the mailbox door again before taking a wide berth around the area.

Todd grasped his mother's hands. "Mom, look at me."

Deb took a shaky breath then complied, a tear rolling down her cheek. "I'm sorry."

"I know." He moistened his lips then asked, "Was the van there when you turned around and saw Hailey was gone?"

Deb's eyes drifted closed and her lower lip turned in. She bit it and shook her head. "No. They'd pulled into the Rothburg's driveway and were backing up to turn around."

Todd stood and squinted at the road and driveway. Nodding, he pulled out his cell phone and punched a couple of numbers. "Brad? My daughter's been snatched. Might be tire tracks in the neighbor's driveway. Maybe trace near the mailbox. And track her cell.

She knows to keep it in her pocket."

Todd pulled away from the phone to tell everyone to cordon off the Rothburg's driveway, all of the Decker's yard, and everything in a wedge-shaped area between the leaf sack and the road. All unoccupied officers rushed to help.

Mindy marveled at his ability to command the men and to control his own certain rage and panic. *I'd be a whimpering basket case. Useless.*

Another siren approached as Todd finished up with Brad. He pocketed the phone took a breath as he turned to his mother and Mindy. "Our best investigator is on the way. Just sit tight."

He began pacing, hands clenching and unclenching. Mindy wished she could offer some comfort, but instead she cradled his bawling mother and watched as another sheriff's car pulled up.

A middle-aged man got out and walked to them, his face stern. "Anderson!"

While the other deputies made themselves scarce, Todd watched the official approach. The worry on his face turned into harsh rigidity and defiance. "Yes, sir?"

"You are not on this case."

"Sir, it's my daughter. I'm not leaving."

"You've been assigned to protective detail. I suggest you return to it, immediately, or face disciplinary action."

"I haven't left my detail. Sir." Todd said, holding his ground. "And I will not desert my daughter. She's all I have."

"We'll find her," the older man said, grasping Todd's upper arm. "I'll take over until Jorst gets here, but you need to leave. Now. Your mind's in the wrong place and we all know you can't be impartial."

Todd took a breath and began to speak, but the other man cut him off. "It's not a suggestion. Back down, or hand over your badge and spend your evening sitting in a cell charged with interfering in an investigation."

"We'll find her," one of the younger deputies said, his blue eyes earnest and sure.

Todd muttered a curse then stomped up the steps beside Mindy and thundered into the house. She turned, watching his furious retreat, and wished she could help.

"Go," his mother said. "Help him."

She pushed away from Mindy's consoling embrace then faced the man who peered down at her. "Ask me whatever you need to, Sheriff. Put me on a lie detector. Get me hypnotized, torture me, I don't care. I want my granddaughter back."

"Take her to the police station for an official statement," the sheriff said to the nearest deputy who helped Deb stand and walk to a cruiser. The sheriff turned to the other men and barked orders. Mindy, otherwise ignored, retreated into the house to find Todd.

There were no clocks in the Imaging Services waiting room and all of the magazines were three months old, but at least the TV was showing *Law and Order* reruns. Sean brought Mare another glass of water—they'd instructed her to drink at least a quart of fluid so her full bladder would push up whatever had grown inside her. He sat beside her and reached for her hand.

They'd left the ER a couple of hours before, at his best guess, and while they weren't the only people waiting to be scanned, Mare was, by far, in the best shape. An older couple sat in the corner, the woman twitching and her eyes rolling back in her head. Across sat a young guy, maybe partway through college, whose skin had taken on a greenish cast as he daubed at the endless trickle of blood leaking from his nose. A small child lay across her mother's lap, gasping for breath, and an obese, middle-aged man had leaned into a corner and fallen asleep, but his phlegmy snores had shorted out and stopped a good twenty minutes ago.

Sean tried not to look at the fly crawling in and out of the dead guy's gaping mouth, or the resigned stares from the other patients and their families. He did his best to remain thankful that Mare looked stressed but otherwise fine in her ever-so-stylish double-layered hospital gown and soaking pad.

"Why are you here?" an older woman asked them. She, too, wore a hospital gown that she had to hold at her throat to avoid exposing herself. Her shoulder had grown to an enormous size, as if someone had shoved a cantaloupe beneath her skin, and she wore one gown under that arm, and another draped over. Sean had made a point not to glance her way for fear he'd get yelled at for glimpsing her boob.

"An ultrasound," he said as other waiting patients turned their dying gazes his way.

"Problems with a pregnancy?" an older gentleman asked while his wife snored on his shoulder. She had a lumpy sprawl of crust that covered most of her face and obliterated one eye. When they'd arrived it had mainly been on her lower cheek and chin.

Sean squeezed Mare's hand. *Pregnant. If only.* "No. Not pregnant. A rupture of some kind."

The old fellow nodded with bleak understanding and everyone looked up as an exhausted imaging tech came in with a folder. "Rosemary Knudsen?"

"That's us," Sean said as he helped Mare stand. She hesitated, but took a deep breath and staggered to the technician. Sean grabbed her bloody sitting pad and folded it as he followed them both.

Once Mare was on the table, the tech squirted blue goop over the mass of scars on Mare's lower belly, their presence a fading record of her childhood accident and life-changing surgery.

Sean bit his quivering lip to still it as he watched the tech glide her scanner over the familiar twists, puckers and lines. *Would Mare have chosen me if she'd been whole? Would she have gotten sick sooner? Not at all? How different would life had been with children? How different will it be without her?*

The lines had woven a wall between them, a small wall to be sure, but a wall nonetheless. She had refused to marry him because of those lines, had cried over them, had considered herself diminished because of them. But they had faded. Soon they might be gone. Soon they might take her with them, forever.

Sean choked back a sob and grasped Mare's hand. The ultrasound's computer screen flickered and shifted, showing blood flows and unidentifiable globs. The technician used a measuring tool to mark various things on the screen which, to Sean, looked like everything else, then she moved on to other random mish-mashes of dark and light flickers and splots.

She scanned for a long time on Mare's left side, near the far edge of the scar cluster, returning often to focus on a pair of neighboring globs with smaller dots and fibrous looking structures inside. He thought each larger glob looked like an oblong pomegranate after it had been cut open, round little pods organized around a central fibrous mass. The smaller circles and fiber strands were measured, along with the distance between the two larger masses.

"That's it, isn't it?" Mare asked.

"I can't say, ma'am," the technician replied as she typed something into her keyboard and the image on screen froze.

"Can't or won't? It's my life we're trying to save here."

"Both." Another shift of the scanning wand, another frozen image. "The hospital won't allow me to comment on what I see. I'm just a tech, not a diagnostic specialist or surgeon."

Sean flinched. *She said surgeon.*

Mare didn't flinch, she got mad. "It's my life! I demand to know what you're looking at."

"I can't tell you, other than it's a complete scan of your reproductive system along with special focus on any abnormalities or unexpected findings. If you have questions, please ask your doctor." A few more scans, clicks, and pictures later, the ultrasound finished and they were ushered out with instructions to return to the imaging waiting room.

By the time they got there, the woman with the crust on her face had died.

Chapter Twenty-Five

Mindy watched Todd struggle to control his emotions as he started the SUV and eased away from the police and sheriff vehicles at his mother's. They worked their way across town in the gathering twilight, and he said nothing, merely hitched a catching breath now and then. Mindy sat beside him, unsure what to say to ease his pain.

He pulled into his driveway and turned off the SUV. He sat there, trembling, hands balled on his thighs, while silence closed around them like a dark and deadly shroud. "I want to find him. To *slaughter* him. I need to make him pay for hurting my girl."

"I know," she said, laying her hand on his.

He grasped her hand. Held it. Squeezed it. "How… How can I do nothing?" he asked the windshield. "How can I not track this monster when I know what he'll do to her if I don't stop him?"

"I don't know. What do you tell other parents when…"

His head sagged and he shuddered, silently sobbing for a few moments. "I tell them that we'll do our best to save their child." He took a shaky breath and turned his head to stare at her. "It's all bullshit. Meaningless."

"I know," she said. "But it gives them hope."

"This freak…" He paused, lower lip curling in. "He steals children, cuts off their feet, repeatedly rapes them, disembowels them alive, then rapes them again. And then when those precious kids are cold, rotting husks, he tosses them in a ditch or field to be eaten by bugs and coyotes until some poor soul stumbles over them."

He stared at the windshield. "There is no fucking hope. He's had her almost two hours. Her feet are already gone. She's been raped in every potential orifice. And she's probably been or soon will be gutted. My baby's gone. She's dead. And I couldn't save her."

He shook his head, low, trembling sounds coming from his throat, then he cried, "I couldn't save her from her mother, and I couldn't save her from this. I'm a shitty father, a shitty, shitty—"

"No, you're not!" Mindy said, her voice cutting through the dark. "You're a good father, a good man. Don't take the blame for the actions of a psychopath. It's not your fault."

He bawled in great, heaving sobs, and let her draw him close and cradle him as best she could despite the guns and gadgets in their way. "I swear, it's not your fault," she whispered. "It's not your mom's fault. It's no one's fault but his. Blame him. He deserves your anger. No one else."

They sat there, twisted around the tools of his trade, until he pulled away and fished a handkerchief from his pocket. He blew his nose and settled himself. "Thank you."

"You're welcome. I wish I could do more."

An awkward silence lingered, then Todd cleared his throat. "It's late. I should take you home."

"You don't need to face this alone," she said, touching his hand as he reached for the ignition. "Sean and Mare don't need me. We can stay here, if you want to." She drew her hand away. "Or you can take me back if you'd rather be alone. It's really up to you. I don't want to intrude."

"You're not intruding." He wiped at his eyes. "You sure you can stay? It'll be a long, ugly night."

"I'm sure."

He gathered his files and she followed him to the house. While he paced and cried over marker-makeup Barbie, Mindy made tea. When he stood at the back door, staring out to the night, Mindy rotated laundry and folded the stuff out of the dryer. Midnight approached and the police radio on the counter offered no hope; their concerned chatter led only to dead ends and frustration. So Mindy made more tea. She listened to stories of Hailey, of her birth, her babyhood, of preschool, of how she was a squirrel in the spring play at school.

"Was because of her red hair," Todd said, staring into his steaming mug of Earl Gray. "But Mom made her this tail, a huge bushy thing with a wire frame, the same color as her hair. And she could shake it, the tail, with a hunk of string wrapped around her wrist. Was the cutest thing." He sighed and she saw teardrops fall into his tea and onto the table. "I've called her my squirrel girl ever since."

Mindy squeezed his hand. He'd barely let go since they'd sat at the kitchen table. "You're a great dad."

He nodded and sipped, then stared past her, his eyes growing distant, and she held his hand and waited for him.

"She wanted to go to Disney. I told her we couldn't, it was too expensive. But I already had the trip booked for late August, right before school starts. Just us two. A real vaca—"

His cell phone rang, a perky Celtic tune with a girl singing about touching the sky. He ripped the phone from his pocket and stared at it, crazed laughter burbling from him. "Hailey!" he gasped. "Thank God! Where are y—"

His obvious relief evaporated and he snarled, "Let me talk to my daughter, you fuck!"

Mindy drew back her hand and covered her mouth. *She's alive! Oh, thank you, God for saving her. Thank you, thank—*

Todd pushed something on the face of his phone and thrust it at her. "They want to talk to you."

He stood, moving quickly to a nearby cabinet drawer as Mindy held the phone to her ear, her hand shaking. "He… *Hello*?"

"Yo, bitch," the muffled voice said on speaker phone. "We have a little girl here who *really* wants to see her daddy."

"Give her back." Mindy pulled the phone away from her ear and looked wide-eyed at Todd as he silently laid a tape recorder in front of her and pushed RECORD.

"Oooh, not so fast, spore bitch," the voice said loud enough to be recorded. Todd held a finger to his lips and gently grasped her hand to position the phone near her mouth and directly over the recorder. "We need to make us a little…arrangement."

Mindy reached for Todd and grasped his forearm, holding it against her as if his relieved and quaking presence could keep her steady. "What sort of arrangement?"

"What do you think? You or her. One of you won't make it to morning and the winner is up to you. You willing to kill a kid so you can keep writing some stupid blog? Somehow, I don't think that's in your makeup, Minders."

Minders?!? Fucking goddamn Jeff! she thought, looking at Todd as he mouthed Jeff's name. *I know you're not the creeper so you did all this, you even kidnapped Todd's daughter, because I dared to stand up to you and make you accountable for what you've done?* "Where? How?" Mindy snapped before Todd could coach her otherwise. "Don't you dare hurt her."

The muffled voice laughed. "It's not her you should be worried about. We're going to have a fun time before dawn, oh yes."

Todd thrust a note in front of her nose. *Ask to talk to Hailey. Need proof she's alive.*

Mindy ground her teeth. *So help me God, I will hunt you down and cut off your nuts for this, Jeff.* "Let me talk to Hailey. Now. Or I'm hanging up."

Todd gaped, his eyes wide, and shook his head, mouthing, *No, don't hang up!*

"Eh, whaa..." The voice said, fumbling.

"You heard me, *Jeffy*. Let me talk to the kid. If you want me, if you want to finish teaching me that lesson, you'll have to prove she's all right. I'm not doing squat until I talk to her."

The phone remained silent for a heartbeat of time. Then two. Mindy said, "What's the matter, Jeff? Chicken? Gotta hurt little girls to prove you're still a man?"

"Fucking bitch! Fucking, fucking bitch!" She heard footsteps and a slamming door. "You shoulda stayed dead."

A child whimpered. "No, please! I haven't done anything! Please let me go!"

"Hailey? Is that you?" Mindy asked, looking at Todd, who collapsed to his knees beside the table.

"Who... Who's this?" Hailey asked, crying. "I want my dad. Help me get my dad."

"Right here, baby," he said. "We're coming."

"Daddy!" she wailed. "I'm so sorry, Daddy, it happened so fast, I didn't have a chance to yell or run."

Her voice faded even as she screeched, "Daddy! No! Let me talk to my dad! Please!"

The muffled voice returned. "There. You talked to her. You come alone in a regular car to the address I just texted. I hear one peep about this on the police radio, and I'll crush her ginger skull. I see one police car, I'll crush her ginger skull. I see that fuckwad father of hers..."

"You'll crush her skull. Got it," Mindy said as the phone made a cheerful chirrup sound. A text had arrived. Mindy looked at it and choked back her fear. *Our old house?*

"You have ten minutes, Minders. Don't be late. Time's a wasting."

The call went dead.

Todd grabbed her hand and dragged her to her feet. "Other car's in the garage. Let's go."

Sean yawned and stretched. Hospital TV sucked, especially on a Saturday night.

They'd put Mare in a private room in the obstetrics hall with vague promises that the doctor was coming soon and would explain her medical issues. Even when pressed, when stopped and confronted, the nurses didn't admit to anything else. He heard excuses about being short staffed, over worked, and documentation lost somewhere in various shuffles.

He didn't buy it. It was a freaking hospital, for God's sake. There were supposed to be rules. Practices. Procedures put in place.

Most of the fight in Mare had evaporated after the ultrasound. Her color was still all right, but her eyes had grown distant and numb. She didn't want to talk, didn't want a snack, just wanted to be quiet and rub her left side. Sean held her hand and tried not to lose hope.

About quarter after eleven, a yawning nurse stumbled in to check Mare's vitals, then pulled out a syringe. When Mare asked what it was for, the nurse said, "I've been up for thirty-nine hours and haven't eaten since a cold Pop Tart for breakfast. Everyone's getting a 'be good' shot. Don't like it, you can sue me. I'll get fired. Maybe go to jail. It'll be a blessing."

Before Sean could stop her or Mare could scramble out of bed, she plunged the needle into Mare's thigh and started to stumble back to the hall.

Sean blocked her path. "What the fuck? What'd you just inject her with? You can't just give people shots for no good reason!"

"You want one?" she asked, pulling a sealed, filled syringe from her pocket. "Demerol or Codeine? Personally I'm a Demerol fan. Makes the ladies sweeter."

"No, I don't want one! I want to know what's wrong with Mare!"

"Don't know, don't care," she said around a yawn. "We haven't received patient files for six hours. Too many patients, too few staff. If they're not about to spew out a baby, I honestly don't give a fuck why they're on my floor. I just want them to be good."

She waggled the syringe. "Sure you don't want one, too? You could have a nice nap. A naaaaap. Sleep 'til morning."

He blinked, shocked and furious. "No, I'm fine."

"You sure?" Wiggle waggle. "Naaap!"

"Get away from me."

She shrugged and tottered away. "Ignorant asshole. Don't know what you're missing. I'd sell my soul for a fucking nap."

Sean returned to sit beside the bed while Mare watched him with glassy eyes. "I feel really, really good. Floaty."

"It's the narcotic. Try to rest."

She leaned back, her eyes drifting closed. "I'm not sleepy, exactly, just really relaxed." She sat quietly for a moment while watching an air freshener commercial, then "Oh! My belly stopped hurting."

"Just the narcotic, babe." He raised her hand to his lips and kissed her knuckles.

"No, no, before the shot. No cramps, no anything but the blood." She took a deep breath and let it out. "Maybe it's not a big deal, ya know? Maybe it's treatable. Whatever it is. Maybe my body's fighting it off, us living at Spore Central and all. Wonder spore powers activate!"

He smiled at her old comic book joke. *It never hurts to hope.* "Might be."

"You should go home. Get some sleep." She rolled her head to look at him. "Really. It'll be okay."

"I'm fine." He stretched out his legs and tried to get comfortable.

"You need to finish those inks, and someone needs to be there when those spores come. What if they're kids? What if your uncle breaks in? Who'll help them if you're not there?"

He sat upright, shaking his head. He'd forgotten about the spores. "Babe, I can't leave—"

"What if he hurts them again?" Her voice lowered, cracking with sorrow and fear. "You have to, Sean."

His heart clenched as if it wanted to rip in two. *I can't, I can't! But I have to.* "What if you die?"

"I'm not going to die." Her eyes grew soft. Sleepy. She yawned. "I'll still be here when you get back."

"You promise?" Standing, he caressed her cheek and she turned into his palm, warm skin, warm breath, the lightest touch of her lips. *Oh, Mare!*

"I promise," she whispered against his skin.

He pulled his hand away and kissed her. He murmured, "I love you, Mare Knudsen," against her lips.

"Love you, Sean Casey."

He eased away from her lips to look into her eyes. "Then marry me. Promise me you will."

She looked into his eyes for a long time. "What if I die?"

"What if you live? Just be my wife. For real."

She almost hadn't dated him because she knew he'd wanted kids. Almost hadn't made love with him. Moved in with him. Bought a house with him. For eight long years she'd dodged his proposals. She'd said being married didn't matter. But it did. It mattered to *him*. And, whether she wanted to admit it or not, he'd seen her browsing history on the computer. Wedding gowns. Flowers. Trips to warm, beachy places.

Despite her protests, it mattered to her, too.

A tear leaked from one eye. "It's not fair. You're not fair."

He wiped it away. "Screw fair. I'm not leaving until you promise."

"But you want—"

"Screw my wants. Doesn't matter, Mare. Not anymore. I love you. Just marry me already."

She stared at him, her lip quivering, and at last she nodded. "Only if I live."

He grinned. "Fair enough."

She grinned back. "And I want to go to an island. With a beach. And an ocean. For at least a weekend."

"We'll do a week, maybe two."

"Your mother? She can't plan shit. Our wedding, our choices."

"Fine with me. I'll muzzle her myself if I have to. Maybe lock her in a trunk and ship her to Nepal."

Still grinning, she let out a yawn. "All right. You win. You've made an honest woman out of me."

"About damn time." They shared one last, long kiss.

As he pulled away, her hand trailed across his cheek and over his lips. "Now go. Save the spores."

Part Three
Harvest

Chapter Twenty-Six

Sean almost turned back twice. Once in the lobby, far more crowded than it had been at suppertime, and again at the car. He looked to the sky, the moon, the stars, the clouds gathering in the northwest, and he allowed himself one moment to cry and pray.

Her room faced the other parking lot, but he kissed his fingertips and held them toward the row of patient-room windows, some dark, some lit. "Love you, babe. Be here when I get back."

Heart breaking, he wiped the tears from his cheeks and started the car.

As he pulled out of the parking lot, he was nearly creamed by a silver Ford driven by a woman who looked just like Mindy. She didn't swerve, didn't flash her brakes, she just roared past like a crazed shopper on bargain day.

Sean took a calming breath then turned toward home.

Todd sat in the back seat, fiddling with a case of guns while Mindy barreled across town. Nine minutes remained when she backed out of his driveway, four when they passed the hospital. She slowed to a comparatively sedate thirty-two to take the corner to lead them past the tree-filled lot behind the house, and the Ford's back end skittered and knocked over a recycling can. She straightened and floored it. *Almost there. Almost home.*

"You ever shoot before?" Todd asked, loading a gun.

The wooded lot lay just ahead. She slowed, flicking off her lights. "Yeah. Shotgun. Used to hunt rabbits with Dad."

"Here. Clip this on the keychain," he said, handing over a mini Taser, about the size of a penlight. "The safety's on the side, like a flashlight. I'm taking a chance he's not going to pay attention to your keys."

She dropped the Taser on her lap as she eased to a stop. "Got it." She looked beyond the wooded lot to her old neighborhood. Home of suspicious lesbians. Prison for Hailey Anderson. Future end of Jeff Howard, dipshit banker and all around crappy human being. *Deep breath, Mindy. You can do it. Save Hailey, then worry about Jeff.*

"You don't have to do this," Todd said. He gripped her shoulder with one heavy hand.

"I'll get her. Don't worry. He doesn't scare me anymore." Mindy snapped the mini carabiner-clip onto Todd's key ring. "It's on."

"You don't have to worry about the buttons, all right? It's also pressure sensitive, so just pop off the cap and punch it at him. It'll stun him for about ten seconds. He starts moving while you're helping Hailey, stun him again. There should be six good stuns in there before it loses its punch."

Todd pulled his hand away and muttered a curse. "It's not much, but it's the best I can do. I don't have a gun small enough for you to conceal."

She shrugged despite the frantic slam of her heart. "It'll be okay. You'd better get going or we'll both be late."

"Yeah," he said, gathering up his weaponry. He opened the back door and started out, then paused. "Hey, Mindy?"

"Yes?" she asked, turning her head to smile at him. He looked haggard but determined in the glare of the Ford's dome light.

He leaned close, stretching to reach her, and gave her a quick, light kiss on the mouth. "Be careful. And thank you."

She felt herself blush but, instead of lowering her eyes, she touched his face. "You just get there in time to save my bacon."

"Deal." Then he was out the door and running for the trees.

Mindy made a three-point turn before rushing back the way they'd come. She drove up a few blocks, over one, then sped toward the house so she'd arrive from the correct direction with a minute to spare. In a neighborhood of sleepy homes, one house stood illuminated, shades drawn but every indoor and outdoor light on, including the basement.

She jerked the car to a halt in front of the neighbor's house and got out. Flicking the keys in her hand and imagining jolting the piss out of Jeff's balls, she stomped to the front door. *Isn't he going to be surprised? No meek Mindy this time.*

Teeth clenched, she slammed the side of her fist on the doorbell and casually held the keys in her pocket, thumb resting on the Taser cover. *Come on, Jeff. Don't want to keep me waiting.*

She heard heavy footsteps and the door opened.

She took a step back, mind reeling. He was familiar, but definitely not Jeff, not with the flat-top haircut and beefy muscles under a worn workshirt.

Oh, shit! That asshole cop!

"Mrs. Howard. Was beginning to wonder if you were going to make it," he said, then grabbed her arm and yanked her inside.

Sean sagged from exhaustion. It was just starting to spit rain as he climbed out of the car. No deputy, no picketers, no anyone other than two zombie hunters sitting on his front steps.

"Hey, dudes," he said as he fumbled through his keys. Two weeks of this madness and he still wasn't used to unlocking his front door.

"Yo," one said, making room for Sean to climb the stairs. Lean and bearded, he passed a paper sack covered bottle to the other, and his stocky partner took a good long drink. The bearded guy sniffled then sighed.

Crap. Key ready to insert in the lock, Sean paused. "What's wrong? Why are you here so late all by yourselves?"

"Em died," the stocky zombie hunter said, passing the bottle back. "She was cold and dead when we woke up this morning."

Aw, hell. "Emily? The lady with the braid?"

"Yeah. Sucks, man," bearded guy said, rooting around in his ear. "Lost our woman, lost our home. What a fucking day." He took a sip and burped.

Our? "I'm so sorry. She seemed nice."

"She was fucking awesome," the bearded guy said, flicking something off his finger before passing the bottle over.

Stocky held the bottle but stared at the sky. "Yah. Good job, good cook."

"Good in the sack."

The two men sighed, nodding, and the bottle made another round. Stocky burped. "Buried her in your backyard while some other folks were burying their kid. Hope you don't mind."

Sean shrugged. "Nah, it's cool. I'm kinda used to it. Not sure why everyone wants to use my yard, though. I'd think most anyplace that's damp would do."

"Because you're Sean, the spore guy," the stocky one said. "The news keeps telling everyone it's you. You missed a helluva night, though."

"Oh?" Sean said, not really caring about picketer nonsense. "What happened this time?"

"Your neighbor lady? The purty black gal? Her daughter went outside and never came back."

Sean felt his belly drop. *Steffie? God, no!* "She *what*?"

"Yup. Creeper got her, right around dusk, they think. Cops all left maybe twenty minutes ago."

"Jesus," Sean said, reeling as he looked toward Nic's house. *Steffie! Oh, baby girl.* He took a staggering step. *I should go see if I can help look for her. Something.* "I… I'll talk to you guys later, okay?"

"Nah, don't bother, dude," the stocky guy said. "The mom and the little boy took off hours ago. Came by asking for your woman, but we didn't know nuthin' 'bout it."

Bearded finished his sip then looked up at Sean. "Hey. Where is your woman, anyway? Saw you tear out of here with her this afternoon."

"Hospital," he said, sitting beside them to watch the clouds roll in. His throat clenched. *Mare. Steffie. Goddamn.* He swallowed another sob then said, "She started bleeding and no one will tell us why."

"That's harsh, dude." Stocky passed the bottle to Sean.

"Yeah. Not knowing sucks." He took a swig and coughed. The mystery beverage was cheap and harsh. Burned all the way down.

Bearded chuckled. "Got ourselves a lightweight, Rog."

Rog nudged the bottle back toward Sean. "Take another drag, Mr. Casey. It'll clear your pipes."

"Sean. Just Sean." He shook hands with his new drinking buddies and noted the bearded guy's name was Chuck. Sean took another sip and managed not to cough. The burn wasn't as bad the second time. He returned the bottle to Rog.

"So why you here instead of at her side?" Chuck asked.

"Shit to do," Sean sighed, frowning at his sleeping neighborhood. "Comic's not done and I have spores in the basement. Might be kids. Might be groundhogs." *Steffie's gone, Mare's dying. What the hell am I gonna do? How will I survive?*

Chuck leaned forward, elbows on his knees. "Hmm. I don't think they're groundhogs."

Sean grasped the bottle when it came his way again and took a swig. "I don't think so, either."

"Yep, wrong time of year for Punxsutawney Phil," Rog said.

All three laughed then Chuck contemplated Sean. "What I want to know is why kids are in your basement."

"My uncle. I think he's been killing them. No one will believe me."

"Fuck, dude, I believe you," Rog said, holding out the bottle.

Sean declined this round. Three was enough to make his head feel just a little hazy. "Really?"

"Shit, yeah. He's one creepy ass dude. Come and gone at least twice tonight. Rattles around your house for a few then sneaks off to your neighbor's again." He nodded his head to the north, to Earl and Ruby Simmons' place.

Sean clenched his teeth. *Earl and his goddamn dog. No wonder I always have nightmares.*

"Done it most nights," Chuck said, looking up as Sean stood, hands balled at his sides. "Ah, dude, you didn't know."

Sean shoved his key into the lock. "Nope. He's here most nights, eh?"

"Yeah, the last few anyway," Rog said, standing. "Back and forth, and back and forth. It's like he's checking an oven to see if a pie's browned yet."

Sean knew what was cooking beneath his bedroom and it wasn't pie. He unlocked the door and muttered, "Great. Thanks." *Wish you would've mentioned it days ago.*

Chuck stood and popped his back. "Em made fantastic pie."

"Oh don't get me started on her pie." Rog finished off the bottle and whispered, "Rest in peace, darlin'." He pulled off the bag and tossed it aside before slamming the end of the bottle against the concrete steps.

"What the hell?" Sean yelped, turning to see the jaggedy bottomed bottle winking in Rog's hand.

Rog blinked, confused. "This?" he asked, holding it like a weapon. "He's in there now. Thought you might want backup."

Chuck hiked up his grimy trousers and Sean saw Emily's military-issue pistol peeking out of his pocket. "We're drinking buddies now, dude. And I don't tolerate no kiddy killers."

"Me, either," Sean said. "But you're both drunk. Can you call the sheriff, ask for Deputy Anderson to come over? He knows what's going on." He took a breath and pushed the door open.

Mindy landed on her gut, sprawling face down on plush, cream-colored carpet that smelled like vanilla. The two women tending the yard the day she'd spored lay together in the corner, both with tidy round holes in the middle of their foreheads. Mindy caught a glimpse of their clasped hands then she scrambled to her feet and lunged toward the hall.

A crystal lamp lay on the floor beside the couch. She snatched it up as she ran past, ripping off the shade and tossing behind her. Every door stood open, every room had been ransacked, and she saw no sign of Hailey.

Neck of the heavy lamp clenched in her hands like a stubby bat, she put her spine to the linen closet door and watched the cop saunter toward her. "Where's Hailey?"

He held his hands wide. "I dunno. What'd you do with her?"

Mindy grit her teeth then screamed, "Where is she?"

She heard a muffled squeal and a crash from the basement. *Hailey! Just gotta get past him, get down the stairs… Crap!*

"You're trapped, Minders. Is that what he called you? Minders? Such a stupid name for such an expensive, fucking bitch."

He stepped closer, within range of the lamp, but Mindy made herself freeze, quivering, as he lifted a lock of her hair. "Your old man told me I could play with you first," he said, pulling the lamp out of her hands and tossing it aside. "I could even be rough if I wanted. Teach you some respect."

His breath was hot on her cheek, his hand heavy on her breast, pinching, hurting her. "I never get to be rough, and to get paid for it… Well, that's just a double bonus."

"No, please," she said, flinching away from his cruel kiss. She gasped for breath and released a low squeal while, in her pocket, she flicked off the Taser's cap. "Please don't hurt me. I'll do whatever you want," she said, voice trembling. She swallowed and stilled her panic. *Never gonna be a victim. Never, ever again.*

He held her against the linen closet door with one forearm crushing her ribcage and his other hand reaching into the top of her dress. "Handcuffs. Maybe my belt. This is going to be fun."

Mindy pulled her hand out her pockets to struggle for him, to fight, and she felt his grin along her cheek in the brief moment before she slammed her fist against the side of his throat.

The sizzle filled her ears with an enormous crackling roar and he arched away from her, his voice caught in a silent scream. She pulled her hand away and he fell, twitching and writhing on the floor like an animal that had been struck by a car. Teeth clenched, she pushed away from the closet door and leapt over him, scrambling to the kitchen and down the basement stairs to find a sprawling tangle of wet clothes strewn around a fallen kitchen chair. The air reeked of gasoline.

Mindy stepped into the sodden mess. *Good God, was he going to burn her?!*

"Hailey!" she called out, frantic and sliding through the ruined clothing. She found no sign of the child in the game room, the laundry, nowhere in the tangle she could see. "Where are you?"

The floor above her creaked, his steps heavy and stumbling, and she heard a terrified whine behind her.

Hailey had scuttled behind the water heater, hands and feet bound and her mouth covered with packing tape. Gasoline had soaked her hair, her clothes, her skin, and her eyes were wide and terrified.

"It's me," Mindy soothed, climbing into the narrow space with her. "We're the same, remember?"

Hailey nodded and sagged with relief.

Mindy ripped off the tape and whispered, "Be still," while she worked to untie the binds at Hailey's wrist.

"Dad. Where's my dad?" Hailey whimpered.

"Soon. You'll see him soon." The steps above faltered and she heard a heavy thump, like he'd fallen again. But he'd be out of the hall in a step or two, and only eight, maybe ten steps more to the top of the stairs.

"The car's across the street to the left," she said, finally freeing Hailey's wrists. "When you get out of here, run out the front door to it, hide in the back seat, and lock yourself in. You hear me? You don't let anyone open the doors but your dad."

"'Kay. I can do that." Hailey fumbled as she helped Mindy with her ankle binds.

Steps, surer but still stumbling, reached the kitchen.

Time's up. Todd, where are you?

Mindy held the child's face in her hands. "Do not look back. No matter what you hear, what you see, you do not worry about me. I don't care what else happens, as soon as you hear me fighting him, you *run*." Then she kissed Hailey's gas-slick forehead and eased out from behind the water heater.

"You're a naughty, naughty girl, Minders," the cop said from the top of the stairs. "My little get out of debt free card."

"Where is she, you shit?" Mindy screeched as she flung the hamper into the game room. She followed it, knocking stuff aside, making noise, moving away from the stairs toward the bedroom side of the house, leading his attention away from the trapped child. "Where'd you hide her?"

She heard him skid-stumble down the stairs. *Almost here. Come on, asshole. Come on.* "There she is! Oh my God, Hailey! What have they done to you?" she shrieked, rushing for the basement bathroom to rip back the shower curtain.

The cop, stumbling and dutiful, followed her. "You and I are going to have us a little interrogation. Teach you obedience."

The bathroom door swung inward and Mindy crouched in the shower, ready to pounce. She saw his shadow reach forward, saw his movement in the gap between the door and the jamb, saw the barrel of a gun peek around the door.

Oh, crap, Mindy thought, *I'm toast,* but she lunged forward anyway, tackling the door. The gun went off, the bullet shattering the medicine cabinet and ricocheting off a tile near Mindy's head and the shower surround before embedding in the ceiling.

The cop fell to his knees, grunting, gun still clenched in his hand as he turned it toward her.

Mindy clambered over him, a second shot whizzing past her to hit a furnace pipe well ahead. Her foot slammed into his gut as she fled and she heard a pained whoof of air, but he shifted his legs, tripping her. She fell, once again, sprawling to the floor even as Hailey's light steps sprinted up the stairs and across to the living room.

She's all right! Mindy thought, struggling to regain her footing, but the cop grabbed her ankle and dragged her toward him.

"Gotcha," he snarled, standing while holding her leg. "You're not going anywhere."

Watch me. Mindy rolled to her back and kicked out with her free leg, intending to slam her heel into his balls, but he shifted and flipped her onto her belly again.

He planted a heavy foot between her shoulder blades and, despite her struggles, she was pinned. He leaned forward, weight on the one crushing foot, and she felt the warm barrel of the gun press against the back of her head.

"Don't move or, money or not, I'll blow off your damned spore head," he said, rummaging in her pockets for the keychain, which he tossed forward into the gas-soaked clothing.

He shifted again and she heard the beepty boop of a cell phone. "Got her. She's become real compliant with a pistol pointed at the back of her skull." He paused. "Yep. Face down on the floor. I'll have her at the drop off on time."

She heard another soft boop as he ended the call.

He knelt, knee replacing the heavy foot, and he put the gun away long enough to cuff her hands behind her and drag her to her feet. Mindy heard a creak from the kitchen—Todd!—and she turned to spit in the cop's face, hoping to distract him from the noise.

"Bitch," he snapped before backhanding her across the face. "You brought this on yourself."

She fell to her knees and licked the corner of her mouth, tasting blood. Above her, the floor creaked again. "Big man, beating up a bound woman half his size," she muttered, forcing herself to turn on her knees and glare at him through the mussed tangle of her bangs. "Can't get it up unless you knock the crap out of a girl first, can you?"

His eyes narrowed and he hit her again, this time with the side of the gun. "Shut up."

Hit a nerve there, didn't I? God, you're pathetic. She grinned and spoke louder, hoping to lead Todd to them. "Do all your talking with a gun, don'tcha, copper? Bang, bang! Just like the old gangster movies!" Then she started laughing.

"I said shut. Up." He grabbed her by the throat and dragged her to her feet.

Mindy glurgled, unable to fight back, unable to breathe. She tried to knee him in the groin but he dodged it.

"You need to learn a little respect," he snarled in her face before slapping her with the gun again. "Spore bitch. Nasty fungaloid piece of ass. If you weren't worth so much money I'd—"

"Let her go, Hendrix," Todd said. "Drop the gun and put your hands behind your head."

Mindy couldn't see anything, her vision had become hazy, but she managed to kick Hendrix in the leg.

He yelped and stumbled back a single step. His gun went off—a vicious bee stung her left bicep—and, behind her, Todd grunted.

She heard another shot, then another as she fell, once again face-down on the floor. Hendrix collapsed on her, shifting to raise his gun one more time, but a final shot echoed through the basement and he fell backwards, unmoving, his leg across her forearms and lower back.

Todd limped to her, an injured bull in a too-tight hallway. "Mindy! God, Mindy!"

"I'm okay," she mumbled, trying to push Hendrix's weight off her and sit, actions apparently impossible with bound hands. "Think I got shot, though." She rolled and her shot bicep became smeared with gasoline and grit. "Ow, crap! That stings!"

She felt Todd's hands on her, lifting her, pulling her out from the stink and the dead weight of Hendrix.

"Let me see," he insisted, examining her arm. "You'll need stitches, but you'll live." He uncuffed her hands then lifted her chin to scrutinize her battered face. "Where's Hailey?"

"You didn't see her?"

"No. I haven't had a chance to look for her." He limped away, holding his leg as if it barely supported his weight. "Hailey!!"

Mindy grabbed his hand. "She's outside. In the car. She got away."

He turned, gaping, and grasped her shoulders. "She's what?"

"I sent her to the car." Mindy swallowed and felt a clench of queasiness. The left leg of his jeans had turned black and glossy with blood. "Your thigh. You've been—"

"Shot. I know. Third time." Grinning, he draped an arm over her shoulders. "They lie. You never get used to it. Hurts like a bitch."

She helped him up the stairs and outside, but he staggered to the car on his own power, calling his daughter's name.

Hailey peeked up from the back seat and burst into a wide and bawling grin. She scrambled from the car and ran into his arms as he stumbled and fell to his knees in the middle of the road. They held each other, crying and kissing their relief.

Grasping her bleeding bicep, Mindy limped toward the curb, intending to sit and let the little family have their private moment while she caught her breath.

"Oh no you don't. Get back here." Todd stretched to grasp the hand of her injured arm and he pulled her to them, down to the road and into their embrace.

Chapter Twenty-Seven

The living room looked all right, but the house reeked of spore funk, heavy and pungent. Sean paused to listen—*is Paul upstairs? In the basement?*—but heard nothing but the soft whirr of the refrigerator. *Crap.*

Knowing his steps would echo downstairs, he took a breath and strode in as if he owned the place and belonged there. Which he did. It still was his house whether Paul liked it or not and he'd be damned if he'd let his uncle hurt any more kids. He released a loud and facetious yawn despite his heart slamming and his muscles thrumming like every fiber had been electrified.

Is this fear? Adrenaline? Something else? Sean thought as he rounded the corner into the kitchen and took the few steps to the fridge. He opened the freezer and reached in.

"Looking for something?" Paul leaned against the doorjamb leading to Sean and

Mare's bedroom. He was covered with dirt and mud, stunk of spore, and the awful tattoo seemed to glow in the light spilling from the bedroom.

"Popsicle," Sean said, heart slamming in his ears. "Maybe an ice cream bar. Something cold. Too damn hot out there." He made himself look away from Paul and grab the box of diet fudge bars. He closed his eyes for a moment, relieved at his luck. *Still heavy. Just shoot the bastard and let the cops sort it out.*

He glanced over the door at Paul as he tipped the box in his hand and let the gun slide out, plastic baggie and all, while keeping it hidden in the freezer. "Want one?"

"Nah. Maybe later," Paul said, returning to the bedroom.

Sean unbagged and checked the gun. Still loaded. *Holy freaking crap, it's cold!*

Trying to settle himself, Sean gripped the icy gun and took a deep breath. "Oh, by the way, what the holy hell are you doing in my bedroom?"

"Ain't yours, kiddo," Paul said from beyond the door. "I built this fucking room. Built it special just for me. So what do you do? Wait 'til I'm gone and change the fucking locks, then you nail the goddamn window shut? Go fuck yourself, Seanny, and go back to your doodles. It's my place."

"Bullshit. I've told you before it's *my* house." Gun clasped in both hands, Sean pushed the door open with his foot.

Their bed had been flipped over to stand against the south wall along with both dressers and a slumping roll of threadbare carpet. All of their knick knacks and personal clutter had been dashed aside and strewn about, leaving broken bits and loose hair ties scattered on what remained of the floor, which wasn't much.

Four large, rectangular panels of sub-floor had been removed, exposing the muddy cellar beneath the room. One floor panel stood in the mud to lean between joists near the bathroom door, cross-bars running horizontal like a ladder, while the rest lay against the bedroom wall beside the window.

A deep hole had been dug in each corner of the muddy cellar floor and all had seeped full of ground water. Spore slime quivered in three of the holes, one foaming and about to melt away, another so small it barely rippled the water.

"Figured a house-stealing thief like you'd bring the gun," Paul said, coming around the open door with Mare's aluminum softball bat in his hands. He swung, low and fast.

Sean tried to turn and leap back, but the bat hit him hard across the side of the hip. He crumpled, yelping in pain, and tried to shoot Paul. He missed and hit the mattress instead.

"Cowardly fuck! We're done with this shit," Paul said, swinging downward.

Fuck! Sean covered his head with his hands, but the bat hit him across the middle of his back and he fell flat and sprawling to the floor. The gun skittered away.

Sean's diaphragm seized, fighting to draw in air, and he was helpless to resist as Paul grasped him by the scruff of the collar and threw him into the muddy pit.

While Sean lay there in pain and unable to breathe, Paul jumped down with the gun in his hand. "I wondered where your crazy bitch hid it," he said, opening the cylinder. "Freezer? I didn't expect that." He shook out the bullets and flung them, then the gun, into the kitchen and knelt in front of Sean.

"Guns are cheating." Paul grabbed Sean by the hair and wrenched his head up. "What we have…" he said, dragging a finger down Sean's cheek. "What we're gonna do… It's too personal for that."

Sean tried to tell his uncle to fuck himself, but with no air yet coming in or out of his lungs, he could only manage a pained squeak.

"Worthless cream-puff," Paul said. Shoving Sean aside, he crouched to stroke the largest wad of slime, toying with bubbles filtering up through his fingers. "If you came here looking for that little neighbor girl, you're too late. She's buried over there beneath the dressers," he said, shrugging toward that side of the pit. "I never liked the little ones. They give up too quick. Guess she'll never get all her quarters, will she?"

Oh, Steffie! Sean managed to draw in a slip of a breath, then another. He rolled to his side and coughed out, "You're a sick fuck," as his lungs loosened again.

"You should know, kiddo." The slime bubbled from several places and had begun to melt away. It flexed, the life inside moving and pushing out with an elbow or heel. "C'mon, baby," Paul cooed. "Papa's got a present for you."

Sean got to his hands and knees despite the pain in his left hip and back. "Get away from that spore."

Spore froth spewed over Paul's hand as he stroked the quivering mass. "Oh shut your pie hole and wait your turn. Been waiting days for this little treat to come back to me. We still have so much left to do, don't we, Princess?"

Get up, Sean, get UP! He managed to get one foot forward, and he sagged, still struggling to breathe smoothly. "Get away from her."

A swirl of slime faded away, then another, and Paul grinned. "Princess and I had such fun; now we get to do it all again while Sean watches us! It's gonna be sweet!"

You twisted monster. Sean managed to get to his feet, but sagged, his left leg not totally working.

More slime twirled then faded away, and Sean saw a child's hand reach out of the water then slip beneath the surface again. Paul chuckled and stood to unzip his jeans, his back to Sean.

No! I can save this one. Have to save this one. Sean staggered forward, both hands clasped together, and he swung, using body momentum to slam the side of Paul's head with his fists.

The blow sent Paul reeling toward the far corner. Sean gasped for breath and fell to his knees beside the hole.

Most of the goop had melted and a little girl, perhaps six or seven years old and covered with spore-slime, burst out of the water, gasping. She blinked at Sean with her odd purple eyes, still mindless and gone.

"C'mon," Sean said. "We have to go!"

"My house, my spore-kid," Paul snarled. He grabbed Sean by the hair and punched him in the face, bloodying his nose. "Mine," he said, punching again. "Get me, Seanny? I don't care how many times I have to kill you, this house, these kids, are *mine*! You wait your fucking turn!"

Sean squawked and swung blindly, striking Paul's throat. Paul cursed and his grip slipped away, leaving Sean to crawl back to the girl while blood ran freely from his nose, nearly choking him.

Paul chuckled and reached for the child. "Now, now, Princess, come to Papa. We have things to do."

The girl's head turned, perhaps drawn by the sound, and she babbled, "Aaah bada bah!"

"Stay away from her, you sick freak!" Sean shoved himself between Paul and the little girl and batted Paul's hands away. He coughed at the cloying musty stink of spore slime as it soaked his jeans, but he pressed himself backward, nudging the spore child out of the hole. He felt her grasp at his shirt, heard her cry out in mindless panic and fear as she crawled into the shadows beyond the makeshift ladder, but she was safe. For the moment, at least. Paul loomed, glowering and blocking any retreat to the kitchen and the gun.

Sean tried to control his rising panic even as he reached back to locate the girl. *There's no way I can get both of us past him. We're trapped. What the hell do I do?*

Paul rubbed his throat as he contemplated his nephew. "Thought you were feisty the first time, Sean. You got away from me, almost escaped." He spat blood onto the churned up dirt. "No one ever managed that before."

Sean kept his mouth closed, trying to hide his surprised fear. *The first time? So Paul DID hurt me. The cops must have gotten the dates wrong!* "What do you mean I almost escaped? I did get away from you, you sick fuck."

"You always were a tricky bastard, weren't you, Sean? A crafty little prick who took away my chance to fuck away that thing's first breath." Paul knelt before Sean, eye to eye, leaving Sean paralyzed with fear. "It's okay, it's all right," he soothed, smoothing Sean's hair. "I took your last breath back then. How about I take it again? Maybe you won't come back this time and steal my shit."

Come back? How the fuck do you know I die in my dreams? The floor panel serving as a ladder dug into his back, promising a quick escape to the bathroom if he'd only abandon the girl. His heart slammed and his hands grasped for the ladder, his entire body, his soul, demanding he flee to relative safety, but, as he shifted upward, ready to bolt, he remembered the girl. *Shit! Without me she'll be helpless. Paul'll rape her, maim her…kill her. And it'll be all my fault.*

He swallowed, panting as he struggled to control his panic. *I can't, I can't leave her. I can't let her die because of my fucking fears!*

Growling, he took a breath and lunged, turning his head to bite Paul's forearm.

Paul screeched and tried to yank his arm away, but Sean grabbed him and held on, sinking his teeth deeper into his uncle's flesh despite Paul beating him about the head with his free hand.

Paul managed to jerk away from Sean's bite and he fell, ass first, into the girl's sporing pit, good hand clamped on his forearm and his legs flailing for purchase while Sean tried to grab the girl.

"I killed you once, you fucking prick!" Paul snarled. "Fucking killed you and fed you to Lulu."

Sean's vision swam as the girl scuttled away from him and deeper into the darkened corner. *Lulu, the same dog the Minotaur said.* Sean turned, hands clenching. *Oh, crap, oh hell. My nightmares can't really be memories.*

Paul grunted and climbed out of the hole. "Grown or not, I'm gonna teach you a fucking lesson, just like I did twenty years ago. Gonna bust you up and I'll fuck you until I'm tired of your screams, then gut you and watch you die. Only this time I'm gonna burn your fucking corpse after I'm done playing with it."

"Ahmba dagah?" the child said, perhaps drawn by Paul's voice.

He's too strong, too fast. I need a weapon. Something to even the odds. Sean stayed between Paul and the girl while trying not to stare at Mare's bat, glimmering on the dirt behind Paul. "You never killed me. I'm obviously still here."

"Only because your fussy-bitch mama worked at that cloning lab. Bet she grew you back in a petri dish."

Sean swallowed. *Cloning?* "You're lying."

Paul pointed to a swath of ground under the dressers. "No. No lie. I buried what was left of you right over there."

Sean shook his head. *I'm a…clone? A spore? It's not possible! Mom, what did you do?*

Paul laughed and dragged himself upright. "You really didn't know that, did you? And here I thought you were all horny for the spores and their stupid rights because you're one yourself."

Still blocking the girl, Sean managed to stand despite his throbbing hip. "No. I had a childhood. I have memories."

"Memories don't mean shit. I really did kill you," Paul said. "God, you were a pain in the ass, always getting yourself untied and trying to escape, even without your feet. You almost did it once. Hid in a ditch full of dead leaves. Tricky little shit."

Mind reeling, Sean struggled to breathe. *My dreams? They really happened?*

Paul sidled closer. "My stupid brother knew how I felt about children. He never let me hang out with you, even when you were in diapers. Was sad, really. You and I had such fun playing when we were finally alone together. Now with this spore-stuff, we can do it over and over and over!"

We? Oh, hell, Todd said the killings continued after you died. Goddammit, you had partners and they're still around!?

Paul leapt, hands encircling Sean's throat. He flung Sean to the ground and dragged him toward the nearest hole. "Gonna make sure you don't come back this time!"

Sean beat him with his fists, but Paul didn't let go, he just continued to crush Sean's throat, then shoved his head under water, darkening his vision to a fine, bright point. Sean bucked and kicked, desperate, but Paul had leverage. *Too strong, he's just too strong!*

Trachea creaking beneath Paul's grip, Sean's head swam with memories: the stink of Minotaur and dead leaves, hazy scrapes and bloody, child-sized handprints on cinderblock walls.

He managed to shove Paul off with his feet and roll aside, coughing up slimy water, but Paul returned. Sean cried out as Paul pummeled his face and throat, gouged his face, and kicked his ribs and back. He tried to crawl away, but he was weak. Hurt. Exhausted.

Panting, Paul grabbed Sean by the shoulder and flung him far away from the whimpering girl. Sean's fingers skittered over something cold. Mare's bat. He grasped it and dragged it to him.

"Fuck you. I'm not dead yet," he said, blinking past the blood in his eyes, even as he tried, and failed, to get his feet beneath him. His head swam and his vision was a dark flickering sea of red. One blink Paul grinned at him, the next the Minotaur. The beast took a step toward him, his breath a stinking hiss, and Sean pulled back to swing the bat at its great and terrible head. It laughed at him in dark, jolly glee.

"Get the fuck away from me!" Sean swung, but the Minotaur dodged, snarling.

Then it was Paul again, wrenching the bat from Sean's hand and flinging it away. He beat Sean across the face with his fists, bringing dazzling pain to his cheekbone, and Sean fell to his side, gasping through the blood and pain. "Run. Please," he said to the little girl, her eyes glittering in the shadows beyond the ladder, but she was too far away, and he was too weak.

Laughing, Paul hoisted himself up onto the remaining flooring and into the kitchen, returning a heartbeat later with their chef's knife.

"See this? It has a lot to do tonight, and so do you."

"No, please," Sean said, turning his face away as Paul laid the blade against his cheek. He thought of Mare, alone and maybe dying, of Steffie already dead, and closed his eyes. *Oh, babe, oh Stef, I am so sorry I failed you.* He opened them and almost made out a dark blur near the newest sporing hole, but filmy blood over his eyes made it difficult to see.

Paul crouched and muttered into Sean's ear. "Oh, not you, not yet. See, you're going to watch. First, we're gonna cut off her feet so she can't get away, so she'll see them lying there, pieces that used to be part of her. And then I'm going to fuck her. Ass. Face. Cunt. In that order. If I feel like it, I might share her with my friends next door and watch them do it again. You know my old buddy Earl, right? We've been hunting together since high school."

That's why the deaths continued! Sean reasoned. *Earl consults all over the country. Travels constantly with his fucking dog.*

"When we're done, I'll cut her open, from here," Paul touched the knife to the base of Sean's sternum, "to here," he said, dragging it past Sean's belt buckle.

"I'll rip her guts out, and hopefully she'll last long enough to feel it this time. And then before I toss her out, I'll fuck her open and empty carcass while it's still warm. How's that sound, Seanny?"

"You sick bastard! She's just a kid. A helpless innocent kid!" Sean tried to push himself up enough to crawl away, but his arms quavered and he crumpled down again. *Have to save her. Somehow.*

"No, this one, she's a spore. They heal, remember? No telling how long she'll last. Probably a lot longer than you did. And we fucked you off and on for two days before I cut your guts out. I bet she'll last twice as long. And so will the rest I've planted here." He grabbed the back of Sean's head by the hair and yanked Sean's face toward him. The tattoo on Paul's arm flexed and seemed to grin in dark glee. "So, so much play time. What do you think?"

Sean spat his mouthful of blood at Paul. "I think you're a sick fuck."

"Yeah, a sick fuck who keeps kicking your worthless cream-puff ass." Paul laughed and stood, letting Sean slump again to the ground. He kicked Sean in the face before unzipping his pants, unzipping his skin, until the Minotaur stood there, towering and vile. "You're going to have a front row seat as I get to know my little spore princess, so enjoy the show. After I'm done with her first round, I'll do the same to you. Only this time, I'll burn your body. No more second chances, Sean. Not this time."

Sean blinked, Paul, Minotaur, Minotaur, Paul, each hazy and red, walked to the ladder. The Minotaur crouched, tail swishing, and held out a clawed paw. "Come, child, come to Papa Paul. Let's play."

She whined. The Minotaur snarled, "I said get your goddamn spore ass back here so we can fucking play!"

Sean tried again to push himself up, but failed. Defeated and lightheaded, he turned his head away, unwilling to bear witness—

Is that my shovel?

His own garden shovel lay beside the hole, just a good stretch away. *Get it, get it, get it!!*

"Get your fucking ass back here, you little bitch!" the Minotaur bellowed while Sean crawled, reaching, stretching.

He wrapped his hand around the shaft and allowed himself one breath of rest, then rolled back toward the Minotaur who was dragging the screaming child out from behind the ladder panel.

Get up, get up, GET UP!!

Her skin was still wet and slick from spore foam, and she slipped from the Minotaur's grip and scuttled away.

Sean sat, panting, the shovel across his lap and his head a reeling vat of dizziness and pain as he struggled to remain conscious. *Don't you hurt her, you filthy shit.* He slumped back to the dirt once, then he shoved himself to his knees again. *Don't you dare. Don't you fucking dare.*

Another breath and his vision cleared. He tottered to his feet, free hand holding his forehead in place, and staggered toward the vile beast. He heard a soft siren or maybe desperate ringing in his ears as he stumbled forward. *I won't let you! I was a kid then. Helpless. Not anymore.*

The Minotaur's hairy back arched as it bent, straining to reach the kid, lumps of knotty backbone in a row down its spine. Laughing, it dragged the child to it and reached for the knife.

Head swimming in rhythm with the squeal ringing in his ears, Sean drew the shovel over his shoulder, like he was prepping Mare's softball bat for a good pitch. He wobbled, but found his balance and swung.

Sean hit the Minotaur square in the topknot. It fell forward, gasping, its clawed hands clenching into the dirt.

"I said, get your filthy fucking hands off her!" Sean stumbled under his momentum but caught himself and swung again, against the back of the thing's massive head.

It turned, snarling, breath stinking of death and decay, and Sean smacked it square in the face again and again and again. It became Paul, nose mashed and bleeding, forehead split open, but Sean swung again. The Minotaur, one eye bludgeoned shut. Another swing. Paul. The Minotaur.

The cheap shovel's shaft snapped, but he continued the beating. "No one's hurting any more kids in my goddamn house!" he screamed, still swinging. "No one's hurting any more kids, you fucking freak!"

He screeched his fury as hands grabbed him and dragged him off Paul, and he fought to get back to killing the filthy thing that had taken his hope, his life away. He screamed, kicked, and flailed, but three deputies forcibly removed him from the basement and through the house while others rushed past, heading back toward Paul and the spore girl. Sean was still screaming, still fighting, when they carried him outside to a gentle summer rain.

"You really ought to go to the hospital," the EMT said as she stretched a butterfly bandage over Sean's split cheek.

"Nah, I'm good," he said, voice muffled behind the swollen lip and his head swimming despite the icepack he held to his brow. *They've taken my statement, said I could go, but I'm not going anywhere until I know that fucking lunatic is locked up and gone.*

"Suit yourself," she said, moving on to the next gash or contusion. "But your cheek's busted. Someone needs to look at it."

"So noted," he sighed, stretching to see another pair of EMTs drag Paul out of the house on a stretcher. *Least I was able to walk afterward,* he thought.

The little girl sat in the backseat of a deputy's cruiser, clutching a blanket close as she watched Paul get hauled away. She blinked at Sean and smiled, shy, hopefully still innocent. At least until her memories returned.

"Give me a minute," he said to the EMT as he stood. Ignoring her protests, he staggered to the cruiser.

"Hey," he said, afraid to kneel before her because he might not be able to get back up.

She looked up at him, her blue eyes huge as she tightened the blanket around her.

"You beat up that monster."

"Yeah. I guess I did. You all right?"

She nodded. "He just scared me. That's all."

Good. "Scared me, too. What's your name?"

"Luchie Fawkes."

"Sean Casey." He held out his hand and she shook it, gracing him with another shy smile. "I'm glad you're all right."

"Just wish my mom would get here," she said, staring at the officers and flashing lights. "They said they'd called her."

"She'll come. Want me to stay with you 'til she does?"

She nodded in relief, tears brimming in her eyes. "You won't let anyone hurt me. Not even scary monsters."

He leaned against the car for balance and she grasped his hand. "No, sweetie, I won't," he promised as he blinked back tears. "Let's just wait for your mom."

They didn't wait long, a couple of minutes, then a minivan skidded to a stop beyond the ambulances. A haggard but hopeful couple scrambled out, followed by a teenage boy and another girl a few years older than Luchie.

"It's them! It's them!" Luchie squealed as she slid out of the cruiser, still holding Sean's hand.

The dad grabbed the nearest deputy. "Where is she? Where's our daughter?" He muttered something Sean couldn't hear, then the whole family ran to them, smiling and crying and hugging Luchie.

Sean smiled and said goodbye as he turned to walk around the thankful family.

"Oh, my baby," the mother cried, holding Luchie close and rocking her. "We thought we'd lost you!"

The teenage boy looked up, gaping and pointing at Sean. "It's him. It's the guy from TV."

The dad lurched to his feet, one hand on the back of his daughter's head, and grabbed Sean's arm, turning him to face him. "You… You did this? For my family?"

"That's Sean. He saved me from the monster, Daddy," Luchie said, voice muffled against her mother's bosom.

The dad choked back a sob. "I know who he is, baby." He took a breath and looked Sean in the eye. "We can't ever repay you, I know that. But if you ever need *anything* you call me, okay?"

"Thank you, but I'm good," Sean said, grasping the father's shoulder. "Really. She saved me, too. We're even. Right, Luchie?"

He couldn't hear her response, but it didn't matter. She was safe with her family again. Head throbbing, he was stumbling back to the glowering EMT when he heard his mother scream his name.

He sat in the ambulance's open doorway, teeth clenching as Paul's taunts banged around in his head. He wasn't ready to see her. Not yet, maybe not ever.

Helene scurried to him. "Sean! Oh my God! What happened?"

He looked away, fury and disgust rising at the sight of her. *All these years she knew. She knew what happened, why I had the crippling dreams, why I'm messed up, but never told me. Even when I asked her for the truth.* "Not now, Mom. Go home."

"My son looks like he's been through a garbage disposal. I am *not* going home. Tell me what happened!"

Fine. "I put Paul on a stretcher," he muttered, gesturing to the ambulance surrounded by armed deputies. Glowering, he turned to stare at his mother. "He'd buried kids under my bedroom. That little girl over there was one of them. He was going to kill her *again*. A second damned time! Know anything about that, *Mother*?"

She took a step back, then smoothed her blouse and said, "Sean, sweetheart, I have no idea what you're insinuating."

"Right, Mom. Paul told me your lab made clones. Look what's been happening lately. Makes all kinds of sense now, doesn't it?"

Helene turned pale and, shaking her head, reached for Sean. "No, no, they didn't make clones. That's absurd!"

"Don't lie to me, Mom," he snapped. "All my life, all the nightmares, you knew my uncle killed me. You knew you had your stupid job clone me back. Don't you think—"

"That's not what happened! Your father, he suspected what Paul did. Was all over the news, the missing kids, and your father… He hated Paul. But he never told me why!"

She sobbed, her breath shaky. "Your father was on a hunting trip when my mom took a bad turn and I had to go to Des Moines. I needed a babysitter for a couple of days. I couldn't leave you alone, not with a pervert running loose, so I called your uncle. *I* called him, *I* asked him to babysit. Me. *I* even dropped you off at this filthy house!"

Sean stood and pushed the EMT aside. "You *what*?"

"By the time I got back, it had been three days. You weren't here, no one was. But the house… It reeked. Smelled like death and blood. I was afraid and went looking for you, but all I found in the basement were your feet. There were so many feet! Boys. Girls. All chewed up. And it smelled so bad, so awful down there. I'd seen the news and realized it was him, all along, *him*, and he'd killed my baby."

She didn't notice the deputy who walked up behind her and stopped to listen. She clutched Sean's arm. "I didn't know what to do, I was so frantic. Screaming. I went looking for him. Paul was up on the highway, walking his rotten dog. I couldn't help myself. It just happened."

Sean's head throbbed and he thought he might crumple but he gritted his teeth and remained standing. "What just happened, Mom?"

"I drove over him. With your father's truck. Then I backed up and did it again."

Sean staggered back to slump in the ambulance doorway. "You? You killed him?"

"I had to," she snarled. "He killed you! Killed all those other children. Once it was done, I went back to his house. There was nothing in the car, no blood, nothing, so I searched everywhere. I finally found fresh dirt dug up in the basement, under that room he'd just built. It stank so badly down there, Sean. I dug and dug. I found rotting children. They were so nasty. And I found you."

The deputy spoke into his radio, asking for assistance, as Sean regained his feet.

"So it really happened? He really buried me there?"

"You and some others, three, four, I don't remember, but I put you all in the truck and dropped the others off in the woods. You, I took to the lab. You… You weren't stinking yet."

She fell to her knees and looked up at Sean, pleading. "I didn't know what else to do. I had to get you back, get my life back, make everything right. The lab had been closed for years but I knew where they'd buried the barrels. I dug one up, got it open, and put some in a milk jug. I still have the jug, in the basement, just in case I needed to save you again."

"Why didn't you tell me? You had twenty goddamn years to tell me! All the nightmares, the madness. Why didn't you tell me?!"

"Because it worked!" she wailed, her grip on him slipping as he lurched away. "I took you to the lab, washed you in the big sink, my baby, my sweet Sean, and spread the growth medium on you, like lotion. It was just like lotion! Don't you see? I took care of you, soothed you! Made it all better. But it needed to stay wet, so I filled the sink. The next morning, a slimy thing had spouted on your poor ruined chest. It was working! A miracle!"

Damn her. If I'd known I could have faced it. Somehow. No wonder Dad left her. "Mom, no. How could you? What about Dad?"

She nodded. "Your father? He was easy. I called him at the lodge to tell him his brother had died in an accident. Then when he got home a few days later, I pretended I was frantic, that you'd gone off riding your bike that afternoon and hadn't come home. No one knew what had happened. What Paul had done."

She blinked away desperate tears. "Every day I went out to the lab to check on you.

The slime got bigger and bigger, then one evening there you were, wet and blinking up at me. I couldn't tell you! All I could do was save you. Let you be found and rescued, let it all be okay again."

He leaned over her even as two deputies grasped her arms. "But you threw the other kids away. Even after you killed Paul, you threw the other kids away like garbage and left me to suffer with your secrets. And this time, when you knew what he was, when you knew kids were dying, you did *nothing*!" He turned and walked away, toward his own car.

"Because everyone would know about you!" she screamed after him. "I tried to protect *you*!"

All the other kids! They could have been found, saving their families two freaking decades of grief and pain. The toxic mess could have been cleaned up, back then twenty years ago. He turned back, glaring. "No. You tried to protect yourself. You'd have to explain what you'd done back then how you chose to spore me but not the others. You should have come forward as soon as you found out Paul came back, and you should have saved the other dead kids!"

"But they were dirty! Rotted and slimy and filthy!" Crying, she struggled to break free from the deputies and reach for him. "Sean, please. Try to understand. I wanted to help them, but I couldn't wash their rotted filth! I had to run the truck through the super-scrub car wash five times before I could park it in the driveway, how could I stand to put lotion on their rotted flesh? I tried but I couldn't! It was so awful, I still scrub my hands, scrub everything, to get their stink off me. I did the best I could. I saved and protected *you*."

None of this would have happened. Not the spores, not the sickness, not Steffie. None of it. It's all her fault. "This was never about me. It's always been about you. You had two chances to make things right, and both times you took the cowardly way. I'm done talking to you." He resumed walking away, hands clenched at his sides.

"Sean! Please! I even killed Evie before you could ask her about the lab. You have to understand that I only did it to protect you! I've done everything to protect you, to save you!"

He heard a scuffle but kept walking.

"Let me go!" she screeched. "I have to help my son!"

A detective stopped Sean. "Can I have a moment?"

"Sure." He glanced over at his bawling mother being stuffed into the back of a cruiser and found he felt only disgust and lingering pity. "What can I do for you?"

"I need to ask you about your dog."

Sean tilted his head, confused. "We don't have a dog. I can't stand dogs." *Now I know why. Thanks for that, too, Mom.*

"You see, Mr. Casey, all of our victims have been…"

"Their legs and feet chewed up? Yeah, I heard. I still don't see why you're asking me. We *really* don't have a dog."

"Your uncle had one somewhere. Any ideas where he might have stashed it?"

Beyond the police cruisers and ambulances, Earl Simmons and his wife scooted out their front door, pulling Peaches behind them on a muzzle and leash.

Sean pointed. "Paul spent a lot of time with them, said they helped him hunt and kill the kids. They have a mean dog. Talk to them."

The detective nodded his thanks then trotted toward the couple as they threw luggage into the back of their minivan.

Earl noticed the approaching detective, dropped his overnight bag, and ran. Two young deputies pursued while Earl's wife fell to her knees and put her hands on her head.

A news crew caught the incident on camera then while the deputies tossed Earl onto the ground beside his prone wife and snarling dog, a reporter stepped in front of Sean. "Mr. Casey! Excitement has found you again. Care to make a statement?"

She seemed familiar, surely a reporter he'd talked to before, but he was in no mood to indulge her agenda tonight. "No. I have no comment," he muttered, stepping around her.

"But Mr. Casey, these events have unfolded here, at your home in Pinell. Surely—"

He turned, glaring, and snapped, "I have no fucking comment. Now get off my lawn."

While she stood there, he slammed himself into his car and fumbled out his keys. *My whole body hurts. I'm furious, exhausted, and grieving. No idea how I'm going to get out of here with all the mess, but I have to. Somehow. Or I'll go mad.*

He'd just slammed the key into the ignition when he heard a light tap on his window.

What now? He ground his teeth and glared at Rog and Chuck, the two zombie hunters. *Oh, it's just you.* He managed a tired nod as he cranked down the window. "Hey guys."

Chuck grinned at the madness. "Dude, this is intense!"

Rog nudged him in the ribs. "Knock it off." He gave Sean a worried smile. "You all right?"

Mare dying, Mom off to jail, Steffie and other dead kids sporing beneath my bedroom? Oh, and I'm a spore, too. I'm fanfuckingtastic. "Yeah, I'll live. What's up?"

"We heard you fighting in there. Hope it was okay we called the cops."

"It was. Thank you." He extended his hand and both Rog and Chuck shook it. "Can you do me one little favor?"

"Anything, dude!"

"Can you clear a path so I can get out of here? I really want to get back to the hospital, back to Mare."

"Sure thing," Rog said, then tapped the roof of Sean's car as he turned to walk down the drive. "Backing up now," he hollered, shooing people out of the way. "Make room."

Sean managed to back onto the road and maneuver around the sheriff's cruisers. A few minutes later, he yawned as he pulled onto the highway toward Boone.

Chapter Twenty-Eight

Todd lay in his undershorts on an examination table and winced as a bleary-eyed doctor poked and prodded the bullet hole in his thigh. A knock rapped on the doorframe and Todd reached for his gun, his gaze darting to Mindy dozing on the chair in the corner. Her own wounds had already been tended by the same doctor, and she held Hailey cuddled close and sleeping on her lap.

They're fine, and by God they're going to stay that way. He wrapped his hand around the gun and drew it close to his belly. "Come on in."

The sheriff entered. "How are you feeling?"

Todd released the gun, but kept his hand close. *How much did you know about the cover-up of Mindy's accident, boss? Shot one deputy for hurting my girls, why not a sheriff, too? I'll be investigated, either way.* "Great. Nothing like having a pair of new holes to ooze blood out of. What brings you here to check on a poor lowly deputy, sir?"

"Just wanted to tell you we caught the guy. The creeper."

Mindy lifted her head and stared at the sheriff while holding Hailey a little closer. *'Bout damned time.*

"I've already read your statement on what happened tonight. Good job. State police have apprehended her husband." He glanced at Mindy before returning his gaze to Todd. "We'll give you a full briefing on the creeper tomorrow."

"You can give it to me now," Todd said, pointing at his leg. "Planning on taking a couple of days off. Workman's comp injury."

"When you come back then," the sheriff said.

He turned to go, but stopped when Mindy asked, "Who was it?"

"Paul Casey. Uncle of the guy that took you in. But we have him and his accomplices in custody. They'd killed a neighbor, girl, though. Poor kid."

"Steffie?" Mindy whispered, curling around Hailey again. "Oh my God."

Todd swallowed down the rancid taste of bile. Sean had claimed his uncle was involved and insisted the slimes beneath his bedroom were kids. He'd ignored him, thinking it was just another one of Sean's irrational fears. *Crap.* "Sir?" The sheriff paused in the doorway and turned. "Did you find kids in the cellar?"

"One. Sean Casey saved her and the others still growing, including the neighbor girl the suspect had already buried. If you want to know more, be at the briefing in the morning."

No idea how to do that while guarding Mindy, but okay. Todd laid his head on his arm as the doctor probed the front of his thigh. *Thank the good Lord for narcotics or I'd be screaming my head off about now.* "Yes, sir. In the morning, sir."

"Um, wait," Mindy asked and the sheriff paused again. "Are Sean and Mare all right? Where are they staying?"

"I don't know. I was informed he left the scene despite the instructions of the EMT and she was not present at the incident."

He left and Mindy murmured, "I hope they're all right."

Me, too. And the poor kids. Todd gave her a hopeful smile then winced as the doctor pulled out a blood-soaked swab. "How's it looking, Doc? Didn't seem so bad to me, all things considered."

"It missed the femur and major blood vessels, so you lucked out there." The doctor walked to the cabinets and unlocked them. "But there's considerable muscle damage, especially near the exit wound, as well as a great deal of debris and what smells like gasoline. You didn't immediately wrap it, did you?"

"No, I was rather preoccupied with trying to stop the bad guy from killing the three of us. You know, minor distractions."

"Ha ha. Cops. Always with the jokes." The doctor returned to the table with various bottles, syringes, and suturing implements. "I'll get it cleaned up, and after a few stitches and some antibiotics, you can be on your way."

'Bout damned time. Todd tried to relax while the doctor stitched him up. Three stitches in front, five in back. Not so bad. After the doctor finished then left, Todd sat and reached for his stiff, bloody jeans. Mindy still cradled Hailey, who slept on, innocent and oblivious. Todd managed to wrangle his bad leg into his pants. "Did you want to go to a hotel?"

Mindy raised her head to blink at him and he saw a glimmer of a sweet smile. "That's a little forward, don't you think?"

He felt himself blush as he zipped up and found his shoes. "No, not like that. Since Sean's house is a crime scene, you can't stay there. With that in mind, is there somewhere else you want to go, or would you rather go to a hotel?"

"She wants to go home with us," Hailey murmured around a yawn before nuzzling in again. "I like her."

It'll probably cost me my job, but I like her, too.

"Shh. Sleep." Mindy stroked Hailey's hair and laid her cheek on Hailey's head, watching Todd all the while. "I don't know what I want," she whispered.

Todd wrestled on his shoes and limped to her. "Me either," he admitted. "But the department will spring for a hotel room. Or…"

"Or?"

"We have a guest room. It's not very big, but we have plen—"

Hailey opened one eye and glared at him as she squeezed Mindy. "She's staying with us."

Mindy chuckled and stood, still holding Hailey as if she'd been doing it forever. She met Todd's gaze. Her coffee-brown eyes were warm, depthless. Confident. The same, yet so different from the timid doe eyes she'd had when she'd first come out of the trees. Again, she smiled at him, nearly making his knees buckle. "Guess we've been told, eh?"

Todd fell in beside her as they left the examination room. He couldn't help but smile as he draped a protective arm around his girls. *Yeah, I guess we have.*

Sean limped into Mare's room with dread pounding in his heart, but he let out a sigh of relief when he approached the bed. She slept, illuminated only by a dim side light. Her breath came even and relaxed, and, when he leaned over to kiss her forehead, she felt warm and alive.

Thankful and exhausted, he sat beside her, grasped her hand, and stretched out his legs, hoping that sleep would find him.

He'd barely closed his eyes when he heard her exclaim, "What the hell happened?"

He blinked, squinting at the bright window. *Urgh. What time is it?* He yawned and rubbed his face awake, then immediately yanked his hands away. *Holy crap, that hurts.*

She frowned and gingerly reached out to touch his face. "You're a mess. What happened?"

The morning light hurt and he forced himself to his feet—*Pain! Ohshit! Holyfuckinghell! Holyfuckinggoddamnhellonastick!*—and staggered to the window to lower the shade. "Paul kicked my ass, then I kicked his. Cops have him and I'm here, so I guess I won." Sean's eyes ached a little less, but everything else continued to complain, so he shuffled back to his chair and sat. "And, oh, I saved a little girl. Luchie. Nice kid. Grateful parents. Yadda yadda yadda."

He leaned back in the chair and let out a pained sigh. "I really need some morphine. Or tequila. Hell, at this point, I'll take ibuprofen and BenGay."

A woman bustled in with a breakfast tray, giving Sean a worried glance and a wide berth to set it on Mare's beside table.

"You're not gonna get off that easy," Mare said as she lifted the lid. Scrambled eggs, bacon, toast and juice. "Wanna share?"

"No, you go ahead," Sean said. The way his cheek felt, surely eating would be worse.

Mare sipped her juice. "You all right?"

Sean leaned back and closed his eyes. "Yeah, just sore. I'll be fine."

As Mare ate he told her what had happened, from the two zombie hunters on the steps to his mother being stuffed into a sheriff's cruiser.

Mare said little during the tale. When he finished, he opened one eye to watch her as she lay back upon the pillows. *Don't leave me, babe. Not because you're sick, and not because I'm a spore.*

"Sorry about your mom," she said, grasping his hand.

His heart clenched for a moment, then resumed its usual rhythm. "She did some pretty bad things."

Mare sat upright and leaned over to run her hand through his hair and caress his unbroken cheek. "Maybe so, but she brought you back. I can forgive pretty much everything for that. Even years of treating me like crap." She smiled into his eyes and stretched to kiss him. "I don't know what I'd do if I'd never met you."

"Same here," he said, savoring her kiss. "Have you heard anything about your…" He swallowed, hating the taste of the words. "Your condition?"

"Nothing." She relaxed into her pillows and squeezed his hand. "I have no idea what's going on. But as soon as we find out, as soon as we make a decision, whatever it might be, you need to get looked at. Get antibiotics at least."

And some pain killers. "Deal."

He dozed while she watched TV, some Sunday morning news show discussing the latest riot reports coming out of St. Louis, Cairo, and London. Both looked over when a man in scrubs walked in, skimming the file he carried.

Mare's hand tightened in Sean's. He felt her fear slam against him in waves and he held fast, intending to be her rock. Her bruised, battered, and partially broken rock, but her rock nonetheless.

"Morning," the fellow said, glancing up at them before returning his attention to the file. "Rosemary Knudsen?"

Mare's voice sounded dry. Lost. "That's me."

The man peered at Sean. "And you are?"

"Sean Casey. Her fiancé."

"I know that name," he mumbled as he pulled a chair from the corner. "I'm sure I do."

Sean shrugged. *Almost everyone does.* "Who are you, and what can you tell us about Mare?"

"Neil Hathstone," he said, extending his hand to each of them. His handshake felt friendly and confident. "I'm an OB-Gyn specialist from Iowa City, and the local powers that be have decided to give you to me, or me to you. However you want to look at it. I'd hoped to talk with you earlier, but it's been a heckuva morning. Four births since I got here at six AM, including a vaginal breech and a preemie by C-section. Busy, busy day. But a good one, so far at least. Happy moms, happy babies. Can't ask for much more than that!"

He sat, took another look at the file then snapped it closed. "So! How are we feeling this morning?"

"I'm scared out of my wits and Sean kicked the shit out of a pedophile. How do you think we're feeling?"

Hathstone laughed. "Ah, feisty, I like that!" He tsk-tsked and shook a finger at Sean. "And you, the biggest news story in the country sitting there being all coy."

"I don't really care about the news. I care about Mare."

"Understandable. Both of you." He leaned forward to contemplate them. "I've been over all of your sonograms, your history, and the results of your pap. What part do you want first? The good news, or the bad?"

Sean moistened his lips and Mare's hand in his twitched. "Tell me what's wrong," she said.

"All right. When you acquired the systemic replicating fungal infection, or the spore fungus as it's commonly called, it replaced your missing uterus." He pulled a pen out of his pocket and drew a tubular shape on the back of the folder. "Let's say this is your vagina. The fungus regrew your cervix first."

While he drew a plumpish donut shape on the folder, Sean reached over to wrap Mare in his arm. She shook and he smelled her fear.

Hathstone continued to draw as he talked. "The fungus happily moved on and created your uterus, from the bottom up—very fascinating stuff—then outward with fallopian tubes, then a pair of lovely little ovaries."

He paused in his drawing to glance up at them. "You with me so far?"

Both nodded.

"All right," he said, returning to the folder. "The problem is your original ovary." He drew a second oval partly over the left side ovary. "They're fighting for space. That's the abdominal discomfort you've been having."

Sean and Mare looked at each other. "That's it?" she asked. "I have an extra ovary?"

"Yes," Hathstone said as he opened the folder. "It's uncommon, but not unheard of for women to have oddly shaped uteruses with three, even four sets of fallopian tubes and ovaries, they can even have vaginas that split into two separate paths leading to two separate uterine systems. Your new uterus, however, is plain and typical, rounded with two fallopian tubes. It's quite lovely, really. The issue at hand is the extra ovary."

He paused to look each of them in the eye. "Plenty of women are born with three ovaries, but it's unnatural for *you* and we're just not sure what the hormones will do, or if you'll feel any adverse effects at all. Also, the two on the left are vying for the same space and fallopian tube. This may, or may not, impact your fertility."

Sean's heart quickened. *Fertility?*

Mare gaped, her eyes wide. "You're telling me I can get *pregnant*?"

Hathstone glanced into the folder. "I don't see why not. Everything looks great, it's in the right place and, to be perfectly honest, the two new ovaries look like they belong to an exceptionally healthy thirteen-year-old, not a woman a year or so shy of thirty." He grinned. "They are chock full of eggs. Great for making babies, not so great when you're looking at menopause when you're in your late sixties or early seventies."

Mare stared at the doctor, unable to speak and Sean, too, found himself tongue tied.

"So, congratulations on getting your first period, but be ready for all the normal pubescent changes that teenagers deal with. Mood swings, acne, sore breasts." He grinned at Sean and said, "No guarantees they'll get bigger. They might, they might not. We're stepping into uncharted territory here."

"Uh, sure," Sean said, still shocked at the news.

"How… How is this bad?" Mare asked.

"It's bad because we just don't know how you're going to manage three times your previous hormones, if the hormone levels will self-regulate on their own, or if you might have a greater risk of ectopic pregnancy. *We don't know.* That's the problem, this is all new science."

"Sure, okay," Mare said, nodding.

Sean sighed his relief. *I don't think it sounds bad at all.*

"So, what I suggest is that over the next, say, two to four months, you get your hormone levels checked daily. We have some home test kits I can get for you, but you'll need to come in for bloodwork and a sonogram once a week, all right? Just for those couple of months or so."

"Okay," Mare said. "Bloodwork. Sonogram. Sure."

"Depending on what we find, we'll make more decisions from there. You might need to have the extra ovary removed. You might not. We don't know. But we'll find out, all right? Then we'll reassess."

"So no cancer?" Sean asked.

"Nope. Everything looks fantastic. Like I said, she has the reproductive organs of a pubescent teenager. They're about as close to perfect as they come."

Sean and Mare looked at each other, both grinning in joy and relief. He leaned over to kiss her, and she kissed him back, still grinning against his lips. *It's a miracle!*

Hathstone stood. "Oh! One more thing. Since we're trying to assess the impact of suddenly adding two ovaries, I'd rather you didn't get pregnant until we know what's going on. Can't put you on the pill or implants, it'd make the tests inaccurate, and I'd rather not put an IUD in such a new uterus. I strongly suggest condoms along with a spermicide *and* a diaphragm. No babies, okay? Not yet."

"But I, we…" Mare looked at Sean, then the doctor, then back to Sean. "We really can get pregnant?"

"As long as his swimmers don't get lost, sure. You can have all the babies you want. Just try not to until after we've completed the tests." He winked. "Might ruin my chances to get published in *The American Journal of Obstetrics and Gynecology*."

Hathstone fished a business card out of his pocket and handed it to Mare. "Great to meet you folks," he said, shaking their hands. "Do you have any other questions before

I go?"

Mare stared at the card as if it were magical.

"I think we're good," Sean said, still grinning. He stood and shook the doctor's hand again. "Thank you."

"You bet." He leaned in and squinted at Sean's battered face. "Better get that cheek looked at before it turns septic."

He patted Sean's upper arm then turned to go. "You kids have fun, but stock up on condoms first."

"We will," Sean called after him. He turned back to Mare to see her clamber out of bed and rush to him. She threw herself into his embrace and, laughing despite the pain, he spun her around and kissed her. *Mare's all right! Better than all right!*

"We can have babies!" She squealed, giddy. "Oh, babe, what fantastic news!"

Sean couldn't agree more.

Too excited to sit still, Mare buzzed around the room to gather her things and get dressed while Sean eased back into the chair to await her release papers. "Once we're out of here, we're going right down to emergency," she said as she pulled on her pants. "So help me, we're not leaving this hospital until—"

Mare turned, falling silent as the news switched to coverage of banker Jeffrey Howard being arrested on charges of kidnapping and murder for hire while his victims had been treated and released from a local hospital.

"Oh my God," Mare said, taking a step toward Sean but her gaze still riveted on the TV. She reached for his hand. "Todd's daughter? Mindy?"

"Least they caught him. And Mindy and Hailey are okay."

She turned to face him, lower lip curled in, while behind her the news turned to exploding cancer deaths that were expected to impact billions worldwide.

"I'm celebrating a stupid new uterus and all this bad stuff's happening. People are *dying*," she said, searching his eyes. "Millions, maybe billions of people. What's wrong with me?"

"Nothing," he assured her as he stood again and drew her close. "You're perfect. You've always been perfect." He closed his eyes as he relished the bliss of her in his arms.

He thought of the spore sickness, the dying, the no longer dead, and of their future children and what sort of unknown world they'd be born into. With a sudden population decrease, would it be plagued by rampant disease and fear, or brightened with hope and prosperity?

At last he said, "The future's never been certain. Good or bad, as long as we're together, we'll make it through just fine."

About the Author

Tamara Jones started her academic career as a science geek, earned a degree in art, and now writes full time. She's an avid quilter as well as a wife, mother, and cat wrangler. Despite the gruesome and often violent nature of her work, Tam's easygoing and friendly. Not sick and twisted at all. Honest! Visit her online at www.tamara-jones.net.

Acknowledgments

I'd like to thank Bill, Laura, and LittleMiss for all of their support, patience, and indulgences as I worked through this novel. Next, I want to thank my agent, Laura Bradford, and editor, Don D'Auria, for their guidance in bringing Sean's story to print. Also, a huge, humble thank you to Sam Arnold, Stephen Bagley, Kat BarronMiller, Lisa Blair, Wendy Blanton, Tom Burns, Joely Sue Burkhart, Shirley Damsgaard, Jon Dearman, Kat Fireblade, Margaret Fisk, Gemma Godwin, Alison Kent, Joyce Kopecky, Tina Kulesa, Elle Lassiter, Michele Maakestad, Darren Magedy, AR Miller, Josh Rode, Jean Schara, Maripat Sluyter, and Tori Swanson for reading, bouncing story ideas around, and generally putting up with me. You guys rock! I'd like to add another thank you to everyone who donated photos for the artwork.

Lastly, I want to thank the Boone County Sheriff's Office and Iowa State University fungi expert Thomas C. Harington for willingly answering all of my "what if" questions, even the crazy ones. If there are mistakes, they're because I didn't know what else to ask.

#GoSpore

There's a killer on the road...

White Knuckle

© 2015 Eric Red

He's a big rig truck driver who goes by the CB handle White Knuckle, and he's Jack the Ripper on eighteen wheels. For thirty years he has murdered hundreds of women in unimaginable ways, imprisoning them in a secret compartment in his truck, abducting them in one state and dumping their dead bodies across the country.

Dedicated FBI agent Sharon Ormsby is on a mission to hunt down and stop White Knuckle. She goes undercover as a truck driver with a helpful long hauler named Rudy in a cross-country pursuit that will ultimately bring her face-to-face with White Knuckle in a pedal-to-the-metal, high-octane climax on a highway to Hell.

Enjoy the following excerpt for White Knuckle:

Carrie was wide-awake all right.

The rearview mirror burned blinding white as four headlamps of two big rigs fast approached, one in the left passing lane and one in the right truck lane. The eighteen-wheelers surged forward and bellowed past her, rocking her vehicle back and forth in the wet hurricane of their afterblows. The nurse whimpered and gritted her teeth against the terrible noise of the rampaging diesels rushing by, sandwiching her car between a hundred and forty tons of wheeled steel. She decelerated to aid in their departure ahead, shaking like a leaf as she did so. Within moments they were red-jeweled pinpricks of taillights twinkling out in the watery darkness up the road.

Blacktop and broken white lines unfurled.

Thwap. Thwap. Thwap.

Her mouth seriously smarted.

A greenish blob floated out of the inky murk ahead in the windshield. Reflective words became discernable. "Johnstown. Next exit." She passed the sign.

Fifteen minutes would bring her to her exit.

Twenty minutes and she'd be pulling into her driveway.

A few minutes later, she'd be safe in bed.

Please God, just get me home.

Mouth hurts.

The radio. *Turn it on.* Static. *Flip up the dial.* Static. Static. More static. *Ugh. Turn the thing off.*

Thwap. Thwap. Thwap.

The blackness ahead was melting like oil in the smear of the windshield wipers. A glance into her mirrors showed only darkness behind.

Twinkle.

Headlights.

Coming on fast.

Two big saucer eye headlamps inflated in her back windshield, filling her car with stark illumination that violated her safe confines like a kind of rape. The front grill was vaguely outlined and resembled a grinning demon. *Oh c'mon, just get past me,* she thought. The rig must have had its high beams on because her rear and side view mirrors were a white-out of blinding triangular reflection that made it impossible for her to see or move her eyes anywhere. *Just get past me!* The trembling thunder and low register vibration of the tractor-trailer shuddered her vehicle as it hauled itself up alongside on the right. Carrie held on to the steering wheel for dear life, waiting for the truck to pass.

But it didn't.

The monster eighteen-wheeler, a towering shadow silhouette on the passenger side, just hung there—as if it sensed her anxiety on some animal predatory level and was toying with her. It had slowed to her speed as she was nose to nose with the cab. She decelerated to get behind the speeding big rig.

Its taillights flared and hellish red light inflamed the inside of her car.

The truck had slowed, too.

Neck and neck again.

OK, fine! The nurse stepped on the gas and her Prius shot ahead up the unfurling blacktop and broken white lines of the highway that was now empty except for she and her seventy-ton unwelcome companion. Carrie felt her car hydroplane on the unsafe wet tarmac and she struggled to wrest the vehicle back under control.

A throaty diesel engine roared behind her and the cough of smokestacks, jutting up like twin chromium steer horns on the cab in the sopping back windshield, belched smoke that sinisterly wreathed the truck. It heaved forward, easily pulling up alongside her again and now she was scared.

Carrie threw an anxious glance at the cab and driver door window of the big rig keeping pace beside her. Through her rain speckled passenger's window an empty seat away, she could see nothing but the lower edge of the driver's window. There was a shadowy silhouette of a head with a cap on the trucker inside. A light went on inside the cockpit of the flanking truck, and now she could make out that the blurry oval of his face was Caucasian and male. The rain on the window glass made his distorted features look like melted candle wax. Fear jolted her body like sparking jumper cables and she decelerated down to 30 mph, but without missing a beat, in a hydraulic hiss of brakes, the truck slowed too, so that his window and the face beyond hovered over hers. The driver was looking at her, staring at her—she could feel it, if not see it, beyond the walls of glass and rain.

Suddenly a bright light exploded in her car, lighting her up and she heard herself scream. It was coming from an industrial flashlight the stalking trucker shone out his window, aiming it right in her face. Terror flared as she realized he was trying to make her out. Then, just as quick, the flashlight switched off.

And the tractor-trailer edged inwards to impact the side of her car!

CRANNN-NNNG!

Now Carrie screamed and screamed, releasing the steering wheel. The truck veered like a gigantic rattlesnake and hit her passenger side again. Metal buckled and glass cracked as she skidded out of control, sideways. She was going to die. He was going to kill her. *But why?* Seizing control of the rotating steering wheel, she wrestled it into alignment with both white-knuckled fists and somehow kept her wits enough to steer into the skid, regaining traction as she pumped the brakes and slowed as fast as she dared, coming to a near standstill on the shoulder of the fast lane.

The eighteen-wheeler could not stop as fast and didn't try, just plunged on ahead. As her little vehicle came to rest on the bad side of the road, Carrie watched the red taillights recede up the highway. The maniac was picking up speed and getting the hell out of there, his lethal prank over. No question, he was speeding off and that must mean she was safe. The truck was gone, thank God and blessed Jesus.

Sitting, sobbing and shaking behind the wheel, the nurse found her jeans were soaking and at first thought it was rain but then realized she'd pissed herself. Was still emptying her bladder all over the vinyl car seat. Her breath and heart were sledgehammering in her chest as she sat paralyzed and alone. The inside of her car stank of urine.

The front and back windshields were black as melting onyx in the muddy rain. The highway was otherwise deserted, and it was just her. Carrie couldn't move, frozen in place with indecision. No way she was going to get back on the road after that close shave, even though the exit was a mile away. The mad trucker might be waiting for her. But she couldn't stay here, could she? What to do. *Gotta do something,* her mind raced. What?

Fumbling her cell phone out of her purse, the nurse punched in "911."

The phone rang. "Police emergency." A man's voice.

"H-H-H—"

"Ma'am, this is police emergency. I can't understand you."

Shit, her mouth wasn't working. *Use your words*, like her mother always told her as a child.

"Ma'am, this is an emergency line. Are you hurt?"

Once Carrie spat out the first syllable, she couldn't stop talking. "Help me, please! A big truck just ran me off the road! He smashed into my car on purpose! Tried to kill me! Help! Please! Send the cops!"

"Where are you now?'

"I'm in my car. I'm on the 80 about a mile north of the Johnstown exit." Good, her RN training was coming back to her and she was lucid and articulate. It was going to be all right. *Give the 911 dispatcher the information. Be calm.* "My name is Carrie Brown. I'm a nurse at County General and I was driving home from my shift and this big rig just came up on me and knocked me off the road." She heard the sound of a keyboard tapping on the other end of the line as the 911 dispatcher took down her information.

"Are you injured?"

"No, just shaken up."

"Stay in your car, Ms. Brown. Lock your doors. Do not leave your vehicle. We have a Highway Patrol unit in Johnstown and he is on his way."

A flare of headlights in her windshield came from the oncoming lanes on the other side of the road and her brief rush of expectant relief that it was the authorities turned into a chill as she saw it was yet another truck, hurtling in the opposite direction. Then there was red glow in her car as the big rig disappeared behind her and all was dark again.

"Can you hear me, ma'am?"

"Yes, I'm sorry, yes. Stay in the car. Lock the doors." She pressed the master plunger lock button and heard the locks on all four doors all drop with a soft *thunk*. "Don't worry, I'm not getting out."

"We have a unit on his way. Should be there in ten minutes."

"Thank you."

"Sit tight."

The call disconnected. Carrie put the phone in her pants pocket. She lay in her own water on the driver's seat, gasping for breath. The body heat of her wild fear was fogging up the windows. Outside, the night highway was desolate and empty, barely visible in the thrashing sheets of torrential rain. Blackness embraced her. The nurse waited, counting the seconds, then switched on her blinkers. A yellow pulsing glimmer broke the black void outside that was broken only by her headlights, which seemed so weak. Wiping snot from her face with her shirtsleeve, she smelt the acrid tang of her pee filling the car and permitted herself the luxury of embarrassment worrying about the state trooper discovering her in this condition. That was the least of her problems, she decided. As the moments passed, listening to the *thwap thwap thwap* of the wipers and the *click click click* of her blinkers, she grew restless and felt her skin crawl, trapped in her car like she was out on the great big scary empty Interstate. Fear spread.

Then stygian darkness brightened.

Two white pinpricks to her rear.

Somehow, Carrie knew two things right away.

It was not a police car.

And the trucker was back.

CPSIA information can be obtained at www.ICGtesting.com
Printed in the USA
BVOW04s1453270515

402065BV00003BA/141/P